PRAISE FOR JANE ORCUTT'S PREVIOUS WORK

"4 Stars. Troubled heroes are nothing new in romantic fiction, but Ms. Orcutt has elevated this archetype to a new level of excellence in this stirring romance [*The Fugitive Heart*]. Add vivid description to a fast-moving plot and read until done."

—Romantic Times

"Jane Orcutt has created a memorable tale with a pair of strong, passionate characters faced with a seemingly impossible situation. Samantha's faith is as natural to her as her skin and enhances the romance. *The Fugitive Heart* carries the reader at a fast clip to the sweet conclusion! Orcutt weaves a masterful tale! Carry this one with you, you won't want to miss a page!"

—The Literary Times

"Ms. Orcutt is a powerful storyteller. I've read inspirational romance before that left me longing for more tension-filled romance. At last, Ms. Orcutt has combined a beautiful, realistic faith in God with the passion of true romance [in *The Fugitive Heart*]."

—AOL Reviewer Board

"This book [*The Hidden Heart*] stands out among the many prairie romances. Recommended."

—Library Journal

"4½ Stars. Pick of the Month. In this beautiful love story [*The Hidden Heart*], two hearts seek God's redemption, one sin-scarred, and the other wounded and terrified of falling in love. Jane Orcutt's name may be fairly new to readers, but her work is every bit as fantastic as veteran authors, and like cream, she's certain to rise to the top."

—Romantic Times

"Jane Orcutt has a deft touch with historical details and the often harsh realities of the American West. The reader will laugh and cry with Elizabeth and Caleb and share the peace of Anna's wisdom. A worthy sequel…that will lure the reader from page to page! Share this one with a friend! It can only enhance the relationship!"

—*The Literary Times*

"*The Hidden Heart* is an incredible tale that has your heart racing and your emotions in full gear from the first page. I wept and rejoiced right along with Elizabeth and Caleb. Ms. Orcutt has done a marvelous job of combining the senses of great romance with the indescribable joy of a relationship with Christ."

—*AOL Reviewer Board*

"The four up-and-coming romance writers featured in this charming collection [*Porch Swings & Picket Fences*] are all in top form, delivering stories that are both romantic and funny, with subtle spiritual messages. If patrons are demanding light summer reading, libraries won't go wrong with this title."

—*Library Journal*

"The cream of this collection book [*Porch Swings & Picket Fences*] is Jane Orcutt's 'Texas Two-Step.' This is an author we'll be hearing a lot about. Ms. Orcutt's previous full-length novels are both nominated for RWA's coveted Rita Awards this year. Jane Orcutt is certainly a writer who knows how to tell a page-turning story. *Humorous, charming* and *romantic* describe the love story told in the backdrop of a town so small it has a population of 532 people."

—*RomCom.com*

The Living Stone

The Living Stone

A NOVEL

JANE ORCUTT

WATERBROOK
PRESS

THE LIVING STONE
PUBLISHED BY WATERBROOK PRESS
2375 Telstar Drive, Suite 160
Colorado Springs, Colorado 80920
A division of Random House, Inc.

Scripture taken from the *New American Standard Bible*® (NASB). © Copyright
The Lockman Foundation 1960, 1962, 1963, 1968, 1971, 1972, 1973, 1975,
1977. Used by permission. (www.Lockman.org)

The characters and events in this book are fictional, and any resemblance
to actual persons or events is coincidental.

ISBN 1-57856-292-9

Published in association with the literary agency of Janet Kobobel Grant,
Books & Such, 3093 Maiden Lane, Altadena, CA 91001.

Library of Congress Cataloging-in-Publication Data
Orcutt, Jane.
    The living stone / Jane Orcutt.--1st ed.
        p. cm.
    ISBN 1-57856-292-9 (pbk.)
    1. Traffic accident victims—Family relationships—Fiction. 2. Drunk
driving—Fiction. 3. Friendship—Fiction. 4. Widows—Fiction. I. Title.
PS3565.R37 L58 2000
813'.54—dc21
                                                    00-033368

Printed in the United States of America
2000—First Edition

10 9 8 7 6 5 4 3 2 1

To Robin Heath

Acknowledgments

This book could not have been written without the expert help and opinions from the following people:

J. J. Wagner for police work, Rita Maddux-Potter for paramedic/ER details, Peggy Johnson for chaplain questions, Ann Diamond and Shawn Paschall for legal and courtroom procedure, Al Sibello for baseball consultation, Becky Brooks for critiquing, Yolanda Martinez and Arcadia Camacho for help with Spanish, Lisa Bergren and Traci DePree for editing, Paul Hawley for a stellar job of copyediting, Sandra Byrd for being the best first line of literary defense a grrrl could have, and Janet K. Grant for her constant encouragement and patient agenting.

Thank you one and all. Any errors or discrepancies are mine alone.

And special thanks to Jay Bond for relating his personal experience with the loss of a loved one to drunk driving.

May all victims experience beauty instead of ashes and the oil of gladness instead of mourning.

And coming to Him
as to a living stone, rejected by men,
but choice and precious in the sight of God,
you also, as living stones,
are being built up as a spiritual house
for a holy priesthood,
to offer up spiritual sacrifices acceptable
to God through Jesus Christ.

1 PETER 2:4-5

Chapter One

"Maybe we should have gotten an earlier start for home." Leah Travers stared into the dusk descending beyond the Corolla's headlights, then checked the backseat. Her two-year-old son waved a sleepy fist, yawning as he scattered cracker crumbs.

Leah's husband, Perry, tightened his hands around the steering wheel. "Galen'll probably fall asleep before we even get home, Leah. Your parents practically wore him out." He set his mouth in a grim line and flipped on the radio. LeAnn Rimes warbled, "You light up my life."

Perry jabbed the preset buttons until he landed on a Smashing Pumpkins tune, then cranked the volume up two notches. Leah winced. "Galen'll never get to sleep that way."

Perry snapped the music down but not off.

Leah crossed her arms and settled back into the worn vinyl passenger seat. Would they never get home? Perry had fumed all the way from Houston on a journey they'd made countless times. Even in this twilight, driving north up I-45 to Fort Worth should be as comfortable and familiar as Leah's favorite sneakers—easy to slip into and easy to wear. She knew all the road signs by heart.

Corsicana, 12 miles

She peeked in the backseat. Galen was fast asleep.

"Did you get somebody to replace you in the church nursery this morning?" Perry asked.

Leah prayed a breath of thankfulness for Perry's first efforts at decent conversation in the past three hours. "Barbara filled in for me. She knows we visit my parents every month or two."

The headlights of an oncoming car flickered across Perry's tightened jaw. "I'd think you'd get tired of kids, Leah. You take care of Galen all day, then you watch other people's kids every Sunday morning."

"I love children," she said softly. "In fact, Mom asked me if I was pregnant again. She said I had that glow."

"Oh, really?" Perry turned his head sharply.

"I don't know anything…yet. But there's always that possibility. Mom said…"

Perry scowled and turned his full attention back to the road. "Your mom talks too much."

Leah twisted her hands together in her lap. "She and Dad are just concerned about us."

"They made that clear enough when they said I could make more money at accounting in Houston than in Fort Worth. They don't think I'm taking good care of you and Galen."

"They never said that."

"They didn't have to. I saw your father slip you those hundred-dollar bills."

Leah's face warmed with shame. She'd hoped Perry hadn't seen. She'd planned to tell him later—at home, when he was more relaxed. "The money was just for a swing set for Galen. The kind with a fort attached."

Perry turned, his expression pained. "We agreed to build him one together, remember?"

"As Mom said, it'd take us weeks to finish. It'd be nice for Galen to have it now before the weather turns cold."

Perry turned up the radio. He stared straight ahead at the road.

Leah sighed. "I'll give Daddy back the money," she said loudly, over the rock music. "Will that make you feel better?"

He clenched his jaw. "It doesn't matter."

"Yes, it does. Obviously it bothers you to accept this gift. Daddy's just trying to help. He knows how busy we—"

"It's not the money, Leah! Don't you get it? They want you under their thumb. It kills them that you live too far away for them to run your life. That's one of the reasons I took this job in Fort Worth after Galen was born. But even long distance, your parents tell you what to do. Everything from what stocks to invest in for Galen, the best drain cleaner to use…even how to cut your hair. And you always go along with whatever they say!"

Leah absent-mindedly fingered her newly shorn locks. The truth was, she didn't like the short cut as much as she'd hoped, nor did she think it made her look as beautiful as her mother had predicted. It reminded her of the pixie cuts she'd had as a girl, but she wouldn't give Perry the satisfaction of knowing that.

"It's a practical hairstyle," she said.

Perry just looked at her. "Leah, I'm doing my best to take care of you and Galen. I *love* you. We've been married seven years, but in a lot of ways, you've never left your parents' home."

Stung by his words, Leah turned toward the window. Didn't he realize how much she loved her parents, how much she wanted to raise Galen as she'd been raised? She'd had a wonderful childhood. Her mother had never worked outside the home and had always had time for Leah and her older sister and brother. Their father had worked hard to provide for them but had made time for a week-long family car trip every summer.

Perry's parents were divorced. Maybe he was just jealous.

Leah heard the flip of a switch then the *click, click, click* of the turn indicator. The car slowed. She sat up straight. "What's wrong?"

"Nothing." Perry headed the car off the highway and onto the access road. "I'm taking the Ennis cutoff tonight."

Leah blinked. Her normally practical husband took the inter-states whenever possible, preferring speed and predictability to more winding back roads. "You always say it's faster to take the highway."

Perry steered the car left and across the overpass. "Relax, Leah. How much traffic can be going this way on a Sunday night? And the car's low on gas." He glanced sideways at her. "Besides, this is the way your father always goes, isn't it?"

Leah sighed, knowing that anything she said would be mis-construed. *Soon. Soon we'll be home. Then Perry will feel better, and we can put this mess behind us.*

Perry pulled into a sleepy filling station, the Czech Pit. He got out of the car and slammed the door shut, then yanked the gas hose from the pump.

Leah looked past him to winking house lights and families set-tling in for a quiet Sunday evening. Last spring she and Perry and Galen had come to Ennis for the town's annual polka festival. The day had been sunny with wildflowers in bloom, and they'd eaten sausages and kolaches while tapping their feet to oompah bands. The locals greeted each other and onlookers equally, welcoming the tourists like old friends.

But now everything felt different. Darkness shadowed the small-town streets. A gust of wind scuttled newspapers against a peeling picket fence, and a dog howled at length then suddenly went silent.

Leah rubbed her arms. Why hadn't Perry filled up the car before they left Houston? If he hadn't been so angry, zooming out of her parents' driveway, he might have remembered.

Keeping an eye on him through the glass while he pumped fuel into the Corolla, she covertly flipped the radio knob off.

At last he paid the yawning attendant and the driver's door opened, chiming. Perry started the car, glaring at her as he cranked the radio back on, then peeled onto the road. Gravel churned in their wake.

Tapping his hand against the steering wheel to an old Blue Oyster Cult tune, Perry kicked on the high beams. The twin lights cut through the thick night and magnified the starkness of each zipping white divider line.

Waxahachie, 13 miles

Perry was right about one thing; there was hardly anybody on the road, certainly no one traveling in their direction.

Midlothian, 10 miles

The tires hummed against the road, accentuating the stony silence. Leah mentally formulated tomorrow's to-do list. Two of Perry's suits and shirts to the cleaners. Clean the refrigerator. Then grocery shop to restock it. Before she'd had Galen, she'd assumed stay-at-home moms had lots of time.

Mansfield, 2 miles

Perry turned onto a farm road that took them through Mansfield, then Crowley. Then there were no more mileage signs—they were within Fort Worth's city limits.

Darkness gave way to a multitude of business security lights. Leah sat up straighter, anticipating the familiarity of the road. Here was the Dairy Queen where she'd taken Galen for a cone. Beyond that was an auto parts store where Perry had once sent her for a new radiator hose. There was the small family-run café they frequented.

Parked on the shoulder in front of an antiques shop was a battered Buick. It listed at the rear of the driver's side.

"Bad time for a flat," Perry said.

As the Corolla zipped past, Leah glimpsed an elderly woman inside the Buick. She thought of her mother, then shook off the notion. Somebody was probably already on the way to help.

Perry slowed the car. "I'm going back. It shouldn't take too long to change a tire." He turned around in a brightly lit all-night gas station.

You'll stop to help a stranger, but you'll hardly talk to me, she started to say, then felt ashamed. The woman had looked frightened, and who wouldn't be? Being stranded was bad enough, but being stranded in the dark was unbearable.

The woman was still sitting in her car, and she hunched in her seat when they pulled up behind her.

Perry set the brake and shut off the engine. "Come with me, Leah. If I go by myself, she'll probably be more nervous." He yanked the key from the ignition, and she followed him from the car after a quick glance at Galen. She'd be back soon.

Several cars zipped past in both directions, but no one stopped to ask if they needed help. When they reached the Buick, Perry let Leah move ahead. The woman inched away from the door, trembling. "S-someone's already coming for me," she said loudly, clutching her keys and her purse.

Leah bent to the window and held out her hands. "If you need help, we'd like to change your flat tire," she said through the window, hoping her voice was gentle but loud enough for an elderly woman to hear.

The woman eyed Leah cautiously.

"This is my husband," Leah continued, gesturing behind herself, trying to think of anything that would put the woman at ease. "And our son is back there, asleep in his car seat."

"Car seat? You have a baby?" That seemed to get her attention.

Leah nodded. "Yes ma'am. A two-year-old. Do you need help?"

The woman studied her, then Perry, who stepped forward so she could see him better. "I'd be glad to change your tire, ma'am," he said, "but you'll have to get out of the car. You shouldn't stay inside while the tire's being changed."

The woman eyed them again, then opened the passenger-side door. Still clutching her keys and purse, she stood staring at Leah and Perry across the hood. "I'm not usually out this late," she said, "but I wanted to finish watching *Touched by an Angel* with my son and his wife." She made an effort to straighten. "If he had any sense at all, he would have followed me home."

Leah walked slowly around the front of the car. "I like *Touched by an Angel* too. My name's Leah, and my husband's name is Perry. He'll change your tire, and you can be on your way."

"Ma'am, I need you to open your trunk so I can get your spare," Perry said behind her.

The woman looked startled, then relaxed when Perry didn't move past Leah. She grudgingly nodded, then moved toward the trunk. Her hands shook as she fumbled for the right key and inserted it into the lock. "I think that son of mine said there was a spare in here… Oh dear, I can't tell!"

Perry moved beside her and peered into the open trunk. "Yes ma'am, there's one right under this flooring here, see? Would you like to wait in our car with my wife? This'll take a few minutes."

She was obviously nervous again; Leah could see her hands tremble faster. Her grandmother had had that same reaction many times. *Probably arthritis as much as fear. She really needs to sit down.*

"There's a bench in front of that antiques shop," Leah said. "Would you rather wait there?"

The woman relaxed her shoulders. "That'd be just fine." Her face fell a little. "Can you help me over there? All this excitement has me a bit flustered."

Leah smiled. "Let me check on my son first." She peeked in the rear passenger window. Galen had his cheek pressed against the soft material of his car seat cover, his chubby fists covering each other over the belt. He smiled in his sleep, deep in a pleasant toddler dream.

Straightening, Leah reluctantly turned from the car and headed for the darkened antiques shop. She hoped it wouldn't take Perry too long.

Beside her, the woman hobbled on heavy, orthopedic shoes. Her foot slipped on the gravel walkway, and Leah caught her by the elbow. The woman covered her heart with her hand. "Thank you," she said breathlessly.

"Just a few more steps." Leah helped her to the bench, then sat beside her. She could see Perry hunkered down on the ground, jacking up the flat tire.

The woman wiped a gnarled hand across her eyes. "I'm sorry if I was so suspicious. A body can't be too careful these days, and I get so scared sometimes by myself. I knew I should have left earlier!"

Leah smiled at the echo of her own previous words to Perry. Perry rose and headed for the trunk, then bounced out the spare tire. Thank goodness he'd gone running that afternoon—she'd known he just wanted to get out of her parents' house for a while, but at least now he wasn't wearing his dress shoes. The Nikes had to be more comfortable for this sort of work.

A pickup truck full of laughing teenagers sped past, honking, the horn fading as they disappeared toward Fort Worth.

The woman sniffed. "Most folks don't have any respect these days. I'm Orvilla Ivers. You and your husband are good people to stop for an old lady."

"We're happy to help." Distracted, Leah concentrated on the Corolla, straining to see Galen in the darkness. Surely she would hear him if he cried out. She wouldn't want him to awaken and be afraid at being alone. She rose, then hesitated. Glancing down at Orvilla, Leah saw that her hands were trembling again.

Leah cupped her hands around her mouth. "Perry! Can you check on Galen?"

He propped the spare against the Buick and waved his acknowledgment. She watched as he strolled back to the Corolla and peered in Galen's window, pressing his hand against the glass.

Perry straightened and waved back at her. "He's still asleep! He's..."

Behind the Corolla, headlights wavered over, then illuminated, the road. Axles ground their protest at sharp overcompensation, and tires screeched against the blacktop. Still standing, Leah felt her knees inexplicably weaken and her heart lurch to her throat.

Puzzled, Perry turned. Then he, Galen, and the Corolla were engulfed by the oncoming lights and the crunch of metal and shattered glass.

Chapter Two

"Perry!" Leah found her voice, but her body momentarily froze in shock. A battered pickup was jammed against the Corolla, which had accordioned into Orvilla's Buick like a smashed paper cup.

Oh, Jesus, help me! Galen! Surely he was safe in his little car seat.

A man kicked open the driver's door of the pickup and stumbled out. He held his hand to his head, and blood oozed between his fingers as he wobbled into the oncoming lane. A car screeched to brake just short of hitting him, and he shouted something in Spanish before staggering across the road.

Cars stopped and dozens of people rushed toward the wreckage, clustering around the three cars. Several knelt around something farther up the road. Everywhere were lights and noise...yelling, crying.

"...just in front of the antiques shop," someone was saying. "Yeah, this is a cell phone. You'd better hurry!"

Terror flooded through Leah, pumping adrenaline into her shocked system. She ran toward the mangled pile. "Galen!" She slammed to a stop with her hands against the passenger side of the crumpled Corolla and lost her footing on a patch of broken glass.

A siren wailed through the darkness, and several firemen jumped off a hook and ladder before it came to a complete halt. One of them gripped her arms and helped her to her feet. "Stay back, ma'am."

"But…but my son!" Another fireman was lifting out the car seat, a motionless Galen still strapped in. Panic knotted in Leah's stomach, a cry strangling in her throat as she tried to muscle past the fireman holding her back. *"Galen!"*

The fireman glanced over his shoulder then gripped her arms tighter. "Stay back. The paramedics will—"

"No! I want to see him!"

Sirens blaring, lights flashing, an ambulance pulled up alongside the circle of people gathered down the road. Two paramedics slammed open the back doors and bounced a gurney to the ground. The crowd parted but not enough for Leah to see what they surrounded. As the paramedics rolled the gurney forward, she saw a pair of men's Nikes strewn in the road, alongside a pool of blood.

Her stomach clenched, and she tried to make another break. "Perry!"

The fireman restrained her, his hands digging into her arms. "Let the paramedics take care of them both until CareFlite gets here, ma'am. You can't help them."

CareFlite! "I have to see him! I have to see my son!"

"They'll both be taken to the hospital. CareFlite's the fastest way. They'll be here in just a moment." His tone softened. "Is there someone you'd like us to call for you?"

Leah shook her head, hugging herself for warmth. *Oh, God, let this be a bad dream!*

A police officer with a clipboard called to the fireman, who excused himself. They conferred briefly, then returned. The fireman cleared his throat. "This is Officer Seton, and he'd like to ask you a few questions if he could."

"I'll be as brief as possible, ma'am," Seton said. He looked scarcely older than Leah, but he was all authority. "I know this is all a shock, but the sooner we have our information, the better. Let's start with your name and the name of the occupants of the car."

Someone slipped a jacket around Leah's shoulders. The presence of a police officer—authority—made her heart pound, yet kept her from racing down the road to where the paramedics worked. "M-my name's Leah Travers. My husband is Perry Travers, and our son is Galen."

"Can you tell me what happened, as you saw it?"

"I...I don't really know," she said, shaking at the thought of having to relive those quick, awful seconds. "I was sitting over there. My husband was changing the tire on a lady's...Orvilla, I think she said her name was...car—"

"The Buick?" The officer wrote on his clipboard without looking up.

Leah nodded. "Then I asked my husband to check on our son."

"Your son was in his car seat in back of the Corolla?"

"Y-yes."

"How old is your son?"

"Two." Leah's eyes filled with tears. "All of a sudden, I saw headlights coming toward them, from behind them, then... then..." She blinked. "I just remember the headlights. It happened so fast, it's like I didn't even see it happen."

The officer looked up from his writing, his face grim. "We apprehended the driver of the pickup as he was trying to flee the scene. We've given him a Breathalyzer test, and it looks like he's over the legal intoxication limit."

"He was…drunk? A…a drunk driver?" Such things happened on the ten o'clock news or in a newspaper article. Not in Leah's secure world.

"Yes ma'am." The officer continued to scribble. "Can we call someone for you? Someone to take you to the hospital?"

"Can't I ride with my husband and son? I want to see them."

Officer Seton shook his head. "There's no room in the helicopter. You can ride with me in my car."

"I want to see my husband! I want to see my son!" Leah had never yelled at anyone in authority in her life, and the emotional force of her words shocked her. Seton lowered the clipboard and stared at her.

Blades pounded overhead, and bright lights strafed the ground. The skids of the CareFlite helicopter touched down in a field alongside the road.

"Ma'am," Seton said gently, "your husband and child have both been badly injured." He paused. "But if it were my family, I'd want to see them too. Come with me."

Her heart pounding, Leah followed the police officer toward the grassy area. They passed Orvilla standing alongside the twisted wreckage, weeping while a police officer patiently tried to take her statement.

Near the helicopter, Seton cautioned Leah back. "Let me talk to the attendants first. Stay here."

She nodded, trying to breathe deeply. *One, two. In, out.*

Seton grabbed a paramedic and spoke rapidly. The young man shook his head, swiping the back of his hand against his brow. He rubbed his palm against his white shirt, leaving a red stain. Seton gestured at Leah, and the paramedic straightened.

The policeman motioned her forward.

"This is Mrs. Travers," he said. "Her husband's name is Perry, and their son is Galen."

"We've done all we can for them," the paramedic said. "Now it's up to CareFlite. The faster they get to the hospital, the better their chances. I want to prepare you, though. It doesn't look good."

An icy finger trailed down Leah's spine. "They'll be okay, won't they?"

The paramedic looked her square in the eye. "They've both suffered internal injuries. Head injuries, too, from what we can tell."

Leah trembled. Seton steadied her.

"The CareFlite crew's the best there is," the paramedic went on. "Your best bet is to go to the hospital with the officer and wait for word there."

Leah straightened. "I want to see them."

The paramedic sighed. "Mrs. Travers, I'm not sure you want to do that. They're both unconscious. They don't look—"

"I want to see them *now*."

The young man sighed, then gestured toward the helicopter. "You can watch them being loaded."

From within the circle of people, a female CareFlite attendant rose, holding an IV bag high. "Everybody *get back!* Give us room!"

The crowd dutifully parted, and a second paramedic pulled a gurney forward with the woman running alongside toward the helicopter. A male attendant stooped alongside also, squeezing a clear bag attached to a tube stuck down the throat of the man on the gurney.

"Perry," Leah whispered, stepping forward. It had to be her husband, yet the figure looked nothing like him. His neck was wrapped in a thick collar, and his legs and arms were each wrapped in inflatable plastic. His clothes had been cut off, and someone had partially covered him with a blanket. The IV tube disappeared under its edge.

His face was bruised and bloody. A deep gash raked the side of his head, and his eyes were fixed and unblinking.

"Get out of the way!" the woman barked at Leah, then Officer Seton. "Can't you keep these people back?"

"It's her husband!" he yelled over the whirring of the blades, but by then the woman and the gurney with Perry had already disappeared into the helicopter.

A paramedic helping them yelled, "Where's the kid?"

"Here!" Another CareFlite attendant rolled an identical gurney forward. This time Officer Seton held her back, but Leah caught a glimpse of Galen, his small body stark against the adult-sized gurney. He looked like his father, with a blanket thrown over him, tubes running out of his body, and an attendant continually squeezing a bag attached to a tube down his throat.

Unlike Perry, Galen's eyes were closed, his face barely visible around the bag. Before Leah could even touch his hair, he was whisked away.

"Go, go, go!" The paramedic helped them into the helicopter, then slammed the door. "Everybody back!"

The crowd obeyed, and the helicopter lifted off, tilted at an angle, then circled back through the night toward Fort Worth. The sound of the blades grew fainter. The paramedic watched for a moment, sighing.

Officer Seton cleared his throat. "This is Mrs. Travers, the wife and mother. Can you tell her anything about her family?"

The paramedic turned, and all the energy he'd previously exhibited drained from his eyes. "We think your husband has severe internal bleeding, most of it in his head. He's also probably suffered several broken bones in his extremities. His ribs are fractured, which might have caused damage to his lungs."

Leah swallowed hard. "And Galen?"

"Internal bleeding, from what we can tell." He stepped forward, his eyes sad. "Get to the hospital, Mrs. Travers."

"I'll put the sirens and lights on." Officer Seton touched her shoulder. "Ready, ma'am?"

She nodded, clutching the jacket on her shoulders as she followed him.

She'd never been inside a police car before, but then this was a night of many firsts. Leah sat in the front seat, numb, as Seton ran the sirens and lights all the way into town and straight to the emergency room.

She was at the automatic doors and inside before Seton passed her, striding toward a young woman behind the information desk. "This is Mrs. Travers. Her family was brought in on CareFlite."

The woman held out a clipboard with papers. "She'll need to fill out—"

Officer Seton grabbed the board. "She'll take care of them later."

The woman flushed. "She needs to fill them out now."

Officer Seton leaned slightly over the counter. "*She'll fill them out.* Just tell the doctors she's here. I'll take her to the waiting room."

"Y-yes sir." The woman scrambled from her chair and disappeared through an entryway.

Officer Seton pushed through a swinging door that said "No Unauthorized Personnel" and led Leah down a long, tiled hallway. Farther down she could see various open doors with bright light spilling out over the scuffed linoleum. She heard the bustle of metal carts and voices, loud and clipped, barking out orders in the medical language of hospital staff.

Leah trembled and clutched the jacket closer. Mortified, she realized she didn't know who it belonged to. How was she ever going to find the owner now?

Officer Seton opened a door and flipped on the meager light of a small waiting room. A durable tweed sofa and four matching chairs made a U in the center of the room. Along the near wall stood a table with a coffee machine, where the dregs of a cold pot languished alongside opened packets of NutraSweet and used plastic stirrers. On the far side of the room, the blinds to a small, lone window were pulled tightly shut.

In one corner beneath the sill was a low table scattered with dog-eared magazines, and in the other was a plastic chest filled with toddler toys.

Leah brought her fist to her mouth and pressed hard.

"Mrs. Travers, can't I call someone for you?"

She shook her head, unable to speak for the tears clogging her throat. "I don't have any family in town," she whispered.

"A friend? A neighbor?" he said gently. "You shouldn't be alone now."

Who should she call? Rob and Joyce from Sunday school class? Greg and Sharon from the supper group? Maybe Ed and Tracie from next door? The thought of enduring any of their friends' sympathy, of even having to talk, was more than she could bear.

She shook her head again. "I'll be all right."

Officer Seton sighed and gestured at the sofa. "Have a seat. I'll go get some fresh coffee."

"I don't drink it," she said, obediently sitting.

Seton tossed the clipboard on a chair. "I'll get some anyway." He pulled the door open, and Leah blinked at the intrusion of the bright hallway light. The door swung shut, and she dropped her head into her hands.

"Oh, God," she whispered, "how could you let this happen? Why are you punishing us? The man who caused this should be the one suffering—he was drunk!"

The door swung open. Leah jerked her head up, swiping at her eyes. An Asian woman entered and extended her hand. "Mrs. Travers?" she said in slightly accented English. "I am Nora Chan, the hospital chaplain. I came to see if I can do anything for you."

"Do you know anything about my husband? About my son?"

Nora sat beside Leah and shook her head, her short dark hair swinging slightly. "The doctors will come as soon as they can." She smiled gently. "Your family is in good hands. Not just the doctors', but the Lord's."

Leah drew a deep breath. "Then why is my family here? Why did the man who hit them walk away from the accident?"

"I do not know, Mrs. Travers. Here in the hospital I see many horrible things happen to good people. Things no one can explain or justify. But he is a good God—I cling to that. And we will pray for your husband and son." She held out her hands as if in question.

Leah sagged and wearily placed her hands in Nora's. She bowed her head, and Nora began to pray. "Father, thank you that you love us, even when our human eyes cannot see it. We do not understand—"

The door swung open. Dropping Nora's hands, Leah raised her head expectantly. An older and a younger man, both in street clothes, entered slowly, their expressions stoic. Stethoscopes hung around their necks.

Leah rose, her heart pounding. Nora stood beside her.

"Mrs. Travers," the older man said, "I'm Dr. Pender, the head ER physician. This is Dr. Andross, my senior resident."

"I'm so sorry, Mrs. Travers," Andross said gently. "But the force of the car's impact was too much for your son. We weren't able to save him."

"But he was in his car seat! He was supposed to be safe!" Leah vaguely felt Nora's arm wrap around her shoulders. *Galen gone? There must be a mistake!*

"Even though he was strapped in correctly, the force of the car that hit yours was enough to cause major internal trauma. The paramedics and CareFlite personnel did their best, but your son wasn't even breathing on his own when they brought him in. We did everything we could, but there was too much damage." Dr. Andross's eyes clouded. "He slipped away just awhile ago."

"No," Leah whispered. Grief welled inside her, explosive, and she shook with its force. "Oh, God, no. Not Galen!"

"Mrs. Travers...," Dr. Pender said slowly.

Leah straightened, bracing herself. *Please, Jesus. Not more.*

"Your husband didn't make it either. He also had massive abdominal injuries, but he died from a torn artery that caused a rapid hematoma—buildup of blood within his skull. Ultimately, his brain was compressed."

Leah's knees buckled, and Nora held her up.

Dr. Pender drew a deep breath. "I'm so sorry. I want you to know we don't believe either your son or your husband suffered.

And while it's normal for survivors to feel a certain amount of guilt, there was absolutely nothing you could have done. They had the best care available." He paused. "I understand this was a drunk driving accident."

Leah closed her eyes, unable to speak. She nodded briefly. How could what had happened to her family ever be called an accident?

"Then there will be an investigation," Pender said, "and be assured that Dr. Andross and I will make certain that all the facts are straight so that justice will be served."

Leah nodded again, her eyes filling with tears. "Thank you."

"Do you have any questions?" Dr. Andross said gently.

"Can I see them?" Leah whispered.

The doctors glanced at each other, then Nora. She tipped her head slightly, then squeezed Leah's hand. "I will go with you. Doctors, can you please tell Mrs. Travers how to expect her husband and son to look?"

"I saw them as they were being loaded on the helicopter," Leah said. "But they had tubes…and things…attached."

"Those will be removed before you see them," Dr. Pender said. "If you'll follow us…"

Nora held on to Leah's hand, and Dr. Andross walked on her other side. They followed Dr. Pender, who led them farther down the brightly lit hall.

"Your husband and son will be covered with a sheet," Dr. Andross said. "If you've seen them already, you know that they have bruises and lacerations. Your husband had broken bones as well."

"Will…will their skin still be warm?" Leah had never seen anyone dead before.

"Yes. And their eyes have been closed."

Just like the movies.

Dr. Pender stopped and turned. "Mrs. Travers, do you want to see your son or your husband first?"

"My son," she said automatically.

"This way." Dr. Pender gestured to an open door.

Inside, Leah saw a man at a desk, writing, and a woman bustling to return a full metal supply cart to its corner.

Another woman stood over a small sheet-covered form, her hand resting on the head. Her eyes were closed, and her lips moved silently. Nora led Leah to her side, and the doctors stood at the foot of the gurney. "This is Mary," Nora said softly.

Mary opened her eyes and turned. "I was one of the nurses," she said softly. "Would you like to see your son...Galen?"

Leah nodded, her throat thick. Mary slowly pulled back the sheet to his shoulders, and Leah sobbed once, then clung to Nora for support. "My little boy," she whispered. "My precious...little boy." She stretched out her shaking hand, then withdrew it.

"You can touch him if you'd like," Mary said. "You can even hold him."

Leah gently fingered his hair. "I'd like that."

Nora drew up a chair for Leah to sit. Mary lifted Galen's sheet-wrapped body and laid it in Leah's arms. Studying his face, she held him close, remembering the first time a nurse had given him to her. He had squalled and kicked, red-faced, furious with his new world. Now he was white and silent, and if she believed the Bible, he was in another new world.

She felt Nora's hand on her shoulder. "He was a beautiful boy. Galen is a beautiful name."

"It means 'little bright one.'"

Nora knelt on the linoleum to Leah's level. "Would you like for me to say a few words?"

Leah nodded, holding Galen closer.

"'Let not your heart be troubled; believe in God, believe also in Me. In My Father's house are many dwelling places; if it were not so, I would have told you; for I go to prepare a place for you.... And He shall wipe away every tear from their eyes; and there shall no longer be any death; there shall no longer be any mourning, or crying, or pain; the first things have passed away.'"

Leah closed her eyes and rocked wordlessly, a tear falling on Galen's hair. How could she ever release him from her arms? She couldn't imagine life without her only child.

"Galen," she whispered to his still face, "you were the child Daddy and I prayed for." She bent and kissed his small forehead. "Mommy loves you, darling. Good-bye."

She held him closer, pressing her face against his cheek. *If I don't let go now, I never will. Lord, do you know how much this hurts? Why is this happening?*

Turning her face, she wordlessly held him out. Mary lifted him gently, and Leah rose and forced herself to step toward the doctors. "Where is Perry?"

"This way." Dr. Pender led her into the room next door. This time she was prepared for the sight of the covered body and the lowering of the sheet.

Leah looked at Perry's battered face. His lips curved up slightly, a shadow of his usual smile. *Can you believe this mess, Leah?* he seemed to say.

The thought made her smile briefly, and she raised his hand to her cheek. "I love you. Take good care of Galen...okay?"

She trembled, clutching his hand with both of hers. *Wake up, please wake up. Tell me this isn't real. Sit up and tell me this is all just*

*a horrible practical joke, then we'll go home and laugh about it.
Okay?...All right?*

"Perry!" she sobbed brokenly.

"Oh, Lord," Nora said softly behind her. "This is not a path
Leah would have chosen. But you are with her. Let her feel your
arms of comfort as she walks this difficult road."

Nora continued to pray, even though Leah wasn't listening.
When at last the chaplain's words penetrated her grief, Leah
straightened. Embarrassed at her outburst, she lowered Perry's
hand to the gurney. She kissed him gently. "I love you," she whispered, then blindly made her way from the room.

Outside, she leaned against the wall, shaking. She was cold, so
cold. Nora and the doctors joined her, all of them waiting for her
to speak, it seemed.

She drew a steadying breath. "What happens to them now?"

"They'll be taken to the morgue for autopsy," Dr. Pender said.
"After that they'll be released to you for burial or cremation."

Leah closed her eyes. She couldn't fall apart. She *wouldn't* fall
apart.

He touched her shoulder. "Please don't hesitate to call either
Dr. Andross or me if you have any questions."

"Thank you," she managed to mumble. She heard them leave,
their rubber soles squeaking and fading down the hall.

Nora embraced her. "I am so sorry, Mrs. Travers," she said. "I
have no words."

And I have no family. Leah briefly pressed her cheek against
Nora's shoulder then awkwardly pulled away. "Thank you for your
help."

"Is someone coming to get you?" the chaplain said. "Where are
you going now?"

Leah felt her lips tremble, and she pressed them together. "I don't know," she whispered. "I'm not sure."

Jacobo Martinez bent over the heavy law book at his desk and ran a hand through his shoulder-length hair. He glanced at the clock radio emitting soft jazz and groaned. Three o'clock in the morning, and he had a class at eight. Not only was he exhausted, but the humidity was horrible this fall, even for Austin. No breeze blew past the scraped paint of the old house's window.

Someone rapped softly on the door. "You still awake, Jocko?" The way Eric pronounced it used to grate on Jacobo until he realized his housemate meant no disrespect. "You've got a phone call— a woman, and she's babbling Spanish something fierce."

Grateful for the interruption, Jacobo rose and stretched, opening the door. "Probably that pretty Consuelo I met at the Student Union. You know how we Latino men are—women just can't keep away."

"Yeah, well tell them to call at a decent hour." Eric yawned, stumbling back toward his bedroom. "Some of us Anglo types like to get our sleep."

Jacobo grinned and padded barefoot down the scuffed hardwood hall to the house's one telephone. He lifted the receiver from its side on the dented coffee table and flopped down onto the secondhand plaid couch. *"¿Bueno?"*

"¡Jacobo!"

Sobbing pierced his ears, and Jacobo sat upright at the sound of his younger sister's voice. *"¡Dolores! ¿Qué pasó?"*

"¡Es Manuel...borracho...!"

Drunk. It figured. It seemed to be her husband's constant occupation. Jacobo gripped the phone. "Did he hurt you, Dolores? The kids?"

"¡Muerto!"

"Manuel's dead?" His heart lifted momentarily. Then, ashamed at the thought, he crossed himself in a vestige of tradition.

"¡No! Un hombre y...y su hijo." She wailed anew, unable to speak further.

Jacobo drew a deep breath. *"Dolores, escúcheme,"* he said in the firm tone that had always kept his younger brothers and sister in line. "Tell me exactly what happened."

She stopped sobbing, and when she spoke again, her words came out more slowly. Jacobo listened intently, grief knotting his stomach. Dolores started weeping again, this time softly, and he murmured reassurances. When she finished, he issued temporary plans for her and the children.

He hung up the phone, drained. He wanted to sink back on the couch and fall into a deep sleep or at least return to his sweltering bedroom and the law book. He was tired of fighting his family's battles, tired of being the one they turned to in a crisis. Hadn't he at last earned the right to his own life?

"Lord, forgive me," he murmured instantly. "My sister and her family need me. And tonight there are two people dead. May you receive them into your kingdom and comfort their family."

Jacobo trudged back down the hall, knocked on Eric's door, then entered without waiting for an answer. "I have to leave town. Now. Can you loan me some money?"

Eric sat up, rubbing his eyes even as he switched on the bedside lamp. "What's up?"

"I have to go home to Fort Worth. Emergency." Jacobo turned away, already mentally calculating what he'd need to take.

Eric was right behind him. "I can probably get enough cash from a teller machine for you to catch a plane."

Eric's unquestioning generosity never failed to amaze Jacobo. "My motorcycle will be just as fast." Jacobo pulled a bag out of his closet. "It beats sitting around the airport waiting for a flight. And I'll need the bike once I get home. My sister's Plymouth is unreliable." He yanked a few shirts from their hangers and tossed them in the bag.

Eric leaned against the doorjamb, yawning. "You've got classes tomorrow, man. It must be some emergency if you're ducking out."

Jacobo pitched underwear and socks on top of the shirts and tried to keep the anger out of his voice. "My brother-in-law got drunk and drove with a suspended license—again. Only this time he wasn't lucky enough to just get arrested. He hit and killed a man and his son." Jacobo snapped the bag shut. "So now my sister and her kids need me."

Again, he wanted to add. But didn't.

Chapter Three

Leah stared blankly at the wall, watching the evening shadows deepen. Mentally she traced the swirls and patterns of the roses-and-lace wallpaper that had decorated her room since she was twelve years old. She'd sat on the pink ruffled bed countless times, first as a moody adolescent, then as a heartbroken teenager, nursing the latest emotional catastrophe in her young life.

My parents don't understand me... Everybody else gets to wear makeup, why can't I?... I didn't make the swim team... Jeff Murray asked Susan Sharpe to the dance instead of me...

Leah folded her legs up against her chest and pressed her eyes against her knees.

She felt young again, so young that things were once again spinning beyond her control. Only this time there was no growing up to anticipate, no tiny spark of realization that she would one day be able to decide for herself. No, her decisions were all gone, snatched away by some drunk on the road. And she was a helpless bystander. A little girl on the inside, wanting to cry and yell and find some way to make it all better.

Yet, as though they couldn't see the little girl trapped in her woman's body, strangers—especially the press—had turned to her in the past few days for quotes regarding the wreck. She'd refused, shaking her head and scurrying away from personal contact, letting the answering machine handle the rest.

Worse still were the strangers who wanted specific answers to their myriad questions: Burial or cremation? Memorial service or graveside? Scriptures? Songs?

How could she decide the fate of Perry and Galen's bodies? Leah vaguely remembered Perry once joking that he would prefer to be cremated, yet the brochure sounded like the script to a horror movie. "Cremation reduces the body to small portions through intense heat," the brochure said. "Pulverization then reduces the portions to dust or ashes, which can then be interred, inurned, or scattered in accordance with local laws."

The other choice, burial, hadn't seemed any more pleasant. The thought of worms eating away at what was left of her baby's poor, tiny body...

Her father had mercifully taken charge, dealing with the questions as confidently as he invested his clients' lifetime savings. A true man of business, Hart Tyler navigated the waters of death as smoothly as those of retirement. So when he pronounced interment in a solid oak casket to be the most cost-effective yet dignified method of disposition, she had numbly agreed.

They flew to her side immediately, her parents, flanking her, knowing exactly—as always—what to do. Her mother contacted someone to watch Leah and Perry's home while her father arranged for the bodies to be taken to Houston for the funeral services. They never asked Leah if she might prefer to have the burial in Fort Worth, assuming instead that Perry and Galen rightfully belonged in Houston, where she and Perry had grown up. She'd silently ridden in the limousine that reversed their fateful journey, murmuring a quiet prayer of thanks when her father curtly ordered the driver to take a different route than the road that had claimed Perry and Galen.

Leah wrapped her arms tighter around her legs and pressed them against the empty ache in her chest. She'd halfway expected Perry and Galen to be waiting for her, alive, at her parents' house in Houston. Instead, she'd proceeded dazedly through the double funeral. Surrounded by a blur of family and friends, she hadn't believed one word from the verses Reverend Kiley read as she clenched her hands in her lap and stared at the long, flower-draped coffin and the pitifully smaller one beside it.

The Lord is near to the brokenhearted, and saves those who are crushed in spirit.

Thankfully, Perry's divorced parents had gone their separate ways back to Louisiana right after the funeral. She didn't want to see them—she couldn't stand the sadness in their eyes.

"Leah?" A firm knock sounded on the door. "Leah, there's food on the table. And Aunt Dorothy and Uncle March are here with your cousins. Not to mention people from the church."

Leah closed her eyes and pressed them against her knees. Her kneecap pushed against her eye socket, and she winced at the pain. She'd never realized how hard bone could be, yet how easily broken. She thought of Perry's shattered body.

...the brokenhearted...crushed in spirit...

The door clicked open, and she knew from the silence that her mother stood watching her. "Leah, you have to come out," Emily Tyler said firmly. "What will people think about you hiding out in here?"

Leah raised her face and stared at the wall. "I don't really care, Mom." She'd agonized over and abdicated many decisions the past few days, but this one, so blessedly easy, she'd make on her own.

"You have to eat something," her mother said, trying a new tack, a mother's tack. One that she herself might have used to persuade a pouting Galen.

"I'm not hungry." She doubted she would ever be hungry again.

"You'll make yourself sick if you don't eat." Her mother swept into the room and flicked on the bedside lamp. "That's not what Perry or Galen would want. Now come out and acknowledge everyone here. They were good enough to stop by."

Leah drew a deep, tired breath. She was weary of everyone's murmured sympathies and stares as though she were the latest attraction in a freak show. "Mom—"

"It's the thing to do. For them as well as for you. It's painful, but it's one of the first steps on the road to healing. Now dry your eyes and come out to the dining room. Once you put some food on a plate, you'll feel like eating."

Resigned, Leah rose and followed her mother's ramrod-straight figure down the hallway toward the staircase. Her own body felt like Jell-O. It had always been easier to give in and do what was expected, what her parents thought was needed. And the heavy pit in her stomach would be present no matter where she was, whether she was alone or not.

Halfway down the stairs, she heard the hushed tones of the gathered mourners. She stopped, bracing her hand on the wall just below last year's gilt-framed Christmas portrait of herself with Perry and Galen.

Three steps down, her mother turned to see what was keeping her and promptly mistook her hesitation for an attempt at composure. "That's good, take deep breaths." She walked up two steps and clasped Leah's arms. "Be a strong young woman. You'll get through this. Don't look so glum, darling."

Leah obediently stretched the corners of her mouth, and her mother cupped her trembling chin. "They know you're hurting." Emily glanced at the Christmas portrait, and her hazel eyes misted. "We're all hurting."

"Oh, Mom…" Leah covered her mother's hand with her own, wanting to crawl up into her lap right there on the stairs. She felt a tear trickle down her cheek.

"No tears now, darling. We'll talk later." Her mother wiped her face, then straightened Leah's rumpled navy dress. She squared her own unwrinkled shoulders and smiled wryly. "First things first."

"Em? Is she—?" Hart Tyler stopped at the bottom of the stairs and smiled sadly. "Leah." He held out his arms.

Leah brushed past her mother and into her father's embrace. He held her warmly, securely, and she pressed her face against his black wool suit. The faint odor of cigar lingered among the threads, evidence that he'd sneaked out for a smoke, against Emily Tyler's standing wishes. The pungent smell reminded Leah of when she was a girl, when she'd bury her face against his neck for a hug and be pleasantly enveloped in the contrasting smells of an expensive Macanudo and Old Spice aftershave. Smells that she forever identified with her father.

He gave her one more hug then wrapped an arm around her shoulders. "Come greet our guests. It's just family and friends. Most of them didn't get to talk to you at the graveside." He drew her toward the den.

Leah gripped the newel post, panic filling the empty spaces of her heart. He acted as though he wanted her to put in an appearance at one of his business parties, as she'd often done while growing up. Did he and her mother really believe she was capable of small talk today? Of handling a host of sympathetic murmurs and pitying glances? "But, Daddy—" she whispered.

"Leah!" Aunt Dorothy drew her away from her father in a suffocating embrace. "How are you, dear? I was so proud of you at the funeral and at the graveside. So brave."

"Hello, doll." Uncle March grabbed her next, his wispy white beard scratching the top of her head. "Such a shame. Such a shame."

"God's will is so hard to understand," Aunt Dorothy said. "At least you're young. You have your whole life ahead of you."

"Oh my, yes." Aunt Laurie boomed over her shoulder. "Just turn it over to God. You'll be all right."

Leah panicked, feeling the press of the crowd that swelled from the dining room into the hallway. "Daddy—" She looked around helplessly for rescue, but it was her mother who freed her from the clutches of her family and steered her away.

"Now, now, Leah needs to eat," Emily said with the authority that had ruled a multitude of PTA and hospital volunteer boards. "I don't think I've seen her put one bite in her mouth since she's been home."

The universal plea of food had its effect, for the relatives parted way, murmuring regret for their thoughtless behavior. Leah felt her mother's grip on her elbow all the way to the overburdened sideboard. A plate was thrust in her hands.

"Look, dear," her mother said, "there's chicken and ham from the Ladies' Bethany Class and Waldorf, Caesar, and ambrosia salads from the wives of the early service ushers. And over there are several lovely casseroles," her mother dropped her voice, "though I have no idea what they are. I certainly can't say that I recommend them, based on looks alone."

None of it looked appetizing or even edible, but to appease her mother, Leah dutifully scooped a few items onto her plate. She avoided the questionable casseroles.

"I've saved you a chair over in the corner by me." Leah's older sister, Danni, leaned forward and whispered, "Maybe away from the buffet table, all these old biddies and geezers won't notice you so much."

Leah suppressed a smile as she followed her sister's plump figure to their father's favorite leather wing chairs. Good old Danni. She'd always stuck up for Leah.

As Leah sat down, Danni set a glass of iced tea on the low table between the chairs. "Here's something for you to sip on."

Leah reset the glass on a circle of sandstone, then made a stern face in imitation of their mother. "Danielle Catherine, how many times do I have to tell you to use a coaster?"

Danni snickered, and Leah smothered a giggle herself. The moment felt good, the best she'd had since the accident.

Danni's expression sobered, and she touched Leah's hand. "I'm so sorry. I can't imagine what you're going through."

Leah swallowed hard. She and her sister had never shared their innermost thoughts and dreams, but maybe Danni would at least let her express the dark grief and anger that battled for control of her heart. "I..."

"Aunt Leah." Danni's daughter, Jennifer, touched Leah's knee.

Leah set aside her plate and smiled at the four-year-old. "What is it, sweetie?"

The little girl's blue eyes filled with tears. "Mommy says I can't play with Galen anymore. Is that true?"

Danni looked stricken. "Jennifer!"

"It's okay. Jennifer, your mom's right." Leah drew her niece into the circle of her arm. "Galen's gone to—"

"Jen, come upstairs with me and see the new Beanie Baby I bought for you." Emily Travers drew her granddaughter away from Leah, casting a sharp glance at Danni. Leah watched them retreat up the stairs, then turned to her sister.

Danni's eyes were filled with tears. "I'm so sorry, Leah. Jennifer doesn't understand. Derek and I tried to explain things to her on the flight here from Chicago, but I think she's still too little."

"It's okay." Leah took Danni's hand, her own eyes filling with tears at the sight of her sister's distress. "At least she wants to talk about it."

"Oh, Leah…"

Danni rose and Leah met her in a fierce embrace. "It's okay, Danni," she whispered.

"Mom warned us not to say anything upsetting… You know how she is." Danni laughed shakily, clinging to Leah. "And you know how I am, always wearing my heart on my sleeve. I guess Jennifer takes after me."

"I'm glad she does," Leah whispered, holding her sister closer.

Danni sniffled loudly then drew back. She glanced nervously over her shoulder, and Leah saw Aunt Dorothy and Aunt Laurie moving in. Danni wiped her eyes and gave Leah a little push. "Go on. Head for the bathroom or something. I'll keep them at bay. I know you probably don't feel like talking to anybody."

Leah squeezed Danni's arm in silent thanks and took a shortcut through the kitchen to the downstairs bathroom. Her face did feel warm; a splash of cold water would help her regain her composure. She certainly wasn't about to fall apart in front of all these people, not because her mother decreed it but because she didn't want them hovering around her, feasting on the carrion of her soul.

Passing by her father's study, she heard his low voice. "I have a lawyer friend who has connections with the district attorney's office. I've learned quite a bit already about the driver."

Leah stopped short. Her father had already looked into what had happened? He hadn't said anything to her. What exactly did he know about the driver of the other car? ·

"Not only was that Mexican way beyond the legal limit, he didn't even have a valid driver's license."

"You know how they are," Owen, her older brother, said disdainfully. "They cross the river illegally and make just enough money to own a car, but not enough to cover the responsibility."

"This one's license had been suspended. Evidently he'd been arrested for drunk driving before. More than once, in fact."

Leah shook, clenching her hands. If he'd been caught before, who had let that killer loose to drive? Why hadn't his family stopped him?

Hart Tyler's voice tightened. "That wetback'll be an old man before he sees the light of day. Perry and Galen's deaths will put him away for a long time." His voice shook. "I saw the reports from the hospital, Owen. I didn't tell Leah, but their bodies were mangled so badly internally that no organs could be harvested for donation. The funeral director told me that it was a good thing Leah didn't see anything below their necks at the hospital. He said both Perry and Galen's bodies were in the worst shape he'd seen from an auto accident."

Leah pressed a fist to her mouth and hurried past the open door. "Leah?" She heard her father step into the hall behind her.

She rushed into the bathroom and locked the door, then climbed into the shower. Whipping the curtain closed, she sank into the privacy of the tub.

Why did Perry and Galen have to suffer so that this awful man—this *killer*—would finally be punished? Their bodies had been mangled…her strong husband who worked out at the gym three times a week…her precious Galen, with his baby-soft skin and dimpled little bottom. Their killer would go to prison, but he'd still be alive. His family could still see him, could still talk and laugh and cry with him, while she'd never again get to be with Perry and Galen in this lifetime.

That man had chosen to drink too much, had chosen to sin. Why did Perry and Galen have to suffer for his choice?

"Leah?" Her father knocked on the door. "Are you all right?"

She swiped at her eyes. "Y-yes, Daddy."

"Leah?" Her mother's voice accompanied the rattling of the knob. "Honey, open the door."

She hugged her knees to her chest. Couldn't they just leave her in peace? "I'm okay, Mom," she yelled.

"Em, she's allowed to use the bathroom, for crying out loud," her father said.

"But what if she heard you talking?" Leah detected an anxious edge to her mother's voice. "Leah, dear…"

"I…I think I'm going to take a shower," she said, trying to buy time.

"Leah!" Her mother sounded frantic now. "Hart, don't let her—"

To tune her out, Leah turned the faucets on full force. The water hit her in the face, surprising and confusing her. Yet the flow felt warm and comforting, even over her clothes. She held her bowed head under the showerhead and wept.

The door banged open, startling her so that she jumped back. The curtain snapped open, and her mother's concerned expression quickly changed to chagrin. "What are you doing?"

Her father stood beside her, holding up a full medicine bottle. "The sleeping pills were in the medicine cabinet, Em. Completely full. I told you she wouldn't do anything foolish."

"She's foolish enough to take a shower fully dressed." Her mother shut off the faucets, then stared at Leah, her eyes sorrowful. "What's wrong with you?"

Without waiting for an answer, Emily left the bathroom.

Leah stood in the tub, dripping. Would her mother have been more pleased if she *had* swallowed the pills? At least it would have been the conventional thing to do.

"Leah..." Her father handed her a towel, his eyes sad. He quickly smiled, obviously trying to lighten the moment. "If I'd known you really were taking a shower, I wouldn't have kicked the door in. But your mother was afraid..."

She touched his arm. "I know, Daddy."

Danni appeared in the doorway, her face white. She saw Leah standing in the tub, and her shoulders relaxed. "I'll bring you some dry clothes." She turned, then paused. "Mom's making excuses for you and sending everybody away."

Leah sighed inwardly. At least she'd achieved that much. "Thanks, Danni."

Her father cleared his throat. "Have yourself a real shower, then." He opened the medicine cabinet, then sheepishly pocketed the pills. "It'll make your mother rest better if you don't know where they are."

"I wouldn't take them, Daddy."

"I know, but you seem so—"

"So upset?"

"Distant," he amended.

"Isn't that what she wants me to be? Cool and collected? The properly grieving widow?"

"Leah…"

"Never mind. Take the pills with you." She was too weary to try to explain what no one wanted to hear anyway.

He patted her wet shoulder awkwardly, then retreated. When she was alone again, Leah stripped out of her wet clothes and turned the faucets back on, letting the water heat as high as she could stand. She stepped into the spray, and it stung her scalp and skin in a hot flood, sapping her small reserve of strength. She'd showered early that morning after a night of insomnia, but it had been a perfunctory washing. This felt more like a ritual, a symbolic cleansing.

Closing her eyes, she leaned against the tiles. If only Perry were here to tell her how to deal with her family. He'd stand up to them, then chastise her privately about letting them run her life.

On the other hand, he usually interpreted their every kindness as an attempt to control her. The two hundred dollars her father had given her to buy Galen's swing set and fort still burned in her wallet, the subject of her final conversation with Perry.

She let the tears come. Why had they argued on that trip home? Why couldn't she have seen things his way and stood up to her family, at least that last weekend they'd spent here?

What she wouldn't give to undo that journey to Fort Worth.

Leah smacked a palm against the tiles. "Why did you have to take that different route? You were so angry, you stubborn man. Look where it got you! If you'd only taken the interstate like you did every other trip, this wouldn't have happened! Now you're in heaven someplace, probably having a great time, and you've left me here."

She let out a strangling sob. "And you took Galen, too! Couldn't you have at least left him with me?"

The water beat down. Leah crossed her arms over her chest, sobbing, and sank under its relentless flow to the porcelain. "Oh, God. Oh, *God!*"

What was she supposed to do now? If Galen alone had died, she would at least have Perry to grieve with. Or if only Perry had died, she would have Galen to pour her energy and love into. With them both dead, her future was destroyed.

The water slowly become lukewarm, cool, then ice cold. Oblivious, Leah curled tight into a ball, shivering, until Danni shut off the faucets, wrapped her in a large, thick towel, and put her to bed.

Chapter Four

Jacobo let the tattered front screen door bang shut behind him as he stepped out into the night. He sank to the well-worn vinyl couch on the porch and absently pushed some stuffing back into one of several holes. He'd have to warn Dolores that it'd make a great nest for mice and rats and tell her to get it repaired. Better yet, he should patch the holes himself or have the thing carted off altogether.

But then where would he sleep?

A car honked as it pulled up to the curb, radio blaring Tejano music through its open windows. Laughing, Manuel slammed the passenger door shut and traded amusing obscenities with his friend. Manuel playfully kicked the door, stumbled, then waved away the driver, who honked again and accelerated noisily up the street. Still laughing, Manuel turned and swaggered up the pockmarked sidewalk.

When he saw Jacobo, he cursed loudly. "Go back home. Nobody wants you here anymore."

"I'm not leaving until things are settled."

Manuel cursed again, flopping down at the other end of the couch. "They won't be settled until the trial's over. You planning to stick around that long?"

"If I have to."

Manuel laughed and leaned back, sprawling lazily. "You won't quit school."

Jacobo tightened his jaw. "I'll do whatever I have to for Dolores and the kids."

"Yeah, that's right. That's all I've ever heard. Jacobo the brave, Jacobo the good, Jacobo the smart one. *Oye,* if you're so smart, go back to school. We can manage without you."

You couldn't manage bail without me, Jacobo started to say, then decided that the reminder wouldn't help matters. He was here to encourage his sister's marriage, not tear it apart. No matter what his true feelings had always been about her choice of a husband.

"I'm here until Dolores tells me she doesn't need me," he said.

"She doesn't need you. I'm walking the straight and narrow— I'm not drinking. Not since they put that interlock *mecanismo* on Dolores's car and take a urine sample once a week. Can you believe that?"

"There's a good reason for those precautions."

"Why?"

"*Why?* You've twice been convicted of DWI. Your license was suspended. You killed two people, Manuel!"

He spread his hands out. "It was dark. So what if I had a few drinks? It could have happened to anybody."

Anybody who was drunk, Jacobo wanted to say, but looked away in disgust. The man wasn't even repentant.

Manuel sighed loudly, then leaned his head back and closed his eyes, immediately starting to snore.

Jacobo nudged him with his foot. "Hey! Go to bed already."

"What?" Manuel jerked his head up from the couch.

"Go to bed. This is where I'm sleeping."

Manuel stumbled to his feet and headed for the door. "You should be sleeping in Austin. Why don't you go back there and leave us alone?"

The screen door slapped shut, followed by the front door. Jacobo heard Manuel fumble with the lock until it engaged.

Shaking his head, he retrieved the pillow and blankets Dolores had left for him—as she had nightly—in the rusted Adirondack chair. Arranging them over the couch, he blessed the night's balminess and knew that he wouldn't be as cold as he'd been two nights ago when a blue norther had forced him to seek refuge in Dolores's Plymouth.

Since his mother had died, he no longer had a home base in Fort Worth. Between Dolores, Manuel, and their five kids, the Garcias' two-bedroom house was crowded already. But he wanted to stick close to Dolores for the time being. Manuel needed to know he was being watched by more than just the bondsman who'd put up the $50,000 bail in exchange for the $5,000 Jacobo had put up from his law school savings. Savings he'd only been able to amass since the sale of his mother's house last summer. Savings he'd never see again.

Jacobo stretched out on the couch and contemplated the moon hanging in the space of black sky between the porch rail and roof. Reaching under the couch, he touched the stack of newspapers he'd stashed to spare Dolores and the kids from seeing the articles about the wreck and its aftermath.

Recently the *Star-Telegram* had run obituaries for the victims, Perry and Galen Travers. Two of the most Anglo names Jacobo had ever heard and enough to convict Manuel on the spot. If that didn't do it, the single picture of the two victims certainly would. It looked like a Christmas portrait, with a third party cropped from sight. The protective female arm around the little boy was just barely visible, but it had to belong to the wife and mother of the dead.

Leah Travers, Jacobo remembered, every word of the simple obituary's text committed to memory. The surviving widow and mother, with no children left to comfort her in her grief. She had family in Houston and Chicago. The dead husband had family in Louisiana.

According to today's article, the double funeral had been held in Houston. Jacobo guessed that until the trial, it would be the last published report or news broadcast about the accident. The father-son deaths had grabbed media attention and stirred public outrage, from the cop and medical attendants on the scene being quoted to local politicians calling for stiffer drunk driving laws. The only silent principals had been Manuel, who'd been advised by his court-appointed attorney not to speak to the press, and Leah Travers.

Jacobo draped his arm over his eyes, blocking his view of the moon. How could his brother-in-law be so cavalier? He'd bawled long and hard when they'd finally sprung him from jail, promising to Mary, Joseph, and every saint he could recall that he'd straighten up. He'd get his life together and show the law that though he'd done wrong, he was truly a changed man.

Then he'd sobered up, and only because of the random urinalysis did he stay sober. But he had never expressed regret for the wreck, nor did he seem to worry about actually serving time in prison.

Jacobo rolled to his side, facing into the couch, wishing for the comfort of his futon back in Austin. Or even the sagging single bed back at his mother's old place four blocks over.

Tomorrow, Jacobo planned to have a stern talk with Manuel about taking care of his family until the trial. Then Jacobo would head back to school.

He laughed bitterly. And what? If he was blessed, they'd excuse the days he'd missed and let him finish the year. If he was even further blessed, he might even pass. Then he'd have to spend the summer earning money for a fall semester he might not even be able to attend. Whenever the trial started, Dolores would need Jacobo's support. He was the only family she had in town.

Jacobo flopped to his back. The moon had disappeared behind a bank of clouds. He pulled the covers tight under his chin and said an extra, selfish prayer that his sister would learn a little self-reliance for a change.

Inside her father's Cadillac, Leah hugged herself around the waist, marveling at the secret she'd been able to keep even from her mother. She wanted to treasure it alone for a while before she shared the news with anyone, especially her family.

Out of the ashes of her life, God had granted her this precious gift—a baby growing in her womb. He'd given her hope, a reason to get out of bed in the morning, a reason, even now, to travel back to her home in Fort Worth to take care of the final details of her old life.

Just like her pregnancy with Galen, she'd been unable to eat much of anything for the several weeks she'd been in Houston. She was constantly tired, sleeping solidly all night but good chunks of the day as well. And the most promising sign of all, her period was well past a month overdue. During her first pregnancy, that had been the clincher.

She turned to the window, her spirit once again deflated. *Galen...*

Her father cleared his throat. "Your mother said some people from your church had brought food out to your house. I met those who drove down for the funeral. They seemed like nice folks."

"They are." She didn't move her gaze from the rushing scenery outside.

"Maybe we can enlist some of them to help us load your stuff in the U-Haul." He readjusted his grip on the steering wheel. "Have you thought about what big items you want to keep?"

Leah's stomach flipped. Why did she have to decide now? Her parents had said she needed to get on with her life and move back in with them. At least until she decided what she wanted to do.

As if she had any decisions to make.

Right now she just wanted to touch Galen and Perry's clothes to remind herself that they'd once lived, that they'd once been a part of her life. She wanted to hold their pillows close to her face so that she could smell their scents one last time. She wanted to cuddle Galen's stuffed animals and play with his favorite toys.

She wanted to sleep in the queen-sized bed she'd shared with Perry and pretend that she was bothered by his snoring and cover stealing.

"Well, anyway," her father continued when she didn't answer, "I'm sure you'll want to keep a few knickknacks. And photo albums, of course."

She pulled her gaze from the window. "I don't understand why Mom and Danni went up yesterday without us."

Her father shifted uncomfortably. "They wanted to clean the house for visitors, Leah. More people will stop by once they know you're back in Fort Worth. Your mother and sister didn't think you needed to be worrying about scrubbing toilets or washing floors."

She sighed inwardly. It would probably do her good to push a broom or a dust rag. Of course, Galen did have all those Winnie-the-Pooh figurines that were so difficult to get completely clean...

Her throat welled with emotion, but one sidelong glance at her father and she swallowed hard. *No, don't cry. It would only embarrass him. And you. Hold it until you're alone.*

The car slowed, and Leah sat up straighter. "Where are you going?"

"I'm taking the cutoff through Ennis," he said calmly.

"No! Oh, Daddy, please!"

He turned to look at her, his eyes steady. "Trust me, Leah. It's time. This is for you."

For her? She shook with grief. How could taking her on this road possibly help? Her father had drilled into her since childhood that if she fell off a bike, she had to get right back on. But this... this was...

She squeezed her eyes shut. This was one bicycle she would not climb back on.

Her father drove in silence, and the miles clicked by as she mentally replayed that night. Surely now they'd passed Ennis, passed the gas station where Perry had refueled. Passed the turnoff to Waxahachie, then Midlothian...

Don't you get it? They want you under their thumb. It kills them that you live too far away for them to run your life... We've been married seven years, but in a lot of ways, you've never left your parents' home.

49

The car pulled off the road, then stopped. Leah's heart pounded. She could hear the rush of traffic on their left, and she knew exactly where they were.

"Open your eyes, Leah. I want you to get out of the car and see something."

She laughed hollowly. "What, Daddy? Skid marks? Blood-stains? Is that your idea of making me face reality? Of forcing me to *get on with my life,* as you and Mom keep insisting?"

The driver's door chimed as he got out, then she heard an identical chime as he opened her door. He stood there waiting, but still she kept her eyes tightly closed, battling not only his presence but her own morbid curiosity.

She clenched her teeth. He would have to drag her from the car.

She felt a touch on her shoulder. "This isn't for me. It's for you," he said softly. "Please, Leah."

It was the *please* that broke her resolve. She could never remember hearing her father ask anything of her beyond what he needed. In his voice she heard only his concern for her, only his desire for her healing.

She slowly opened her eyes. Her father smiled and helped her from the car. Her legs were shaking so hard she didn't think she could stand; he had parked in front of the antiques shop. The bench was still by the front door.

Leah immediately dropped her gaze to the gravel. Her father tucked her arm in his and slowly led her up the road. "Your mother and I talked about doing this, but it seems that several of your church friends beat us to it." He stopped. "Look there, Leah," he said softly.

She raised her gaze. In the grass just beyond a trail of shattered glass stood a white cross with Perry's picture glued in the middle.

Alongside it was a smaller white cross with Galen's. Lying at both bases were dozens of fresh white carnations, roses, and lilies.

Her father put his arm around her and wiped his cheek. "It's beautiful, isn't it, honey?"

Leah trembled, pressing her lips together hard to fight back the rising bile. "No."

Her father turned. "Why, what's—"

She broke from his embrace and ran for the safety of the car. Slamming the door, she dropped her head to her knees and sobbed until her stomach twisted. She hastily opened the door and leaned out to throw up.

From inside the car, her father handed her a handkerchief. Humiliated, she wiped her mouth and shut the door, wanting to shut out the rest of the world forever. A sob broke in her throat, followed by a hiccup.

"Lean back and catch your breath." Her father smiled sadly. "I thought you would be pleased. I thought you'd like the memorial."

"It's not a memorial, it's a...a shrine. It makes Perry and Galen look like some kind of gods." Her eyes filled with tears. "This isn't sacred ground. It's the most profane place in the world. I don't want to remember it, I want to forget!"

Sighing heavily, her father reached over and buckled her seat belt, then started the car. As he drove past the crosses, Leah deliberately avoided looking out the window.

"I'll see that they're taken down," he said. "We didn't realize it would hurt you so much. We thought you'd be happy."

"Happy?" Leah trembled so hard that she had to wrap her arms around herself. "Do any of you honestly think I can ever be happy again? I lost my husband, Daddy. I lost my child!" Even the baby could never replace Galen and Perry.

Hart Tyler ran his hand through his hair and glanced at his watch. "Look, Leah, I'm not very good at this sort of thing. But I do know that you have to—"

"I know, Daddy. Get on with my life. Move along. Keep walking down the road. I've heard that so many times in the past few weeks from you and Mom and Owen, not to mention all the other family and neighbors. Danni's the only one who doesn't offer me platitudes."

"It's easy for your sister; she won't be here later," he said tightly. "She'll go back home to Chicago and won't be around when you have to face that killer in court."

Leah's spine tingled. "Daddy, I don't want to talk about the trial. Not today." Not ever.

"We need to talk about it, Leah. I've held off, knowing that you needed some time to collect yourself. But now that we're heading back to Fort Worth, you're going to have to prepare yourself for a lot of questions. People will be contacting you— police officers, lawyers, insurance agents—and you're going to have to go over the accident again and again, detail by detail. If you want Perry and Galen's killer brought to justice, you can't fall apart."

He glanced significantly at her. "And right now I'd say you're pretty close to the edge."

The edge of what? Where was the line between reality and insanity? Was what had happened to Perry and Galen sane? Was what she felt now—like she was drowning in a bottomless black pit—insanity?

Was the fact that somewhere her family's killer was eating, sleeping, and breathing sane?

She squeezed her eyes shut. "I hurt, Daddy. I hurt so bad."

"I know, Leah, but you're going to have to toughen up. You're going to have to be strong for Perry and Galen. You've got to be their witness, their voice, when this thing comes to trial. The sooner you get over the emotional aspects, the better."

Leah turned away from her father. What was the use?

He drove the rest of the way in silence. When they reached the house, Emily Tyler and Danni met them in the driveway.

"I believe there's a little color in your cheeks," her mother said, herding her inside.

As she stepped over the threshold, a bittersweet wave of familiarity hit. Leah drew in her breath. She'd been home so little since the accident, she hadn't had time to absorb the idea that Perry and Galen would never be back here.

The place already felt different. Normally Perry would have the wide-screen TV blaring full-blast, and Galen would be racing through the house in a superhero costume. Now all was quiet and still. The two-bedroom rental tract home only had eleven hundred square feet, but it had never seemed so large.

Or empty.

Leah frowned. All the pictures had been taken down and stacked along a wall in the family room. Lamps were unplugged and set on the floor. The media shelf was dismantled, CDs and videos arranged neatly in open moving boxes.

Taped shut, several larger boxes lined the hall beyond the family room. "What are those?" Leah said.

Danni glanced at their mother, deferring the question. Emily Tyler smiled confidently. "Danni and I did some boxing today, dear."

"So I see. What did you box up?"

Her mother put an arm around her, and her eyes misted. "Galen and Perry's clothes. Galen's toys. Perry's—"

Leah shrugged out of her embrace and headed to Galen's small room. They couldn't! Surely they wouldn't!

Once filled with two crammed bookcases and a toy box overflowing with plastic figures and stuffed animals, the room Leah had lovingly decorated with an airplane-and-train motif was bare. Even the bed had been stripped of its linens and the curtains taken down.

Except for a rolled-up *101 Dalmatians* sleeping bag and several partially deflated beach toys, the closet was also empty.

Leah stood dumbfounded.

"We wanted to save you from having to see his things," Emily said. "We thought it would be too painful."

Leah turned to her sister. "I suppose my bedroom looks the same...all of Perry's items gone?"

Danni nodded solemnly.

"It wasn't easy. Everything was a reminder of—"

"They should have been *my* reminders, Mom," Leah said in a low voice, clenching her trembling hands into fists. "How could you do this? I wanted to be near them again!"

Danni's eyes welled with tears. "I didn't think about that, Leah. I'm sorry. Let me help you unpack the boxes."

"Perry and Galen are gone, Leah," Emily said. "These are just...things."

"But *their* things, Mom! Things that they touched and loved." Leah shook, making no effort to wipe the tears from her cheeks. "Do you think that by removing their possessions I can forget them as easily? I won't ever forget!"

"None of us will, darling." Her mother touched her shoulder. "But life is for the living." Emily glanced at Hart, standing back in the hall. "Your father talked to you about the trial?"

"Yes. *No.*" Leah shook off her mother's hand. "I'm not ready to talk about it yet."

"But that's why we're in Fort Worth. We'll stay in town long enough for you to give the necessary statements to the authorities, then we'll take you back to Houston."

"And then what? What will I do—mope around and write sad poetry like Emily Dickinson?"

"If that's what you want."

Leah crossed her arms. "What about a job?"

"Leah, be realistic, dear. You haven't held one since you were in high school. Maybe you can take some courses at the community college. Painting or writing—you always did like to write." Her mother probably had already secured a catalog from the local campus and circled the courses she thought best.

"So I'm supposed to live the rest of my life in your home as the grieving widow, is that it?"

"Leah, I don't think she means it that way. Please let me help you unpack the boxes."

"You stay out of this, Danni," Leah said. "You don't understand either. I'm tired of all of you making my decisions. You don't ask, you just act."

"Honey, we're only trying to do what's best for you," her father said, stepping into the room. "Lord knows you're under enough stress."

"And none of you are making it any easier." Leah drew a deep breath, trying to hold in the sobs. "I *know* Perry and Galen are gone. I know nothing can bring them back. But I'm not ready to put them out of my mind as easily as you boxed up their belongings. I want to feel them with me, don't you see?"

Emily gripped Leah's arms. "I see that you're a mess. Get ahold of yourself. Hart, get a cup of water and some of those sleeping pills."

"No," Leah said, stepping back. Calm descended over her, along with a renewed sense of purpose. "I'm not taking any pills, and I'm not going back with you. I'm staying here in Fort Worth."

Her mother frowned. "Darling, you're just upset."

"Of course I'm upset. But I'm serious. I'm staying."

"Alone? You wouldn't last a week."

Stung by her words, Leah looked at her father. "Is that what you think too?"

Hart shifted uncomfortably. "Honey, you're not in very good shape to take care of yourself. Much less make major decisions."

And her parents were? They'd been making decisions for her right and left ever since the accident. Even before that.

Perry had been right all along.

And now she'd never get the chance to tell him so.

"I'm staying," she repeated.

After several hours of tearful pleas, her family gathered their things—her mother a wall of silence, Danni on the verge of tears. Her father slipped her some money along with a good-bye kiss and told her she was always welcome. She tearfully nodded, then shut the door behind them. Shutting the door on her previous life.

She puttered around the house, tentatively opening boxes but finding the physical memories of Galen and Perry indeed painful. Though she pressed a multitude of clothing to her face, she couldn't smell anything except detergent and fabric softener. Her mother's efficiency had seen everything laundered, even the dirty clothes Leah remembered leaving in the laundry basket.

She opened Perry's closet and found empty shelves and a handful of coat hangers. Wedged under a shoetree was a pair of beat-up Adidas that he'd always worn while cutting the grass. Leah removed her flats and slipped into the oversized sneakers. She clomped down the hall back to Galen's room, searching for something personal—anything—that had belonged to him too.

Finding nothing, she sank wearily to the carpet beside the closet. A vinyl raft, still partially inflated from their summer vacation at the Gulf, tipped over into her lap. Closing her eyes, she held the raft to her face and breathed in the faint odors of sand and salt. When Perry realized he'd forgotten the pump, he and Galen had laughed hard, taking turns blowing life into the raft.

Leah put her mouth around the air stem and opened the valve. Pinching the sides of the stem, she carefully inhaled the air that hissed out. When she was crying so hard that her mouth slipped, she painstakingly capped the valve and lay on the floor, hugging the raft to her body.

Jacobo stood at the edge of the road alongside the antiques store. From reading the investigating officer's report, he knew that Manuel's pickup must have made impact right about here. He would have known it even if the two crosses hadn't marked the spot.

He knelt before them and looked at the victims' pictures. They were cut from the same Christmas picture that had accompanied the obituaries. The woman's arm wasn't visible.

Jacobo rocked back on his heels, ignoring the traffic whizzing past. Several cars honked—in sympathy, he hoped, for they had no way of knowing who he was, who he was related to.

He knew from the medical reports that the father and son hadn't died here, but later, at the hospital. Yet this place had the feel of death about it. Had the woman...Leah...been here?

He touched the wilting pile of flowers. Had she brought these? He'd never liked these highway memorials, but maybe it comforted her to know that her loved ones were publicly honored. He should associate the crosses with Jesus, the man whose life and death they truly honored, but he couldn't take comfort in their presence here without knowing whether the slain man had been a believer.

Father, I don't know what the condition of the man's soul was. But the little one... I know he's already in your arms. Thank you for your blood that was shed for our sins and covers even the blood that was spilled here.

Jacobo reached inside his leather jacket and laid a single red carnation in front of each cross before he got back on his motorcycle and headed home to Austin.

Chapter Five

The doorbell rang, and Leah sighed. Not another casserole from the church. She had a refrigerator full of sympathy food that hadn't even been touched.

Glancing through the peephole, she saw two of her fellow nursery workers. She started to ignore the doorbell's second chime, then decided against it. They'd just come back later.

"Hi, Leah! Oh, my gosh, don't you look good. You look so *thin!*" Debra Marty held out a covered dish. "I brought you some food. I am *so* sorry about Perry and Galen."

"I'm sorry too," Julia Rowler said, her voice subdued. Where Debra's wide, red lips were stretched in a smile, Julia's eyes looked softly sad. "May I hug you, Leah?"

"Sure," Leah said, automatically stiffening. She'd been grabbed so many times in the past few weeks that physical contact had lost its ability to reach her.

But something felt different about Julia's embrace, something genuine. She didn't cling as if she expected Leah to support her, but she held Leah in a solid, warm hug, gently patting her back the way a mother would.

Leah winked back a tear. Horrified that she might get emotional, she started to pull away, but Julia released her first. Her eyes still looked sad, but she didn't say anything, didn't offer any useless words.

"One from me too," Debra shoved her casserole into Julia's hands and snaked her arms around Leah, rocking her sideways. "Oh, I know how hard this is for you! But it was God's will. I guess he needed two more angels in heaven."

Leah bit her lip. If she heard that one more time, she'd say exactly what she thought about a God with a will cruel enough to demand the lives of a loving husband and her precious child. She jerked away from Debra and snatched the casserole from Julia's hands. "Thank you for stopping by. It was very nice of you."

Debra looked confused for a moment, then she smiled gamely. "We miss you in the nursery. When are you coming back?"

Julia stepped forward. "Nobody expects you to work in the nursery, Leah. But I do miss you." She glanced at Debra. "You're a good listener."

Something clicked in Leah's memory, something about Julia living at home with her dying mother. Many times Leah had drawn out of the reticent Julia how painful it was to watch her mother slowly succumb to cancer.

But what was cancer compared to what she'd suffered? With cancer, there was time to prepare. Time to make any needed peace and say good-bye. What was losing a mother, compared to a spouse and child?

Julia touched her arm and smiled gently. "We've kept you long enough. You've probably got a house full of family."

"No, I'm all alone. It was nice of you to stop by, though. And thank you for the food." *Would they never leave?*

Debra craned her neck to look past Leah. "Well, if you're all alone, maybe we could come in and—"

"Is there anything we can do to help around the house?" Julia smiled gently. "I don't mind cleaning bathrooms or doing laundry."

"No, really." Leah retreated a step and put a hand on the door-knob. "Thank you again."

"I'll pray for you. I miss you, Leah," Julia said softly.

Debra opened her mouth to speak, but Leah shut the door in their faces. She didn't need what the church called "fellowship" right now.

Casserole in hand, she sagged against the door. When would people stop coming by? When would they stop calling with their useless words of sympathy? Nothing anybody could say or do would bring Perry and Galen back. *Nothing.*

Leah carried the dish to the kitchen and set it on the counter without even looking at the contents under the foil. She had little interest in food. When her stomach growled past the point of pain, she ate a handful of crackers. She knew she should eat better, for the baby, but even the saltines tasted like sawdust.

Sifting through the piled-up mail, she noticed the red light blinking furiously on the answering machine. Six or seven messages waiting, messages she'd never heard because she'd turned down the volume early that morning.

She tossed out the junk mail, making the easy decision first. The rest she stacked in neat piles: bills, Perry's personal mail, and cards of sympathy. Maybe later she'd have the strength to work through it all. Right now, she was tired. There were always so many decisions to make: bills, insurance payments, canceling Perry's subscriptions to *Sports Illustrated* and his accountant's magazines.

Then there were the endless calls regarding the pending trial. Calls from the police department regarding the investigation. Calls from a Jill Strickland, the assistant district attorney who'd been assigned to the case. Each time, Leah was forced to relive the most horrifying moments of her life with strangers who had never even met Perry and Galen. What interest could anyone have in a trial that wouldn't bring Perry and Galen back no matter what the outcome?

Leah fingered the letter she'd received two days ago, a simple letter that began *Because we care...* It was signed by Mothers Against Drunk Driving and expressed their consolation and readiness to help in any way.

Leah threw the letter in the trash. She didn't want to talk to anybody.

A thousand times she wished she'd died with Perry and Galen. She didn't have the strength to see beyond each day, much less to the trial, and beyond that, the rest of her life. She didn't see any reason why God had spared her life, unless it was because she was carrying a child. If she could hold on to that belief for the next seven months, until she held Perry's baby in her arms, maybe she would make it. Maybe then she would see a reason for living.

Leah awoke in the night, as she did every night, to the dark stillness pressing around her. But something else intruded, something beyond the customary fear and grief.

She felt painful cramps, wet and sticky, and in a moment she was out of bed and in the bathroom. Her face looked ghostly white in the mirror as she flicked on the light switch.

Oh, Lord, not the baby. Please, *not the baby!*

Immediately she was on the phone to her OB-GYN, crying and sobbing so hard that she could scarcely get her message across to his answering service. When he called back right away, she was no less calm, especially when he firmly told her to have her husband drive her to the emergency room and that he'd meet them there.

Sobbing, Leah cleaned herself and changed clothes. Why wasn't Perry here to help her through this? Was she going to have to go through everything alone? Who could she call in the middle of the night? *Oh, by the way, I'm having a miscarriage. Could you please drive me to the hospital?*

She bundled up as best she could and clenched her teeth against the pain as she drove to the emergency room. She knew in her heart it was too late; driving herself couldn't possibly make any difference. It was far better than relying on others.

The doctor shook his head after a quick examination. "You're all right, Mrs. Travers."

"But…the baby?" Surely a little one couldn't survive such cramping.

Dr. Harolds came to the side of the table and touched her shoulder. "I see no signs of pregnancy, Mrs. Travers. You're just having an abnormally heavy period. I can give you something for the cramping, for the pain."

"No baby?" she whispered. How could that be? "But I had all the signs! It's just like it was with…with…"

Dr. Harolds helped her to a sitting position. "The nurse told me you recently lost your husband and child. It's natural that your body would react so strongly. Grief can affect us physically in many different ways." He scribbled on a pad of paper. "I want you to consider seeing this woman. She's a colleague—a counselor." He ripped the paper from the pad. "She's worked with many victims of drunk drivers."

After he left, Leah dressed slowly, dazed. She shoved the paper into her skirt pocket and scarcely heard the nurse's instructions as she handed Leah the medicine. It was still dark when she walked back to her car, and she rested her head against the steering wheel.

No baby. There had never been a baby. There had never been a future for her.

She started the car and drove aimlessly through the deserted parking lot. She didn't want to go back to the empty house that was no longer home. She wanted her husband's arms and comfort, his gentle voice telling her that it was all right, that they could still have children. She wanted to look in on her sleeping child and kiss his soft forehead and listen to his baby snores.

Leah drove past her street and headed for the interstate. She didn't realize what was she doing until she merged onto the freeway. Her heart pounded, and she gripped the steering wheel. The car had plenty of gas, enough that she wouldn't have to stop unless she chose to.

The road was nearly empty, and the freeway lights glared down, solemnly showing the way. Leah wondered at her calm. She'd never driven by herself so late at night, heading so far from home.

She drove for miles, through Corsicana then Richland. The sun appeared faintly on the horizon by the time she reached Buffalo and fully rose by the time she passed Huntsville. Morning traffic surrounded her in Conroe, pressing her in the rush of commuters headed for Houston. She drove steadily, ignoring the dull ache between her shoulder blades and the sharper pain of grief in her stomach.

She passed the exit to her parents' home, thinking it would be ironic indeed if they were to see her. Then she remembered that they'd never seen the Dodge Neon she'd worked up the courage to buy on her own.

No one knew where she was; no one knew where she was going. What would normally have been frightening to her before, when she'd been sheltered and protected, now felt oddly liberating.

Clouds obscured the sun as she negotiated the Houston traffic. At last she crossed onto Galveston Island, and she headed east along the seawall, then down a private road. When she reached the coast, she parked the car beside a small house on stilts and shut off the engine.

The waves lapped before her, beckoning. Leah got out of the car and left the door open with everything inside.

Here was where she and Perry and Galen had vacationed last summer. She wrapped her arms around herself and remembered Perry diving into the surf and Galen squealing with delight as he retreated from the rushing tide.

Leah kicked off her shoes and socks and walked to the water's edge. A cold breeze blew water droplets at her face. The surf chilled her toes, and she hiked back up the beach to sit on the packed sand. Hugging her knees, she huddled in her gauze dress.

How different everything looked in winter than summer. There was nothing inviting about this water, nothing to entice her to play. Even the rental house looked vacant and sad; the stairs leading from the beach up past the stilts to the door had rotted.

Leah dropped her head to her knees and shut her eyes. A gull squawked overhead, while the wind whistled through a loose board in the decayed stairs. The tide hit the shore then retreated, hit then retreated. Relentlessly in motion, relentlessly reshaping the shoreline.

Leah rose and walked into the water. It lapped around her ankles and wet the hem of her skirt. The sky brewed gray, hiding the sun. A storm rolled in from the sea, and thick drops pelted on the shore and her skin, pricking and stinging.

Shaking with the cold, Leah threw her arms out wide. "Lord, where are you?" she screamed into the rain. "You were supposed to walk on water, you were supposed to help Peter walk on water. I'm not asking for miracles—I'm just tired of sinking! Why aren't you helping me?"

She clenched her hands into fists, raging. Where was the mercy she'd always heard about? Where was the *justice?* The killer walked free on bail; her family was dead. Didn't God care? Wasn't he supposed to take care of his children?

Weeping, she knelt in the surf. Waves slapped against her, and she angrily struggled to keep her balance. What did God want from her?

Maybe her mother had been right to worry; maybe Leah hadn't really considered the best solution. She should walk into the water and let it draw her down to its depths. If Perry and Galen were in heaven, she wanted to join them. She was too tired to carry on alone.

A surging wave knocked her flat, pulling her into the tide. Tossed end over end, she flailed her arms, struggling for purchase as she scraped the sandy bottom.

Helpless, her body instinctively reacted by lurching up, forward—anything to escape the powerful, suffocating force.

She gasped for air and swallowed salt water.

Her lungs burned. She grappled for safety and found nothing. *Oh, Lord...oh, God, help me. Help me!*

The tide heaved her onto shore, then withdrew in a great rush. Choking and panting, she coughed until her breath returned in racking gasps.

She burst into tears, crying until she felt nothing but the hollowness of her body and soul. Spent, she pressed her cheek against the coarse sand and opened her clenched hands into the grit.

Take courage. It is I. Don't be afraid.

Leah weakly raised her head. A hermit crab scuttled back into the water, but she was alone on the beach.

"Lord," she whispered hoarsely, brokenly. "Oh, Lord…"

Come.

"I…I can't. I'm too weak!"

Come.

Aching and bruised, Leah slowly got to her feet. She straightened her clothes and trudged back to the car. Dripping wet, she sank into the driver's seat and rested her head against the steering wheel. She buried her hands in her pockets, and her fingers jammed against a forgotten wet slip of paper.

Staring at the counselor's name, she considered her options. She could end her life—here or elsewhere; she could try to make it on her own; or she could move back in with her parents.

Come.

Leah crumpled the paper and tossed it on the beach. Professional help was not an option she would consider; if she was going to live, she would do it alone. She shut the door and buckled her seat belt, then turned around and headed back for the highway. When she reached Houston, she passed her parents' exit without a glance and continued straight to Fort Worth.

Chapter Six

Wanda Voss, director of Engineering Associates Publishing Production Department, folded her hands over the application papers on her desk. "Your proofreading test looks good, Mrs. Travers. But your application shows that you've never held a job since you've been out of college."

"I...I got married and helped my husband with his career." Leah clenched her hands in the lap of her new wool suit.

"Hmm. But you wrote for the TCU *Daily Skiff* when you were in school."

Leah nodded. It was where she'd met Perry, who'd been dating another reporter at the time.

"And you've edited your church bulletin, and you like to read." Wanda removed her reading glasses. "What's the last book you read?"

Leah blinked, taken aback. "I...I don't remember, really. I haven't been reading much lately. My husband passed away recently...along with my son."

Leah twisted her hands in her lap, feeling miserable. She'd applied for countless openings listed in the *Star-Telegram,* and now she was failing the only interview she'd been granted.

Wanda's face softened. "I'm sorry to hear that." She went back to reading Leah's application.

Leah studied the older woman and decided that she liked her. Graying slightly at the temples, Wanda was stylishly dressed in a designer suit. She looked all business, yet the desktop photos of her whooping it up in the snow with several children revealed a warmer, more personal side.

Wanda caught Leah staring at the pictures. "Those are my grandkids," she said proudly. "They live in Wisconsin."

"They're lovely." Leah smiled wistfully.

Wanda looked at her a moment longer, then leaned forward. "I don't know how it feels to lose a child, but I understand about being a widow. I lost my husband several years ago to cancer. Look, Leah." She stacked the papers and smiled. "I'd like to have you work for us. I think you'd do a good job."

Leah let out her breath. "Really?"

"It's an entry-level position, but we have great benefits. Best of all, the people around here are not only professional, but friendly."

She named a salary, and Leah winced. Her budget would be tight.

"There's room for advancement, though." Wanda must have read the skepticism on her face.

Leah studied the woman, deciding she could trust her. She had to trust her. "I'd like to take the job, Mrs. Voss, but I'll have to go to court sometime in the next year. My husband and child were killed by a drunk driver, and his case will come to trial then."

Wanda's face softened. "You can have all the time off you need. We'll work something out when the time comes."

While Leah struggled to unlock her front door, the phone rang incessantly. The queue on the answering machine must have filled again.

Clutching a bag of groceries, she nearly tripped over a stack of cardboard boxes as she maneuvered through the maze in the family room to find the phone.

"Where have you been, Leah?" her mother demanded. "I've been phoning for days. Your father was ready to jump in the car and come after you."

Leah flopped down with the full grocery sack on the couch and kicked off her pumps. How was she going to stand wearing high heels every day? She adjusted the phone against her shoulder and caught the sack before it upended. "I'm sorry I haven't called, Mom. I've been busy. I'm packing up to move, and I got a job today."

"A job?"

"I can't live on the insurance money forever." Leah stuffed a bunch of bananas and three apples back into the bag. "I'll be a proofreader with a publishing company. They publish engineering manuals—guidance books for professionals."

"Sounds boring, Leah. I know you're bound and determined to make it on your own, but your father could find you a more interesting job if you'd come home."

"I *am* home. And I've never dealt with things on my own. Now I have to, and I'm going it alone. When the trial starts—"

"Speaking of which, have that assistant D.A. phone your father. He wants to talk to her."

Oh, Mom. You never believe me. You never listen.

"I have to go," Leah said. "I've got a carton of Blue Bell Homemade Vanilla that's going to melt if I don't get it in the freezer. I'll call you as soon as I find a new place. I promise."

Leah hung up the phone and carried the groceries into the kitchen to unpack. Shopping for one was lonely. She missed Galen helping her put the groceries away, his little hands grasping for whatever she'd hand him—a can, a bag of chips—to set in the pantry.

She leaned against the counter, pushing down the ache in her chest. She had a job now and new resolve to get a grip on herself. It was time to hunt for an apartment. Staying in this house was getting harder by the day.

The phone rang again. Leah sighed as she lifted the receiver, expecting to hear her father this time. Lately he and her mother had been calling in tandem.

"Leah, hi! This is Joyce Panger from the Young Couples Sunday school class."

Leah wrapped the cord around her finger. Joyce and Rob had brought over a chicken pot pie when Leah had first returned to town. "Hi, Joyce."

"I wondered if you'd like to go out to dinner Friday night with some of the class. Nothing fancy, just Chili's. Rob and I would love to pick you up."

Leah drew a quiet breath. Go along with them as a fifth wheel? Be the odd woman out in a group of couples?

Joyce was probably just calling as a gentle reminder that Leah hadn't been back to church since Perry and Galen died.

"Thanks, but I'm busy that night. I'm getting ready to move."

"Really? I'd love to help you pack, Leah. I'm pretty good at it by now; Rob and I have moved five times since we married."

Leah bristled. "I've got it under control."

"Well, how about we all get together and rent a U-haul and get some of those burly guys to tote boxes and—"

"It's all taken care of, Joyce. But thanks again for the invitation. Have a wonderful time."

Leah set the receiver in the phone's cradle.

But more than once she wished Perry were still alive, to help her make decisions. The irony of the situation made her smile wryly as she studied the city apartment guide with all its options.

This apartment was more expensive, but it had a built-in washer and dryer. That one had more square footage than most, but it was in a questionable neighborhood.

In the end she ignored the pictures and descriptions and used two criteria: location and rent. After visiting several, she instantly fell in love with a small complex that had been popular with married TCU students during the 1940s, or so the landlord informed her. It was hardly larger than an efficiency, with its bedroom separated from the main room by only a wall. The kitchen was so small, she could stand in the middle and touch both the refrigerator and the sink, set at opposite ends.

But she loved its worn but elegant hardwood floors, blue-tiled bathroom, and the way her front door opened into a small courtyard blooming with pansies. Her neighbors appeared to be a mix of elderly people and serious-minded young cultural types—two groups who would no doubt keep out of her daily life and expect her to keep out of theirs.

The rent was affordable, and she could walk to an eclectic row of shops that looked intriguing—a vintage thrift store, a coffee shop, and an organic grocer's.

Places that families weren't likely to frequent, families whose presence would only intensify the empty ache in her heart.

At her request, Salvation Army came and carted off nearly all the physical reminders of Perry and Galen. She gave them all the furniture—everything from the beds to the sofa and lamps—and nearly all of Galen's toys. She kept his Winnie-the-Pooh stuffed animal set, minus the precious Tigger with whom he'd been buried. Of Perry's belongings she kept little, saving his watch and the pen and pencil set she'd given him when he'd passed his CPA exam soon after they married. She kept all the photo albums and books and one large bookcase to house them all. Nearly everything else she gave away for someone else to use.

Danni and her mother had been right. The sight of so many memories of Perry and Galen was disturbing.

She filled her new living quarters with the bare essentials: a single bed, night table with lamp, and dresser in the bedroom; a sofa, end table, and small black-and-white TV for the living area; a small wooden table with two straight-backed chairs for eating by the window; and only the most basic of kitchen utensils.

Her new home was small and definitely built for one. She didn't plan to entertain.

She would regroup what was left of herself, alone. She would be an island, a rock. Hadn't her parents taught her to keep her emotions locked up tightly? In this new life, no one knew who she was. No one except Wanda knew about Perry and Galen. If she didn't talk about it, no one else would either, leaving her to explore her grief on her own, at her own pace. No questions, no insincere hugs, no casseroles. She would be in the world, but not of it.

The day she started her job, she placed her wedding ring in a small velvet box and tucked it in the back of her dresser drawer.

"Welcome aboard, Leah." Wanda met her at the door to the department to let her in. A special code had to be punched into a keypad for entrance, and Wanda showed her the sequence.

Leah thought that surely any company with such James Bond–type security must not be very sociable, for which she was grateful. She was here strictly to earn a living.

Wanda steered her through a maze of cubicles, calling out greetings as they passed. Most of the workers glanced curiously at Leah, smiling.

"You'll know everybody in short order," Wanda said. "That's why we have nameplates on the cubicles. As long as people stay where they're supposed to be, everything works fine."

Was that a hint of humor Leah detected in Wanda's voice or a warning? She squared her shoulders. *She* certainly intended to stay where she was supposed to be.

Wanda paused outside an office, waiting for a woman to get off the phone. The nameplate on the door said *Betsy Culligan*.

"The department is comprised of three groups, and Betsy is your group's manager," Wanda said. "Within each group are two teams, and Jim McArthur is your team's leader."

Betsy saw them, waved, and indicated she was wrapping up the call. Leah heard her babbling about print quantities and the merits of electronic versus traditional printing. She was beginning to doubt the wisdom of accepting a job for which she was so woefully behind the times, when Wanda touched her shoulder.

"Before I introduce you to Betsy, I want you to know that I haven't told anyone about your husband and child. That's only anyone's business if you want it to be."

Leah smiled gratefully, and she heard Betsy replace the receiver and bound for the door. "You must be Leah," she said, smiling, holding out a hand of welcome. "We're so glad you're going to be part of our group."

"I'll leave you two to get acquainted." Wanda winked at Leah. "Good luck. You'll do great."

Leah shook the outstretched hand, squelching her doubts. "Hello, Ms. Culligan. I'm glad to be here."

Jacobo hung up the phone and leaned back in the fraying recliner Eric had liberated from the curbside of one of Austin's better neighborhoods. He closed his eyes and tried to work up the enthusiasm for praying.

"Bad news from your sister?" Eric looked over from where he sprawled along the couch, studying a book about constitutional law.

"She's already talking about me coming back for the summer."

"What about the fellowship you applied for?"

"I guess it doesn't matter now whether I get accepted or not." Jacobo raked his hands through his hair. "I don't know why I ever even wanted to go to law school."

"Because you wanted to make a difference."

Jacobo laughed. "You sound like a public service announcement... 'You too can make a difference in the Hispanic community...one degree at a time.'" He laughed again, briefly wishing he could trade places with Eric for just one day. Eric was an only child.

"I'm serious." Eric sat up and set the book on the table. "You told me how many years you saved your money so you could come here, so you could help your family. And yes, the Hispanic community."

"Apparently my family wants their help now, not when I get a degree. Nobody except my mother understood why I wanted to go to undergraduate school, and nobody understands why I want to be here. When my mother died—"

He broke off, reluctant to say more. Rosa Martinez had understood the years her eldest child had shouldered the family's burdens after his father died. Jacobo had still been at North Side High the year of his father's heart attack, but he'd stepped in as breadwinner without complaint. He'd seen in her eyes that she hadn't wanted him to, but they both knew there was no choice. She had herself and four children to feed.

Unemployed, Rosa spoke little English, and besides Jacobo, only fourteen-year-old Dolores was old enough to get a job. Then she'd gotten pregnant one month before her *quinceañera*—the coming-of-age celebration for fifteen-year-old girls. Jacobo and Rosa scraped together enough money to give her a decent wedding instead, then helped her move into Manuel's house.

Jacobo abandoned his dream of undergraduate school for several years, taking a few community college courses here and there. Saving every penny and every extra moment for study, he finally attended the University of Texas at Arlington and received a history degree. And promptly waited three more years to apply for law school, only when he had once again saved enough money to support Mama and his two younger brothers still living at home.

The sale of the house after Mama's death had provided him with the final means to attend UT's law school, one of the best in the country.

Jacobo sighed. "If I go back to Fort Worth, I can probably find a job as a law clerk."

"And if you stay in Austin, you might be eligible for a fellowship doing community work. That's all you've talked about."

All he'd talked about before Manuel chose to not only take two lives but destroy the life of everyone in Jacobo's family.

Jacobo closed his eyes again. Once Manuel was convicted and sent to prison, Jacobo would have no choice but to step in once again. His younger brothers had struck out for California years ago, and Manuel's only family lived in Mexico.

Dolores and her kids had no one to turn to.

Lord, am I always going to have to be my family's keeper?

"More coffee, hon?" The waitress poised the carafe over Leah's table.

"Sure." Leah set aside the morning paper and pushed her cup closer. The waitress dutifully refilled it, then bustled off to check another of her myriad tables.

The Purple Onion Coffee Shop was a great place for Leah to begin her morning. No one in the breakfast crowd noticed if she sat in the back booth and just watched. She was amused by the regulars who appeared nearly every day: the group of octogenarians who sat on the other side of the low wall and argued state politics; the young professionals in their crisp shirts and suits, studying the daily stock market report; the table of elderly women who alternately stared over their Belgian waffles at the elderly men and argued about a running bridge game.

Here she could study them all, young and old alike, with their human frailties—wheezes, nose blowings, and imperfect skin—

and their strengths—a kind word, a gentle touch, a smile. She wanted to tell them all to enjoy the day, to revel in their frailties as well as their strengths, because it could all be taken away in a moment.

"More coffee?"

"No thanks." Leah glanced at her watch. "Time to get to work."

The waitress smiled, and the light caught her black nametag: Louise.

Leah looked away, ashamed. She didn't want to know such a personal detail about the woman who'd waited on her.

"See you later, hon," Louise said, winking at Leah then heading to another booth, whistling.

Leah tucked the paper under her arm and left a good tip.

Riding up the elevator to the office, she thought about the stack of folders waiting on her desk to be proofread. She didn't mind her job, even if it grew tedious at times. It was work—something to occupy her mind. There were actually moments when she became so absorbed in the intricacies of the engineering lingo that she forgot about Perry and Galen. Then the memory would crash through her, and darkness would descend once again.

"Mornin', Leah." Ed Spivey, who occupied the cubicle across from hers, smiled as he got off another elevator at the same time she reached her floor.

"Hi." She ducked her head and punched in the code to the department's door. Ed slid in behind her and dogged her steps to the lane of their cubicles.

"Are you going out to lunch with us today? We're celebrating Evelyn's birthday."

Leah groaned inwardly. These people celebrated everything. Birthday lunches, bridal and baby showers, potluck lunches in the department's kitchen for no special reason, cake once a month for birthday celebrants, get-togethers after work...

She'd been here several months already, and she still couldn't get over how much time they shared socially. All she wanted was to stay at her desk, do her job, and go home every night.

She flashed him a quick smile so he wouldn't think she was rude. "I'd like to, but I have a mountain of work. One of my books is going to the printer's next week." She laughed. "I'm still trying to get the hang of this."

"I understand. But it's okay to take a break occasionally. You don't have to stay in that cubicle all the time."

So he'd noticed. "I'm just a Type-A kind of gal, I guess." She laughed again.

He smiled. "Okay. But if you ever do want to go to lunch, there's a great Chinese restaurant just up the street."

"I don't like Chinese," she said flatly. They'd reached their work areas, and she thumped her purse down on the desk. Couldn't this guy take a hint?

Ed leaned against her cubicle, still smiling. "Italian?"

Leah turned. "I don't think it's a good idea for me to go out for lunch at all. There's still so much I need to learn."

"Okay, okay." Ed held up his hands, not seeming offended in the least. He backed toward his own work area, shaking his head, then turned away to sit in front of his computer.

Alice Brett, the department's administrative assistant, handed Leah a work folder. She tilted her head in Ed's direction. "He's got a crush on you, you know," she said in a low voice.

Leah's face burned. She hadn't asked for any attention. "I'm sure he's just being polite."

"He just wonders why a pretty woman like you isn't attached." Alice laughed, but it was friendly, not mocking. "He's a nice guy, Leah. Not the type to give a new girl the rush. I've known him a long time, and he's more likely to just want to be a friend—not a jump in the sack. You might consider giving him a chance."

Leah set the folder on her desk and sat down, hoping Alice would catch the hint that she was ready to start in. "Thanks for the work," she said, opening the folder to emphasize her intentions.

"Sure." Alice sounded hurt. Leah knew Alice was still watching her, as if she wanted to ask something, but Alice turned away, the sound of her high heels muffled by the thick carpet.

Leah picked up her red pen and concentrated on the words in the folder's document. When it was time to go to lunch, nobody stopped at her cubicle.

On the drive home, she deviated from her normal route to pick up her dry cleaning. She passed a neighborhood church, and even though it wasn't yet six o'clock on a Wednesday night, people were already heading inside the sanctuary. The front doors were open wide, and warm light spilled out into the twilight. The joyful fervor of a gospel choir was punctuated by trumpets and drums.

Leah pulled the car over, mesmerized. *Here is the church, and here is the steeple. Open the door...*

She shook her head. It was Wednesday night—what did she expect? These people were probably just ritualistic about their mid-week service. Maybe she was imagining the smiles on their faces as they walked inside, many hand in hand. And if not, well, after all, they were probably a tight-knit group. It was a small church; they probably all knew each other well.

She cranked down the window. An indescribable longing swept over her to get out of her car and join them. But she didn't know them, nor they her. She would be out of place, and they would feel obligated to welcome her. It would be awkward. She pulled back into traffic.

She hadn't even been back to her own church since Perry and Galen died. Only recently had the calls stopped coming.

No one seemed to understand that her life had been forever changed. She didn't want to attend social gatherings, she didn't want to hear any more trivial sympathy. She could take her hurt and doubts directly to God without worshiping alongside others. He could refuse to answer her questions when she was alone as easily as in a crowd.

Letting herself into the security of her apartment, Leah was trying to decide whether to heat up the frozen single serving of macaroni and cheese or lasagna when she heard the answering machine pick up.

"Hi, Leah. This is Jill Strickland from the D.A.'s office. Call me back as soon as you can. The trial date's been set."

Chapter Seven

From that moment, Leah felt as if she were hurtling through a long dark tunnel toward no light, toward no visible opening. Although the trial had always been in the back of her mind since the accident—nearly three months now—she'd persistently shoved it to the dim recesses, refusing to think about meeting her family's killer in court.

Besides, in little over half a year, it was the state, not she, who'd be the prosecution. Nowhere were she or Galen or Perry mentioned in the *State of Texas v. Garcia.*

Garcia. Manuel Garcia. She'd known the driver had a name, but *Garcia* seemed so harmless, so normal, like the name of someone in a high school homeroom roll call: Fulton, Gabbert, Garcia...

She continued to think about him as the months wore on leading to the trial. Jill Strickland confirmed he'd been convicted of DWI before—why had he been back out on the road? Was he remorseful? Had he known that night what he'd done? Did he even *remember* that night?

Christmas passed, a holiday made more mournful to Leah because of its emphasis on children. She forced herself to spend a few days at her parents', but she would have preferred to stay in her apartment, alone. Danni and her family came from Illinois, and they all gathered around a small artificial tree and halfheartedly opened packages. Leah felt sorry for her niece, Jennifer. The little girl worked hard at containing her enthusiasm, especially around Leah. She'd probably been cautioned by her grandmother, as well as her mother.

Leah kept an emotional distance from them all, even Danni. Where once she might have opened up emotionally to her sister, she no longer had the energy or inclination. She was settling into her life of solitude, and she had no desire to upset it by sharing her grief and letting anyone into her heart.

After the new year, she followed a routine of going to work every day and spending the weekends holed up in her apartment—mostly sleeping and watching TV—seldom venturing beyond her neighborhood. Occasionally she received an invitation to a Tupperware or jewelry party given by someone at work, but she never accepted. She wanted to be alone.

As friendly as her coworkers were, as persistent as some of them were in trying to get to know her, she maintained a wall of silence. She'd rather let them think her unfriendly than divulge the sad details of her life. She'd allowed that she was originally from Houston and had graduated from TCU, but beyond that, she offered no clues to herself. She heard it rumored that she was divorced, but she did nothing to set the record straight. If she started talking about Perry or Galen, her carefully constructed wall would crumble and anyone would be free to march through her emotions. She saved her grieving for nights alone, in bed, where every morning she awoke to a tear-wet pillow.

Winter melted into spring, which bloomed into the green and heat of summer. A sore throat and cough that Leah developed at

Christmas recurred intermittently into June, along with a nervous stomach that prevented her from eating many of the spicy foods she'd previously enjoyed. She'd had little appetite for anything since the wreck, and she'd dropped two dress sizes. Slender to begin with, she now found herself shopping in the petite section. Several women at work noticed her new shape and voiced their pleasant envy. She smiled and accepted their compliments, wondering what they would say if she told them the real reason for her weight loss.

She knew what they'd say. They'd look shocked, then they'd back-pedal. Then fawn. And no one would ever look at her the same way again. Suddenly she would be the Grieving Widow and Mother.

Far easier—and less painful—to be the Unsociable Outcast.

As the date drew nearer for the trial, she wondered how she would manage to have the time off without arousing anyone's suspicions, not to mention keeping them from seeing Perry's and Galen's names in the newspaper. Until then, she would go about the daily business of living, as unobtrusively as possible.

Jacobo knelt and looked one final time under the couch to make sure he hadn't missed any dirty socks. All he saw were dust puffs that had accumulated since the last good sweeping.

When he rose, Eric and his girlfriend, Karen, were standing by the couch, their faces long.

Jacobo grinned. "It's not like I'll be gone forever. Lots of people leave law school for a while and then come back."

Karen smiled. "It's not just that. We'll miss you. Besides, who's going to watch out for this one?" She elbowed Eric.

Jacobo smiled. Karen was an elementary grade teacher at an Austin Christian school and, in Jacobo's opinion, perfectly suited for the overly studious and analytically minded Eric. Jacobo and Karen were forever teasing Eric that he needed a keeper to see that he took time to eat. "Why don't you go ahead and marry him, Karen?" Jacobo said. "Then you can move in and make sure he eats his vegetables."

Eric and Karen laughed, breaking the tension. Jacobo smiled too, knowing he would miss watching their easygoing relationship. He did hope they eventually got married, but he could understand Eric's wanting to finish law school first. He wondered briefly if they would still be living in Austin by the time he returned to school, then shoved down the thought. *Día a día,* his mother had always said.

He cleared his throat. "Well..." Squaring his shoulders, he headed for the door. Karen and Eric followed him onto the porch.

"We'll miss you." Karen stood on her toes and briefly hugged him, kissing him quickly on the cheek. "I think you're doing a wonderful thing. *Vaya con Dios,*" she whispered, stepping back.

"If that's the only Spanish you know, you're doing all right," he said, wiping a tear from her cheek. He cupped her face gently, as he would one of Dolores's little ones, and smiled. "Thank you."

Eric held out his hand. "See you around, Jocko. Let us know how things are going."

Jacobo grasped his hand, then pulled him into a quick hug. "You too. You've got my home number and the number of the law office where I'll be clerking this summer. Call me if you need anything."

Eric nodded, stepping back. He wrapped his arm around Karen. They watched Jacobo as he headed for his motorcycle, and they were still watching him, waving, as he drove up the street and out of Austin.

———⟨⟨———

"You mean you haven't told anyone? Not even Betsy?" Wanda Voss shook her head. "I've heard of private people before, but you win the prize."

Leah didn't know whether to take that as a compliment or an insult, so she said nothing.

"And the trial's next week, and you need the time off."

Leah cleared her throat. "Yes."

Maybe she should have said something before. Wanda didn't look too happy; maybe she'd tell Betsy to mark it against Leah. Evaluations were going on right now. *Lacks communication skills,* the review would read, and Leah would be denied a raise.

She was having enough trouble making ends meet as it was.

Wanda picked up the phone, then set it down. "Look." She crossed her hands on the desk and leaned closer. "I can't make you divulge personal information to your supervisors. You can ask for a week off and not say a word when the inevitable questions come up about where you're going for vacation."

"Do you think if I told them, they'd be more pleased with my work?"

Wanda laughed. "Jim and Betsy are both extremely pleased with your work. They said you've picked up the job faster than anybody they've ever trained. You're always working, always on time, and never object to staying late."

"Then—"

"What I'm concerned about is *you*, Leah. Not your work. Not even that everyone know what's going on. We're a company that cares about its employees, and we want you to know that we're behind you. In whatever way we can help. I assumed you would have told someone long before the trial started."

Leah locked her fingers together. "I never saw the need. If you think I should, I'll at least tell Jim and Betsy."

"Would you feel better if I called them up here now? No one would see you in Betsy's office and wonder what was going on. I'd be glad to help out if the talking gets too difficult for you..."

Leah nodded. She might as well get this over with.

Wanda phoned Betsy and told her and Jim to come to her office. She paused, then said, "Leah's up here."

While they waited, Wanda brought Leah a cup of coffee. She accepted it, grateful to have something to do with her hands as Betsy and Jim settled themselves on Wanda's plush leather sofa. Wanda came around from behind her desk and took a chair beside Leah.

"What's up, Wanda?" Betsy didn't believe in wasting any time.

"Leah has asked for next week off."

Betsy looked at Jim, who shrugged. "You could have come to us about that, Leah," Betsy said, sounding hurt.

"Wanda knew about...my situation when she hired me," Leah said. "She knew that I would need a week off...to attend a trial."

"What she means—" Wanda said gently, trying to help.

"What I mean is that my husband and child were killed by a drunk driver nearly a year ago, and the killer's trial is next week. I have to testify, but I also want to be there—especially for the outcome."

Jim and Betsy glanced at each other, then Leah. "We had no idea," Betsy said, clearly shocked. "We thought—"

"The people on the floor said—" Jim cut in.

Leah smiled wryly. "That I was divorced? That I was standoffish?"

"Well, yes," he said. "You never want to do anything with anybody else... You never even talk to anybody else."

Betsy leaned toward Leah and took her hand. "Why didn't you tell us?"

Leah gently eased her hand away. "It's not something I like to talk about. But Wanda felt I should let you know the reason I need the time off."

"You can have all the time you need," Betsy said.

Jim nodded. "We'll all help to cover your work load."

While he and Betsy discussed what assignments they would farm out to whom, Leah settled into her seat, silent. A dull ache formed in her stomach. Now everyone would know. Everyone would stare, then, after working up the courage to approach her, offer up greeting card sympathies or ask questions that would make her relive the accident over and over. No one would ask about Perry or Galen, what they had been like, what did she miss most about them... They would only want gory details about their deaths or offer advice as to how she should face the future.

As if she hadn't been doing just fine on her own.

The next day, Thursday, the day jury selection began for next week's trial, Leah phoned in sick at work, and the following day as well.

Monday morning Jill Strickland met her at the doorway to the Tarrant County Criminal Justice Center. She hustled Leah through the metal detector, talking almost as fast as her high-heeled shoes tapped against the linoleum. "How are you? I know you can't believe this day is finally here. Your parents are meeting us in the waiting room, right? Do they know where to go?"

Leah nodded. Hart and Emily had spent the weekend at a downtown hotel, offering but not delivering moral support for Leah.

Jill ushered Leah inside the waiting room. Maintained solely for victims—who, as future trial witnesses, were prevented from hearing others' testimonies—the room was filled with deep-cushioned sofas and chairs. Tables and plants were strategically placed around the room. The smell of freshly brewed coffee wafted from a full pot in the coffee maker. A morning talk show aired on a television in the corner.

Hart and Emily rose from the largest sofa and greeted Leah with a hug, then Jill with a handshake. Leah sat next to her father, and Jill drew up a chair beside them.

"The lawyer's name is Gabriel Herrera, and he's well respected. Especially in the Hispanic community. I can't believe Garcia's pleaded not guilty, but there you are," Jill said, plunging right in. "I've seen defense lawyers try to prove all kinds of things, and I don't expect this one to be any different."

Leah didn't realize her hand was shaking until her father drew it into his own. "He won't try to play a racism card, will he?" Hart said.

"He might, to a certain degree. Mostly he'll be trying to prove that we the prosecution can't prove that the defendant is guilty. That we don't have enough evidence."

"But I saw it happen!" Leah said. She and Jill had gone over this several times before, but now that she was here, she couldn't believe the man wouldn't just say he was guilty and serve his time.

Jill smiled. "I know, Leah. And that's what you're going to tell the jury. I'm calling you as my last witness. I want them to remember you, even if they forget the testimony of the policeman, the doctors, and all the other technical experts. There are mothers and fathers on that jury, men and women who are husbands and wives. I want them to see that night through your eyes." She paused. "And that, if nothing else, is going to send Manuel Garcia to prison for a very long time."

Leah's eyes filled with tears. Her father squeezed her hand, and Jill gave her a reassuring hug. "I have to go into court now. I wish you could watch."

Leah pulled a photograph from the pocket of her jacket and handed it to Jill. "If you can somehow show this to the jury..." she whispered.

Jill looked at the close-up shot of Perry and Galen, taken on Galveston beach. Galen was snuggled in Perry's embrace, his small arms hugging his father's neck. They were both smiling at the camera.

Jill smiled, tucking the photo in her jacket pocket. "They'll be there, Leah. I promise you that the jury will know they're there. I know it's hard, but sit tight here, and I'll report back when there's a break." She touched Leah's arm. "You okay?"

Leah nodded, unable to speak. She'd spent all last night staring at that photo; trusting it to Jill was more difficult than she'd imagined.

Jill patted her arm. "Good. It's going to be all right, Leah. Just hang in here and be patient. Meantime, have some coffee, make yourself at home. You're welcome to get yourselves something to eat. There's not a cafeteria in the building, but you can go across the street to the outlet mall's food court and bring it back here, if you want. This room is for the victims' family only. The offender's family isn't allowed here."

Hart extended a hand. "Thank you so much, Ms. Strickland. For all you've done."

Jill shook his hand and gathered her briefcase and purse. "It's going to be fine, Mr. Tyler, Mrs. Tyler. Leah…okay? It's going to be fine."

"Yes." Leah forced a smile. "I know you'll do your best."

Jill nodded, then she swished efficiently from the room, her high heels clicking down the hall.

"Well." Emily rose and headed for the coffee maker. "I could use a good strong cup. Anybody else?"

Leah shook her head, her throat tight. As much as it terrified her, as much as she dreaded reliving her worst memories, she wanted to be in the courtroom. She wanted to see Perry and Galen's killer face to face.

She'd imagined him many times, many ways. Sometimes he was swarthy and mean-looking, eyes glazed and body dissipated from years of drinking; at others, he was small and thin, scared, deeply remorseful and henceforth sober.

She'd also imagined what she might do, given the chance to be in the same room with him. She even dreamed about it, waking up in a cold sweat with the realization that her subconscious was much more violent than she'd ever fathomed.

She'd shot him, stabbed him, even run him over with a car. She'd also seen him injured and dying, though not by her hand, and she'd turned her back.

Never once in all her various dream states did Perry and Galen come back to life.

Betsy and Wanda entered, smiling when they saw Leah. "We wanted to be here with you," Betsy said, taking a seat beside her. "In case you need anything."

"Hart Tyler." All business, Leah's father stepped in, holding out his hand. "And you are…"

"Betsy Culligan. I'm Leah's supervisor."

"And I'm Wanda Voss, *Betsy's* supervisor," the older woman said, laughing gently, extending a hand to Leah's father. "We couldn't imagine not being here. We think of Leah as family."

Leah raised her eyebrows. When had she ever given them cause to think of her as family? Guiltily, she remembered that she'd phoned in sick last Thursday and Friday.

"It was good of you to come. I'm Leah's mother, Emily Tyler." Leah's mother stepped in, balancing a steaming Styrofoam cup with one hand and extending the other. "So nice to meet you. I wish it were under different circumstances."

"Yes." Wanda took a seat and turned toward Hart. "You must live in Houston."

As Wanda made polite conversation with Leah's parents, Betsy drew Leah to the side. "You don't have to talk to me or anything. I know you must be a bundle of nerves. At least I would be."

Leah shrugged. She was very nervous, but she wasn't about to admit it to her boss.

"If you're wondering, Wanda and I told the others at work. They sent you this." She fumbled in her purse and drew out an envelope.

It's a little late for a sympathy card. Leah opened the envelope and tried to smile. "That was very thoughtful of them."

"They're a good group, Leah. They're concerned."

Leah pulled out a card with a picture of a woman sitting on a hill, staring at the faraway horizon. The caption underneath, in simple scrolled letters, said *Thinking of you.*

Everyone in the department had signed it, each person including a brief message of encouragement and hope. Many included specific Scriptures or promises that they were praying. Several specifically mentioned Perry and Galen. No one merely signed a name.

Leah drew a deep breath, too overcome to speak.

"You should see what they put on birthday cards," Betsy said.

Choking on a sob, Leah laughed. What a sweet, crazy group. And Betsy was a sweet, crazy boss. "Thanks," she whispered. "And tell everybody else thanks too."

Her eyes welled with tears, and she ducked her head.

Betsy took her hand. "It's okay, Leah," she said softly.

Leah wiped the tears under her eyes and sniffled. "I...I have to go get a Kleenex. I'll be..."

She couldn't reach the door fast enough. Keeping her head down, she cruised down the hall then suddenly realized she had no idea where the bathroom was.

Wham! Leah collided with someone, and she stumbled. Horrified and humiliated, she backed away. "I'm so sor—"

The stranger steadied her. "Are you all right?"

Leah looked up. A Hispanic man dropped his hands from her arms, his concerned look shifting to wariness.

Manuel Garcia!

Leah relaxed, realizing the defendant probably wouldn't be roaming the court's hallways by himself. Still, he was wearing a nicely tailored suit—the sort of outfit a defendant would wear to impress a jury—and his long hair, though held back in a ponytail, gave him a criminal air.

"I...I'm fine. S-sorry," she mumbled and stepped away. Scurrying past a bank of elevators, she dodged inside a rest room, discovered it empty, and hurried into a stall.

Shaking, she leaned against the locked door and let the tears flow in a rush of confusing emotions. The grief she'd grown accustomed to was joined by fear, brought on by the man in the hallway—whether or not he was Manuel Garcia.

She was going to have to get on a witness stand in a room full of strangers and recount the details of Perry and Galen's deaths. And their killer would be present to hear every word.

What if she fell apart on the stand? What if she couldn't testify well enough to convince the jury of his guilt?

Leah clenched her fists. The man had killed her family—the police had caught him at the scene. There couldn't be any question. Why did everyone have to go through the motions of this trial? Why couldn't he just be honest?

It seemed so grossly unfair; he was able to sit in the courtroom, able to hear every word of testimony, yet she was here hiding in a bathroom stall, sobbing, barred from the trial as though she were the guilty person.

The door to the bathroom squeaked open.

"And *then* guess what he had the nerve to say!"

"He wanted to see you again?"

"Yes! I told him…" Water ran in the sink, muffling the rest of the conversation.

Leah pressed a wad of toilet paper against her eyes. *I can't even grieve in peace.*

She should probably get back to the waiting room anyway. Not because her parents or Betsy and Wanda expected her, but because she wanted to be there when Jill arrived with any news. If she couldn't be present at the trial, she at least wanted to know every detail. She wanted to be prepared when her time came to walk into the courtroom.

Chapter Eight

But her time didn't come that day. Jill bustled back to the victims' waiting room as often as possible and kept them apprised of the trial's progress.

"Gabe's doing everything as an attorney that I imagined he would," Jill said. "He's trying to prove—or at least plant doubt in the jury's mind—that the evidence is flimsy. Garcia's blood sample might have been contaminated. The machine calibration might have been faulty. The training of the officer who performed the gaze nystagmus—the eye-tracking check—on Garcia might not have been sufficient. Garcia might have been blinded by oncoming headlights. Your car probably wasn't pulled over far enough…"

"That's absurd!" Leah clenched her hands. "All those things are illogical. Especially…" She swallowed hard. "Especially the last one. Perry pulled over on the shoulder."

"Maybe so, but the lawyer's planted doubt, Leah. Don't worry. Your testimony will set things straight."

Leah drew a deep breath. She had to know. "How does he look? Manuel Garcia, I mean."

"He looks completely respectable, as I knew he would. He appears sober and clean-cut, and he's wearing a nice suit."

"He...he doesn't have a ponytail, does he?"

"No, in fact, I'd say he has a fresh, short haircut."

Leah breathed an inward sigh of relief.

"Gabe—the defense attorney—is also playing up the fact that Manuel Garcia is Hispanic and Perry and Galen were Anglo."

"Why..." Hart Tyler got to his feet, but Emily laid a restraining hand on his arm.

"Let Ms. Strickland finish," she said.

Hart sheepishly sat back down.

"He's not playing a racist card as you might suspect, Mr. Tyler, he's simply playing on the jury's sympathy that Garcia is a hard-working blue-collar man with a wife and kids to support."

"And by implication, Leah, being Anglo, hasn't lost much at all, is that it?" Hart said. "After all, she doesn't have anyone to support except herself."

"It's not quite like that, Mr.—"

"I know what it's like. I expected this, Ms. Strickland. Everybody's a victim these days, except the true victims."

"Mr. Tyler," Jill said softly but firmly. "I just want Leah to be aware of the situation. The local TV news has been hanging around—not to mention newspaper reporters—and they'll probably want to talk to her. I want her to be prepared for the questions they might ask."

Leah hadn't thought about the press. She'd thought they had long ago lost interest. "I don't want to talk to anybody."

"She doesn't have to, does she?" Emily looked worried.

"Of course not. I'll walk you out of the building every day to fend off any questions. I know it can be disconcerting, but if they aim cameras and lights at you, hold your head high, Leah. You're not the criminal. Okay?"

Leah nodded. How could this all be happening? She suddenly had the urge to run to her apartment, jump into bed, and pull the covers up high.

She steeled herself inwardly. If she could get through this trial, everything would be all right. Then, at last—finally, *surely*—she would have what was left of her life on an even keel.

—◯⤴

Jill faithfully escorted Leah and her grim-faced family from the building late that afternoon. As she'd predicted, the media waited like a pack of dogs at a rabbit hunt.

"Mrs. Travers! Over here! What do you think of Manuel Garcia?"

"Mrs. Travers! Leah! Do you think he'll be convicted?"

"Do you have any animosity toward him because he's Hispanic?"

Jill's high heels momentarily ceased their resolute rhythm against the sidewalk, and she turned to face the reporters and cameras. "My client has nothing to say about this trial," she said. "We believe justice will be served." She gripped Leah's arm and hustled her down the street.

The reporters trailed after them. "Justice? What does that mean?" one of them shouted.

Jill stuffed Leah in the backseat of her parents' Cadillac, and Hart and Emily bustled into the front. Hart pulled away from the curb, and the question rang in Leah's ears as the reporters turned away, disappointed.

After everything was over, what would justice mean?

The next day, Leah stayed in the victims' waiting room all day, pacing, trying not to sit next to her mother, who nervously laughed at Regis and Kathie Lee's antics on television, or her father, who grumbled about the slowness of the legal system.

Wanda came alone, finally switching off the TV and engaging Emily Tyler in a lengthy discussion about volunteer work and the current state of hospitals. Leah made occasional forays to the bathroom for a change of scenery, eyeing the closed courtroom door as she passed, even pausing occasionally, hoping to be present when they called a recess or, better still, when she was called to the stand.

Wednesday she drank a strong cup of coffee on an empty stomach and felt queasy all morning. She bypassed the pastries her parents brought to the waiting room for breakfast and had settled in to watch a morning game show when one of Jill's assistants came through the door. "Mrs. Travers? It's time for your testimony."

Leah's stomach somersaulted, and she wished she'd eaten something after all. Rising to her feet, she vaguely heard her mother sobbing gently. "We'll be right there, Leah," her father said.

Betsy, bless her heart, who had shown up that morning for the day's vigil, clasped Leah's hand. "I'll be praying for you, Leah. Don't worry. You'll have just the right words."

Leah smiled bleakly. "Right now I'd rather have a good dose of courage first."

"You'll have that, too." Betsy patted her hand.

Leah went to the assistant, who waited patiently by the door, then followed her down the empty hallway and pushed through the heavy courtroom door. Most of the crowd turned as she entered. She hadn't felt this nervous since she'd walked down the aisle for her wedding.

She sensed her parents slipping into the back row as she walked alone past the crowd and up to the front. The bailiff held out a Bible, just as Jill had said he would, and Leah placed her hand on it, swearing to tell the truth.

As if she could tell anything else.

Seated on the stand, Leah relaxed as Jill walked toward her, smiling. "Would you please state your name and address for the court?"

Never taking her eyes from Jill, Leah complied, then answered more routine questions about her relationship to Perry and Galen. As she relaxed, she let her gaze drift to the defendant's table.

And there he sat.

He looked everything and yet nothing like she'd imagined. Dressed in a nice three-piece suit, hair carefully groomed, he did indeed look like a hard-working man. A man she could easily imagine as a husband and the father of children. But not the killer she knew he was.

Just behind him, in the spectator's section, sat the ponytailed man.

Leah's hands shook, and she realized Jill had asked her another question. "I'm sorry. Could you repeat that, please?"

Jill frowned, fixing Leah with a look that said *concentrate*. They'd been over this many times—how she should act, where she should look, how she should answer, even down to the navy blue dress and matching shoes she was wearing.

Justice, apparently, was quite a calculated business.

"Leah." Jill moved closer and softened her voice. "Please tell the court what happened on the night in question."

Leah drew a deep breath. As she raised her chin, her gaze landed on the ponytailed man. He crossed his arms and frowned. Leah jerked her gaze back to Jill and let the story spill out as rehearsed.

As she spoke, searching for just the right words to convey the horror of that evening, she noticed Jill drift to the prosecutor's table. Confused, Leah stumbled over her words, but continued. When she was finished, she drew a thankful breath that she hadn't fallen apart on the stand as she'd dreaded.

Jill didn't say anything for a moment, then reached under the table. "Leah...do you recognize this?"

Leah froze. Jill was holding Galen's car seat. She set it on the table and watched Leah expectantly.

"Yes," Leah whispered, blinking.

"Would you tell the court what it is?"

"It's my son's car seat."

"The one you strapped him into the night he died?"

Leah nodded.

"Please answer verbally," Jill said gently.

"Yes," she said softly, her eyes filling with tears.

Jill carried the car seat toward the witness stand, walking slowly. "Leah, did you strap your son into this seat, believing that he would be safe?"

Leah could see various stains on the restraining straps, some that she recalled distinctly as food stains. Others were unrecognizable. Her eyes were watering now, and she wiped them. "Y-yes." She thought she saw several female members of the jury wiping their eyes also.

Jill paused in front of the witness stand, then mercifully removed the car seat from sight. She lifted a folder and walked to a display easel set in full view of the witness stand and the jury. She withdrew a photo from the folder, placed it on the easel, then stepped back. "Do you recognize this?"

Leah stared at an autopsy photo of Galen. To her utter horror, she heard herself sob. "Y-yes. That's my son. G-galen."

"How about this one?"

Jill put up an autopsy photo of Perry. He looked as eerie and lifeless as Galen, a stark contrast to the vacation photo Leah had given Jill when the trial began.

Leah's voice cracked. "Th-that's my husband, Perry." She felt her shoulders jerking, and another sob escaped. A murmur rippled through the crowd, and she bowed her head, embarrassed at her emotional display. What was Jill doing to her?

"Thank you, your honor." Jill whipped the pictures from the easel and returned them to the folder. "No further questions."

She headed for the table, passing the defense attorney, Gabriel Herrera, as he rose and approached the witness stand. He also carried a folder.

Leah sniffled furiously. Herrera smiled gently, handing her the handkerchief from his breast pocket. "Mrs. Travers…may I call you Leah?"

"Yes." She accepted the handkerchief and wiped her eyes and nose.

"Leah." He rested a hand on the witness stand. "That night was very painful…probably the most painful in your life, wouldn't you say?"

"Yes," she said, wary. Jill had warned her that he would probably appear sympathetic.

"Sometimes when people are in pain, they don't always remember things the way they think they do later."

"Objection, your honor," Jill said.

"Sustained. Mr. Herrera, please get to your point."

Herrera withdrew a piece of paper from the folder and held it up for Leah's inspection. "Do you know what this is?"

She could barely make out the words "investigation" and "report." "No," she said truthfully.

"It's the report from the police officer who took your statement the night of the accident. Do you remember what you told him?"

"No sir, I don't."

Herrera cleared his throat. "'All of a sudden, I saw headlights coming toward them, from behind them, then…I just remember the headlights. It happened so fast, it's like I didn't even see it happen.'" He paused and looked up at Leah. "Did you say this?"

"I…I must have."

"So if I were to ask you exactly what happened, we wouldn't have any way of knowing whether it was really the truth or not."

"Objection. Counselor is implying that the witness is a liar."

Herrera turned toward the judge. "Your honor, I'm merely trying to establish that it's possible her memory is not what we've been led to believe. That a person like Mrs. Travers who has admittedly undergone a traumatic experience might have an impaired memory."

The judge thought for a moment. "Overruled. Mr. Herrera, please keep your line of thinking a bit more clear."

"Thank you, your honor. I'll try." Herrera leaned forward again, smiling gently and lowering his voice. "Leah, you said in your statement that you remembered headlights. And that everything happened quickly. Is it possible, then, that you didn't even see the actual impact at all?"

Leah gazed desperately at the crowd. Manuel Garcia leaned back in his chair, his expression passive. The ponytailed man was still frowning. She lowered her gaze. "It's possible," she mumbled.

"I'm sorry, I couldn't hear you."

She raised her chin. "I said, it's possible."

Herrera smiled. "Thank you, Leah. No further questions, your honor."

"Ms. Strickland, redirect?" the judge said.

"No, your honor." Jill was scribbling furiously on a piece of paper.

"Thank you, Mrs. Travers," the judge said. "You may step down."

That was it? Now that she was up here, she wanted to stay. She wanted to tell the jury how much she missed Perry and Galen, how the man sitting at the defendant's table had taken not only their lives but mangled her own beyond repair. That his actions had nothing to do with the metal and glass of automobiles or even a bottle of liquor, but about his willfully choosing to abandon common sense and violating the sacred trust of strangers.

Leah clenched her fists, frustrated and helpless. Gabriel Herrera sat calmly scribbling on paper; Manuel was studying the far wall, clearly bored; and even Jill was preoccupied with something in her briefcase.

"Mrs. Travers…," the judge said gently.

She nodded, rising and somehow making her way from the stand. As she walked to the back of the room and her waiting parents, she paused at the defendant's table. Manuel Garcia never looked up. A woman sat behind him, glowering at Leah. Ponytail Man whispered something in her ear.

Jill touched Leah's arm. "You did fine," she whispered. "We'll talk later. Now go to your parents."

Leah pushed open the low wooden gate and headed to the back. Her father led the way into the corridor and back to the waiting room. Once there, he embraced her tightly. "You were wonderful, honey."

Her mother touched her shoulder. "We're so proud of you."

"Was I okay?" Leah twisted her hands together. "I sounded ridiculous...like I didn't even see it happen. Maybe I didn't."

"Of course you did, dear." Her mother patted her arm.

Jill bustled into the room, all smiles. "Leah, you were *wonderful.* The jury will..."

"Why did you do that to me?" Leah stepped away from her parents. "I looked like an idiot up there, crying. Why didn't you tell me you were going to show me Galen's car seat? Or their pictures?"

Jill folded her arms. "I wanted the jury to see your honest reaction...grief. Pain. Heartbreak. They're going to remember that a lot longer than Gabe Herrera's quibbling about whether or not you actually saw the accident. If I'd told you in advance what I was going to do, you would have subconsciously steeled yourself for it. Your reaction wouldn't have been as genuine."

"So I'm just a pawn, then. This is just one big chess game, isn't it? From the clothes we all wear to how we act in the courtroom. It's just a game of who's the better manipulator, you or Herrera."

"I know it seems like that," Jill said. "And I know you're tired. You've been cooped up in here for days and suddenly you're thrust into the courtroom. Gabe has an ethical responsibility to represent his client, as do I. The truth is being presented, but yes, some of its impact is in the method of delivery. In a sense, we're handing the jury all the puzzle pieces, but they're the ones who have to put them together to get the true picture. And they will, Leah. They'll find Garcia guilty."

Leah sank to the sofa, cradling her head in her hands. How would she ever forget the sight of Perry and Galen's autopsy photos?

Jill sat beside her and wrapped an arm around her shoulders. "I know it's tough. I admire what you did today. It's difficult to think about the crash, much less recount it for a roomful of strangers."

"I just want it to all be over," Leah mumbled. "I just want him behind bars where he can't hurt anybody else."

"It'll be over soon. You were my last witness, so the judge recessed the trial for lunch. After that the defense will call their witnesses. Then there will be rebuttal testimony and closing arguments. Then the jury will be excused for deliberation. I expect we'll have a verdict either late today or tomorrow."

"Really?" Leah raised her head. Surely she would feel better when this was all over.

Her father leaned down, smiling. "I'll go get some lunch. Ms. Strickland, would you like to join us?"

"Thanks, but I've got a few things I want to check on during this break." She gave Leah's shoulders one final squeeze then headed for the door. Hart held it open, then trailed after her, smiling at Leah as he went.

Leah dropped her head back into her hands and closed her eyes. She felt her mother sit beside her on the sofa, then she felt a hesitant arm wrap around her. Leah leaned into her mother's embrace and rested her head on her shoulder.

"Dolores, slow down already!" Jacobo braced open the heavy door of the criminal justice building. His sister was already down the steps and at the corner to cross the street.

Jacobo grabbed her arm, and she shook it off, fishing in her bag and coming up with a pack of cigarettes. She lit one, shooting Jacobo a defiant look as she exhaled smoke. "Yeah, I haven't quit yet," she said in Spanish. "Don't look at me like that."

Jacobo spread his hands out, tired. It had been a long morning. "Like what?"

"Like a big brother."

"It's what I am, Dolores. What do you want me to do?"

She turned away and watched a group of people cross the street at the light. "Look there." She jerked her head at the crowd and took a drag on the cigarette. "The daddy."

Jacobo followed her gaze and saw the man he'd figured as Leah Travers's father crossing the street to the outlet mall.

"That woman makes me sick," Dolores said. "Crying up there on the witness stand. That was a pretty smart move."

"That was the car seat her son was in when he was killed, Dolores. Don't you think you'd feel the same way if it had been Rosita or Carlos?"

"I know, I know." Dolores threw the cigarette on the sidewalk and ground it out with her heel. "But when's the jury going to hear about us? When are they going to hear how I'm going to be left alone to support five kids because of my idiot husband?"

"They'll probably hear about it during the punishment phase. Gabe'll mention it then, hoping they'll give Manuel a lighter prison sentence."

Dolores laughed. "It doesn't matter how much time they give him—he still won't be home. Not that he's much help even when he's there."

"Come on. Let's get some lunch." Jacobo took her by the arm and led her to the crosswalk. She was silent as they negotiated the street, then on the other side, she stopped abruptly.

"Why do you always take his side?" she said angrily. "You don't like him either."

Jacobo pulled her away from the curb, out of the path of pedestrians. "No, I *don't* like him, Dolores. He's been nothing but trouble for you since you met him. But he's your husband. You can't just throw away your marriage because times are tough."

"You sound like Mama," she said, frowning. "Or the church."

"The Catholic Church doesn't have a monopoly against divorce. The Bible teaches against it too," Jacobo said. "And as for Mama…"

"Sorry I brought it up." Dolores walked toward the mall, head high and trim hips swinging.

Jacobo shook his head as he followed, glowering at several men who gave Dolores the once-over.

"The defendant will please rise."

Manuel Garcia got to his feet. Leah held her breath, and her parents, on either side of her, clutched her hands. The jury had deliberated for less than half an hour before returning with their verdict.

"Ladies and gentlemen of the jury, have you reached your verdict?"

"We have, your honor," the foreman said, then cleared his throat. "We the jury find the defendant guilty of two counts of intoxication manslaughter."

A ripple of approval swept through the courtroom. Hart Tyler punched his fist in the air. Jill Strickland turned to Leah and her family and smiled.

Manuel Garcia's shoulders slumped, and the woman sitting behind him burst into tears. "Manuel!"

The man with the ponytail took her into his arms, and she sobbed against his shoulder.

Jill quietly tucked Perry and Galen's autopsy photos—along with the vacation snapshot Leah had given her—back into her heavy leather briefcase. She clicked the latch shut.

Leah's satisfaction felt hollow, as hollow as the ever-present ache in her stomach.

Chapter Nine

The punishment phase began the next morning. Manuel Garcia was given the maximum sentence, two twenty-year sentences, to run consecutively. He wouldn't be eligible for parole for twenty years.

Wanda called Leah later that night to offer her quiet congratulations and also to tell her that she wasn't expected back at work until she felt ready. "You're on short-term disability leave," Wanda said.

Leah's parents tried in vain to persuade her to come back to Houston. "Come stay in your old room for a while," Emily said. "Let us pamper you."

"It wouldn't hurt, honey," Hart said. "You need some time to regroup."

Leah shook her head. "This is my home. I might as well stay here"—she smiled wryly—"and get on with my life."

She felt an odd mixture of relief and sorrow that the trial was over. But now she was at loose ends. What did she have to look forward to anymore?

Leah padded around her apartment, not even venturing down to the Purple Onion for her breakfast. She'd lost interest in the regulars.

She'd lost interest in her own life.

Staying up late every night, she huddled in a blanket on the couch, the darkened living room bathed by the glow of television. She flipped listlessly through the channels, pausing only on the ones that required the least amount of concentration: the shopping channel, late night talk shows, wrestling matches.

In the morning, she'd awaken with the TV still blaring, the remote control still in her hand. Sometimes she crawled into bed and slept until early afternoon. She ate little, usually one small meal per day, and her weight dropped lower than it had been in high school.

She suffered a variety of aches and pains that refused to subside: headaches, stomachaches, a heavy feeling in her chest. She developed the flu and lay in bed, weak and helpless, barely able to get to the kitchen for a glass of water. She thought about calling someone for help, then remembered they all had their own lives to lead. Betsy or Wanda called faithfully every few days, but Leah masked her illness, not wanting to be a bother. The entire department would probably bring her food.

When the aching finally subsided, she ventured to the organic store for juices and vegetables. "Where ya been, Ms. Travers?" Pete, one of the clerks, said cheerfully. "You look kinda pale. You need some supplements or something?"

Leah shook her head and scurried back home. Once inside, she thumped the grocery bags on the table, dismayed to see the apartment anew, after venturing out for the first time in days.

Dirty dishes filled the sink. Dust covered the furniture. Dirty laundry was stacked up in one corner of her tiny bedroom.

What kind of mad woman lived here?

Leah sank to the sofa, too exhausted to deal with it. Why did everything take so much effort?

She wrapped her arms around her knees and cried. She'd thought she'd feel better after the trial was over and Manuel Garcia was in prison. Instead, she felt worse. Justice was as unpalatable as a sour apple, not sweet to the taste as she'd imagined. Justice hadn't changed anything. It hadn't brought Perry and Galen back. It hadn't given her a fresh outlook on life.

She'd been allowed in the courtroom for the punishment phase. Manuel Garcia had never said he was sorry or expressed any sign of remorse. He hadn't even taken the stand. His wife—the woman who'd been sitting behind him—had testified and cried buckets, pleading with the court for mercy. That he was really a good man at heart. That he was the sole support of her and their five children.

Leah had sat, unmoved by her tears, clenching her teeth.

Then the brother-in-law—the man with the ponytail—had testified. To Leah's shock, Jacobo Martinez told the court in a quiet but confident voice that he had left law school in Austin to take care of his sister and her children. He was a clerk in a law firm. Leah noticed that he didn't try to redeem Garcia's character; in fact, Gabe Herrera seemed intent on proving Jacobo's good character instead. He focused on how stable Jacobo had always been and what he was giving up to take care of his family because of Manuel's "miscalculation."

Leah's anger stirred at Herrera's use of the word, but when Martinez stepped down, he glanced almost apologetically at her. He looked away quickly, but she'd seen an unguarded moment, an anger, that left her studying him covertly.

After the sentencing, she read aloud her victim impact statement, but it seemed superfluous after Garcia's conviction.

"My name is Leah Travers. My husband and child were killed in a car accident that I will never be able to forget. I saw it happen, saw firsthand the aftermath of broken glass and twisted metal and heard the ambulance sirens and CareFlite helicopter blades. What I didn't see were my husband and child conscious, ever again. What I didn't hear were their voices. Nor did they see or hear me ever again. They both died shortly after they were taken to the hospital.

"We were coming back from a trip to visit my family. I was thinking about getting home, about getting back to my daily routine. I wasn't thinking about losing my husband and two-year-old son, or about my life being forever, inexplicably, terrifyingly altered. But even while my grief was still fresh and raw, I was forced to move out of the only home my baby had ever known and into a tiny apartment. Previously, I hadn't worked outside the home, preferring instead to take care of my family. Without my husband's salary, I was forced to seek employment.

"I lost the two most precious people in the world to me. Now I live alone. I passed their birthdays this year, alone. Even a year later, I cannot look forward to a life without my family, yet looking back is too painful."

Dry eyed, she'd stepped down from the stand and walked straight to her seat. A few women in the audience dabbed their eyes. Manuel stared straight ahead, not even looking back at his wailing wife, who cried her husband's name against Jacobo Martinez's shoulder.

Leah had glanced away, feeling only a cold knot of satisfaction in her stomach. A knot that hadn't loosened even now, after the trial and sentencing were over. She couldn't forget Manuel Garcia's casual attitude, his stoicism about what he'd done. Didn't he care at all? Hadn't it sunk in that he'd killed two people?

And his wife. The knot tightened whenever Leah thought of Dolores Garcia's emotional outbursts. How dare she—as if she had been the one to lose a husband and child. Though he was headed for prison, *her* husband was still alive. *Her* children could still be kissed each evening as they were tucked into bed.

She even had five children of her own. Five! What kind of cruel God would take Leah's only son and let all the children of the murderer survive?

Leah raised her head from where she'd pressed her face against her knees, hoping that the apartment wouldn't look quite so messy. But it did, just like her life. Cleaning up either one would take more energy than she now had.

She grabbed the phone book and thumbed through it, her heart racing. There were surprisingly few Manuel Garcias listed. She quickly found the street name she recalled from the court documents, snatched up her purse, and headed out the door. It was well past suppertime, and though she made a habit of not going out after dark, she headed for her car.

She wanted to see, she *had* to see, where the Garcias lived. What did the house of a killer look like? Did the neighbors know who he was and what he'd done?

As she drove toward the north side of town, rage built, and her imagination soared. All the dreams she'd had of exacting revenge for Perry and Galen rushed in her head.

Her fingers drummed the steering wheel as she turned into his neighborhood. Here the obviously once grand houses showed signs of disrepair. Rotting porches were gathering places for groups of men under yellow bug lights. Mothers called in Spanish through screen doors to children playing in yards. Several women watered pots of geraniums and pansies.

Leah turned onto the street and drove slowly, searching for house numbers.

And there it was. The house. *His* house.

Run-down was her first thought. Shingles were missing from the roof. The concrete steps were crumbling. The wide porch was still intact, but a beat-up sofa gave it an air of tackiness.

Leah had half expected to see children spilling out all over the porch and yard. But the house was quiet, save for the glare of the porch's bare yellow bulb and the glow of a lamp through the thin, closed draperies of the front window.

What was going on behind that window?

Someone honked and zipped around her car, yelling out the open passenger window something about slow drivers. The Garcias' front door opened, and Leah pressed the accelerator and headed down the street, her hands shaking.

Mixing in with the traffic on a major thoroughfare, she relaxed her hands on the steering wheel and laughed out loud. Who could possibly have spotted her? And even if they had, so what? She had a right to be on any street in the city, including Manuel Garcia's.

Back at her apartment, she shut and locked her door, grabbed the remote control, and sank to the couch. Yawning, she switched off the light and huddled into the blanket and another mindless marathon of television watching. But even as she forced herself to blink while flipping between a controversial talk show and a sexy sitcom, she felt a tiny coal smoldering in the midst of the empty ache.

She closed her eyes and envisioned Garcia's house—the porch, the door, the window with the closed curtains.

Someone lived there. His family survived and moved around and went about the daily business of living. She would trade places with them in that dilapidated house in a minute, if she could only have Perry and Galen back.

Yet it was as if Manuel Garcia had left that house on the North Side and come into her neighborhood and snatched her family out of her home. Even though he was in prison, it was as though he were hiding behind that closed door, behind that curtained window, laughing at what he had taken from her and dragged back to his own home for the enjoyment of his own family.

Something clawed inside the empty ache, and Leah randomly flicked the channel button to a documentary about the metamorphosis of a caterpillar. She watched it spin a cocoon around itself, wondering with distaste if the caterpillar had any idea what was in store for itself. Did it work tirelessly, knowing that it would reap the benefits of its labor? Or did purely unemotional instinct compel it to weave its own coffin?

Tossing the remote control aside, Leah rolled down to the couch and covered her head with the blanket, breathing in the dark, musty odors. When she was a child, she had often wondered if she would suffocate if she slept all night with her head under the covers.

"You've got a letter from Austin." Dolores dropped the envelope onto the table.

Jacobo looked up from his bowl of Raisin Bran, yawning. He'd been up late last night with the kids, playing a game of touch football in the yard well past dark. He lifted the envelope and noticed the flour clinging to it, a sign that Dolores hadn't been home long from her job at the bakery. She had to be there bright and early on Saturday mornings, but she was home before noon.

"Your roommate?" Dolores poured Lucky Charms into a bowl and sat down beside him.

Jacobo nodded, setting the envelope aside to read later. "Eric's a good guy. You should meet him sometime."

Dolores smiled wearily as she poured milk. "When am I ever going to get a chance to go to Austin?" She capped the jug and started to eat, yawning in between bites.

Touched, Jacobo covered her hand with his own. "I know you're working hard, Dolores. It won't always be like this. When we get a little money saved…"

"That's not going to happen. There's always something that needs to be paid for. Things you shouldn't have to worry about. You should be back at school, doing what you always planned to do with your life. Not just settling for being a clerk to somebody else with a law degree."

"Law school will keep for a while," he said quietly. "I can always go back."

"When? You can't stay away until Manuel gets out. That'll be years!"

"I know that, Dolores. But you and the kids can't make it on your own. Not yet, anyway."

She set down her spoon and hunched over, her eyes filling with tears. Jacobo looked up and saw her shoulders shaking. "Hey, what's wrong?"

She shook her head, but the tears fell faster. Jacobo wrapped an arm around her, trying to comfort her as he had when they were kids. "What's the matter, Dolores?"

"You…you've been so good to us. And we're…I'm…" Her voice broke on a sob. "I think I'm pregnant."

Stunned, Jacobo let her cry. Pregnant?

Oh, Lord, Lord. How could you let this happen? Why now?

"Shh, it's okay. It'll be okay," he said automatically, even though his heart said otherwise. Where were they going to find room for another? Or the money? They were practically living on boxed macaroni and cheese as it was. A baby meant Dolores had to have the best to eat. A baby meant new clothes. Diapers. Hospital and doctor bills.

Dolores raised her head, her tears subsided to sniffles. "Lupe at work said she knows where I could get it taken care of real cheap. Manuel would never even have to know, Jacobo. Then we wouldn't have to worry."

Her words—the solution to the dilemma—came so swiftly that he caught his breath. Then reason crashed against his heart, and he gripped her hand. "No, Dolores. No. That's not the answer. That's never the answer. We'll find a way. God always makes a way."

She pulled free of his embrace. "You're just saying that because of what the church says about abortion. You don't want it on your conscience. I'm not afraid of the church anymore, all right?"

"You should be afraid of *God,* Dolores. I don't want it on *your* conscience. It might seem like the right thing to do now, but it's not. Murder is never justified."

"Then what about what Manuel did? How could God let that happen? Doesn't he see that we're down here practically starving to death, while Manuel's getting three square meals a day in prison? That winter's setting in, and I'm not sure we can even pay the heating bill? Why did he let me get pregnant, Jacobo? Huh? Or did you leave the church because you couldn't find the answers to questions like that either?"

"The Catholic Church can't answer a lot of questions. Neither can the Protestant churches," he said. "Only the Lord can answer some things, and we still won't know all the answers till we get to heaven. But until then, I walk by faith. Which is what we're going to do with this baby. He'll provide, Dolores. He always has."

"Sure he will." She smiled bitterly. "There's always your law school money savings, what's left of it after Manuel's bail money. You said so yourself. Maybe that's what God has in mind, huh? We can live on that."

Jacobo's stomach sank, but he looked his sister straight in the eyes. "If that's what he wants, then that's what we'll do."

Bills piled up unopened on Leah's kitchen table. Milk spoiled in the carton in the refrigerator, but she let it sit. A second wave of the flu hit, and she lived on the couch with a tumbler of tap water and a box of Kleenex beside her.

When the illness passed, she rose from her sickbed, weak but determined. It had been three months since the trial's conclusion. She had to do something. Wanda had stopped by with some homemade chicken noodle soup two days ago, and even in her illness, Leah hadn't failed to see the disgust in her employer's eyes.

She showered and then made an attempt to tidy the apartment, hauling armload after armload of dirty clothes and linens to the laundry room. She leaned against the folding table, resting for a moment after pulling the final load from the dryer, fighting tears.

During her latest illness, she'd begged God to take her life. She was too much of a coward to do so herself—her trip to Galveston had proven that. Yet she couldn't go on. She just couldn't. Wanda had told her she had to be back at work on Monday, and Leah suspected the edict had more to do with her boss's assessment of Leah's misery than an actual need for her proofreading services.

Leah snapped a towel into an orderly pile. Manuel Garcia's family was probably doing just fine. The brother-in-law—Jacobo—was probably already back in law school, learning how to defend other criminals. She thought momentarily of Manuel's wife and kids, then angrily brushed them aside. They weren't her concern.

Or were they?

She hugged the towel to her chest. What had they been doing while she wished for her own death? It was daylight now; maybe the curtain to that front window would be open. Maybe she could see exactly what they were doing.

She tossed the rest of her laundry into the basket.

Anger churned in her empty stomach as she drove faster than normal up University Drive toward the north side of town.

The Garcias were probably all healthy. And happy. Happy to have the killer out of their home.

Leah changed lanes quickly, and someone honked. Frowning, she pressed the accelerator harder and sped away from the person she'd offended. She turned off Northside Drive and into the predominantly Hispanic neighborhoods. Rounding the corner onto the Garcias' street, she felt her heart pounding as she neared their block.

The house came into view, but before she could glance at the front window to check for open curtains, she blinked.

A child, a little girl not more than five years old, chased a cat into the street, directly in front of Leah's Neon.

"Oh, God!" Leah slammed on the brakes, instinctively swerving. The tires screeched and the car hit with a hard, neck-snapping jolt.

Whoosh! The airbag deployed, and the car rocked for a moment, then went still.

For a moment, Leah was frozen. Then the memory of a dark two-lane road came in a rush, and she heard herself scream.

Her car door jerked open, and a man reached toward her. "It's okay. You're all right. Rosita's all right too. Thank God you had your seat belt on. Here, let me help you out."

She felt her seat belt being unfastened, but she couldn't focus. The man helped her out, and her knees buckled when she tried to stand on the pavement.

The car had come to rest against a telephone pole. Steam hissed up from under the Neon's hood, which crumpled up toward the windshield.

"It's okay, you had a bad scare. And your forehead's bleeding. Here. Sit down."

The man helped her to the curb. Embarrassed, Leah couldn't look at him. She wrapped her arms around her knees, surprised to find she was shaking hard. "I...I'm okay. The little girl...?"

"My niece is okay too. I'm sorry she ran out in the street. She knows better."

"I...I'm glad." Leah was aware that several people had stepped out onto their porches, watching her and her unknown helper, and she ducked her head even more. *Oh, Lord, what on earth am I doing here?* She started to rise, but found her legs still unsteady. "Thank you for your help. I'm just going to go home now."

The man put a restraining hand on her arm, easing her back to the curb. His voice was patient, as though he were speaking to the little girl. "You can't go home with your car like this. It isn't drivable."

Panic swept through her as she realized the truth of his statement. She was stranded in Manuel Garcia's neighborhood.

"I'll call a tow truck for you. Then we'll see about getting you home." The man paused, handing her a handkerchief. "Or maybe to a doctor. You're bleeding pretty hard."

She pressed her forehead with the cloth, surprised when it indeed pulled away bloody.

She licked her lips; her mouth was so dry. "I'm fine. And I can walk to a phone. I can call..."

Who? She didn't have any friends. She didn't even know the name of a towing service. Why hadn't Perry ever thought to sign her up for the Auto Club? Didn't he know there might be a time like this?

To her horror, she started sobbing. Tears ran down her cheeks, and she covered her face with her hands, trying desperately to control her emotions.

"Hey. It's all right," the man said softly. "Leah? It's all right."

The sound of her name made her look the man full in the face. Manuel Garcia's brother-in-law looked back at her. "Y-you recognize me?"

"I saw you at the trial."

All along she'd been watching them, and now it seemed they'd been watching her too. "And you're..."

"Jacobo Martinez," he said, then smiled wryly as if he too recognized the irony—and absurdity—of the situation. He must have read the panic in her eyes, for his expression gentled. "Please, Leah. Let me call someone for you."

She shrank back. His very presence terrified her. He was related to her family's killer. He'd spoken on Manuel Garcia's behalf—no matter how vaguely—at the trial.

He was the enemy.

But what choice did she have? She couldn't get back in her car and zoom away. She couldn't dream away her foolish action of driving to this neighborhood. She couldn't close her eyes and wake up on the sofa in her apartment.

He probably thought she was crazy. He was probably angry at her for nearly running over the little girl. He probably hated her for helping send Manuel Garcia to prison.

Why should she care what he thought?

Defiant, Leah raised her chin, and when she did, her eyes met his. "I don't have anyone to call."

"Then I'll call a tow truck for you." He held out his hand to help her up. "Come inside while I call so that I can get a look at that forehead. Do you hurt anywhere else?"

She stared back at him, refusing to answer. Sighing, he shoved his hands into his pockets. "Look...at least come sit on the porch. There's a couch. You'll be more comfortable than sitting here on the curb."

"I'm fine right here." Her head had begun to ache, and her mouth was dry as sandpaper. She clenched her teeth to keep them from chattering. Not for the world would she let him know how miserable she really was.

Jacobo looked as though he wanted to say something, but he nodded. Leah watched him walk toward the house, then she turned toward her wrecked car and dropped her head in her hands. She wanted to cry again, but she'd already embarrassed herself once.

"Señora?" A soft voice spoke at her side, and she raised her head. A middle-aged woman held out a glass of water. "Would you like a drink?"

Leah wanted to refuse, but thirst bested pride. "Thank you," she said, accepting the glass.

"I saw the accident." The woman settled herself on the curb. "You were very brave to avoid hitting Rosita. Are you all right?"

Leah nodded over the rim of the glass, gripping it tightly. Her hands were still shaking.

"I live across the street from the Garcias," the woman went on. "It would have been tragic if something had happened to the niña. The family has been through so much already."

"Oh, really?" Leah set down the glass and pressed Jacobo's handkerchief against her forehead. The bleeding had slowed but still hadn't stopped completely.

"Yes. They have tried so hard, especially—"

"I called the tow truck." Jacobo sat on the other side of Leah and handed her a wet rag. He gestured at her forehead. "Are you sure you don't want me to take you to the emergency room?"

She shook her head, pressing the fresh cloth against her throbbing head. She hoped the tow truck didn't take long; she was feeling a little lightheaded.

The woman beside her said something to Jacobo in Spanish, and Leah caught the word "Rosita." "She's fine," Jacobo said in English. "The bigger kids are taking care of her."

The woman babbled something else, rapidly, and Leah's head pounded sharply. She wished the woman would either be quiet or speak in English. It was rude of her to speak in a language she didn't understand and even ruder to talk about the Garcias like they were the ones who had suffered.

The street suddenly rose, tilting, and the next thing she knew, she had her head tucked between her knees.

"Leah?" The voice sounded far away, and the pats on her hand grew more insistent. "Leah?"

The wet rag slipped down her neck as she raised her head. Jacobo was rubbing her hands, his eyes concerned. He looked relieved when he saw her looking back. "Let me call an ambulance."

"No." Horrified, she brushed away his hand and sat up. She was ready to burst into tears again. She didn't care about the car—surely the insurance company could deal with it later. She wanted to settle in the nest on the couch, safe and comfortable behind her locked door. "Please…call me a cab. I want to go home."

Jacobo said something to the woman in Spanish, and she scurried off. He pressed the cloth against the back of Leah's neck and encouraged her to lean over. "Just take it easy. Someone will be here soon."

Leah shut her eyes and concentrated on not passing out. She was so tired.

When the cab arrived, she stumbled as she rose. Jacobo helped her into the backseat. "Give me your address and your number. I'll call you later about your car," he said.

Too weary to argue, she mumbled a response. He nodded and shut the car door, then leaned over and gave her address to the cab-driver, *again in Spanish.*

She rested her aching head back against the seat.

"Leah, I'll call you," Jacobo shouted through the window glass. She nodded numbly. As the cab pulled away from the curb, she closed her eyes so she wouldn't have to look at Jacobo Martinez or Manuel Garcia's neighborhood any longer.

When they reached her apartment, she wearily got out. She tried to pay the driver, but he shook his head and said it was covered. Shrugging, she trudged inside, locked the door, and collapsed on the couch.

Chapter Ten

Jacobo called the next morning, immediately apologizing into the answering machine that he hadn't called earlier. "I didn't want to burden you with any details. I thought you might not be feeling well or—"

Leah snatched up the receiver. "I'm fine." Did this guy feel so guilty that he had to hover over her? "I slept most of the rest of the day and all night. That's all I needed...a good rest."

"Sleep is dangerous if you have a concussion," he said. "You didn't go to a doctor?"

"No. Like I keep telling you, I'm fine. My head doesn't hurt at all." She was lying, for her head, though no longer throbbing, did ache with residual pain around the gash. But a large Band-Aid had stanched the bleeding.

"I hope so. Listen, I had your car sent to a body shop I know. A friend of mine owns it, and he said he'd personally take care of the work."

Leah gripped the phone. Great. A friend. No doubt a Hispanic friend who would probably charge an arm and a leg just out of spite for who Leah was.

"He said that as bad as it looked, most of the damage was to the exterior. The frame's all right. He thinks it'll need to be realigned and the brakes redone, but—"

"How much is all this going to cost me? Will he give me a written estimate?"

"I told him to go ahead and fix it."

"You *what?* You had no right to do that!"

Jacobo was silent for a moment. "I didn't think you knew any shops, and I trust this guy with any repair work my sister's car needs. I'm sorry if I've overstepped—"

"Overstepped? That's a pretty mild word for what you did." Leah's head was pounding again, and she drew a deep breath. She had to steady herself and get out of this situation as quickly as possible. "Look, just tell me where this place is and I'll go talk to the guy. Maybe I can stop him before he starts any work. Or who knows?" She laughed. "Maybe I can even afford what he's charging."

"Leah—"

"The address?"

She heard him sigh, then he gave her the name and location of a body shop on the northeast side of town. She scribbled down the street, grimacing. She might have known it wouldn't be in a decent neighborhood.

"Look," he said. "I'm really sorry if—"

"Never mind. I'm sure you were just trying to help. Thank you for the information. Good-bye." She hung up before he could answer, feeling smug about getting the last word. Thankfully, that would be the last she'd hear of Mr. Jacobo Martinez. Or any of the Garcia family. She'd learned her lesson—they were every bit as awful as she'd imagined. Children running loose in the street, brothers taking charge of the situation and sending *her* car to some two-bit body shop...

She bit her lip, realizing that now she'd have to find a ride to the shop to retrieve her car. And leaving the apartment meant showering, dressing, and putting on some kind of makeup—all the tedious little details that made life so difficult.

Not to mention wrangling with Jacobo's *friend* about her car.

She took a cab, her anger growing with each mile, anger at Jacobo Martinez and anger at herself for not being assertive enough to have seen that the Neon was towed to a repair shop near her apartment.

Anger at Perry for dying on her and leaving her to manage on her own.

The body shop—American Body Works—was located in the heart of a Vietnamese neighborhood. Leah paid the cab driver and warily eyed the shop. Many businesses on the street bore Asian names—restaurants, markets, tailors—and she felt like a tourist in a foreign land.

Shrugging off her discomfort, she entered the shop. She'd have them stop work on the car and have it towed to Sears. At least she could charge it there.

Shabby, though clean, the shop looked like countless other auto repair establishments with its tattered car and motorcycle magazines, ancient vending machine, half-full coffeepot, two vinyl chairs, and a bookcase stuffed with auto manuals. Leah settled in a chair that had the best view of the repair bays through the windowed door.

The door suddenly opened, and an Asian man stopped short. "Mrs. Travers? You're here sooner than I expected."

Leah rose. "Who told you I was coming?" The question sounded foolish, for she knew the answer. "Where's my car? I'd like to take it, please."

"I'm sorry, but it's not ready. Didn't Jacobo tell you that? We probably won't be…"

"Are you the owner of this shop? I'm sure you do wonderful work, but you see, Mr. Martinez brought the car here without my consent. And I'd like to take it."

"Yes, I'm the owner. Tran Nguyen. Please…come see, Mrs. Travers. We're hard at work on it. I'm sure the damage looked bad, but it was primarily the body. That's easier to fix than damage to the frame."

Leah hesitated.

"Please." He gestured toward the repair area. "Have a look."

Reluctantly, she followed him through the door. He walked to the far end, past three other cars being worked on. The sound of drills and sanders and hammering was nearly deafening.

The Neon looked half-naked. Stripped of both front quarter panels, the hood, and the grill, it looked more like a toy car than a real vehicle. At a word from Tran, another Asian man rolled out from under the car with a greasy rag and monkey wrench in hand.

"You can see it's not quite ready. But it's in good shape. Look here," Tran shouted over the shop's noise. "No damage to the engine. That's good. It needs a new radiator, but we found one in perfect shape at a junkyard. And the—"

"How much is this going to cost me?" Leah shouted back.

Tran pulled a bill from his pocket and handed it over. She let out her breath, shocked. Three years ago, Perry had had a new car-buretor and battery put in the Toyota, and they had cost more than the figure on this bill.

"This is the final amount?" she said, suspicious. Surely this was just for their initial work.

She turned the paper over and saw *"Paid in full"* written on the back.

Tran took the bill back, grinning at her shocked expression. "He didn't tell you, did he?"

"Jacobo…Mr. Martinez paid for this?"

"In advance. But if you have any problems with your car after you take it home, bring it right back and we'll fix it. He paid for the work, but you're my customer."

"I…" Leah wished she could slide under the car. "I… Thank you."

"No sweat." Tran grinned. "I'm glad you came out to check our work. We stand by it, but I'm always glad to see interested customers. Would you like some coffee? Can I answer any more questions for you?"

"Tran!" Three bays down, a worker raised his head from under a pickup's hood. "Come look at this!"

Tran looked apologetic. "Please excuse me. If you'll wait in the reception area where it's less noisy, I can give you a better idea of what time your car will be ready tomorrow. We can bring it to your home so that you won't have to make another trip back here."

Leah nodded and headed for the waiting area. She shut the door behind her and sank into a chair, grateful for the quiet so that she could collect herself.

Why was the bill so low? And why did she care? She didn't know much about cars, but it looked as though they were doing a respectable repair job.

Maybe they were cutting corners.

The front door opened, and Jacobo entered. He smiled when he saw her. "You got here fast."

She nodded, twisting her hands in her lap. "They've done a lot of work already. He said it'd be ready tomorrow."

Jacobo sat in the other chair, setting a motorcycle helmet on the low table between them. "Tran does good, fast work. He's the best in town."

"And has the best prices, apparently." Leah cleared her throat. "You've already paid the bill," she said, then cringed at the accusing sound of the words.

"It seemed fair. It was because of my niece that you had an accident."

"So you're grateful to pay an auto rather than a hospital bill, is that it?"

"Yes," he said, his gaze level with hers. "I *am* grateful. Cars can be fixed."

She lifted her chin. "Not always. After Manuel Garcia hit it, my Toyota couldn't be."

Jacobo rose and moved to the coffeepot. "Would you like a cup?"

"Sure. Why not?" She settled into her chair. What did he want from her? Instant forgiveness for his sudden largess? Was that supposed to make her feel bad that Manuel Garcia was in prison where he rightly belonged?

"Cream? Sugar?"

"Black is fine." Funny that she never drank coffee before Perry and Galen died.

He handed her a small Styrofoam cup full of thick dark liquid. "It looks like it's been sitting for a while, but it seems hot enough."

She took a sip. It tasted strong, but good. "It's fine."

Jacobo took a few sips from his own cup, then set it down beside the helmet. "Look, I know you're probably thinking that I paid for the repairs because I want you to feel bad."

"You're darn right that's what I think. It's great PR for the Garcia family, isn't it?"

"I didn't do it to make the family look good," he said in a low voice. "I did it because I figured you've had enough problems and didn't need to add this to the list."

Leah laughed. "What's one more? Besides, I've gotten used to dealing with the aftermath of car wrecks. They're not a problem. You just pick up the pieces and try to go on."

Jacobo leaned back. "*Have* you picked up the pieces?"

"From which wreck?" she shot back. His question was discomforting. She wasn't about to let him pull out her emotions one by one, like the parts from the Neon.

Jacobo took a quick sip of coffee. "That wasn't a question I have any right to ask. I'm sorry." He set down the half-drained cup and checked his watch. "I have to get to work. I'm sure Tran'll let you know when your car's ready." He took up his helmet and held it between his hands. "My niece wants to apologize to you."

Leah thought of Galen, and a lump rose in her throat. "That's not necessary. I'm sure you've scolded her enough."

"She needs to say it."

"Tell her it's all right."

"It's not that simple, Leah." Jacobo met her eyes. "I want her to understand that forgiveness must be asked for. I want her to understand that we all have to confess our sins. Especially to those we've wronged."

Do you want the same thing for Manuel? Why hasn't he apologized to me?

Leah gritted her teeth. "Tell her it's all right."

Jacobo laid his hand only inches from hers on the table. "Please," he said softly.

He was practically begging her to listen to the poor child apologize, as though Leah were a queen who could bestow a royal pardon. Yet he looked so earnest, so intent on her agreeing to his request, that she knew instinctively he had only the girl's best interests at heart.

"All right. I'll meet with her."

She knew she'd regret it. She wanted to be free of Manuel Garcia's family.

Didn't she? Or did the part of her that had wanted to drive by his house not once but twice still want to find out more about them?

Jacobo's face expressed his relief. "Thank you. Can you come to the house?" He smiled wryly. "I think you know where it is."

Leah stiffened. "I said I'd meet with her, but I didn't agree to come to your home."

"Then you pick the place."

The first one that came to mind was the coffee shop near her apartment, but she quickly rejected the notion. Too close to her own home.

Then she remembered that she'd already given him her address, so it didn't matter. "The Purple Onion Coffee Shop. Meet me there Saturday morning at nine o'clock."

"We'll be there." He put the helmet on his head, but she could still see his eyes—or did she just imagine them?—looking at her.

That evening Jacobo roared up the driveway and parked the bike near the house. Instantly he was swarmed by a flock of kids— nieces, nephews, even neighbor kids. "Jacobo! Tío Jacobo!"

"Hey, guys." He quickly took off his helmet and gave each one a hug or backslap, according to age. "Carlitos, Frankie, Maria… What have you been up to today?"

"School!" they answered nearly in unison, including the ones who were too young even for kindergarten. The exclamation was followed by gagging sounds from some of the boys, and Jacobo smiled.

"Good for you. *La escuela es muy importante.* You want to be able to grow up and do important things, sí?"

"Sí!" several answered enthusiastically.

"Sí," others—all boys—mumbled, scuffing their shoes against the brown grass.

Jacobo's heart went out to them. He'd felt the same way when he was in elementary school, that it didn't matter whether he learned the dates of the Alamo or when the first man walked on the moon. Those things had little meaning when he'd watched his father toil from dawn to dusk at a job that scarcely kept the family fed.

Then he thought about Leah, and for the first time that day, he belatedly—ashamedly—remembered to be thankful for his current circumstances. *Thank you, Lord. Please open these children's hearts to you.*

"Tío Jacobo!" The screen door banged shut, and his eldest nephew, Marcos, ran down the stairs. "Mama wants you. She's in the kitchen."

"Stay and play! Come on!" Several kids tugged at his hands.

Smiling, Jacobo retrieved his helmet from the head of a neighbor kid who'd tried it on for size. "After dinner. When your homework's done—*and only when it's done*—come outside and we'll throw the football."

Whooping with delight, the neighbor children dispersed from the yard, hopefully to start their homework. It was later than he usually arrived home, and there wouldn't be much light after dinner.

In the kitchen, he found Dolores whacking celery into bite-size pieces, a cigarette dangling from her mouth. The radio blared a tune by Bobby Pulido.

Jacobo frowned. "I thought you were going to quit smoking. You don't want to hurt the baby."

"And I thought you'd be home sooner." Dolores set down the knife and swiped her wrist across her brow. "Where were you? I was counting on you to keep the kids entertained. They were cranky when they came home from Mrs. Vasquez's, and now dinner is late."

"I had to work late to make up for some time I took off this morning." Jacobo loosened his tie and tossed his leather jacket over a chair.

Dolores stubbed out the cigarette in a half-full ashtray and blew a final long puff of smoke above her head. He gave her a scolding look, and she sighed. "All right. I'll quit." She dumped the entire ashtray into the garbage, then went back to chopping. "What'd you have to do this morning?"

"I made sure the woman whose car was wrecked was satisfied with Tran's work."

"What do you care what she thinks? She nearly hit Rosita. She deserves to have her car smashed."

"I'm grateful she was willing to risk her own life to avoid hitting Rosita. I'm paying for her car repairs."

Dolores turned. "You're what?"

"I'm paying for the damage to her car."

"Why? Do you suddenly have money to toss around? You could have bought Marcos new shoes to replace the ones he's outgrown. Or Maria a new dress. Not to mention the things the baby will need."

"God will provide those things, Dolores."

She smiled bitterly. "Yeah, right. Maybe he'll throw in a winning lottery ticket, too."

She turned back to the chopping, and Jacobo heard her soft crying. Moved, he put his hands on her trembling shoulders. "Dolores," he said softly. "I know you're tired and that you're under a lot of strain. I know you're working hard down at the bakery."

"I hate having to work. I miss my kids. Do you know how awful I felt when I came home from work and you told me that Rosita had nearly been killed? I felt like it was my fault for not being here. Mama was never away from us when we were growing up."

"Your life is different from Mama's."

"Don't I know." She laughed. "I hate Manuel, Jacobo. I hate what he's finally done to us. He's disgraced the entire family. Do you know what it's like every day at the bakery? People point and whisper—'Look, there's Dolores Garcia. Her husband's the drunk who killed a man and a baby.' Do you know what the kids go through at school because of their father?"

"They've told me," Jacobo said, grimacing.

"Papa would never have done such a horrible thing to Mama. Or to us."

"Papa was a good man, but he wasn't perfect. Neither is Manuel. Maybe all this will bring him around again. God always brings good out of bad for his people."

"What makes you think Manuel's part of his people?"

He turned her around again. "I know *you* are, Dolores. You've told me you believe in Jesus. And I know your kids love the Lord too. He knows what you're all going through, and he cares. He *will* provide for you."

"You have a lot of faith if you're tossing several hundred dollars away for that woman's repairs. God knows the whole thing was her fault."

"I'm not tossing any money away, and God knows *Rosita* was to blame. She's old enough to know not to run into the street. Speaking of which, I'm taking her Saturday morning to meet with the woman."

"Why?" Dolores glared at him suspiciously.

"I want Rosita to apologize."

"Apolo—?" Dolores clamped her mouth shut. "Fine. You seem to have everything under control, as usual. Pay the woman's bills. Make Rosita apologize. You can be the one to explain to all the kids that we don't have enough food to eat next month, but hey, it doesn't matter. We've done the right thing. God sees us. He'll *provide* for us." She angrily swept the chopped vegetables into a bowl and headed for the far end of the kitchen.

Jacobo turned away, sighing. He'd never hear the end of it if Dolores found out the identity of the woman who nearly hit Rosita. Better that she not know. After all, when Saturday's meeting was over, he'd never be in contact with Leah Travers again.

Chapter Eleven

Leah made certain she arrived at the Purple Onion well before the scheduled nine o'clock meeting so that she could watch for Jacobo and his niece. She couldn't remember the last Saturday morning she'd been down to the coffee shop. The weekend clientele was distinctly different.

Instead of the usual old men, young professionals, and blue-haired women, the booths and tables were populated by scruffy college-aged kids who were either engaged in deep philosophical conversations or who propped up thick textbooks against the napkin dispenser and obliviously drank cup after cup of black coffee.

Leah watched them, fascinated. At a nearby table, a young man waved a piece of toast while discussing the works of Verlaine and Mallarmé. His companion, a young woman dressed entirely in black, nodded solemnly while sipping what looked like prune juice.

At another table, four clean-cut young men nodded over plates of bacon and eggs, bleary-eyed as they gulped hot coffee. Eventually they pushed away their plates and held their heads to nurse their hangovers.

"More coffee, hon?"

Startled, Leah glanced up. She hadn't expected to see Louise, her usual waitress, but then she hadn't been to the Purple Onion for quite a while. "Sure."

Louise poured the hot brew, nodding at the rest of the room. "Haven't seen you in a spell. It's a different crowd here on the weekend, ain't it? I'm surprised it's taken you this long to come in on a Saturday."

Leah couldn't resist asking. "Why?"

"You look like you could fit easily into either group. Or maybe neither. You sit here morning after morning, all by yourself. I seen you just watching people—you scared of them, or do you want them to be scared of you?"

"I don't know what you mean." Leah took a quick sip that burned her tongue.

"Sure you do." Louise smiled, holding the half-full carafe aloft like a hunting trophy. "You're young enough to fit into this college crowd, yet you seem kind and savvy enough to mix with the seniors and weekday professionals. Yet you steer clear of everybody. Why do you come here?"

Leah shrugged, smiling back. She and Louise had never exchanged words beyond "More coffee?" and "Sure," yet Louise's question seemed more curiously friendly than probing. "I like the coffee?"

Louise turned. Leah followed her gaze and saw Jacobo standing behind the waitress. He looked scruffy yet clean in faded jeans, and his long hair fell loose over a slightly wrinkled cotton shirt. A little girl clung to his hand. He smiled when he caught Leah's eye, and she realized with a start, for the first time, that he was probably what a lot of women considered attractive. "Good morning."

"Well!" Louise stepped aside for Jacobo and the girl to slide into the booth opposite Leah. She grinned down at Leah. "Now I see what you've been waiting for all this time. You two need a menu?"

"Just coffee for me," Jacobo said. "Rosita?"

Eyes downcast, the little girl shook her head. Jacobo nudged her gently. "How about some milk?"

"We have white and chocolate, sweetie," Louise said, smiling. "Nice and cold."

Rosita looked up tentatively. "Chocolate," she whispered.

"Comin' right up." Louise winked at Leah.

Leah was certain that she blushed. Thankfully, Jacobo was busy helping Rosita unfold her paper napkin. When he looked up, he smiled. "You and the waitress good friends?"

She shrugged. "I come here often. She just remembers my face."

"Do you remember this face? This is Rosita. Rosita, this is Mrs. Travers."

"How are you, Rosita?" Leah nodded.

"I'm okay," she whispered. The little girl bit her lip and glanced up at Jacobo.

"What did we talk about?" he said softly.

Rosita's gaze flickered to Leah, then she lowered her head. "Tío Jacobo says that I should tell you that I know I did something wrong."

Leah frowned. Couldn't Jacobo Martinez see this was painful for the little girl? Why did he insist on forcing her to acknowledge her mistake? "I told your uncle you didn't need to say anything to me."

Rosita's eyes widened. "But I *am* sorry! He told me that Jesus would want me to say so. Jacobo told me I could have been hurt— or that you could have been hurt—because I ran out in front of your car." Her lips quivered, and a tear rolled from her eye. "I was just chasing the neighbor's kitty out of the street."

Leah blinked back her own tear. This little girl was probably about five—three years older than Galen had been when he died. He would have turned three this year. Leah had talked to him about Jesus, but he had been too young to understand much more than the basic beliefs expressed in "Jesus Loves Me."

Would he have apologized as easily as Rosita, if he were her age? And would she and Perry have truly raised him to love Jesus, or would they have settled for merely a weekly nod to him on Sunday morning?

What would have happened if Galen and Perry had lived?

"Leah?" Jacobo said softly, leaning forward.

She smiled weakly at Rosita. "It's okay, honey," Leah said hoarsely. "Jesus knows you're sorry. I do too."

Rosita exhaled a long sigh of relief. "I feel better already! Tío said I would. And that the person who says it's okay would too."

She looked so sweet and hopeful, so innocent of what could happen in just a matter of seconds. Horrified, Leah realized the tears were welling up again, and this time she didn't think she'd be able to stop them.

What if she'd hit Rosita? What if the little girl had been killed? Leah would never have forgiven herself for taking a life.

"Leah, are you okay?"

She closed her eyes and lowered her head, unwilling that Jacobo see her tears. How was she going to get out of here without him knowing how all this was affecting her, how many painful thoughts and memories it brought back?

Memories that she'd locked carefully away from prying eyes. Especially those of strangers.

"Tío?" Rosita tugged at his sleeve. "Can I go look at the jukebox over there?"

"Sure," Leah heard him say, but he sounded distracted.

The vinyl booth squeaked as Rosita pushed past her uncle. Leah wished she could push past her emotions as easily. She blinked hard, but her vision only clouded more. A tear rolled down her nose and onto the edge of the table.

Jacobo slid into the booth beside her. "Here." He handed her a napkin from the dispenser. She accepted it without looking up, blotting her eyes. Great. Now what little eyeliner she wore would be smeared around her eyes. She probably looked like a raccoon.

He handed her another napkin. "Your nose…" he said softly, gesturing.

Horrified, she realized it was running. "Thanks," she said, muffling the word as she pressed the paper against her nose.

"No problem." He leaned back against the vinyl seat and glanced around the coffee shop for Rosita.

"Is she okay?" Leah asked with automatic maternal concern.

"Yeah, I see her. She's fine." He looked at Leah. "Thank you for meeting with us today. I'm sure it wasn't easy."

"On a lot of levels," she said, fishing another napkin out of the dispenser. Emotions back under control, she edged away from Jacobo, putting space between them.

Jacobo propped his elbow against the back of the booth and rested his head against his hand. "What kind of levels?"

Straightening, she studied him carefully. Was he hoping to draw her out so that he could laugh about her later with his family, or was he genuinely curious?

He smiled gently. "You're wondering why I'm interested and whether or not to trust me."

"Well…" Caught off guard, she stalled for time by not answering. How could he read her so easily?

"This isn't a witness stand," he said. "You don't have to answer if you don't want to."

She cleared her throat. "You're a law student, aren't you?"

"I'm on a temporary leave."

"To take care of your family, as I recall the defense attorney said."

He nodded, his eyes never leaving her face. "What else do you want to know?"

Leah shifted. She had a million questions, and he was offering her the opportunity to ask them. Judging from his relaxed posture, he'd answer each one until she was finished. "Why?" she said, reaching for the all-encompassing question that had haunted her over the past year.

"Why do I ask or why...?" He gestured her to finish the sentence.

She couldn't help but grin. "Why do you keep turning the tables on me?"

"This is your interview."

"Interview?"

He nodded, curling his hand under his cheek as though settling in. "Start big, start small. Ask whatever you want."

"All right." She settled into the vinyl cushion. Two could play this game. "Why did you really want to meet me here?"

"I wanted Rosita to apologize. I want her to understand how confession and forgiveness work."

"Can't she learn that at church? You and your family are Catholic, aren't you?"

"My family is. I'm a member of a nondenominational church now."

"Why?"

He smiled. "Let's just say I got tired of the ritual. Next question?"

As a former churchgoer herself, she wanted to know more about his worship change, but she had more pressing inquiries. "So bringing Rosita to apologize was your only reason to come here today?"

"Yes." He paused. "I want her to learn what God wants for us. She doesn't understand the full reason why her daddy's not at home anymore, but someday she will."

Leah bristled. "I'm still waiting for the full reason why my family's not at home anymore too."

Jacobo's deep brown eyes softened. "I know you are," he said gently. "I wish I had the answer for that one myself. I would gladly give it to you."

Leah took a sip of her rapidly chilling coffee. Where was Louise, anyway? Usually she was Johnny-on-the-spot with refills.

"Next question."

"Look." Leah set down her cup. "I should probably get going. I think I've heard enough."

"No you haven't." Jacobo sat up straight. "You haven't heard nearly enough. You haven't even asked enough. Neither have I."

Leah frowned. "What do *you* want to know?"

"Well, how about, why were you driving down my family's street that day?"

Unnerved, Leah looked away. "It's a public street," she mumbled.

"Yes, but a tucked-away residential one. Did you have a special reason for being there?"

She whipped her gaze back to his. "What kind of question is that? Do you think I tried to hit Rosita? Do you think I would, that I *could*, do *anything* to hurt your family the way Manuel Garcia hurt me?"

"No, I don't. And I don't believe you were out to hurt anybody. But it still doesn't explain why you were there."

Leah sighed, letting her shoulders sag. "I don't know. I wanted…
somehow I thought if I could see…"

"See what?"

Leah closed her eyes, trying to remember what had been going
through her mind. "I wanted to see where he'd lived, his family's
home. I thought maybe I'd understand why all his family was still
alive, and all of mine had been taken."

"Was that the first time you'd driven by?"

"No. I drove by one other time. At night."

Jacobo was silent a moment. "It must be very painful to live with
such grief. Have you talked to anybody about it, a counselor maybe?"

She laughed curtly. "Why should I? I'm not the one who killed
anybody."

"No, but you lost your entire family. How do you deal with it?
Do you talk to your family? Friends?"

"I don't have any friends. And my family is miles away, thank
goodness."

"Why do you say that?"

"Because they'd run my life if I let them."

Jacobo was silent again. He reached for the sugar shaker and,
with deliberate movements, as though he were thinking carefully
about what he was doing, poured a small amount in his coffee. "If
you don't have friends, and you're staying away from your family,
how do you cope?"

"The secret is to be like stone. Immovable, unshakeable."

Jacobo made slow circles in his coffee with his spoon. "And
does this work?"

"Most of the time."

"Really? Because I've heard that if you harden your emotions,
you don't get any pain, true, but you also don't get any joy."

Leah frowned. "Why should I want any joy? Why should I even expect any?"

Rosita hurled herself at her uncle. "Can we go now? You said we could go to the zoo when we were finished."

"Okay, *mija*, in a minute."

Leah collected her purse. "That's all right. I'm ready to go too." It was a good time to leave. The conversation was over, as far as she was concerned. Jacobo Martinez hadn't told her anything that eased her mind.

Jacobo studied her while he put his arm around Rosita. The little girl wriggled impatiently. "Please? Can't we go *now*?"

Jacobo smiled at Leah. "Why don't you come with us?"

She inched across the booth, indicating that he should let her out. "No, I couldn't."

"Why not? It's a beautiful day. The zoo's close by. You can meet us there. You don't have to ride with us."

Leah blushed. Did he think she didn't want to be seen with them? Or that she didn't trust him to drive her?

"You did get your car back from Tran, right? I'd like to hear your opinion of his work."

So now he was trying to make her feel guilty, reminding her that he'd arranged to have her car fixed! She hiked her purse strap higher on her shoulder and inched closer, until their knees were almost touching. "Look—"

"Please?" Rosita said. "Tío Jacobo always takes me to the children's petting zoo and lets me buy food to feed the sheep and goats. I bet he'd let you feed them too!"

Leah swallowed a lump in her throat. Rosita's small face scrunched up with worry the same way Galen's did when he was afraid she was displeased with him.

The same way Galen's face *had*.

The last time she'd been to the zoo was with Galen and Perry. They'd purchased a five-year family membership, which they'd used only once.

She knew without even looking that just the picture on her zoo membership card could bring back memories that would make her cry. Galen had pitched a fit just before they reached the zoo. He'd calmed down by the time they'd had their photos snapped, but the film had recorded her frazzled look as she smiled grimly at the camera, dressed in a mother's all-purpose uniform of flannel shirt and jeans.

How had she reacted to Galen's tantrum? She couldn't even remember. Had she been too firm? Not loving enough? Maybe he'd thrown the fit because she'd somehow irritated him. Why hadn't she seen that her child needed her love and attention?

How she wished she had the chance to do it all over again.

"Honey..." Leah blinked quickly. "Rosita."

"*Please?*"

"Rosita," Jacobo said, then bent and murmured something in Spanish.

"But I told her I was sorry! Doesn't she believe me?" Rosita looked near tears.

"Of course she does," Jacobo said, then straightened. "Leah," he said gently. "Won't you share this gorgeous morning with us? Winter will be here soon enough."

Her life had been the bitterest of winters since the accident. Did he think one morning gawking at monkeys and elephants would change things, would somehow miraculously remind her of the beauty of creation and give her the strength to carry on?

Yet, Rosita...innocent Rosita. What a day at the zoo must mean to her. A beautiful morning, a glorious lifetime. It had been so long since Leah had seen such innocence and exuberance. It was painful, the memories it evoked, but surely it was no worse than the memories she dredged up on her own back in her dingy little apartment.

"All right," she said, sighing. "I'll go. I'll meet you at the entrance."

Rosita beamed. Jacobo nodded gravely. "Go ahead. I'll pay for your coffee."

"You've paid for enough. You two go ahead, and I'll settle up with Louise."

"Fair enough. We'll see you there." Jacobo took Rosita's hand and headed toward the door. The little girl fairly skipped, but she turned back and flashed a small, satisfied wave.

Leah waved back, feeling her throat tighten. Louise sidled up beside her, check in hand. "They belong to you?"

"No!" Leah said, startled. "They're just...they're just..."

Louise raised her eyebrows, her mouth curving up at its red-lipsticked corners.

"They're *just*," Leah said lamely, pressing several bills into Louise's hands. "Here. Keep the change."

Louise grinned. "Thanks, hon. Good to see you again."

Jacobo leaned against a wooden elephant sign by the ticket booth, searching for Leah among the gathered knots of people heading for the zoo's entrance. Judging from the crowd, it looked like half the county had the same idea to enjoy the beautiful day.

Young parents pushed single strollers as though they ferried royalty; older, more relaxed parents patiently herded two or three children between them; others carried newborns in body-snuggling carriers, held hands with toddlers, and called out pleasantly to several older children.

Everywhere, balloons, laughter, and the sense of togetherness, of belonging, filled the air.

Jacobo straightened, shielding his eyes against the sun's glare. He could barely make out Leah walking toward him from the farthest end of the parking lot. Evidently she'd had to park in the overflow lot across the street. Hands stuffed in the pockets of her brown corduroy jacket, brunette head down against the fall breeze, she walked briskly—like a scuttling autumn leaf—toward the entrance.

He cupped his hands around his mouth. "Leah! Over here!"

She raised her head, looking lost and confused in the sea of people. "Here!" he yelled again, waving his arm. She caught sight of him and nodded solemnly. Rosita yanked on his free hand, impatient to see the animals.

When Leah reached them, Jacobo stepped up to the ticket window. "Two adults and one child."

"No!" Leah said hastily.

Jacobo turned, money in hand, annoyed. Wouldn't she accept anything from him? "You can pay me later."

Leah fished in her purse and pulled out a card. "No, I mean I have a membership."

Jacobo glanced at the white plastic with her photo. "Okay, *one* adult and one child."

He shoved the extra money back in his wallet and gestured at her card. "It's not a very good likeness," he said, trying to compliment, to put her at ease.

She glanced at it briefly, then, without comment, tucked it back into her purse.

Jacobo took his niece's hand and led her through the turnstile. "What do you want to see first, Rosita?"

The little girl ran ahead to the bridge and leaned over, pointing. "Look at the funny pink birds."

"Those are flamingos," Jacobo said. "See how they stand on one leg?"

Leah trailed behind, but appeared to be listening—if only half-heartedly—as he discussed the birds with Rosita.

He glanced surreptitiously back while Rosita prattled on. Leah held herself aloof from both them and the other people pressing around, but she studied the children as they passed. Her eyes looked sad, and her face drawn, but here and there she smiled faintly at a childish giggle or stepped aside so that a youngster could have a better view.

Jacobo considered her carefully. It'd been a year since her family had died, but he had a strong feeling that she hadn't gotten out much since then. Could there be a worse place to bring a woman who was grieving the loss of her family? She'd probably rather be home, hiding, as he suspected she had done most of the past year.

Yet she'd agreed to meet them here. Why? What was the chink in her armor?

"Everybody has a weakness, Jacobo," Mama had said softly long ago. "And often, it is also the key to their strength."

"Let's go see the monkeys!" Rosita tugged his hand and headed up the path. He laughed and let her lead him to the double glass doors that enclosed the apes' and chimpanzees' indoor housing.

Once inside, Rosita ran straight to the plate glass and pressed her nose against it to watch the chimps. In the crush of other families, Jacobo stood protectively behind her, pointing out various chimps and exclaiming about their antics. Everyone laughed when a young chimp roughhoused with his siblings, then playfully took on his mother. She pretended outrage, but swatted him back with familial companionship.

Human mothers and fathers howled with delight, identifying with the simian behavior. Children squealed their pleasure. "Look, Mommy! Look, Daddy!"

Jacobo watched Leah out of the corner of his eye. She was studying the children, not the monkeys. Smiling when they smiled, eyes lighting up when theirs did the same.

"Come on, Tío." Rosita tugged at his hand. "Let's go see the big gorilla. And the orangutans are outside! Then the giraffes and the hippos and the rhinos and the bears!"

Jacobo let her lead him from exhibit to exhibit. He saw them all through Rosita's child's eyes—the playfulness of the meerkats, the majesty of the resting white tiger, the hideous fascination with the snakes in the reptile house.

Yet he also saw Leah watching Rosita and other children, and he saw through her eyes as well.

He saw a woman who had lost her only child, and by also losing her husband, any apparent chance at having more children. He saw the pain in her eyes as she studied the passing families—yet still she watched and spoke gently to Rosita, still she identified. And still, she yearned.

As they slowly moved from one end of the zoo to another, Jacobo noticed something else, too. Rosita gravitated closer and closer to Leah, pointing out interesting sights to her as well as to him, until it was he, rather than Leah, who trailed behind.

When Rosita casually slipped her hand into Leah's while they watched the penguins dive and swim, Jacobo smiled.

Against her will, Leah found herself drawn into the cheerful atmosphere of the zoo.

She didn't want to be around happy families...children. Seeing so many in one place, so much happiness and freedom of spirit, was like salt in the open wound of her maternal soul. She stared down at Rosita's small hand pressed firmly into her own and swallowed a lump in her throat.

Rosita laughed hard when a large penguin slipped into the water, rolled, and gracefully broke into a fast, smooth swim. "Look at him, Leah! Look!"

"I see!" Leah smiled briefly at the penguin, then down at Rosita. The girl's long, dark hair gleamed under the indoor lights, and her face glowed with excitement. She turned, and Leah could see the wonder in her deep brown eyes as well.

"I'm glad you came with us," the little girl whispered. "I don't get to see Mama very much anymore because she's always gone now."

Behind them, Jacobo cleared his throat. "I think you like the penguins best of all the animals, eh, *mija?*"

Unnerved, Leah turned back to the glass and gently slipped her hand from Rosita's grasp. Did Jacobo think she was trying to steal the little girl's affection from her mother? Did he think she was that manipulative? She certainly hadn't invited herself on this outing!

Rosita stood on tiptoe, pressing her face to the glass. The swimming penguin suddenly hopped from the water and waddled to a rock formation, where he preened his feathers.

Rosita laughed.

Forgetting Jacobo, Leah smiled. Galen had loved penguins too. They'd watched every video they could find about the fascinating birds. "They're funny, aren't they?" she said to Rosita. "You ought to go to the Museum of Science and History. They're showing an IMAX film about penguins. But only until the end of the month."

"Can we go, Tío?" Rosita pulled away from the glass, leaving a smudge where her nose had been. "Please? Can Leah go with us?"

Jacobo smiled at the girl. "That's up to her." He glanced at Leah, and his expression sobered. "Would you go with us? Maybe next Saturday?"

"*Please,* Leah?" Rosita hung on Leah's arm.

Leah looked down at the girl's hopeful eyes.

Then she caught Jacobo's gaze, his eyes the same deep brown as his niece's. Leah saw not reluctance, as she'd expected from a man who might be sorry that his niece had issued such an impromptu invitation, but concern.

He wants Rosita to be happy. Poor kid. It's not her fault her father's a killer or that her mother doesn't have time for her anymore. He's a good uncle to step in.

"It won't be any fun if you don't go," Rosita said, tugging again at Leah's arm.

Leah felt a smile rise automatically. How could she say no? "All right. Next Saturday it is."

"Great." Jacobo smiled too. Over Rosita's head, he mouthed the words "thank you."

Leah nodded, then realized with a start that collaborating with this man on such a tender subterfuge for Rosita made her feel pleased and needed.

Chapter Twelve

That evening, Leah's phone rang, and Wanda Voss's voice came over the answering machine speaker. "Leah, I need to know whether you plan to come back to work for us or…"

Leah dropped the rag she'd been using to dust the Venetian blinds and picked up the phone. "Hi, Wanda."

"Well…hello! I thought maybe you'd skipped out of the country."

Leah plopped down on the couch. "No, it's just been a bit of a rough go lately."

"I understand," Wanda said firmly, "and you know we've been behind you all the way. But if you don't think you're able to come back to work, Betsy and I need to consider finding a replacement. I'm sorry to be so blunt, Leah, but your coworkers have taken over your share without complaining. We know they're tired, and it's time to give them a rest."

"I'm ready to come back," Leah said. She'd been thinking about phoning Wanda ever since she'd gotten home from the zoo, but she hadn't worked up the courage.

"You are?" Wanda exhaled a deep, audible breath. "Thank goodness. I was afraid I was going to have to give you my love-us-or-leave-us speech."

"You were ready to fire me?"

"Not *ready*, but backed into a corner far enough. We need you, Leah."

Leah wrapped the phone cord around her fingers. "I'll be in on Monday. And Wanda…thank you for being patient with me."

Wanda harrumphed. "It's part of my job description. You can check the employee handbook."

"See you Monday." Leah grinned.

"I expect you there at eight o'clock."

Leah replaced the receiver in the cradle, a small, thoughtful smile curving her lips.

Jacobo pulled a mock frown as he studied Dolores's kids, standing in line for his inspection as they did every Sunday before they went to church.

Marcos, the oldest at eleven, stood straight and tall, all too serious for a boy his age. Maria, nine, scuffed a worn patent leather toe against the kitchen floor, scowling.

Frankie, eight, had his hands shoved in his pockets, shoulders hunched. He, too, scowled, as he did so often these days. Friday his teacher had sent another note home about a schoolyard fight, and Jacobo supposed as he studied his middle nephew that he should spend some extra time with the boy. Manuel's leaving seemed to have hit him the hardest.

Carlos, at three, crammed a thumb in his mouth and clutched a ratty-looking stuffed bear. Jacobo knelt to his level, his heart aching at the child's sad expression. The little boy had wet the bed repeatedly since his father had been sentenced. "How're you doing, Carlitos?"

"Do we hafta go to church?" he said without removing his thumb. "I don't want to leave Oso."

Jacobo touched the bear's well-worn, well-loved head. Last week some parish children had teasingly taken it from Carlos and threatened to throw it in a nearby creek. They'd meant no real harm, but Carlos had been inconsolable for the rest of the day.

"It's better for him to stay here, don't you think?" Jacobo said. "What if we set him in the window so that he can watch for us until we come home?"

Carlos unhooked his thumb from his mouth and considered Jacobo's suggestion. "Will he be okay by himself?"

"I promise." Jacobo held out his hand. "Let's go check out his view and get him settled."

"Can I watch too?" Rosita tugged on Jacobo's shirt sleeve as he rose.

He smiled down at his youngest niece as Carlos took his hand. "Sure, Ros—"

"Babies!" Frankie spat on the floor, as he'd seen his father do countless times. "I'd have thrown your old bear in the water, Carlos. Then you wouldn't be able to drag it around anymore." He followed the last statement with a curse directed at his younger brother.

"Frankie!" High heels clicking against the linoleum, Dolores stormed into the room and grabbed his arm. "Stop that kind of talk. Leave your brother alone. If he wants to have his bear, what's it to you?"

"It's ugly and it stinks! He's a baby!"

"And you're a nasty little freak," Maria said, giving Frankie a shove.

"Creep!" Frankie shoved her back, then deliberately stepped on her black patent shoes, leaving a dirty imprint.

"Kids!" Dolores moved between them, and Jacobo drew Frankie aside. He heard his sister talking sternly to Maria over Carlos's muffled sobs.

Jacobo sighed. "Frankie," he said in a low voice. "What have I told you about your family?"

"I don't care." He balled his hands into fists. "I hate this family. I don't want to live here anymore. I wish I was dead!"

Jacobo wanted to pull the boy into a hug, but he knew from experience that his sympathy would only meet with stiff resistance and even more anger.

You're loved, he wanted to tell Frankie. *We all love you. Please* let *us love you.* The boy was trying so hard to act older and tough, but Jacobo knew deep inside he was fighting his need to be treated like a little boy again.

Instead of hugging him, Jacobo leaned toward his nephew and whispered, "If your mom says it's okay, do you want to come to church with me instead of your church? We could go grab a burger afterward, just the two of us." He'd planned to spend the afternoon catching up on some legal research he'd brought home from the office, but it could wait.

"I don't want to go to your old church. I don't want to go to *any* church."

Dolores glanced up sharply at Jacobo. "What's this about Frankie going with you?"

"I thought he and I could go to church together, then get something to eat afterward."

"No! Absolutely not!" Dolores shoved past Maria and the other kids, and gripped Frankie's shoulders as though she were afraid Jacobo would snatch him away. "I don't want my children going to that church of yours. We're Catholic. *You* used to be one too."

"Dolores..." Jacobo spread his hands wide. They'd argued this point several times before. He wasn't out to proselytize her or her kids, but he wanted to get Frankie away from the family for a while. Maybe if they spent some time together, alone, he could get a better grasp of what kind of attention Frankie really needed.

Dolores pursed her lips. "And I won't send any child of mine on that motorcycle of yours."

"Anybody who rides on my bike wears a helmet," he said defensively, even though he knew she was probably right. He never felt comfortable with kids on the bike either. He was careful, but some car drivers weren't.

"Just the same, you go to your church, and we'll go to ours. Come on, kids," she said, rounding them up. Frankie scowled at Jacobo, then Dolores, ducking away from her outstretched arm. He shot out of the kitchen's side door, letting the screen bang back, almost in Marcos's face.

"Bye, Jacobo!" Rosita waved, then grabbed her younger brother's hand. "Come on, Carlos. Oso will be fine while you're gone. If Tío said he will, then he will."

Jacobo smiled after his niece as she let the other children go through the door first, then shut it carefully behind herself. "And a little child shall lead them," he murmured.

Riding to the church on the east side of town, he realized he was sorry for the missed opportunity with Frankie, but grateful for the time alone. A biker felt much more a part of the natural surroundings than a driver of an air-conditioned car. And a motor-cycle ride was more intensely personal and solitary. Without several tons of metal and chrome as a cushion of self-assurance, a biker couldn't rely on an airbag and a seat belt for protection. He had to be aware of what was happening around him.

Yet as he drove, alert to the often unforgiving traffic, Jacobo tried to settle in with the hum of the bike's engine. Normally he evaluated his life during this time, praying over problems and rejoicing over answers. Today no praise came readily to mind, however, as he thought about Frankie and the rest of the kids.

He'd noticed this morning that the autumn-colored knit dress Dolores frequently wore to mass revealed the slight bulge of her stomach. Somebody should probably tell the kids that they'd have a new brother or sister in a few months. That ought to go over well, seeing how they were all vying for their mother's attention as it was. Marcos, Maria, and Frankie weren't too young to remember how much time a newborn required.

By the time he'd found a place to park and removed his helmet, he felt more downhearted than he had all year. Other than the money he brought to the household, he didn't seem to be helping Dolores or the kids at all.

If only Mama were still alive. She'd know what to do, what to say to her unhappy grandchildren. She'd had a way of sympathizing with everyone she met and finding out what their emotional needs were—often even before the person knew.

"Jacobo!" Tran stepped away from a knot of people at the entrance to the humble tan brick church. "Did you see Mrs. Travers? Was she pleased with my shop's work?"

Leah.

Jacobo remembered her smile as she watched the penguins with Rosita, and he felt a smile curve his own lips. "You know, Tran, I never heard her say. I'm sure you would have heard from her if she wasn't satisfied."

"Good. But if you see her again, you tell her to call me if she has any problems. Meanwhile…" He gestured at the doorway, where people were slowly entering.

"Yeah, it's about that time. We don't want to be the last ones in, or Nick'll have something to say later."

Tran laughed and led the way to their customary seats on the back row. Jacobo set his helmet on the linoleum beneath his metal folding chair then stood along with the others to clap as they sang about entering the Lord's presence with thanksgiving and praise.

"Hello there, Jacobo!" Theresa Miller, an elderly African-American woman, touched his arm as she moved up the aisle, clapping and dancing in time to the music.

"Hello, Mrs. Miller!" he called after her, then immediately felt several successive touches on his arm.

"Hi, Jacobo!"

"Good to see you."

"Isn't it a beautiful Sunday morning?"

The Landeros family—Arturo, Berta, and their teenage daughter, Carmen—passed by, each one beaming. Before Jacobo could respond, another family—the Smiths—called out greetings as they made their way to their seats.

Tran grinned, never missing a beat while clapping. "That's what you get for taking the aisle seat," he yelled as the singing grew louder.

Jacobo laughed, then clapped and rejoined the song, feeling

the worry slip from his shoulders. Sometimes he did attend mass with Dolores and the kids, and the peaceful stillness of ritual, the reverent holiness of tradition, brought renewal to his soul. Other days he needed boisterous, spontaneous fellowship to remind him that he wasn't alone.

He thought about Frankie and Dolores. He thought about her unborn child. He thought about the money and support the family needed now and in the years until Manuel was released from prison. And slowly—in the midst of the joyful, assembled people—each thought, each burden, fell away.

"I will rejoice, for he has made me glad."

Jacobo laughed again, swept up in the great mystery of the strength of the Lord's joy. It couldn't be explained or weighed like evidence for a verdict in a legal trial. It simply existed for the taking, for those who had the childlike faith to grab it.

The lively praise song segued into another, then another, and at last, began to slow. Many raised their hands high, and many closed their eyes in private worship. Jacobo shut his own eyes, feeling the power of the Spirit, present in the assembled believers, wash over him. Jesus' words about being with them when two or more gathered in his name seemed so mild, yet in reality, in fervent practice, they were stronger than an electric current.

Oblivious to the others, yet feeling the strength in their number, Jacobo sank to the folding chair and bowed his head. *Forgive me, Lord. Forgive me for doubting. Your will be done in my life, in Dolores's life, in the life of the kids. Bring healing to the family, Lord. Be its center. Help us to work together, but always to rely on you.*

An image of Leah, as she'd looked at the zoo, flashed through his mind. "The secret is to be like stone," she'd said. "Immovable, unshakeable."

Jacobo raised his head, suddenly aware of the sound of murmuring, weeping, and heartfelt prayer. The entire congregation seemed to move with one purpose: worship of the same almighty God. Some praised his name. Others petitioned him for blessings. Still others unashamedly confessed their sins. To an outsider it probably sounded like a wild cacophony; to him it was the language of the very angels of heaven.

The room was filled with the spirit and body of Christ. No building, no mortal structure, could hold his sacred presence; instead, each member was itself a stone that fit within the whole, with Jesus himself as the chief cornerstone—the foundation that upheld the entire structure. The admonition not to forsake the assembling of believers was for their own benefit: Throughout the week, each member was to walk within the world, but when they were gathered in his name, they refueled and restrengthened for the days ahead.

Just as stones fit tightly together to form the temple, so did believers rely on each other for support. If even one stone was missing, not only was that stone weakened, the entire temple was weakened.

Again he thought of Leah. He hadn't heard her say, but he felt in his spirit that she was a believer.

Lord, send someone to help her. To show her that you are her strength.

The song slowed to a reverent close, followed by the worship leader's prayer. Heads rose, tears were wiped away, and smiles of joy shone. Without any prodding, people turned to each other, greeting friend and stranger with equal enthusiasm, not bound to those at the periphery of their chosen chair space. The crowd circulated the room to exchange handshakes and hugs, so that when the pastor called the people to attention, Jacobo found himself ten rows from where he'd started.

The worship leaders stepped aside, and Nick Valenti, the church's pastor, took his place at the front. "Thank you all for coming today. Isn't it beautiful outside?"

Murmurs of agreement rippled through the crowd. Jacobo thought about yesterday's outing to the zoo and wished he had something similar planned for today. Maybe he could talk Frankie into doing something outdoors with him.

"Before we continue our worship of the Lord, I have a sad announcement to share," Nick said. "I'm mentioning it now only so that you can keep it in your prayers during our time together. Ilene Makepeace, who's headed up our nursery since this church was founded eight years ago, recently passed away. Not only will she be missed by the little ones, but by us bigger ones as well."

Jacobo bowed his head in prayer. He hadn't heard this news. Ilene had been a sweet, elderly woman who'd tended the children as though they were her own.

"Please keep her family in your prayers. And while we can never find another Ilene, please also pray that we find someone with as much love to share for our church's children."

Another living stone taken from the temple, Jacobo thought.

Leah punched in the code on the numbered keypad, took a deep breath, and entered the production department of Engineering Associates. Coming back to work felt a lot like going to the doctor's office as a child for a booster shot. No matter how much she knew going back to work would help her—probably on more than just a financial level—she still knew it would hurt.

"Hi, Leah."

"Hey! Welcome back."

Several passing coworkers greeted her warmly, but didn't stop for chitchat.

"Hi," she called after them, feeling slightly miffed that they didn't want any details from the trial or her current life.

What's the matter with me? That's the way I've always preferred things!

"Leah!" Betsy reached out for a hug, then drew back as if she'd nearly committed an enormous social sin. "Oh, sorry. I'm just so glad to see you. Welcome back."

"Thanks," Leah said, as Betsy proceeded to the kitchen. Leah headed toward her cubicle, wondering if her coworkers had decorated her work area as they normally did for birthdays or other joyous occasions. She'd always thought that people's cubicles more resembled circus tents, the way they hung balloons and arranged streams of crepe paper into a big-top design, securing the ends under the acoustic ceiling tile.

But her cubicle looked lonely and barren. No crepe paper, no balloons. Not even a card on her chair.

Even the voice mail message light on her phone was unlit, as though to emphasize that no one had needed her during her absence.

Leah stuffed her purse into the cubicle's overhead compartment and shook off a sudden feeling of loneliness.

People spoke to her throughout the rest of the day, smiling warmly, obviously glad to see her again. But no one pressed for details or made what could have been called a fuss about her return. Wanda stopped by for a brief chat, but she didn't linger. Leah ate her sack lunch alone in the corner of the lunchroom, trying not to look like an eavesdropper to the laughter and conversation of the noontime regulars. They smiled pleasantly at her, but didn't ask her to join them as they often had before.

They were finally giving her the privacy she'd always wanted, yet strangely enough, the isolation wasn't comforting, but lonely.

That evening she listlessly ate a bowl of canned lentil soup for dinner, wishing that she had someone or something to talk to. She'd forced herself not to turn on the TV, and the quiet was oddly unsettling.

Maybe she should get a kitten. Or a goldfish.

She thought about Jacobo Martinez and wondered what it was like where he lived. Probably noisy, what with all those kids. And his shrill sister—at least Leah always thought of her as shrill, since she'd been so emotional at the trial. Dolores, wasn't that her name? What was she like?

Leah frowned. What had she been thinking to agree to another meeting with Jacobo? Even if Rosita was heartbreakingly cute and sweet, she certainly didn't need Leah to tag along on a family field trip. She was sorry that the mom—Dolores—was apparently so busy now. That certainly wasn't Leah's fault. Dolores Garcia should have chosen a husband more carefully.

The phone rang, and her heart jumped with excitement. She'd welcome even a telemarketer's call right now.

"Leah?"

"Danni!" Leah settled into the sofa, overjoyed at the sound of her sister's voice. "How are you?"

"I'm fine." Danni sounded suspicious. "Are you okay? You sound funny."

Leah laughed. "I'm just so glad it's you. I was sitting here wishing I had someone to talk to."

"Well, you can always pick up the phone and call somebody. You don't have to wait." Danni hesitated a moment. "Mom and Dad would like to hear from you occasionally."

Leah stiffened. "They call often enough. I don't need to phone them."

"When's the last time they called? Two weeks ago? Three?"

Leah stopped to recall and realized she couldn't. The truth was, their phone calls had slacked off in the past few months, but she supposed she'd been so busy wallowing on the couch that she hadn't noticed.

"Did you know Dad's having a stress test next week?" Danni said.

"No." She probably ought to feel guilty.

"I'm thinking about coming down from Chicago to be there for Mom."

"Is it that bad?" Why hadn't anyone said anything?

"You never know. The truth is, since Galen and Perry died, I've realized how important family is. I don't want to waste any more time where anybody's concerned."

Leah sighed with relief. Daddy was okay. Danni was just on some sort of philosophical tear about the fleetingness of life. "So is everybody else okay? How's Jennifer?"

"She's fine. She started kindergarten."

"I think you told me," Leah hedged, though if Danni had, Leah had forgotten.

"I'll probably take her out of school to come down to Houston with me."

Danni paused, and Leah knew instinctively the next sentence would be the crux of Danni's phone call. *Go on. Out with it, Danni.*

"Leah, I know this is your first day back at work, but maybe you'd be better off moving back in with Mom and Dad."

"*What?*"

"You don't get out at all. You're not doing anything, other than that job of yours. And if working means so much, you can find another job in Houston. Why not at least make them happy, even if you aren't?"

"Who says I'm not happy?" Leah bristled. "Who says I don't get out?"

"*Do* you?"

"Yes! As a matter of fact, I went to the zoo last weekend with a man and his niece. And we're going to the museum this weekend."

Danni went silent over the phone line. "You had a date?" she finally said. "Where'd you meet this guy?"

"It wasn't a date, it was just an outing. And frankly, it's none of your business where we met." Leah didn't feel like explaining the wreck.

"Well, tell me more." Danni's tone turned downright cheerful. "What's he like? What's he look like?"

"He's Hispanic." Leah smiled, anticipating the effect of the bombshell.

"Oh. Wow. Well, I've never cared about a person's background, but you know how Daddy will react. And gee whiz, Leah, you'd think after that Mexican guy killed Perry and Galen…"

Leah sat up straight. "I have to go, Danni. Thanks for letting me know about Daddy's stress test. I'm glad to hear he doesn't have one foot in the grave yet."

"Mom and Dad are concerned about you," Danni said in a low voice. "*I'm* concerned about you too. Especially now. I was hoping you'd get out, maybe even start seeing somebody, but gosh, Leah, for all I know, you met this guy in some biker bar."

"Maybe I did." Leah smiled, remembering Jacobo's motorcycle helmet.

"Won't you even come to Houston when Jennifer and I are there?"

Leah softened. She'd love to see her niece, despite her annoyance with Danni. "I wish I could. But I don't have any time off left at work. I used it all—and then some—during and after the trial."

"Jennifer and I can come visit you."

"You'd better spend your time with Mom and Dad."

Danni sighed. "Keep in touch, okay? If you won't call them, at least call me."

"Only if you promise not to grill me. I'm doing all right, Danni. Really."

Leah was even starting to believe that lie.

Chapter Thirteen

Leah waited for Jacobo and Rosita in the rotunda of the Fort Worth Museum of Science and History. She and Perry had always intended to bring Galen here, but for once she was grateful they'd been lax in their carry through. No memories lingered in this institution.

"Look! It looks like an upside-down bowl!" A little girl stood in the center of a large compass painted on the rotunda floor and pointed skyward at the dome. She lay down on the floor, aligning herself with the west compass point, and gazed upward with awe.

Her mother, instead of scolding her, held out her hand to help her up, laughing gently.

Leah checked her watch. Where were her IMAX companions? The next show started in just fifteen minutes, and already a line was queuing up to enter the theater.

She'd gotten there early, out of boredom, and spent nearly half an hour watching children race to dig for dinosaur bones in the designated area outside. The familiar ache of loneliness had squeezed her heart, but still she felt drawn.

The truth was, she didn't miss only Galen. She missed being close to all kids. Any kids.

Frowning, Leah consulted her watch again.

"I didn't want to come here!"

Leah raised her head in time to see a young Hispanic boy skulk to the outer edge of the floor's compass. Rosita skipped up beside him, followed at a more easy pace by Jacobo.

The boy turned to the man. "I said I didn't want to come here. Why'd you make me? I'd rather be shooting hoops with Bobby Hernandez."

"Bobby's five years older than you, Frankie. And a bad influence."

"He's my *friend*."

Leah frowned, unwilling to interrupt the serious exchange, but afraid they would all miss the penguin show because of the boy's belligerence. Apparently this was another of Manuel Garcia's offspring.

"Leah!" Rosita skipped toward her, pulling Jacobo along by the hand.

"Hi, Rosita." Leah rose, smoothing her palms against the side of her denim skirt. She'd agonized for nearly half an hour over what to wear and finally decided the skirt was dressy enough to look nice but casual enough not to send the wrong message.

"Hi, Leah." Jacobo pulled the boy forward from where he tried to hide behind a moon rock display. "I hope you don't mind that we brought someone along. This is Frankie, Rosita's brother."

"Hi, Frankie," Leah said, trying to sound cheerful, when her stomach was tying up in knots. Rosita was one thing, but this was Manuel Garcia's son. He even looked like the man.

"Hi," Frankie mumbled, keeping his gaze on the floor. He crossed his arms and nudged Jacobo with his elbow. "Can we go now?"

"Let's see the penguin show first, then if you're still bored, we'll go straight home," Jacobo said. "If you're not, maybe we can see the museum. Have you ever been here before?"

Frankie shrugged. "Can't remember. Maybe in school. My parents sure never brought me."

Jacobo glanced at Leah. "What time is it? Are we going to be late?"

"Not if we hurry."

Leah headed for the ticket booth, but Jacobo stepped ahead of her. "Unless you have a season pass, this ticket's on me. After all, Rosita talked you into coming with us."

Leah started to protest, but she caught the sparkle in his eyes. She smiled. "Then I accept. Thank you. And thank you, Rosita, for inviting me."

Rosita slipped her hand into Leah's. "I'm glad you came. And I'm glad you can meet Frankie."

The sullen boy glared at his sister, caught Leah's gaze, then lowered his head again.

Leah frowned. *What a disagreeable kid. Well, what else could be expected from an alcoholic's son?*

Jacobo held up tickets. "They're keeping the doors open for us, guys. Let's go."

"Yay!" Rosita dragged Leah toward the theater's entrance. "Come on, Leah. You can sit by me. Frankie can sit by Jacobo."

"Okay." Leah laughed, struggling to keep up with the girl as they negotiated their way through a roped-off maze and into the theater. The lights were already dim, but Rosita pounded confidently up the stairs to an empty row near the top and plopped down in a middle seat. Leah sat beside her. She wasn't certain if Jacobo and the disagreeable Frankie had kept up with them, but they could always find each other after the movie.

"This is really neat!" Rosita bounced in her chair, twisting around.

Leah's stomach felt queasy. Underneath the rounded screen that stretched from the bottom stair to the top row, seating was at a steep incline. She felt as though she were falling forward, and she closed her eyes to stop the dizzying sensation.

"You get used to it."

Leah opened her eyes. Jacobo had sat down beside her. "This is the first time I've been here," she said. "Apparently it's not bothering Rosita."

Jacobo glanced over her head at his niece and smiled. "She adapts easily."

"What about that one?" Leah nodded at Frankie, who'd refused to sit next to Jacobo, but had chosen a seat two down from his uncle.

"I'm praying he'll come around too. That's why I invited him along today."

"He's a troublemaker, huh?" Leah watched Frankie quietly fiddle with the backpack straps of the girl sitting in front of him.

"He's had a lot of trouble thrown his way, and he's trying to sort it out."

Humph. Little hooligan. Why wasn't his mom taking her errant son places, instead of his overtaxed uncle? "Is that your therapy for troubled people? To take them out in public?"

"That's part of it." Jacobo looked at her.

Leah crossed her arms and settled into her seat. Thankfully the lights began to dim. "Isn't this fun?" Rosita whispered loudly.

No, it's not, Leah wanted to reply, but whispered back, "Yes."

The lights in back of the screen went on to reveal several banks of giant speakers. "Cool!" Frankie said loudly, and the people around them laughed.

Then the show began, a preliminary film shot from a helicopter flying over Fort Worth. Leah felt twice as dizzy now. Amid the sounds of the film's twangy music, the helicopter's blades, and the audience's cheers as the film's speed increased, she shut her eyes tight.

"You okay?" Jacobo leaned toward her. "The regular film won't be quite so unnerving."

Leah sucked in her breath, her panic at the theater and the film replaced by something new. *Unnerving* was the word she would have used to describe the way she felt with Jacobo leaning toward her. "I'm fine," she managed to whisper, then opened her eyes just as the helicopter ride slowed again to a normal speed.

At last the feature film began, a slow-moving shot of a group of penguins. Leah breathed a sigh of relief and settled in.

"How'd you like it?" Leah heard Jacobo whisper to Frankie.

"It was okay," Frankie whispered back loudly, cocky, but Leah realized the boy had moved to the chair next to his uncle.

Rosita sat mesmerized throughout the film, her mouth open with awe at the gigantic screen. Leah herself was amazed, not only at the sheer size of the movie but at the subject matter. She'd never known penguins were so interesting, and the way the filmmaker had so cleverly captured them, they almost seemed to have human emotions.

The documentary followed a male and female courting, then the female's laying an egg. The male guarded the egg on top of his feet until it hatched.

Leah thought about how tenderly Perry had always watched over Galen, and a lump rose in her throat.

The baby penguin grew, and the story followed the family's life in a rookery—their food, anatomical structure and environment, and their miraculous swimming capabilities. Leah laughed as hard as Rosita when the penguins dove and paddled with comically swift ease.

Suddenly a multitude of sea lions encircled an isolated group of swimming penguins. The camera zeroed in on the baby and its frantic efforts to outswim the predators to shore and safety.

Small and helpless, it was easily overtaken and killed.

Leah gripped the armrest, swallowing hard. The first movie she'd seen in over a year… She was *not* going to break down.

The penguin mother stood at the shore, watching for her baby, searching frantically among the penguins fleeing the carnage in the water. When at last it was obvious even to her that her youngster wouldn't be returning, she still looked out over the water.

A tear slid down Leah's cheek, and she furtively wiped it away. Jacobo leaned toward Frankie, whispering something, and Rosita sat quietly, absorbed in the film.

What does anybody in this theater know about that penguin mom? Do they know that she probably wanted to throw herself into the water and join her baby, no matter how horrible death would be? And do they have any idea how quickly life can be snatched away with the speed of that sea lion and the strength of his teeth?

Leah clenched her hands. *And do they realize that the bullies of the world always win?*

The show continued by extolling the magical regeneration of life as the rest of the rookery continued to thrive.

So that's the message. It doesn't matter if an individual dies. The group goes on, no matter what. As if the one had never lived, had never had any impact on their lives.

All the more reason to be alone.

Leah wiped her eyes. *Can't I even watch a stupid penguin movie without getting weepy? Without having it apply to me?*

The lights went up, and Leah realized she was still gripping the armrest. Her expression was probably pretty grim too. She forced herself to smile at Rosita. "How did you like the—"

Rosita's lips were trembling, and her eyes were wet. "It was so sad," she whispered. She slipped her hand into Leah's. "The little baby died."

Leah swallowed, her own grief compounded by the girl's. Jacobo touched Leah's shoulder, and she turned, annoyed by the intrusion. "What?"

"Why don't we go down to the DinoDig area?" he said.

Rosita immediately brightened, pulling her hand from Leah's as she bounded out of her chair. "After that can we go see the big skeleton dinosaurs?"

"Sure. We have lots of time."

Leah glanced up at him sharply, resentful suddenly that he could enjoy having time on his hands. To her, time meant only a series of blank, useless days. Why was she the only one who felt that way?

Walking down the steps from the theater, Rosita chattered endlessly about the film. Jacobo only half listened to her animated conversation, surreptitiously studying Leah. She hadn't stopped frowning since the movie was over, and the only time she even vaguely smiled was when Rosita asked her a direct question.

Frankie, too, was quiet, unusually so, not just sullen. Once they reached the exit, however, he pushed his way through the glass doors and ripped off his shoes and socks to play in the area outside where children could dig up imitation dinosaur bones and artifacts.

"There, *chica*, go play." Jacobo helped Rosita remove her socks and shoes and turned her loose in the sand. She happily raced to a large embedded bone and took up a spoon to dig with a group of other kids about her age.

Leah sank to a large stone shelf designed for weary parents, and Jacobo sat a respectful distance away. She wiped her eyes and straightened, tucking one foot under herself, out of the way of the happy, screaming kids who dashed around them. He studied her face, and she turned her head to avoid his gaze.

"Leah?" Jacobo said softly.

She didn't move.

"Did the movie upset you?"

She squared her shoulders, but didn't turn around. "Only because I like penguins."

He knew there was more to it than that, but he let it drop. Jacobo drew a deep breath. "Leah, are you a believer? A Christian?"

She turned slowly. "Why do you ask?"

He rested his elbows against his knees, trying to affect a casual air even though his heart was pounding. *Lord, I want to help in any way I can. Use her weakness to show her your strength.*

"I saw the crosses," he said, surprising even himself with his directness. He started to tell her about the carnations he'd brought, about the prayers he'd said there, but he waited for her response.

Leah frowned. "What crosses?"

"The ones where your husband and son died."

"Oh." She looked down at her hands. "Those weren't my idea."

"I thought maybe you'd had them put up."

She shook her head. "My father said he'd have them removed. I hope he did. I hated the whole idea. As if where people died has any bearing on the kind of life they lived, the kind of people they were."

Surprised, Jacobo studied her a moment. It wasn't what he'd expected to hear. He'd pictured her approving the memorial gesture, if not ordering it. Knowing differently, he felt relieved. And pleased that she'd shared this insight. "I've never liked those things either."

Leah glanced up, caution registering in her eyes. "You never liked roadside crosses in general, or just the ones for my husband and child?"

"None of them. To me they're like shrines to the dead." He paused, hoping that he hadn't offended.

She nodded. "Especially with the victims' photos slapped on them."

"Do they have crosses at their graves?"

Leah smiled slightly. "No one I've met since the accident has ever asked me about their gravesites or even their funerals. They have headstones, actually. Galen's has a lamb carved on it. Perry's is pretty plain. He never much cared for fancy stuff."

From the play area, a child screamed. Jacobo saw that the little boy was only howling from fun, but Leah jerked around anxiously, half rising. When she saw the boy's mother at the side of the now laughing child, she sat down sheepishly.

Jacobo saw a blush steal over her face, and he wanted to tell her that it was all right. That the Lord didn't expect her to lose her maternal instincts just because her child was dead. That there were still many children who needed the warm, empty arms she no doubt ached to have filled.

"Where are your husband and son buried?" he said gently, hoping to keep her talking. If she didn't talk to friends or family about what she was going through, she must have a multitude of hidden emotions. Even her posture indicated it: arms wrapped tightly around her knees, ankles pressed firmly together. To show her he didn't mean to threaten, he loosely clasped his hands together, still leaning forward, relaxed. He'd learned a lot about the importance of body language from studying attorneys in court.

She didn't uncross her arms, but she did relax her shoulders. "They're buried in Houston. That's where Perry and I were from. Sometimes…," she trailed off.

"Sometimes what?" Jacobo rested his cheek against his palm.

"Sometimes…oh, I know it sounds silly…but sometimes I wish they were buried here in Fort Worth so that I could go to their graves and feel close to them." She scowled. "I wish I hadn't let my family talk me into having them buried in Houston."

"Your husband and son will always be close to you…here." Jacobo tapped his fingers against his temple, then laid his hand over his heart. "And here."

Leah sighed. "It sounds so simple to believe that."

"The little one…he's with Jesus."

"I know." She made a face, as if she'd heard that statement many times. "And it's the best place he can be. I do believe that, but he's not with me."

"And your husband?" Jacobo studied her. "Where do you believe he is?"

"He's with Jesus too," Leah said softly. "He believed in him. And yes, to answer your question, so do I."

Jacobo smiled. "I thought you'd forgotten I asked."

"Would it have mattered? You're studying to be a lawyer—you would have found some other way to get the information."

He studied her, hesitating.

"I was kidding," she said. "That's the problem with you lawyer types. You can't take jokes about yourselves."

Jacobo grinned. "Sometimes we're too dense to understand when we're being joked about." He craned his neck to check on Rosita and Frankie among the shrieking children, then turned back to Leah. He wanted to know more about her spiritual situation, but now wasn't the time to press. "Was the trial the first time you'd been in a courtroom?"

She nodded. "I'd never even pulled jury duty before."

"What did you think of the legal process?"

"I thought it was like a show." She frowned. "A game testing which lawyer could perform better than the other. I felt like the truth was the last thing on anybody's mind."

"Sometimes I felt that way too. Those days in the courtroom made me question whether I really wanted to be a lawyer."

"Why? Because your brother-in-law didn't get off? Or at least get a lighter sentence?"

She didn't even try to disguise the bitterness in her voice. He wasn't sure he was ready to tell her his innermost thoughts, but if he wanted her to open up, he should be willing to do the same. "No. Just the opposite. I was afraid he wouldn't get the stiffest sentence."

Surprise crossed her face, then dark suspicion. "Do you think that matters? My family is gone...*dead.* And you're related to the man who killed them. You're looking after his family. Rosita...that, that...*Frankie,*" she said bitterly.

"Ah, Frankie." Jacobo leaned back. "You don't like him, do you?"

"Should I? Should I like any of Manuel Garcia's family?"

Jacobo was silent a moment. "Leah, your son...if he were alive and if he were in trouble, would you still love him?"

"Of course I would." Her eyes filled with tears.

"And you would do anything to help him, especially if he were in trouble because of somebody else's mistakes?"

"Of course."

"Frankie is my sister's son," he said quietly. "He's having a hard time right now because his father's in prison and will be there for a long time—long after Frankie's become an adult. He was a good kid before, and he doesn't understand why his world's suddenly changed. Why his mother isn't home much anymore because she has to work so much. Why the kids at school pick on him and call him names because of what his father did."

She drew in a deep, angry breath. "Do you think I care?"

"Yes. Or you would, if you'd allow yourself to look down inside, underneath that big coat of self-pity you're wearing."

Leah snatched up her purse. "Thank you for the movie ticket. Tell Rosita good-bye for me. Tell her—"

Jacobo touched her hand to keep her from standing. "She'd rather you told her yourself."

Leah jerked her hand away. "I don't know what you want. I don't know why you even want to talk to me. God knows I don't want to talk to you. I don't want to talk to any of you. I'm sorry about the accident with Rosita. I'm glad she's okay. Now will you please leave me alone?"

"You're pushing everyone away, aren't you?" he said. "It's killing you to be out in public, isn't it? You may think it's easier to stay at home with the drapes closed and the door locked, but in the long run, it's not."

She didn't answer.

"Leah…" He leaned forward. "It's hard to come out into the light when you've been in darkness. But your eyes adjust. If you don't come out and stay out, you're going to die as surely as your husband and your son. Do you think that's what they would want?"

Her eyes filled with tears. "You have no idea what they'd want."

He softened. "I'm sorry. I had no right. Let me put it a better way: Do you think God wants you to stay in the darkness? Or do you think maybe, just maybe, he might have a plan for you?"

"The only plan he has for me is suffering and loss. If I weren't so chicken, I'd join my husband and my son. Then maybe I'd be happy again."

"God isn't interested in your happiness."

She laughed. "That's obvious."

"But he is interested in your obedience. And he is interested in your joy. And in giving you peace."

She smiled sardonically. "There's no peace wherever I go, even though I've looked."

"Would you come to my church tomorrow morning?" The words came out before he could even think.

"I've had my fill of church. Casseroles and false sympathy— that's all it is."

"My church is different. No one will know who you are, Leah. No one will ask you about your family or the wreck."

"What church do you attend?" She looked skeptically at him as though she thought he were trying to recruit her for a cult. A new convert to sell flowers on street corners or pass out tracts in the airport.

He suppressed a smile at the notion. "It's nondenominational. The Good Shepherd. It's small and ethnically diverse. Tran's a member too. You'd already know two people, if you're worried about feeling out of place."

She hesitated.

"You said yourself you've looked for peace," he said quietly. "Why don't you try one more time? Run toward something instead of away from it, for a change."

Her eyes snapped. "I'm not running from anything."

"Then I'll pick you up tomorrow morning at ten."

She rose. "I won't be ready."

"It doesn't matter." He smiled. "Dress is casual at the Good Shepherd. You can come in your pajamas."

"I'm not interested in your church."

"Good. The church doesn't want your interest. God does. He's been trying to get it for about a year now. Isn't it time you meet him at least halfway?"

She gritted her teeth. "Fine. I'll go. Then will you leave me alone?"

He nodded solemnly, suppressing the joy he felt inside.

Leah turned without a good-bye and headed for the entrance, her stride firm, head held high. Jacobo watched until she was out of sight, then he turned back to the children's play area, smiling. The body of Christ would have another opportunity to minister to a hurting member.

Chapter Fourteen

Leah glanced in the mirror yet again, patting her hair. She couldn't remember the last time she'd put so much effort into her appearance, even to go to work.

She wasn't worried about looking nice for Jacobo Martinez. But this was church she was going to, a place she hadn't been since Perry and Galen's deaths. Church meant dressing up, so dress up she would.

She pressed her damp palms against the broomstick skirt she'd chosen. The black-flowered pattern was appropriate for such a somber occasion, going to meet God, but would she be underdressed? Would the fact that her blouse and jacket were silk atone for the casualness of the skirt's line?

And how about her hair? Perry had complained about the short cut just before he'd died, and she'd since let it grow out to her shoulders. Usually she wore it loose and straight, but today she'd pinned and sprayed until the strands were obediently styled.

It was important to look mature, even though she didn't feel grown up. The last thing she wanted was for these churchgoers to realize how childlike she still felt toward God. She had questions and anger and doubts that no one would understand. The members would have no concept of the struggles she had reconciling a loving, all-powerful God with the loss of her husband and son.

The doorbell rang, and Leah panicked. She should have called him—looked up his number in the phone book and told him she wasn't feeling well. She should never have agreed to this in the first place. Why did she keep putting herself in Jacobo's path?

She grabbed her purse and opened the door.

"Hi." Jacobo grinned, taking in her outfit. "So you're ready after all."

"Yes." She stepped forward, hand on the doorknob to close it behind her.

Jacobo braced it open with his hand. "You're going to have to change clothes."

Oh, great. Wasn't her outfit nice enough for his church? "Excuse me?"

"You can't wear a dress. Jeans are best."

"You weren't kidding about dressing casual for your church, were you?"

"No." He grinned. "But you need the jeans because we're riding on my motorcycle."

Leah crossed her arms. "I've never ridden a motorcycle before."

"Nothing to it. You can handle it."

What was she supposed to say: "I won't go, I'm a big chicken"? She didn't like doing things she'd never done before.

Jacobo pushed the door open a fraction and stepped forward to glance around. "Can I use your bathroom while you change?"

It looked as if she was committed. He was in her apartment. "Sure," she said weakly, nodding at the only door in the small living room. "Over there."

"Thanks."

She scurried to her bedroom, then ducked into the closet to change. Why had she rented an apartment with no bedroom door? She was uncomfortable enough; the only men who'd been inside this apartment were an air conditioner repairman and her father. Having Jacobo here made her feel guilty, as though she were a college student sneaking a boyfriend into an all-girls' dorm.

Changing out of the skirt and blouse, Leah chided herself for her foolish notions. She didn't have any reason to be ashamed. She certainly wasn't romantically interested in Jacobo Martinez, or any other man, for that matter.

As she slipped on a cotton blouse over jeans, she heard the bathroom door opening and then Jacobo's footsteps as he headed back toward the front door. Leah tossed the broomstick skirt on the bed, then went down the hallway.

Jacobo opened the door. "You ready?"

She nodded, hiking her purse strap high on her shoulder. "Let's get this over with."

Jacobo smiled. "It won't be that bad—the bike or church." He walked outside.

Leah pulled the door shut and engaged the deadbolt with her key. When she turned around, he was waiting for her, watching and smiling.

Leah paused. He stood straight and tall in the middle of the courtyard, looking startlingly handsome in the warm fall sun. His long hair was pulled back in a ponytail, as it had been the first time she saw him, and he wore a leather jacket and black jeans.

She frowned, shaking off the surprising revelation that he might actually be appealing to her. How could she be attracted to any man, let alone this one?

They continued toward the parking lot and a vicious looking motorcycle with *Yamaha* on the side. He held out a helmet. "Here you go. Put this on while I start the bike. Then get on behind me." He straddled the bike and strapped on his own helmet.

Leah stared down at the seat. It looked large, but not nearly large enough to accommodate two near-strangers. Her heart pounded.

Jacobo started the bike, and it roared to life. Leah flinched.

Jacobo held out his hand. "You can handle it," he said over the engine's noise. "Just be sure to hang on."

Leah drew a deep, angry breath. Of course she could handle it. What did he think, that she was some shrinking violet?

Truth be told, she was, but she didn't want him to know that.

She climbed on behind him and let her feet dangle. Now what? Where was she supposed to *hang on,* as he'd recommended?

"Your feet go on these pegs here." He showed her where to rest her feet. "And keep your legs from pressing against the muffler there—it's hot."

"Where do I hold on?" She felt foolish for asking.

"Put your arms around me."

What? Was he crazy? Leah glanced around, panicked. "What about this curved rail behind me?"

He shrugged. "You can use that."

Relieved, Leah put her arms behind her and gripped the metal with her fingers curled tightly into fists.

"Ready?"

She nodded.

Jacobo put the bike into reverse and before she knew it, they were zipping out of the apartment lot and onto the road.

Leah glanced down at the rushing pavement then decided that was a mistake. She focused on the back of Jacobo's leather jacket and his ponytail.

This is crazy.

He stopped at a light, then turned left. The lean was dizzying—and awkward, with her hands clinging behind her for dear life to the rail. She could see how holding on to him, as he'd suggested, would make more sense. But she'd cling to the rail till her hands froze, if it would keep her from pressing up against that leather jacket.

Despite her discomfort, there was something oddly liberating about being on a motorcycle, zipping past cars. She felt more a part of the road and the wind and the sun than the traffic. In a car, she felt just the opposite—only one of many vehicles making its way across the expanse of asphalt.

She was almost sorry when Jacobo roared into the church parking lot and brought the bike to a stop. He cut the engine, steadied the bike, and got off, removing his helmet. He helped her off, and she removed her own helmet, shaking her head to clear it. Her carefully styled hair fell, but she didn't care. The ride had been worth it.

Jacobo smiled. "What did you think?"

It seemed strange to hear him speak, after they'd been silent—yet together—so long. "I thought it was…interesting," she hedged.

"It's strange at first, but you get used to it. Like everything, it takes practice, some time on the road learning to read the driver's language."

"Language?"

"How the driver moves so that you know when to move with him."

"Oh." She fell in step beside him as he headed toward the church's doors. Had he sensed her awkwardness while they were riding?

"Jacobo! Good morning." An elderly Asian man stopped to shake his hand.

"Good morning, Mr. Chao. This is Leah."

"Hello." Leah shifted the helmet to her left hand and extended her right.

"Good morning." Mr. Chao shook her hand, briefly covering it with his left, then moved on to greet someone else.

Jacobo and Leah had barely entered the church when they were greeted again, this time by a young black couple. Again Jacobo introduced her simply as Leah, and they greeted her as warmly as they did him.

By the time they slipped into the middle of the back row of the rapidly filling church, Leah had been introduced to people of all ages and nationalities. No one questioned her relationship with Jacobo, for which she was grateful. She certainly didn't want anyone to think they were dating.

Just as she was beginning to get dizzy with all the names and faces she'd encountered, the music started. And what music! Leah was accustomed to sedate hymns sung from tattered books. But at this church, the words to the lively, contemporary tunes were flashed on a screen down front for all to read and sing along.

And sing they did—joyfully, at full volume, clapping their hands in time with the music. Some even stamped their feet.

Leah politely clapped too, more interested in watching the others than in singing.

They all seemed happy to be here, as if they looked forward to this time on Sunday. All around her were smiles instead of serious expressions, people celebrating from the heart.

Leah's clapping slowed. This didn't feel like church. Church was pews and stained glass, carpet and altars. High ceilings. Crosses. Choir robes.

The people here met in a low squat building that looked like an abandoned office. They sat on metal folding chairs in a cramped linoleum-floored room with utilitarian green-painted walls. There was no choir; only a small group of men and women, a keyboard, a guitarist, a tambourine, and a set of drums. The only pulpit Leah could see was a battered music stand.

The song segued into a more lively one, and Leah clapped in time again. This song she vaguely recognized, maybe from the radio. The words seemed familiar.

As she sang, she studied Jacobo. He sang enthusiastically, occasionally not clapping so that he could close his eyes. Leah felt embarrassed for him, but then she realized others around her were doing the same.

"Hi, Mrs. Travers." Tran, the auto mechanic, slipped into the empty seat beside hers. "Good to see you. Hi, Jacobo."

Jacobo held out a hand for a quick shake. "Hey, Tran. I didn't think you were going to make it."

Tran smiled and started singing.

Leah felt awkward standing between them. She'd never attended church with her auto mechanic before. Or, for that matter, with people from such diverse ethnic backgrounds. She felt plain and...well, boring. She decided to concentrate on singing.

But as the music continued, she found herself drawn to the words. Some of them praised God simply for who he was, some implored him to move in the hearts of his people, others seemed to be simple reminders that God was present, available—that he cared.

Does he? Does he really see me in all my misery? And more impor-tant, does he really care?

And do all these people believe that, too, or are they just hypocrites?

Surely she wasn't the only one here who had gone through rough times, who'd lost loved ones. Probably more time had passed for them, and they were more accustomed to their losses.

Maybe one day she'd reach such a place.

After over a half-hour of singing, the members turned to greet each other. Leah wasn't sure how it happened, but Jacobo somehow led her away from their seats and introduced her to even more people. By the time a man at the front laughingly exhorted them all to find their chairs, Leah and Jacobo were up at the front. She felt her face warm as he led the way to the back row, past the eyes of the congregation.

A man, whom Leah had met as Nick, stood up to the music stand and started talking.

"What does he do?" she whispered to Jacobo.

He grinned. "He's the preacher."

Leah wasn't a bit surprised. What a topsy-turvy day this had been.

When Nick finished talking, there was more singing, then the passing of double-handled baskets for the offering. Jacobo reached inside his leather jacket and extracted a small envelope, which he deposited in the basket.

Leah guiltily dropped in a five-dollar bill, thinking about all the Sundays she'd missed church since Galen and Perry had died.

Nick stood at the music stand once again and gave a few brief announcements. He closed with a plea for nursery workers while the church looked for a nursery director.

"Our little ones deserve the greatest love and attention, and we won't make the selection hastily," he said. "Until we do, we need helpers for both Sunday services."

Leah's guilt increased. She'd never returned to the nursery at her former church. Had they had trouble replacing her? She knew how difficult it could be to get workers—most people seemed to want an hour of peace and quiet in church rather than to teach little ones.

When the final song was over, Leah shook hands with Tran—assuring him that the Neon was indeed running well. She nodded at several other people she thought she'd met earlier, then she and Jacobo walked out to his motorcycle.

"Well...," he said, "I suppose you're ready to go home."

Leah swallowed. The truth was that she didn't feel like staying cooped up in her apartment. The day was mild and sunny—beautiful autumn weather, with multicolored leaves gently falling and the wind blowing only slightly.

"I had a wonderful time," she said.

He brightened, looking pleased. "I was hoping you would. You're welcome any time, and in fact..." He paused. "I'd be glad to give you a ride if you ever need one."

She smiled. "I might take you up on that. In fact, I was thinking about what your preacher said about needing nursery workers."

"Really?" Jacobo shifted the helmet between his hands. "Would you like to have lunch with me? I could tell you more about my church—answer any questions you might have."

"Sure," she said; then, to cover her sudden shyness, she put on her helmet.

Jacobo whistled as he pushed open the front door. He'd brought research work home from the law office, but the afternoon was too warm and sunny to waste cooped up indoors. Maybe he'd take the kids to the park—especially Maria and Carlos. There was still trouble between them and Frankie, and only that morning there'd been yet another fight.

He walked into the kitchen and poured himself a glass of water from the tap and leaned back against the chipped sink.

Speaking of the kids, where were they?

"Church run long today?" Dolores slouched around the corner. "It's nearly three."

Jacobo drained the rest of the water and set the glass in the sink. "I took a friend to lunch."

Dolores cocked an eyebrow. "From the way you're grinning, I'd say it's a woman."

He shrugged. "So?"

"Ahh." Dolores smiled broader, sweeping into the room. "I was wondering how long it would take you to crack. You haven't had a girlfriend since...let's see, was it Rita Estrella? Before you went to law school anyway. Who's this one?"

Jacobo turned away. "You don't know her."

"Well, well. A mystery woman. It's nice to know you're human, anyway, and needing a little physical contact. Just like the rest of us."

Jacobo clenched his teeth. He knew what Dolores was implying. Usually he was tolerant of her beliefs that everyone thought and acted as she and Manuel did. He didn't mind the indictment against himself, but he didn't like such thoughts cast Leah's way...even if Dolores didn't know her identity.

"Where are the kids?" he said.

"Mrs. Vasquez has them over at her house watching a video. I'm going down the street to Marisa's. You want to come?"

"No thanks." He could stand a little time alone.

Dolores shrugged and grabbed a sweater from the back of a chair. "Suit yourself. Mrs. Vasquez said she'd send them home at five." She sighed. "What I wouldn't give for a cigarette."

The front door slammed, and Jacobo was alone.

The house was quiet. Not so quiet that he couldn't bear it. He needed some time to think, and lately the only time he had to himself was when he was riding his bike.

Still thirsty, he rooted around in the refrigerator and found a can of generic cola. Popping the top, he headed for the small living room, where he settled into the sagging tweed sofa and put his feet up on the scarred coffee table.

He swigged from the can and leaned back, allowing himself to close his eyes in contemplation. So often, this was all he wanted. A moment's peace to reflect, to plan, to dream.

But lately he'd had no dreams, except to earn enough money for the family. He couldn't allow himself to imagine a life beyond this house, this obligation. With every passing day, he felt his desire to complete law school fading. When he was younger, he'd been willing to work two jobs and study hard, to accept that his road would be rough. Now he wasn't so sure he could do that anymore. And the money he'd saved was just about gone.

Everything seemed to drain him more, cost him more of an emotional effort. He was willing, but trying to mediate between the kids or scrape up enough money for the bills, or bolster Dolores's flagging spirits, made him bone weary. Some days he even contemplated leaving a good-bye note on the table, hopping on his bike, and heading straight for Austin. Or maybe the coast.

He wanted his own life. He'd had a taste of it that first year in law school, where the only obligations he'd had were to attend class and study. He'd shared a house—no matter how modest—with only one other person. Eric hadn't made any demands or questioned when he came and went or whose company he kept. Hadn't complained like Dolores or whined and fought like the kids.

Jacobo sighed deeply, willing the tension from his body. *Lord, I know I have obligations here. But did you plant the desire for law school in my heart, only to take away the dream? How long do I have to suffer for Manuel's mistake...for Dolores's mistake in marrying him?*

Instantly he felt ashamed. Across town, Leah Travers was suffering—would suffer the rest of her life—for Manuel's mistake.

Jacobo clenched his fists at the thought of Manuel taking the lives of her loved ones.

Let it go. Let your own despair go.

Slowly Jacobo opened his hands. It took so much more energy to hang on to anger than to release it.

He'd wanted to blurt that out to Leah today, over their lunch at the taquería. One minute they'd been talking about the worship service, then she'd stopped talking to eat. He watched her take a mouthful of her taco, and he'd had the sudden impulse to say, *You have to release your grief, Leah. Let it out, then let it go.*

Not that he expected her to forget about her family. That wouldn't be healthy either. But neither was bottling up her grief.

She talked about her husband and son when he asked. He could see that she even *wanted* to talk about them. But they circled the subject without delving deeper into the real issues—such as what she was going to do with the rest of her life. He wanted her on the road of recovery. From the tiny clues she'd given about her isolated life, it was clear she needed healing, badly.

But there was hope. She'd timidly asked if the church might consider her to work in the nursery so that other parents could attend the worship service. She said she'd worked in the nursery at her former church, but when he casually inquired if she was still attending there, she'd clammed up.

Maybe after her family's death the church members had been overly solicitous. Maybe they hadn't been solicitous enough. Maybe the thought of continuing her membership there had just been too painful. At any rate he'd managed to get out of her that she hadn't been to church since her family's funeral.

He had prayed she'd see the love he always felt at his church. He'd been surprised that she'd agreed to come to the service with him. More surprised that she'd gone to lunch with him afterward.

And secretly—ecstatically—pleased because he knew in his heart that despite the trouble it would ultimately cause with Dolores, Jacobo wanted to see more of Leah Travers.

Coffee at the Purple Onion had been for Rosita. So had the trip to the zoo and the penguin show at the museum. Going to his church had been for Leah.

But lunch today had been for him.

He wanted to help her, to bring her back to the land of the living, but there was something more. She wrapped self-protection tightly around herself under the guise of independence, but it was a hard-won self-sufficiency. Given the tragedy in her life, others might have folded, whimpered, and let others take control.

Not Leah. From what she'd said about her life before the accident, she'd probably let her husband take care of the major details of their lives. But since, she'd been forced to assume the yoke of responsibility while picking her way through the ashes of her life.

He wanted to learn more about that independence and the woman underneath. He wanted to help her sift through those ashes and find solid ground.

The solid ground that always upheld him, even when his own life's dreams crumbled into dust.

Jacobo drained the can of cola and glanced around the room. Another crack had appeared in the wall behind the TV. Frankie had left his Sunday clothes strewn on the floor. Somebody had abandoned a half-eaten bowl of cereal on a metal TV tray. Dust accumulated in the corner behind the door.

Jacobo sighed wearily. If there weren't wounded souls here to nurture, there was the house to maintain. Between him and Dolores, it was all they could do to keep the place from falling apart.

And Sunday was supposed to be a day of rest.

Jacobo grabbed the empty can and the cereal bowl and headed for the kitchen. This Sunday, no matter how he looked at it, would be a day of work.

But in five days—Friday night, if he could hold out that long—he'd see Leah again. Somewhere during their innocuous lunchtime conversation about his church, she'd agreed to go to a baseball game with him.

Leah twiddled the red pen between her fingers and swiveled the ergonomic work chair. She'd had a hard time concentrating all week, but especially at work when the tedium of proofreading was at its strongest.

Friday was only two days away.

She blushed even as she thought about Jacobo. It wasn't that she thought of their upcoming outing as a date. He'd casually mentioned that he'd gotten two complimentary tickets to the Rangers game this Friday and asked if she'd like to go with him.

When he'd put it that way—like she was doing him a favor if she went—it'd been easier for her to accept. An outing with a new friend.

And a new friend he was. He was easy to talk to, about any subject. Sometimes Perry and Galen came up in the conversation, and he asked questions about them. Other times, when the topic seemed too painful, he backed off and deftly steered the talk to a more mundane track.

Jacobo was well-read, and reading was something she herself had been doing more of in the evenings instead of watching mindless television. They talked about books—current bestsellers and classics they'd both read. She learned that *Zen and the Art of Motorcycle Maintenance* had been the inspiration for his buying his first bike, a beat-up old Harley he'd restored with his father several years before he'd been old enough even to ride.

She learned that he'd wanted to be a lawyer since he was ten, that he'd thrived in the atmosphere at UT's law school, that his best friend in the world was a guy named Eric in Austin, and that he loved the beach.

He talked about himself, about anything she wanted to know. Except, by unspoken agreement, about Manuel Garcia or Jacobo's sister, Dolores.

The phone jangled, and she snatched it up before the first ring had finished. "Leah Travers."

"Leah. Darling, how are you?"

She stiffened at the sound of her mother's voice. "I'm all right, Mom. How are you and Daddy?"

Emily Tyler paused. "Your father's stress test didn't go well."

Leah twirled the pen in her fingers. Her mother was working overtime at the guilt trip. She'd never called Leah at work before. "Is his cholesterol level still too high?"

"Worse than that, Leah. They think maybe one of his arteries is blocked. They've scheduled an angioplasty in a few weeks."

Danni had babbled something about the stress test last week, about their parents needing Leah. She'd brushed it off as another attempt to get her to return home. She set the pen down carefully on the desk. "Is an angioplasty where they shoot the little balloon into the artery to open it up?"

"Yes. It's not as risky as it used to be. They say they do it all the time." Emily laughed lightly, the fake laugh Leah recognized as the one her mother used when she was nervous.

"But Dad'll have to go into the hospital?"

"Yes. For a few days." A queer tone crept into her voice. "But you don't need to worry. Danni will be here."

Leah felt the sting of her words. She wasn't needed. "I'm glad, Mom. Maybe I can come down the weekend after the surgery."

"Don't worry, Leah. We'll be fine. Owen will be here too. As always."

Leah bristled. "Owen lives in town, Mom. And Danni doesn't have a job. She can come down anytime."

"That's right. All the way from Chicago. I understand, Leah. You don't have to explain how busy you are."

"Mom…" Leah didn't know why she felt she should justify her life, but her mother obviously still had the power to bring out the guilt. "I don't have any more time off from work. You know that. My company gave me a lot of time off during and after the trial."

"Things don't always revolve around you, Leah," Emily said quietly. "Come when you can. If you care to be here at all, that is."

"But..."

The line went dead. Leah stared at the receiver, stunned.

"Everything okay?"

Ed Spivey hesitated at the entrance to her cubicle. Normally Leah would have shrugged off his question with a tight *sure* and cut him off by turning to her work. But she noticed genuine concern on his face and wondered why she'd never seen it before.

"I think so." She smiled sheepishly and replaced the receiver. "But thanks for asking."

Ed cleared his throat. "They're getting together to celebrate Lisa's birthday." He gestured toward the kitchen. "I could bring you some cake, if you're interested."

Leah thought about taking him up on his offer, then realized she didn't want to be alone at the moment. Her mother's attitude had left her shaken inside, more shaken than she cared to admit.

She smiled at Ed. "If you're headed that way, maybe I could just tag along."

"Why...sure." He cleared his throat again and ducked toward his cubicle, across the aisle from Leah's.

Leah pushed back her chair, stretched a little to work out the kinks, then headed toward the department's kitchen with her coworker.

Chapter Fifteen

Leah clung to the motorcycle's back rail as Jacobo zipped through the traffic on I-30. Her teeth chattered; her whole head hummed with the sound of the engine; the hair hanging below her helmet whipped around; and her jacket seemed scant protection for the autumn wind, made colder by the bike's speed.

She couldn't remember the last time she'd enjoyed herself more.

The bouncing—flying, really—across the pavement was exhilarating. At times she still suppressed a squeal when he turned sharply or came to a halt, but she'd learned to trust that he knew what he was doing.

She'd grown more accustomed to the sensation of riding and learned—as he had said she would—to read his body language. She learned that when he turned she should lean with him. Or when he changed lanes that she should hold on.

The Ballpark in Arlington loomed ahead, and Leah stared in awe. She'd been to a few games in the Astrodome with her dad when she was a girl, but she'd never been to a Rangers game.

"Pretty impressive, huh?" Jacobo said, noticing her still staring at the stadium after he'd parked.

She nodded, taking off her helmet. Jacobo took it from her. "We'll leave them with the bike so we don't have to tote them around."

They walked toward the entrance, stepping up their pace as they blended into the crowd. Leah could feel the excitement as the fans poured toward the first-base entrance.

"This is a playoff game, right?" she said after he'd handed over the tickets and they'd gone through the turnstile.

"Almost. This is the last week of the season. If they win tonight's game, they'll be the Western Division champs. Then they'll go to the playoffs." He paused at the concession stand. "Food first or find our seats?"

"I'm not really that hungry," she said. Food still held no real allure for her. Not the way it had when Galen had begged for cotton candy and popcorn at sporting events.

Jacobo grinned. "You have to eat something at a ball game. Peanuts are a must. A hot dog is even better. Come on, Leah. You don't want to defy American tradition, do you?"

She found herself grinning back. "I wouldn't dream of it."

"That's better. But let's go find our seats so you work up more of an appetite. You have to fully appreciate the culinary aspect of the sport."

He took the ticket stubs out of his pocket and checked the section, then consulted the guides over the portals. "This way," he said, casually taking her by the elbow.

Leah felt the warmth of his hand all the way through her denim jacket. Her mouth went dry as he led her through the entrance to their section.

Inside the opening, she stopped short and stared, forgetting all about his touch.

"What's the matter?" Jacobo turned.

Leah took in the high, bright lights, the crowd, the green field and dots of white bases contrasting with the brown warning track. The design of the stadium looked remarkably like a ball field from a bygone era. She felt as though she'd truly stepped into the heart of American tradition.

"I told you it was impressive," Jacobo said. "You've never been here before?"

She shook her head. "Perry was a football fan, not baseball. My dad..." She swallowed hard, suddenly remembering his stress test. "My dad used to take me to some Astros games when I was a kid."

"This is American League, not National, like the 'Stros play in," Jacobo said. "There are a few differences in the rules."

He found the row—the fourth. Their seats were along the first base line. "You're a big baseball fan?" she said, as they settled in.

"One of the biggest. My dad used to take me to games at the old Arlington Stadium. Most of the time we'd sit in the outfield bleachers, but sometimes he'd save his pennies and we'd sit way up high behind home plate." Jacobo glanced around, and she noticed his eyes were shining. "These are the best seats I've ever had."

Leah was touched that he would invite her to something that was obviously so important to him. "I wish your dad were here to share them with you."

Jacobo looked at her and smiled. "It's good to have *you* here, Leah. I'm glad you came with me."

Leah glanced away, pretending to study the giant Jumbotron above right field. The screen was playing baseball bloopers, and Leah laughed as two outfielders harmlessly collided while trying to catch a fly ball. "Look, Jacobo!"

He turned, then laughed along with her. "That must have been last week between the Mets and the Braves. I heard it was quite a game."

"Have you ever seen them play the Rangers here in Arlington?"

"They're National League teams."

"So?"

"So the Rangers are American League."

She looked at him blankly, and he began a discussion about the differences between the two leagues and the few interleague games that were played.

"So the big difference is that the American League has a designated hitter, and the pitcher doesn't have to bat?" she said, when he came up for air.

"Basically. Hey, it looks like the singer's coming on the field for the national anthem."

They all rose, and a local country western singer led them all in the "Star Spangled Banner." Leah felt a thrill down to her toes, and she heard Jacobo's strong voice chiming in beside hers, much as it had at church that past Sunday.

"...and the hooooome...of the...braaaaaave."

The crowd cheered and applauded. "Play ball!" Jacobo said, and a few took up the traditional cry.

Leah laughed as she took her seat. Jacobo leaned toward her as the Angels' first batter came to the plate. "Now watch this guy, Leah. He's a left-handed batter, and the Rangers' pitcher throws left-handed too, so that's good for the Rangers."

Leah blinked. "Why?" She'd never realized something like that could make a difference.

Jacobo patiently launched into an explanation about curves and angles, and Leah absorbed it all. Perry had never taken the time to explain the intricacies of professional sports to her, even when she asked. He was generally too wrapped up in a football game to stop to explain its nuances. She'd always thought she would have enjoyed the sport more if she'd understood it better.

The Rangers' pitcher got three straight strikeouts to retire the Angels, and the crowd roared. Leah clapped and cheered, watching Jacobo all the time. His eyes were shining, and his face was all smiles.

"That was great pitching! Did you see that fastball?"

Leah smiled. "I wouldn't know a fastball from a curve ball."

Jacobo's smile faded. "I'm sorry, Leah. I hope this isn't boring you. We can leave early if it is."

"I'm not bored at all," she said. It was nice of him to consider her happiness more important than great seats at such a crucial game. "I don't know all the details like you do, but I can tell by the scoreboard that the team's doing okay."

His smile returned, and he touched her hand. "Let me know if it does get dull."

Her hand seemed to tingle, and she felt like a high schooler on her first date.

Though the crowd around them was applauding the first Ranger batter, she suddenly felt as if they were the only two in the ballpark. He kept looking at her, his smile reaching all the way up to his eyes, and she knew it was because of her, not from being at the game. Something passed between them, almost like a secret, a warm current of understanding.

Jacobo gently squeezed her hand but didn't remove it. "Are you ready for some peanuts or that hot dog now?"

"Sure," she managed to say, unnerved. What was happening here? No matter how she felt, she *wasn't* a high school girl anymore; she was a widow.

Jacobo signaled to a passing vendor. Leah blew out a long breath, then fixed a smile as Jacobo handed her an aluminum foil-wrapped dog.

She was grateful for the chance to do something with her hands for a while, and even though she wasn't especially hungry, the dog did taste good.

Midway through the top of the fourth inning, a foul tip came their way. Leah watched it float toward them, in slow motion, it seemed. She wanted to duck—knew she should duck—but she couldn't take her eyes off the ball. She was vaguely aware of a kid in front of them scrambling with an outstretched glove, crying, "I got it! I got it!"

The ball flew just inches higher than the boy's glove, and Jacobo reached out and caught it with his bare hands. Everyone around them cheered.

"Good catch, mister," mumbled the boy, who couldn't have been more than eight. He sat back down and cradled his gloved hand in his lap.

Jacobo tossed the ball into the boy's glove. "Here, you keep it. You'd have had it if my hands hadn't been in the way."

"Gee, thanks!" The boy beamed, happily turning the ball over in his hands to examine it carefully.

Leah smiled. "That was a nice thing to do," she whispered.

Jacobo shrugged.

Leah concentrated on the rest of the game and didn't find herself bored in the least. Jacobo knew all about the players, and he explained various plays that she found confusing.

At the bottom of the ninth inning, the score was tied, with two Rangers on base. Rafael Palmeiro stepped up to the plate, and the PA system blared *Charge!* The crowd cheered its encouragement.

"Is he really good or something?" Leah said, noticing that the cheers were louder for him than for many of the other players.

"Good? He's leading the league in RBIs." When Leah scrunched her face, Jacobo smiled. "Runs batted in."

"That's good?"

He chuckled. "Especially right now, with two men on base." He cupped his hands around his mouth. "Come on, Raffy! Tear the cover off the ball!"

Leah held her breath through three balls and two strikes. On the sixth pitch, *crack!* The ball sailed into the seats behind right field. All around Leah, people rose to their feet, screaming, shouting. The Jumbotron flashed *¡Dale un beso y adios!*

The players streamed onto the field, whooping and hollering.

"They won! Leah, they won the division!" Jacobo gripped her arms in excitement.

Again, the tingle passed through her, but she was so caught up in the moment, she assumed it was from the game. "Hooray!"

When the excitement finally died down and they'd caught their breath, Jacobo smiled. "You ready to go?"

No, she wanted to say. *I've had more fun tonight than I have in over a year. At a ball game, no less.*

And she suddenly realized that the reason she'd had so much fun had been largely because of him. Not because of the game. Not because of the division win. But because he'd shared something with her, a side of himself that she hadn't seen before. A side that had nothing to do with family obligations or work, but just plain fun.

While the celebrating was still going on, they headed out of the stadium. The crowd's cheering grew more muffled as they made their way toward the parking lot.

At the motorcycle, Leah stuffed her hands in her pockets, lingering. "It's not even ten-thirty yet. Too early to call it a night for a Friday. Do you want to get some coffee or something?"

She couldn't believe she was asking. She'd never asked for a date in her life, but here she was asking this man—who was different from her in so many ways—if he'd like to extend their time together. He'd probably think she was too forward. Did Hispanic men think that about women? Weren't they supposed to like women who were passive?

Jacobo handed her a helmet and smiled. "I'd like that, Leah. Why don't we head downtown to a coffeehouse I know? They make a mean latté."

"I'm pretty much a plain old black coffee kind of gal, myself," she said, smiling shyly, then put on her helmet to hide the blush she knew covered her face.

Jacobo was still smiling. "Leah?"

"Yes?" She removed the helmet.

He gestured at the rail behind the saddle. "I know it's uncomfortable to ride hanging on to that thing. Don't worry about being shy; you'd be more comfortable if you put your arms around me. And frankly, it's easier for me to ride if you do."

"Oh." Now she was certain her face was crimson. "Okay."

He got on and started the engine, and she got on behind him. Tentatively, she wrapped her arms around his middle, pressing up close.

She felt like a traitor, betraying her husband. This was another man she was holding, even if it was just for a motorcycle ride. And Jacobo felt different than Perry in her arms—leaner...stronger.

Leah loosened her grip and put as much distance as she could between them.

Downtown, Jacobo found a parking space. For several years, the downtown area had been in a process of rejuvenation. Now two large theater complexes showed the latest movies. Several eateries—from fast food to trendy to upscale—lined the streets. A horse and carriage were for hire at one corner. People lined up to enter several clubs, each featuring a different form of music. A large Barnes & Noble sat across the street from a multistoried mirror-tiled office building.

And everywhere, security patrolled the streets on bicycles so that citizens and tourists could enjoy their evening without fear of crime.

"Ever been here?" Jacobo led the way to a coffeehouse in the heart of the revitalized area.

Leah shook her head. "I haven't been downtown before. Oh, except once when I came to the outlet mall. But that was years ago."

She'd been shopping for baby clothes, but she didn't add that.

Jacobo led the way into the coffeehouse, past the crowd filling the tables outside. Inside lounged young professionals and college-aged kids in post-grunge attire. Several older couples perched carefully on the few vinyl-and-chrome barstools, sipping from embossed Styrofoam cups.

Leah had the feeling that if she squinted hard enough, she might imagine herself at the Purple Onion.

"Yeah?" Behind the counter, the uninterested boy with a silver nose ring and shaved head slapped a dishtowel over his shoulder. "Whad'll you have?"

Jacobo turned to Leah. "Black coffee?"

She nodded.

The server smirked. "The special today is Jamocha Jamaican. Three seventy-five for eight ounces. How 'bout it, ma'am?"

At that price, the coffee had better be served by Juan Valdez himself. Leah smiled. "No thanks."

"Two black coffees," Jacobo said.

"Just…coffee. Plain?" The server cocked a finely plucked eyebrow.

"Yes. Just plain," Jacobo said.

The server shook his head and shuffled back to the coffeepot.

Jacobo glanced at Leah, and she covered her mouth to suppress a laugh.

"I don't get it either," he said. "Doesn't anybody appreciate just a good, plain cup of joe anymore?"

"Apparently not. Actually I didn't start drinking coffee until…" Leah's voice trailed off.

The server handed them their coffees, and Jacobo handed back a few bills, dropping the change in a tip jar.

"Gee, thanks," the kid said. "That'll help my college education."

Smiling at the sarcasm, Jacobo gave him a quick salute, then steered Leah toward a vacant corner table. She sat down gingerly on a mod fabric-covered chair and tentatively sipped her coffee. It was hot and strong. Perfect after a night of riding in the cold on a motorcycle.

"You were saying that you didn't start drinking coffee until…," Jacobo reminded her.

"Oh." She'd forgotten that she'd said that. "I first remember drinking coffee the night Perry and Galen were killed. At the hospital."

Jacobo took a sip of his coffee. "We haven't ever talked about that, Leah. Would you like to?"

Did she want to talk about the night a year ago that her world had come apart? To talk about the scenes she replayed over and over in her mind until she woke up in a cold sweat with warm tears running down her pillow? "Jacobo…" She swallowed.

He set down his coffee and covered her hand with his. "Leah, it's okay. You don't have to, if you don't want to. But I'm interested. I want to hear whatever you want to say. Not the version you told the court, but the version you hold in your heart."

Her eyes misted. "I've tried so hard not to tell anybody. At first I wanted to, but my family told me to be brave. Have courage, they said. Don't talk about it."

He shook his head. "They were wrong, Leah. People need to talk about what affects them deeply. What hurts the most. Especially grief." He squeezed her hand. "It's what being a part of the body of Christ is all about. We listen. We offer comfort to each other even when we can't offer solutions."

Leah thought about his church, about the genuine kindness she'd seen etched on every member's face, and she teared up even more. "I…I can't."

"Can't, or don't want to?" he said softly.

She bit her lip, unable to speak.

"Either way, I'm not judging you, Leah. I just want to help."

She smiled ruefully. "What help can you give? My family's dead. They won't come back, no matter what."

"I know," he said gently. "But you can go on. You can find your way back to the body and your place. Life isn't meant to be space you just occupy until your time is up—your place is where you fit. Where you minister to others."

She swiped at her eyes. "How can I minister to anybody? What do I have to offer, except sadness?"

"Exactly. Sadness. You have experiences that can help other people who are grieving. If that's your calling. Maybe it's not.

Maybe the Lord wants you to be a nursery teacher. Or a…an airplane pilot. Or a…a…"

"Butcher, baker, or candlestick maker?" She smiled despite herself, wiping the last of the tears from her eyes.

Jacobo handed her a napkin, smiling also. "Who knows what he has in store for you? But I do know that you'll never find it…never experience the joy he's planned for you if you don't meet him halfway." He leaned forward, his expression serious. "And he wants you to be joyful. That's not the same as happiness, true, but it's much, much better. He wants to lead you into joy, through the valley of the shadow of death that you're stuck in. He's with you, Leah. He doesn't want you to fear any evil."

She sat back. "How is talking about what happened supposed to help me?"

"Because it lessens the power that evil holds over you. By letting it go, you're giving it to God. I'm not saying that just talking about it will do that—the letting go, that is. But it's a beginning. It's a step toward forgiveness."

Her hands shook, and she drew a deep breath to steady herself. "Forgiveness? Oh, that's right. If I'm really a Christian, I'll forgive and forget."

"The Lord doesn't want you to forget your family."

"Does he want me to forget the sight of my husband being hit by a pickup truck? Of being knocked so far that he was jerked out of his tennis shoes? Or the sight of his blood pooling on the road?"

She knew her voice was rising with each sentence, but she didn't care. "Or maybe," she continued, "he wants me to forget my baby…my precious son…lying under a hospital sheet. Dead. Or holding him in my arms, knowing that I would give anything, do anything, to bring life back into his broken little body."

"I'm sorry, Leah," Jacobo said softly. "I know you can't forget those things."

"I wish I could." She closed her eyes against a fresh wave of tears and lifted the cup to take a swallow. The coffee tasted like hot mud, scalding her tongue. "I'd give anything to erase those images from my mind."

"You were sitting away from the car when it happened...with the lady whose car had broken down, right?"

She nodded, unable to speak.

Jacobo leaned forward. "Do you ever wonder why you were spared?"

"I was spared so that I could suffer." She opened her eyes. "I should have stayed with my baby. I shouldn't have fought with Perry on the way home." She smiled bitterly. "You didn't know that, did you? That's something I didn't tell the court. Perry and I fought all the way home from Houston."

"That wasn't your fault, Leah. Family spats happen. People disagree."

"It shouldn't have happened that night. I should have stayed with Galen—maybe I could have saved him. I should have agreed to whatever Perry said, just to keep peace. I should have...I should have..."

I should have told him I loved him. I should have done whatever he wanted. Like not listening to my parents. Or cutting my hair. Then he wouldn't have stopped to help that woman, and he'd still be alive. So would Galen.

"What did you fight about?"

The ultimate irony. "My family. He thought they were overly protective."

"Are they?"

215

"Yes. Isn't that funny? I didn't realize how right Perry was until after he died. I wish I'd listened to him. He'd still be alive today."

"Leah," Jacobo said in a low voice. "You didn't have anything to do with what happened. You didn't kill your husband and your son."

"No, but your brother-in-law did."

He drew a deep breath at her words. "I know. I wish I could change that. I wish I could go back and change other things, too. Maybe if I hadn't gone to law school, if I'd stepped in between Manuel and Dolores and insisted they get help, Manuel wouldn't have continued to drink."

"Now *you're* acting like the accident was your fault. What could you have done?"

"Nothing more than you," he said softly. "We can't change the past anyway. All we can do is deal with today and plan for tomorrow."

"That would make a great saying in a fortune cookie," she said. "Any other words of advice?"

He shook his head. "The only words that ring truth are God's words. That's what I cling to. Manuel's action changed a lot of people's lives, Leah. It's more clear to me now than it's ever been how sin can affect so many people."

Leah leaned back. She felt tired, spent. She'd said more tonight about the accident than she'd ever said to anybody. Yet when she looked at Jacobo, she saw the sag of his own shoulders, the drawn expression on his face that had to rival her own.

You'd care, he'd told her at the museum, *if you'd allow yourself to look deep down inside, underneath that big coat of self-pity you're wearing.*

Leah swallowed the lump in her throat. "Your family," she said softly. "How are they? Rosita, Frankie...your sister."

Jacobo raised his head to look her straight in the eyes. "They're not doing well, I'm sorry to say. Only Rosita bounces forward in life. The others..." He shrugged.

"What about your sister? How's she taking all this?"

He looked at her a moment as if he wanted to say something, then he shrugged again. "She's adjusting. We all are."

She heard the tone in his voice, the lie that things would be better. "Do you have plans to go back to law school?"

He looked down at his coffee and idly swirled a plastic stirrer in the steaming liquid. "I don't see how I can. Dolores and the kids need me. They need my financial support. They need a male presence in the house. They'll need..." He stopped stirring and looked away.

Leah bit her lip. "I'm sorry this has affected you, too. It doesn't seem fair."

He smiled slowly, a faraway look in his eyes. "Rain falls on the just and the unjust."

"Another fortune cookie?"

"The Bible." He turned to look at her, and their gazes locked. "Leah, I'd like to keep seeing you, spending time with you. I'd like to take you to church every Sunday and out to eat or to a movie occasionally. I like talking to you. You're an interesting, intelligent woman."

He drew a deep breath. "But I'd rather know now if you're not interested. It'd be easier for us both."

Leah leaned back, dumbfounded. "I...I can't make any promises, Jacobo."

He nodded. "I understand. When you look at me, you see Manuel."

"It's not just that..." She fumbled for the right words. "It's that we're so..."

"Different?"

"Yes!" Thank goodness he understood. "I mean, you're..."

"Hispanic."

"...a motorcycle rider," she corrected quickly, "and..."

"Hispanic." He smiled.

"...probably younger than me." The teasing expression on his face made her smile too. "And you..."

"Have long hair?" he guessed.

"...are Hispanic." She smiled. "What were those Spanish words they flashed on the scoreboard when Palmeiro hit that home run tonight, anyway? *Dale un...un...*"

"*Dale un beso y adios.* It means, kiss it good-bye."

"Oh."

He smiled at her. "Does it bother you that I'm Hispanic?"

"No. Does it bother you that I'm Anglo?"

"No." He touched her hand lightly. "Not at all."

His look unnerved her. There was nothing suggestive in his eyes or in the way his hand covered hers. Yet she sensed a connection, a bond of friendship.

"Can I take you to church Sunday?" he said softly.

She knew she should say no. Surely no good could come of any relationship with this man. Or *any* relationship she might ever have.

But she was lonely. Most of the hurt was missing Perry and Galen, but some of it—the deep down pain she tried so hard to hide—even she could recognize that it was a human need for companionship. She'd burrowed in the darkness for so long. Maybe it was time, as he'd said, to step out into the light.

She exhaled slowly. "I'd like that, Jacobo."

At church on Sunday, Leah sat through the service with Jacobo, listening and watching intently. Something exciting happened when these people gathered—if she couldn't experience it firsthand, she would be content to be an observer.

The pastor, Nick, once again asked at the end of the service for nursery workers. Leah looked at Jacobo. When he glanced down at her, she smiled.

He smiled back, and when the service was over, he held her hand as they went down to the front to talk to Nick.

Chapter Sixteen

"Mama will be surprised to see us. We've never been here on a Friday after school before," Rosita said, skipping ahead of Jacobo for the glass doors of the bakery. Frankie, Marcos, and Maria raced past her, each yelling to be the first inside. Carlos stuck his small hand, sticky from an afternoon snack of honey roasted peanuts, into Jacobo's. In his other hand, he clutched his beloved stuffed bear.

He looked up at Jacobo. "Mama won't be mad that we came, will she? She's mad a lot lately." He made a face, stubbing a toe against the sidewalk. "Ever since she found out she was having a baby."

Jacobo sighed inwardly. It had been several weeks since Dolores had sat the kids down and told them about their new brother or sister. Except for Rosita, none of them had taken the news well. Frankie was doing worse than ever in school, while Maria was withdrawn and moody. Marcos threw himself into schoolwork but cried whenever he received any grade lower than an A. His classmates had started to pick on him, and more than once he'd come home with a black eye.

Even Carlos resented the impending addition to the family, screaming with fear if anyone tried to take Oso from his arms. He wouldn't let Dolores wash the badly soiled bear. She, in turn, was frequently short-tempered with her youngest son, with all of them. Jacobo often heard her sobbing late at night, behind her closed bedroom door.

Jacobo knelt to Carlos's level. "The baby will need an older brother to look out for him, Carlitos. Just like Oso needs you."

Carlos hugged the bedraggled bear to his body. His eyes widened. "He won't want Oso, will he?"

Jacobo smiled. "Maybe we can get him his own bear, huh? A bear that could be a friend to Oso too."

Carlos frowned. "Oso doesn't have any friends. Neither do I."

Jacobo's heart ached. It was true. None of the kids seemed to have any true friends, except for Frankie—and his friends seemed more intent on getting him into trouble and scrapes than in whiling away the time in companionable fun.

"I'll bet the baby would be your friend," Jacobo said.

"Huh! He'll just be a baby. What will he do?"

Jacobo put his arm around his nephew's shoulders. "The question is, what will you do for him? Your *abuela* used to tell me when I was a boy your age that to get friends, you have to be a friend."

"Well..." Carlos pursed his lips. "I don't know."

Jacobo patted him gently on the back and rose. "You think about it, Carlitos, okay? It'll be nice not to be the youngest anymore, won't it? And you'll be the best person to help the baby because you'll understand what it's like to be the youngest."

From inside the bakery, Marcos pushed open the glass door. "Hurry up, Carlitos! Mama's going to give us each a cookie."

"We're coming." Jacobo took his nephew's hand.

Inside, the bakery was painted bright shades of yellow and green, with red trim. The kids all had their noses pressed up against the glass cases, licking their lips over cookies and cakes. Jacobo could feel the heat from the ovens in the back.

Dolores came in from the kitchen, hefting a large metal tray filled with hot cookies. She set the tray on a table behind the counter and eased up the cookies with a spatula onto a plate. The minute she set the plate on the counter, the kids each grabbed one and scrambled for a nearby table. Jacobo got one for Carlos, who was too short to reach that high. When he'd received his cookie, he, too, ran for the table.

Dolores stayed on the other side of the counter. She put her hand at the small of her back and stretched. Jacobo noticed how her stomach had grown just in the past week, and he wondered how much longer she'd be able to work at the bakery. Already she came home every night complaining of swollen feet and an aching back. The clinic doctor said she was healthy, but Jacobo didn't want her to do anything to endanger the baby.

He reminded himself that he should look into getting some kind of part-time work to make ends meet.

"Why'd you bring 'em here, Jacobo?" she said. "I don't like them to see me working."

He shrugged. "Why not? They know you work. Shouldn't they see where you are, so they can be proud of what you're doing?"

She laughed, pushing the hair net back from her face. "I'm sure they're real proud that their mom works in a bakery."

Jacobo glanced at his nieces and nephews. They were happily munching on their cookies, swinging their feet under their chairs. "Look at them," he said. "Do they look ashamed of you or this place? It may seem like a menial job to you, but to them, this place is heaven."

"Still trying to find that silver lining in every cloud, aren't you?" Dolores shook her head. "Well, I guess I'd be happy too, if I were you. You're stuck with us, but you've managed to find yourself a girl. We don't see much of you anymore, Jacobo. Is it because of her?"

"I'm working a lot of extra hours," he said, feeling defensive, even though he knew he had no reason. "But yes, I'm seeing some-one. I take her out occasionally. We go places...talk."

Dolores's face darkened. "Lucky you. What do you suppose it's like for me? Don't you think I'd like to go out occasionally? Don't you think I'd like a man to pay attention to me?"

Jacobo glanced at the kids and lowered his voice. "Your hus-band's in prison, Dolores. You don't have any business going out with another man. Even if one were to ask you out."

"How do you know no one has?" She drew off her oven mitts and tossed them onto the tray. "Bobby Cedilla was in here the other day, and he said—"

Jacobo rounded the counter and gripped her arms. "Bobby Cedilla's already broken up one marriage, Dolores. Don't listen to what he says. He'd use you and spit you out like sour fruit."

Dolores's eyes teared. "He said he didn't care that I was getting fat or that I had so many kids. He said he thought I was beautiful, Jacobo. Do you know how long it's been since anybody's said that to me? I haven't heard it from Manuel since before Maria was born. Is it so wrong that I just want to be loved?"

She broke into tears, but she angrily wiped them away. "Look at me. I hate being pregnant. I hate being like this. All fat and weepy. Couldn't you stay with the kids one night so that I could go out with Bobby? Just to a movie or dinner?"

"No, I won't. You're a married woman, Dolores. And besides, the kids want to see you."

She laughed shortly. "Why? They like you better."

"That's not true. You're their mother. And Bobby might promise you dinner or a movie, but what he really wants is something else. He's preying on you, Dolores. He knows you're hurt and lonely."

"And desperate," she added. "I don't care about all that. I just want someone to hold me."

"He wants more than holding."

She put her hands on her hips. "You're a fine one to talk. You're a man—you must want more than that from your girl." She looked at him closely. "Unless she's already given you more."

"We're not sleeping together," he said evenly, trying to keep a rein on his anger. "We're just friends."

"Uh-huh." Dolores crossed her arms. "You've been seeing a lot more of your friend lately. First it was church, then it was Saturday night, then Friday night…"

"Not every weekend night, Dolores," he said. "I spend a lot of time with you and the kids, too."

"But not as much." Her voice sounded accusing. "Tell me something. If you're so happy with this *friend,* why haven't you brought her to meet us? Are you ashamed of us?"

Jacobo didn't answer.

She looked closer at him. "That's it, isn't it? She knows who we are…that we're related to Manuel. Well tell me this, then, if she knows that, why is she going out with you?"

"Dolores…"

She squinted at him. "She's not from around here. Somebody would have told me. I'll bet she's Anglo, isn't she?"

"All right." Jacobo spread his hands out. "Yes, she's Anglo. And she doesn't live around here."

Dolores made a little humph-ing noise, then grabbed up a rag and began wiping the glass display cases.

He knew he should let the subject drop, but he was tired of her accusations. She'd be stubborn to her dying day, sticking to her misguided opinions even when she knew them as such.

Jacobo followed her around the cases. "What's bugging you, Dolores? You have Anglo friends too. We've always had Anglo friends!"

Slowly, Dolores straightened from wiping the handprints the kids had left on the glass. "We never *dated* anybody Anglo." She pressed her lips together and went back to her vigorous cleaning. "I knew when you switched churches that it'd be trouble."

"Dolores, if you'd ever once come to my church, you'd see what it's like. I know what you think…that it's a place where only stiff white rich folks while away an hour every Sunday. The truth is, it's more relaxed than the church you attend. I don't go to mass often because the whole ritual doesn't fulfill me anymore."

"You don't go to mass because you can't make any good business contacts there," she said. "You're not interested in the Hispanic community anymore, Jacobo. You want to go out and make a buck just like all those hotshot Anglo lawyers."

"That's not true! I would have been interning at the Hispanic Community Law Clinic in Austin this past summer if it weren't for your stupid husband!"

The children went silent. Jacobo turned slowly, in time to see the shock register on their faces. He groaned inwardly, wishing he'd kept quiet when he knew he should. The Bible was right in saying that the tongue was untamable.

"Kids." He approached them slowly. "I'm sorry I said that about your dad."

They all stared back at him. "That's okay," Frankie piped up. "He *is* stupid."

Jacobo shook his head. "I shouldn't have said that. I'm sorry."

Dolores brushed past him, glaring. "Come on, kids. Go home with Jacobo. I'll be there around dinnertime. Maybe we can play a game or something."

"Chutes and Ladders," Rosita said immediately, clapping her hands.

Marcos looked out the window. "I have to study for a test."

Frankie scowled. "You'll be too tired to play a game, Mama. You always are."

Dolores's shoulders sagged, and an angry look came over her face.

"Come on, guys." Jacobo herded the kids by touching each one on the back. "Your Mom has work to do. Give her a kiss, then let's go."

"Bye, Mama." Marcos shyly kissed her cheek. Jacobo noticed that the anger slipped from her face, and she lightly touched Marcos's cheek.

"Don't study too hard, Marcos, okay?" she said softly.

He nodded, and Rosita wrapped her arms around her mother's legs. "Bye, Mama. I'll be glad when you get home."

Dolores ruffled the girl's hair. "Me too, *mija.*"

Maria touched her mother's hand, then bolted for the door. Frankie scooted clear of Dolores's reach and swaggered outside after the others.

Dolores wiped away a tear and jerked her head at the door. "You'd better follow them. No telling what trouble they're getting into now."

"Yeah." He tried to smile, but only half succeeded. At the doorway, he turned. "There's a letter from Manuel waiting for you. Maybe he's—"

She laughed. "I know what it says. He wants money for cigarettes and candy."

"Don't you think you ought to go see him? And take the kids?"

"No. He said he doesn't want us there. And I don't want to go anyway."

Jacobo felt weary, tired of trying so hard and seeing no results, no changes in anybody's heart, including his own. "Look... Dolores..."

She waved him away. "Go on, Jacobo. There's not much either one of us can do about any of this."

He left the bakery, and the bell jangled merrily behind him. Trudging down the sidewalk, he saw that the kids were already arguing at the Plymouth over who would sit in the front seat with him.

Jacobo sighed. Tonight, Saturday, and Sunday would be family all the way. Leah was away for the weekend, visiting her parents in Houston. Her father was home from the hospital after a successful angioplasty. Jacobo reminded himself to drop a note in the offering plate on Sunday for the prayer team to pray for a full, speedy recovery.

Suddenly he wanted to call Leah, just to hear the sound of her voice. Knowing she was out of the city made him feel empty inside.

Jacobo stuffed his hands in his pockets and hunched his shoulders against the wind. Dolores was right. There didn't seem to be much anybody could do about anything lately.

Leah set aside the novel she'd been staring at for the last ten minutes, unable to get past the page she'd started on. She pulled the covers up high, all the way to her neck, and snuggled under, rolling onto her side.

Beside the lamp, the bedside digital clock glared the lateness of the hour: one-fifteen.

Leah punched her pillow and laid her head back down, frustrated. She should be exhausted. She should be ready to sleep. She'd worked an eight-hour day, skipping lunch so that she could leave early to drive five hours to Houston. By the time she'd gotten to her parents' home, her legs had felt like butter, her eyes burning with road weariness. She didn't even get to see her father, who had already gone to bed.

Leah threw back the blankets and headed downstairs. Maybe a glass of milk would help her sleep.

The light was on in the kitchen, and her mother stood at the stove, her back to the stairs. She stood straight and tall in her dark green silk robe, pajamas, and matching slippers. Leah could see her stirring something in a pan, occasionally stopping to wipe her eyes with the back of her hand.

"Mom?" Leah said softly, so as not to startle her.

Her mother turned, her hand flying to her heart. "Leah! My goodness. Why aren't you asleep?"

Leah smiled, hugging her arms around her flannel pajamas against the chill. "Just like a mom to ask that."

Emily Tyler relaxed, a soft smile spreading across her face. "You never stop being a mom, no matter what."

Leah thought about Galen, and her smile grew bittersweet. "That's true."

Emily cleared her throat and gestured at the pan. "I was making some hot chocolate. Would you like some?"

"Sure." Leah sat at the kitchen table and watched her mother retrieve more milk, sugar, and cocoa. She measured out level spoonfuls of everything, then stirred firmly.

"How's Dad?" Leah said.

"As well as can be expected." Emily continued to stir methodically, her mouth set in a line.

"Is he sleeping well?"

"Most nights."

"This must be one of them, or you wouldn't be out here."

Emily didn't say anything. The spoon smacked rhythmically against the pan—*clack, clack, clack.* "He's fine," she finally said.

"How about you? You don't usually have trouble sleeping."

"Just a little indigestion, I guess." She shrugged.

"So you're treating it with chocolate milk?" Leah grinned. "I hear Pepto-Bismol works better. Come on, Mom, what's really wrong? Are you worried about Daddy?"

Emily set the spoon down in the pan. "Of course I'm worried about your father. What wife wouldn't be?"

"But he came through the angioplasty just fine. The doctor predicts a great recovery. The worst is behind you both."

"He could have another attack. That's how they found this— during his stress test. He had some mild angina then."

"Sure he could have it again. And every one of us faces death every day, Mom. Life can turn on a dime for anybody. But you can't worry about what *might* happen. You have to be grateful for what you have."

Leah realized with a start that she was actually beginning to live as though she were grateful for her life.

"That's easy for you to say." Emily went back to stirring. "The worst that can happen to you is over."

Leah swallowed back her hurt. Did her mother think Perry and Galen's deaths were behind her, like a nightmare recalled during daylight? Or a bad tooth that had been filled at the dentist? "The worst that can happen is with me every day," she said.

Emily looked at her briefly, but never stopped stirring. "Now, Leah. You know what I mean."

"No, I don't." Leah rose and stood beside her mother. "Do you think I've picked up and moved on since Perry and Galen?"

"You seem to be doing well for yourself. You've managed to keep a steady job. You have your own apartment." She pressed her lips together. The spoon clacked louder against the pan. "Danni tells me you have a boyfriend."

"Is that another reason you're so upset?"

"Who says I'm upset?"

Leah smiled. "If you stir any faster, you'll beat a hole in that pan."

Emily set down the spoon and flicked off the burner. "I am not upset. I'm just...worried."

"About Dad."

"And about you. Danni didn't tell your father because she didn't want to upset him, but she told me that this man you're dating is Hispanic."

"I'm not dating him, but yes, he's Hispanic. And he rides a motorcycle. And he's younger than me." *And he's Manuel Garcia's brother-in-law,* she wanted to add for spite. Danni had warned her that their father would hit the roof, but Leah had never thought about their mother.

"How much younger is he than you?"

"A couple of years, I guess." Leah shrugged. "I've never asked him."

"And he rides a motorcycle? What's gotten into you, Leah?"

Leah stewed silently. How could her mother stand in the middle of her spotlessly clean house, in her designer pajamas, and pass judgment on Jacobo? "He's a nice man, Mom. A good friend."

"A friend?" Emily arched an eyebrow. "Men don't want friends out of single women, Leah. They generally want something else."

"Give me a break, Mom." Leah sat back down, suddenly tired. She didn't want to argue with her mother, and she didn't want to talk about Jacobo. Not if her mother didn't want to hear the truth of their relationship.

Emily poured hot chocolate into two mugs and set one in front of Leah. She sat across from her daughter, sipping silently and staring out the window.

Leah sampled hers, found it too hot, and set the mug aside. She followed her mother's gaze at the darkened backyard. Crepe myrtle, honeysuckle, and rosebushes lined the saw-toothed fence. In the spring, azaleas would bloom in profusion back by the gate. Just in front of the window was a small cobblestone courtyard, where a smiling cherub with a pitcher perpetually poured water into a fountain. A wooden and iron bench sat off to the side in an island of ivy ground cover.

Everything in order; everything lovely.

"Leah, your father and I would still like it if you came to live with us," Emily said softly. "The invitation stands."

Leah turned. "It never sounded like an invitation, Mom. More like an order."

Her mother set down her mug. "We've only wanted what's best for you."

"You want to protect me. Now that my husband is gone, you want me to be your little girl again," Leah said. "Don't you see I'm not? I can't live here again like that. I'm a grown woman. I'm making my way on my own and discovering that it's not so scary."

Emily smiled bitterly. "Yes, Gloria Steinem, Mary Richards, and Helen Reddy all rolled into one. You are woman, you can roar."

"Mom…"

"All we want to do is help."

"I'm learning to help other people for a change, Mom. That's what's gotten me out of my apartment. Did I tell you that I'm working in the nursery at church?"

"I think you mentioned it. Though why you'd want to be around so many kids when you lost your own is beyond me."

Leah sighed. "I'll admit it wasn't easy at first. But I still love kids. And they need someone to watch them while their parents are in the church service. It's a way I can help the kids, the parents, and the church."

"I suppose this male friend of yours is Catholic, if he's Hispanic. This isn't *his* church you're talking about, is it?"

"Yes, it's his church. He was nice enough to bring me to it. And no, it's not Catholic. It's nondenominational. He was raised Catholic, though, if it makes you feel any better."

Apparently Leah's attempt at humor was lost on her mother because she didn't laugh. Leah watched her, sipping her hot chocolate daintily, mentally forming her next line of interrogation.

"I suppose his parents live in Mexico. He probably swam across the Rio Grande and worked his way up from migrant worker status."

"His parents are dead," Leah said evenly. "And I don't know when his family first came to Texas. They could have been here before Texas was part of the United States, for all I know. It's not like Hispanics are newcomers to the state."

Emily set down the mug. "Leah, I know you think I'm being prejudiced, but I'm not. I'm not saying Hispanics or anybody else is inferior, but they're different from us. Their culture is different. And that's fine, but I don't want to see you get hurt because of the differences. You probably wouldn't fit in with his family any more than…"

"…he would fit in this one. You haven't even met him, and already you've judged him! Did you know that he wants to be a lawyer? He dropped out of law school because of the wreck just to take care of—"

Leah broke off. She hadn't meant to tell anybody so much about Jacobo yet, not until she was clear herself about where their relationship was headed.

"What wreck?"

She should have remembered that her mother never missed anything. Leah exhaled heavily. "Okay, Mom. You're bound to find out sooner or later. But it won't make you happy. Jacobo…my friend…is Manuel Garcia's brother-in-law."

She expected her mother to be angry. She expected her to purse her lips and make some remark about crime running in the family. What she didn't expect was to see a single tear slip down her mother's cheek. "Oh, Leah…," she said softly.

"He's a nice man," Leah said quickly. "He's taking care of his sister and her family. She has five kids. I've met two of them, Mom. It's hard for them, having a father in prison."

"So I suppose you think he should be set free?"

"No, of course not. But I'm trying to remember that they're just kids. Two of them have been out with Jacobo and me. One of them is really sweet, Mom…a little girl. The other…a boy…well, he's a troublemaker, and to be honest, I'm not crazy about him.

234

But I'm trying to be sympathetic—toward all the kids. They don't really understand what's going on."

"Do you?" Emily folded her hands in front of her. "Because all I know is that my daughter's practically a stranger. She's turned her back on the family who raised her, and now she's turning her back on her dead husband and child."

Tears sprang to Leah's eyes. "Don't do this, Mom. Please don't."

"Are you so lonely that when that…that man came sniffing around, you invited him into your life just like that? Don't you see what he's after? He's using your love for children to get what he wants out of you—which is obviously a physical relationship. And heaven knows what else. Probably to get you to give that murdering family money. Or maybe to speak on behalf of the murderer himself so that he can get out early."

"He didn't come *sniffing around*, Mom," Leah said, blinking back tears. "I went looking for them. I drove by their house… because I wanted to see what it was like, what they were like. And I nearly ran over his little five-year-old niece. I…I wrecked the car, and he took care of everything—made sure I got home safely, even got my car fixed. He's a Christian, Mom. A nice man. Why can't you accept that?"

Emily rose and set her mug in the sink. "I'm going back to bed, Leah. You should do the same. Your father will want to see you tomorrow, and I know you'll want to be rested."

"We're just friends!" Leah clenched her fists. "Would you rather I'd committed suicide? Because I was that close, one way or another."

Emily stopped in the doorway, and her hand went to her head as if to rub away an ache. "Leah, it's late. You drove a long way, and you're tired. You're saying things you don't mean now."

"Stop telling me what I mean or don't mean!" Leah slapped her hands on the table and rose. "You don't know what I mean. You don't know what I feel. You haven't, ever since Perry and Galen died, but you act like you do. All you know is what you want to believe. Daddy's the only one who even halfway tries to understand, and he's—"

Emily kept her back turned, and Leah could see her draw a sharp breath. "Good night, Leah." She flicked off the light switch and swept around the corner toward the master bedroom.

Hands still clenched at her side, Leah stood in the darkness, staring at the spot where her mother had been.

The rest of the weekend, Leah barely spoke with her mother. The longest conversation they shared was the next morning, when Emily drew her aside and whispered furiously that she'd told Leah's father nothing of what Leah had revealed the night before.

"I don't want to endanger your father's health, and something like this could send him right over the edge," she said. "Besides, this itch you seem to have will likely subside, and you'll move on to someone more suitable. Then this whole ugly incident will be nothing but a skeleton you and I keep hidden in the family closet."

Leah hadn't said anything, knowing that to protest would be futile. She concentrated instead on spending time with her father, who looked pale and thinner than she remembered, despite the fact that the doctors had given him a good report.

They'd danced around the subject all morning, and she'd finally worked up the courage to ask. "Nothing to it," he said, smiling. "The angioplasty was a piece of cake."

Leah sat gingerly on the bed, by her father's side. "And they say you're doing okay?"

"Right as rain." He winked at her, the way he'd always done when she was a little girl. "How about you, Leah? You making out all right?"

"I'm fine, Daddy." She smiled, but the effort felt forced.

"Time for lunch!" Emily entered the bedroom, a heavily laden tray balanced across her hands. "Leah, plump up your father's pillows, would you?"

"I'm fine, Em," Hart grumbled, sitting up as Leah dutifully stuffed them higher behind his back. "Your mother spoils me silly," he said, exaggerating a whisper.

"And well she should," Leah said, giving a final pat to the pillows. "You should take it easy. Let yourself be pampered."

"No chance of that. I've got too much work to do." He smiled. "My clients need me. Investments don't wait for an old man to recuperate."

Old man.

Leah looked at her father. He did look old. Suddenly old. Tired. Vulnerable.

Mortal.

Leah swallowed and forced herself to smile. "You take it easy, Daddy. Let one of your partners handle the work."

Emily brushed past Leah and set the tray across her husband's lap. "I'm sure your father knows best, Leah. Besides, he had a good start on the road to recovery while Danni was here."

"I wish I could have come sooner too," Leah said to her father. "But my office—"

He patted her hand. "I know, honey. We didn't think a thing about it."

Emily rattled the lid to the teapot as she poured. "No, darling, of course not. We're just glad you could take time from your busy schedule to come for the weekend."

Leah felt her face warm. "I would have—"

"Hush, dear." Emily smiled. "Not another word. You have no business playing nursemaid when you're still in emotional straits yourself. Isn't that right, Hart?"

He smiled sheepishly at Leah. "You certainly don't need to worry about me. Or your mother," he said. "You have your own life to take care of." He reached out and squeezed her hand, lowering his voice. "I'm very proud of you, honey. I always knew you were a scrapper."

Leah's eyes misted. She didn't feel like a scrapper. More like an unwilling participant in a fight with an invisible adversary—not someone who came out swinging straight to victory.

Emily leaned between Hart and Leah to tuck a napkin into her husband's collar. "Eat your lunch now. Leah, why don't you call some of your old friends and let them know you're in town? You could make a day of it—lunch, shopping at the Galleria..."

"I'm sure they're busy with their families today, Mom. All my friends here in Houston have kids. It's Saturday."

Chewing vigorously, Hart waved the uneaten portion of a cinnamon-raisin bagel, then swallowed. "Why don't you two go out for the day?"

"And leave you alone?" Emily looked shocked. "Of course not!"

"Oh, come on, Em. I'm fine. And if it'd make you feel better, Owen said something about coming over to watch the Golf Channel. You two could have a real girls' day out. You said yourself you'd like some time to look for a new coat."

Emily slanted Leah a look. "If Owen is coming, I'll stay home this afternoon and make something special for dinner."

Hart laughed. "It's not like he doesn't show up nearly every Saturday for a home-cooked meal, Em. Go out with Leah and have some fun."

Leah watched her mother's expression shift for just a moment, then she was smiling the facade that Leah had always thought of as the determined, suffering martyr. "You know I'd love to spend the day with Leah, Hart. But there's so much to be done here. I'll give her the keys to the Cadillac and the American Express card and let her enjoy herself."

Leah gritted her teeth. "I have my own car, Mom. And my own credit card."

"Don't be silly, dear." Emily swiveled toward her as though she had just realized she was in the room. "This is our treat. Go get whatever you'd like. Have a facial. Have a massage. Treat yourself like a lady…for a change."

Leah curled her fingers into her palms and rose. For the sake of her father, she'd ignore her mother's baiting. "If Mom's going to be busy around here, and you and Owen are going to settle in to watch a boring golf game, maybe I will head out to the mall—by myself," she said, with as much breeziness to her voice as she could muster. The truth was, she did need the time alone—but to think, not shop.

"Have some lunch before you go." Her mother smiled sweetly, taking her place at Hart's side.

Faking a smile, Leah shook her head. "I'll grab something at Chick-Fil-A."

"Fine, dear," her mother said vaguely. She'd already turned to her father and started feeding him bites of tuna salad.

"For crying out loud, Em, I'm not paralyzed!"

Leah headed for her car.

Getting away from her mother didn't make her feel any better. She didn't want to shop. She didn't feel like driving around. She wished she were back home—she wouldn't stay holed up in the apartment, but she'd at least be content to go to the Purple Onion and chat with Louise. Or go to the Kimbell Art Museum. She and Jacobo had talked about seeing the latest show, a traveling Picasso exhibit.

Or maybe she'd just be content to ride behind him on the back of his bike, wrapping her arms tightly around him as they zipped in and out of traffic. With each ride, she grew less fearful of and more attuned to the exhilaration of motorcycle riding.

Leah pulled her car into a Mobil station and cut the engine. She leaned back in her seat and closed her eyes.

She missed Jacobo. She wanted to talk to him about her family, to try to get him to understand their quirkiness, then help her figure them out. It hurt that her mom was shutting her out—shutting her out yet still trying to run her life. If she didn't want Leah around, why didn't she just say so? Why did she continue to make Leah feel guilty for not coming to Houston sooner, then make her life miserable once she got there?

What was Jacobo doing? She knew he didn't usually work on Saturday afternoon, but watched his nieces and nephews while his sister worked. He didn't talk about her—Dolores—much, but Leah knew he was devoted to her kids.

Leah grabbed her purse and the car keys and headed toward a bank of pay phones at the side of the gas station. Her heart pounded as she rummaged in her purse for change; she'd never once called Jacobo at home. In fact, she'd never called him at all. Most of the time he phoned her at work to arrange an outing; he seldom even phoned her at home, as though he didn't want to intrude.

She didn't even know his phone number.

"Manuel Garcia," she said at the sound of the information operator's voice, then followed the hated name with the street address. Leah scribbled the number on the cover of a dog-eared phone book, then punched myriad buttons to make the charge to her calling card. Miles away, a phone rang. Leah's heart pounded.

"*¿Bueno?*"

A woman's voice. Dolores. Leah's heart beat double time. "Is…is Jacobo there?"

"Yeah…who wants to know?" the woman said suspiciously. Two children argued in the background, and she shushed them in Spanish, with little success.

"Uh…Gail. From the office." Leah winced at the lie.

"Yeah…" Leah thought she heard Dolores smirk. "Hang on… Jacobo!" She didn't make any attempt to cover the mouthpiece. "It's a *Gail.* From your office."

Leah could hear him walking toward the phone and taking the receiver from his sister. The children's voices grew louder. "Thanks, Dolores… Gail?" he said into the mouthpiece.

Leah let out a long breath, leaning against the plastic side of the open phone booth. "Jacobo. It's me. Leah."

"Yeah, I thought so." He sounded as though he was turning away, for the noise of the children grew muffled. "Is everything okay? Is your dad all right?"

"Yes… No… I don't know…" She had the absurd impulse to weep. "I…I wish I were home."

He drew a deep breath, which she could barely hear. One of the children was now crying. "I wish you were too."

"I thought your sister would be at work."

The children's voices grew distant, as though he were walking as far away as possible from the fighting. The crying followed, however, and then the female Spanish admonitions.

"I'm sorry, but I can't come to the office today," he said. "My sister's home sick from work, and I need to help her with the kids."

She sounds fine to me. Leah bit back the words. "She's right there beside you, isn't she?" She paused, then said in a rush, "I'll be home tomorrow afternoon. Can you come to my apartment for dinner? I'd really like to talk to you." She paused again. "I miss you."

He hesitated just a moment. "Me too. Yes, I think we should meet then and discuss the situation. Tell me when would be a good time for you."

"How about six?"

"That's a good time for me, too." His voice sounded all business. The crying in the background abruptly stopped. "Thank you for calling. I'll be in touch."

Please don't hang up. She couldn't stand the thought of going back to her parents' house. "Okay," she heard herself say. "Good-bye."

The receiver went dead, and she hung it back on the heavy pay phone with a loud *clunk.* Traffic whizzed past at a major intersection, and she trudged back to her car.

She drove idly up and down streets. She didn't want to go to the mall and fight the crowds—she wanted quiet. A place to contemplate everything that was happening in her life—her dad's health, her mother's coldness.

Jacobo.

Leah turned in to the iron-gated cemetery, parked near the entrance, at the chapel, and stepped from her car. A funeral service was in progress, judging by the line of cars behind a black limousine waiting outside the chapel door. The chauffeur leaned against the driver's side door, humming a popular rap tune as he examined his nails. He stopped humming and momentarily lifted his face to the sun, closing his eyes as he drank in the fall warmth.

Leah smiled as she walked past, stepping up her pace. Ordinarily she drove all the way to the back, but today, like the chauffeur, she wanted to enjoy the warmth. The brisk walk felt good, and by the time she reached her destination, her blood was racing.

She veered into the center section, underneath the giant oak, toward the two gravestones set so close together that Perry and Galen could have been holding hands. Here, far back from the street traffic and even the solemn gravel lanes inside the cemetery, all was quiet.

Leah dropped to the grass between the graves. She wished she'd brought flowers. Real ones, not the cheap plastic kind that mourners laid on graves in hopes of a permanent tribute. No, she preferred cut flowers that at least lived in full beauty and abundance before time withered their blooms.

Grass had grown over each grave, and the earthen mounds had been flattened by the wind and rains. Leah stretched out her hands, burying her fingers in the broad-leafed Bermuda. "I miss you both," she said softly.

A breeze rippled her hair. Overhead in the old oak a blue jay squawked.

Leah hugged her knees to her chest and studied the names on the gravestones. *Perry Travers. Galen Travers.* What did strangers walking past think when they saw those names? Could they visualize the man her husband had been, the beautiful child that was her son? Did they notice the identical dates of death and wonder what had caused them to be taken together?

Her stomach clenched. She hoped Manuel Garcia was rotting in prison, was enduring unspeakable torture. Nothing that happened to him could ever equal what he'd done to her family.

243

And Dolores…Leah didn't care what happened to her either. Unlike Leah, Dolores had a choice in the outcome of her life, and she'd chosen to marry a drunkard. Worse still, the woman didn't seem the least bit sorry about that choice. Her overly emotional attitude during the trial…even her voice on the phone today… Why did Jacobo bother to help her?

Instantly Rosita and Frankie and the Garcia children Leah had never met came to mind. Surely they didn't deserve to suffer because of their mother's foolish choice or their father's sin.

Leah thought too of the children in her nursery class at church. Some of them came from broken homes—alcoholic parents, imprisoned parents, divorced parents…

She glanced at Galen's grave, then dropped her head to her knees. "Why him, Lord? Perry and I loved each other, we loved him. We didn't abuse him, we didn't hurt each other. Couldn't you have taken another child? A child who maybe wouldn't have been missed?"

Shame flooded through her. Who was she to say such things? What if someone asked her to pick one child to be killed from the entire nursery class she taught on Sundays? Could she declare that one human was more expendable than another?

And who was she to turn her back on her family—to have not only survived, but to have as her one true friend a close relative of their killer?

In the quiet of the breeze and the shade of the tree, with the normal, perpetual sounds of nature around her here in the land-scape of departed souls, despair rose inside Leah. She stretched out her hands to touch the gravestones—both of them cold and lonely, as cold and lonely as she felt.

Chapter Seventeen

"You're running off to see *her*, aren't you?" Dolores snapped off the hot water faucet and set the final rinsed dish in the drainer. She and the children had already eaten dinner.

"I'm not running off, Dolores." Jacobo shrugged into his leather jacket and struggled to keep a lid on his annoyance. He'd spent the entire weekend with the family, feeling more like a captive than the helper he was supposed to be. Dolores had such a severe backache after returning home from work on Friday that she hadn't been able to go to work on Saturday. And the children had outdone themselves in crankiness, teasing and tormenting and haranguing each other—so much so that with everything going on, Jacobo was glad for the least excuse to leave the house.

And even more glad that it was to see Leah.

Dolores dropped into a chair. "So her name's Gail, huh? That's a good Anglo name."

He turned, exasperated. "Would you stop fishing already, Dolores? Her name's not Gail, it's Leah. A good, strong, biblical name."

If she made the connection between the Leah he was dating and the Leah at Manuel's trial, then so be it. He was sick of her cat-and-mouse games. He'd held off telling her only because he'd wanted her to get used to the idea that he was dating anyone, much less Leah Travers.

"Leah." Dolores looked pensive, then her expression suddenly shifted to a wince. She leaned back in the chair and rubbed her rounded stomach. "This baby is really starting to kick."

Jacobo softened. He moved behind her chair and kneaded her shoulders. "This one's a *luchador,* eh? A fighter."

He felt some of the tension leave her with a sigh. "In more ways than one," she said. "He's been fighting for his life ever since I've known about him. If not for you, he wouldn't be here. I'd have gotten rid of him."

"You would have come to the right decision once you'd had time to get used to the idea. You *did* come to the right decision."

"But I wouldn't, if you hadn't convinced me." She turned and looked up at him. "I don't know why you always bail me out, Jacobo. Especially where Manuel's concerned. You and Mama never lectured when I found out I was pregnant with Marcos—you just went about arranging a wedding for Manuel and me."

"What were we supposed to do? Mama loved you, Dolores. You don't abandon people you love, you support them."

She smiled bitterly. "Then you must love me an awful lot."

"I do." He touched her cheek. "You know I do. I love you and the kids with all my strength, Dolores. I hate seeing you hurt, seeing you suffer."

Dolores sighed, turning her face away from his hand. "Maybe I should just divorce Manuel. Surely God would understand that he hasn't exactly honored our marriage. Maybe it'd be best if I just moved on and found another father for the kids."

"Someone like Bobby Cedilla?" Jacobo drew up a chair and took her hands. "Listen to me, Dolores," he said gently. "I know it's tough. I know what you're going through, what the kids are going through. But one day Manuel will be out of prison. Until then, you're still family."

"Why do I care? That's twenty years from now! Besides, he'll probably just get drunk again and kill somebody else. It could even be one of us next time."

"And maybe he's getting the chance in prison to rethink his life. People do rehabilitate." Jacobo studied her. "Don't you even want to go see him, to ask him in person how he's doing? When's the last time you even wrote him?"

She shrugged. "I don't remember. A few months ago, I guess."

"How do you expect your marriage to get any better if you don't work at it?"

"Marriage isn't supposed to be work."

"But it is supposed to be love. And love takes time. Commitment. Especially through the hard spots. I stood in the church and heard you promise your love to Manuel until death parted you."

She raised defiant eyes. "Death did part us, Jacobo. The death of that man and his little boy. How can I love a killer?"

"You don't have to love what he did, only the man. The man that God sees and loves and forgives even before he asks. If you believe in such a God, a God of mercy, then you have to be willing to seek such a love yourself. Only then can you share it with others. With Manuel. The Lord has to be the foundation of your marriage, Dolores, or it won't stand."

"But I don't want it to stand! I want a clean break and a new start. I want a better life, a better husband for me and father for my kids. Is that so horrible?"

"No. Except that you're looking for a mere man to fulfill those desires when the Lord of all creation is ready to give them to you."

"Jesus." Dolores made a tired face. "You're always talking about him as though he's some kind of magic formula. A cure-all for what hurts."

"He is, Dolores. All you have to do is turn to him. And then you'll find the love you need for Manuel. And I'm praying Manuel will turn to him too."

She smiled ruefully. "I'm glad you don't expect me to be the one to constantly turn the other cheek. Manuel's the one responsible for all this. He should be the one to take the rap for our bad relationship."

Jacobo smiled, squeezing her hands. There was much more he wanted to say, but she wasn't ready to hear. Like so many wounded souls, she was waiting for all the wrongs against her to be righted before she would consider forgiveness. She would have to learn for herself that the Lord didn't operate that way, nor did he expect it of his children.

Dolores groaned, leaning forward as she pressed a fist against the small of her spine. "If my belly isn't hurting, it's my back. It figures that this would be the worst pregnancy I've ever had. God's punishing me."

"No, he's not." Jacobo rose and planted a kiss on the top of her head. "If anything, this pregnancy is more difficult so that your joy will be more complete when you finally get to hold your baby."

He turned toward the doorway. "Marcos! Maria!"

It took a few more tries before they heard him over the sound of the Looney Tunes cartoon blaring from the television, but at last the two eldest children appeared in the doorway.

"Take care of your mom while I'm gone, all right? She's going to go lie down." When Dolores started to protest, he said, "Yes, you take it easy. Marcos and Maria can take care of the other kids while you rest."

Dolores smiled tiredly and rose. "All right, Jacobo. Go and see your Leah. When you come back, maybe you'll tell me why she called herself Gail on the phone." She paused. "Would you consider bringing her around to meet us sometime? Or have you not forgiven us?"

"What's there to forgive?" He shrugged, then made his way toward the door. "Get some rest, Dolores. Take care of yourself."

She looked at him a moment, then nodded. "You too, Jacobo. If you fall, the rest of us do too."

The words felt like a weight on his back as he headed for the motorcycle.

"I'm glad you could come," Leah said, opening her apartment door wide. She held out her hand for his jacket, then hung it up in the small entryway closet.

Jacobo stood just inside the door, unsure and uncomfortable. Always before, he'd only lingered a moment while she grabbed a sweater or made a last-minute check in the mirror before they left. Tonight he was staying, by her invitation.

Immediately, he shoved his discomfort aside. It wasn't as though she'd invited him to spend the night.

She shut the closet door and smiled. "Have a seat. Dinner will be ready soon. I made King Ranch casserole."

"Great," he said, though he had no idea what that was. Probably an Anglo dish, lumpy and bland.

Ay, Jacobo, you're starting to sound like Dolores.

Leah joined him on the couch, seating herself a respectable distance away. She looked pretty tonight—but then she always looked pretty—in black leggings and a thick cotton sweater. Its bulkiness didn't do much to detract from her womanly curves, and he looked away, embarrassed at the turn of his thoughts.

"How's your father?" he heard himself say.

Leah didn't respond, and he chanced a look. She stared down at her hands. "I don't know. They say he's doing well, but he looks old all of a sudden. Maybe I've been too busy with my own grief the past year to notice that he's aged."

"The angioplasty went all right?"

"Yes."

"And your mom? How's she handling this?"

"She hovers over my father, looking after him. But with me…" Leah bit her lip.

"What?"

She raised her face, and he saw tears in her eyes. "She accuses me of not caring about them, about my father, because I didn't visit them sooner. I tried to explain that I couldn't leave my job, but she turned a deaf ear. All weekend long, she criticized me, especially for being too independent."

"Has she treated you like that before?"

"No. But only because I usually did what they wanted. It was what Perry and I argued about the night he died."

Jacobo didn't say anything, waiting for her to continue. Leah looked back down at her hands and clenched them together. "I told her about you," she mumbled. "She wasn't very happy."

"Should she be?"

"Yes." She looked up, incredulity spreading across her face. "Why not? We're friends, Jacobo, aren't we?"

He moved closer, hastening to reassure. "Of course. It's just that on the surface, we have a lot of differences. To other people, anyway."

"She's horrified. No matter what I said, she wouldn't change her mind." Leah glanced away. "She thinks we're sleeping together."

"It's a logical assumption, Leah. According to the world's standards, at least."

"It's ridiculous. She'd know the truth if she saw us together. There's nothing between us."

Jacobo caught her eye, then saw the faint blush across her cheeks. "I'd be lying if I agreed with you," he said. "You're an attractive woman, Leah."

She didn't look away, but smiled shyly. "To be honest, I don't think about how I look to anybody else."

Desirable. Very *desirable.* "You look fine," he said instead, then cleared his throat. "So she knows who I am?"

Leah nodded. "I didn't intend to tell her or anybody else, but it just slipped out—not that I'm ashamed of our friendship," she added hastily.

"You don't have to explain. I understand." He thought about Dolores, and he cringed. Maybe he should have been up-front with her from the beginning. But he'd had no idea he and Leah would develop such a close relationship, and by the time he realized it, Dolores had started prying so intently into his private life that he wanted nothing more than to keep it completely to himself.

He would have to correct that. He couldn't shut Dolores out of his life with Leah, and he couldn't shut Leah out of his life with his family. They were all a part of him—who he was and where he was going.

For better or worse.

"While I was in Houston, I went to see Perry and Galen's graves."

Jacobo looked up. Leah was twisting her hands together in her lap, as though she were trying to keep from saying more. But since she'd brought the subject up—a rare chance for her to vent her grief—he wouldn't let it drop. "How was it?"

"The grass is growing over them. It's very pretty where they're buried, actually. I had a chance to sit and think for a long time."

Jacobo edged closer. "What did you think about?"

"About children. About why mine was taken, when there are so many in the world who are unwanted. Why doesn't God take those?"

Jacobo thought about Dolores's baby, but didn't respond. He didn't have an answer.

"Perry and I loved Galen. I loved Perry. Maybe that's why I'm being punished. Maybe I love too much."

He shook his head. "You can never love too much. The Lord never does."

"Then why does it still hurt so much? Why am I left alone?"

Jacobo wanted to tell her about Dolores—that she, too, felt alone even though her children survived and another was on the way. Loneliness wasn't about people but about a personal relationship with the Lord. To a person estranged from him, loneliness was just a relative word.

"Your road is one that the Lord himself walked…the road of grief. In his hour of need, everyone abandoned him. Including the God of the universe."

Her mouth tipped up. "I'm not the Lord. I don't have his knowledge of the future or his strength."

"No, but you have his promise to be with you always. And you have his joy… That's the key to our strength, Leah."

"Then I have very little strength." She straightened. "While I sat at Galen's grave, wondering why some unwanted child couldn't have taken his place, I remembered something I hadn't thought about in a long time. Something I never told anyone."

She wiped her hand across her eyes. Jacobo instinctively moved closer, until their legs brushed.

"When Perry and Galen died, I thought I might be pregnant. After their funerals, I was certain I was. I held on to that hope of new life so tightly…"

She wiped her eyes again. "I woke up one night bleeding so heavily that I headed straight for the emergency room."

Jacobo's throat tightened. "I'm so sorry."

"The doctor said I'd never even been pregnant." She raised her eyes to meet his. "Can you imagine that? It was a double loss— Perry's child that I thought I was carrying and then the child that I knew I never would have."

"Leah…" He cupped her cheek, wiping away a tear with his thumb. How could God bless Dolores with yet another child and leave this woman with empty arms? "Oh, Leah."

"I drove through the night all the way to the coast… Galveston. I went to the beach where we'd spent our summer vacation. I…I wanted to kill myself."

She closed her eyes, remembering. "I was kneeling in the sand, and a wave knocked me over and pulled me under. I was scared… so scared…"

Jacobo wrapped an arm around her shoulders and drew her

close. He could feel her shaking, feel the tremors of grief emanating from her soul.

"I prayed. I cried for help. And the tide pushed me up onto the beach." She opened her eyes. "I was still alone, but I felt something—I *heard* something—in my heart, telling me to come."

"And you chose to live."

She nodded. "But I've been broken ever since. Some days I think things are better, then I have to go back to the same place, the same grief. Over and over." She closed her eyes again and leaned back, letting her head rest against his shoulder. "I'm so tired."

"Leah…" He could hardly speak past the lump in his throat. "Leah, I've prayed for you from the moment I first got Dolores's phone call about what Manuel had done. I didn't know you then, or when I saw your name listed under your husband and son's obituaries in the paper. Or when I brought a flower to those crosses by the side of the road. But I've been praying for you all along."

She raised her head. "Why?"

He stared into her eyes, wondering why he'd never seen how clear they were, or how deep.

How could he explain that what many in the church might call a burden to pray for her was really more of a privilege?

Jacobo drew a deep breath. "I felt it in my heart," he said. "Just as I feel now that God brought us together for a reason. To help each other."

She smiled bitterly. "How can I help you?"

"By reminding me of hope. Of courage." He touched her cheek. "Of love."

He leaned closer, his heart pounding, his lips mere inches from hers. He started to pull away—knew he should pull away—but she closed her eyes and tilted her head back.

Jacobo couldn't even remember the last time he'd kissed a woman, and he had the absurd thought that maybe he'd forgotten how.

Leah reminded him. She returned his kiss, slowly, wrapping her arms around his neck, drawing him closer, drawing him past the emotional shield she normally pulled around herself for protection.

She turned her head, and his lips touched the soft flesh below her ear. "Jacobo," she murmured, a sigh that slipped past her lips as she subtly, unknowingly, shifted lower on the couch, drawing him over her. An innocent movement as old as time and as enticing as the apple in the garden.

Jacobo closed his eyes and drew a quiet, steadying breath, burying his face in the crook of her neck. She smelled sweet and soft, and her skin felt firm and smooth. Reluctantly, he kissed the tiny pulse in her throat and sat back, putting distance between them.

He raked a hand through his hair. *Lord, what have I done?*

"I'm sorry, Leah," he said hoarsely, as she straightened beside him. "I don't want to endanger our friendship. If I have…"

"No," she said gently, laying a hand on his arm. "Please don't apologize. I…It was…nice. I…I haven't been held in such a long…"

She trailed off and looked away, but not before her expression betrayed her embarrassment at having revealed so much. Jacobo turned her face back with his hand. "Then I'm not sorry. There's nothing wrong with needing another's embrace."

"I just don't want you to think that I'm..." She winced. "I know it's silly in this day, at my age, but I haven't had a date since college."

He looked at her a long moment. "Are we dating now, Leah?" he finally said.

She held his gaze. "Do you ever plan to kiss me again?"

"Yes." He was thinking about kissing her right now, but he couldn't trust his common sense to counteract the adrenaline racing through his veins.

"Then I think we can safely say we're dating."

He draped an arm over the back of the couch. "Does that bother you?"

"No." A slow smile crept across her face.

He couldn't help grinning in return. "What?"

"My mother thinks I'm engaged in a wicked, torrid affair with a Hispanic lover... At least you don't have to face such prejudices."

His smile faded. "Actually, I do. My sister isn't happy that I'm dating an Anglo woman."

"Really? Why?"

"I'm not exactly sure."

Leah frowned. "Why is it your responsibility to take care of her? Can't someone else?"

"Neither of our brothers lives in the area. She's my younger sister, Leah. What would happen to her and the children if I stopped supporting them?"

"Can't you send them money while you go to law school?"

He smiled faintly. "I can barely support myself when I'm in school."

When I'm in school...

The dream was rapidly fading.

"But surely they could get food stamps or government assistance."

"I can't let my family live off the government. The kids need good, solid food. And Dolores needs..."

Leah crossed her legs and swung her foot. Jacobo hated to tell her, hated the irony of the situation.

"Dolores needs good, solid food too." He paused. "She's pregnant."

She stopped swinging her foot, and her face crumpled. "When is her baby due?"

"In about six weeks."

He could see her do the mental calculation. "So this is Manuel's baby."

Jacobo nodded. "Dolores was surprised."

Leah's mouth quirked. "I imagine. I'm surprised myself, though I guess I shouldn't be. God has a strange sense of humor, doesn't he? Taking my child...leaving all of hers...and then giving her another." She hesitated a moment. "Does she even want it?"

When Jacobo didn't immediately say anything, she crossed her arms. "That figures too," she said.

He touched her arm. "Does this change things between us?"

"I don't know. Rosita, I can sympathize with. Frankie, maybe. The other kids I haven't met. I didn't like Dolores's attitude at the trial, and she was rude to me when she thought I was Gail from your office. What does she think of Leah, your friend, the woman whose family her husband killed?"

Jacobo dropped his hands and looked away. He could feel Leah staring at him, and at last he turned to meet her gaze. "She doesn't know. What with the kids and this pregnancy and her working so hard...and she and Manuel haven't spoken or written to each other in months..."

"I'm sorry to hear that," she said bitterly. "I assumed they had a beautiful relationship."

Jacobo frowned. "It hasn't been easy for Dolores either, Leah. People are cruel to her and especially cruel to the kids. They're constantly teased about their father being a child killer."

Tears sprang to Leah's eyes. "They have my complete and utter sympathy."

"Leah..." He spread his hands wide, then clenched them together. He hadn't felt this helpless in a long time. He wanted to help Leah, he wanted to help Dolores. Yet it didn't seem possible to assist both, not without trampling on loyalties one way or another.

Lord, I've been praying and praying, but you don't answer. What do I do?

He didn't want to risk this growing relationship with Leah, but he didn't want to put her through any unnecessary hurt either. He cared for her too much to ask her to endure any more emotional strain. "If you don't want to see me anymore..."

Her expression softened. "I do, Jacobo. I just don't understand. It seems like I should be the one outraged about your family, yet Dolores seems to be more sensitive. I don't know why I should care, but I do."

"That's because *you're* the one who's more sensitive. In a good way. I've come to know you over the past few months, Leah, and your heart is wide open."

"And obviously laying out for anyone to trample on."

"Isn't that better than hiding it?"

"I don't have a heart," she said softly. "It shriveled up a long time ago."

"No, it didn't." Jacobo smiled gently. "It's growing. You first met me at the coffee shop, then the zoo, because you cared for Rosita's feelings. Then you met us again at the museum because you knew how much it meant to Rosita. I watch you on Sunday while you care for your nursery charges. You love them, Leah, even though you lost your own child."

"I've always loved children," she said softly. "That much hasn't changed."

"Exactly. You hid in this apartment for a long time because you were hurt and lonely and scared. Your parents wanted to tell you what to do, and you didn't let them. But while trying to be independent, you shut everybody out."

"Everybody except you," she said. "The one man—related to the one family—that I should have nothing to do with."

"Why, Leah? Because of Manuel? Maybe that's exactly the reason you and I are together."

"Our meeting was just timing, Jacobo. I nearly ran down Rosita, and you happened to be there."

"Timing, yes, but God's timing."

She looked at him hard. "You think there's some ulterior reason for God bringing us together?"

"What do you think?"

Leah drew a deep breath. "I think you want to say that we're together because I'm supposed to forgive Manuel and help Dolores and all her children and then everything will be rosy, and everyone will live happily ever after."

"I hadn't pictured it quite like that."

"But that's basically what you believe."

"I know that God calls us to forgive."

She rose, and he could see her hands shaking. "Forgive what Manuel did? Why? Can forgiveness undo what was done? Are you asking me to grant it so that Manuel can have a future, when I'll always have none? Is he even sorry for what he did? Has he ever shown even a flicker of repentance?"

Jacobo listened to her anger and bitterness, fully expecting it. He knew the deep emotions she carried inside her, yet as she vented them one by one, he was surprised they resonated with those feelings in his own heart.

Had he ever forgiven Manuel for all the wrongs he'd committed down through the years? Had he forgiven Dolores for giving in to the teenage lust that forced her and Manuel to get married? Their wedding had set back his own future, his entrance into college, just as their current dire straits now prevented him from achieving his one dream of graduating from law school.

His heart echoed the cries of Leah's. *Why should I forgive either of them? Have my goals been so sinful that you wouldn't grant them? Yet time and again, I've set them aside so that I could cover the consequences of Manuel's and Dolores's choices.*

Earlier that evening Dolores had acted almost contrite about her past, yet she had asked him point-blank if he'd forgiven them. He'd shrugged off her question with one of his own: What was there to forgive?

Had he never seen the sin of unforgiveness that he harbored in his own heart, or had he merely covered it up all these years so that he wouldn't have to face it?

Lord, oh Lord...

"I wish Manuel was dead," Leah said in a low voice. "I've wished him dead so many times. During the trial I even imagined—*dreamed*—about killing him myself."

Jacobo snapped to attention with her words. "Leah..."

"You wanted to bring me out into the world again, Jacobo, but why? Why should I want to live in a society that allows things like this to happen?"

"He's in prison, according to the law. A law set up by society."

"And according to the law, he wasn't supposed to kill anybody. But he murdered my husband and my baby as surely as if he'd held a gun to their heads."

"I know that, Leah. I'm not saying you should excuse the crime…only forgive a man who made a bad mistake. There are others suffering too. I know you realize that, deep inside. My sister is pregnant, virtually alone, with five children who desperately need their father. Not only for financial support, but to be there for them. To raise them. Love them. Now not only is he gone, but they have to bear the shame of his sin."

"Don't you dare try to make me feel sorry for them, and for him. Don't play on my sympathy for children that way."

Jacobo rose beside her and touched her arms. "I only told you that to make you see that you're not alone. His sin affects many people."

"But you're asking me to forgive based on his wife and children!"

Jacobo shook his head. "I'm not asking anything, Leah. But I do know that the forgiveness you refuse to release is the bitterness that worms its way into your soul. And by holding on to it, you keep yourself from the fullness of God's joy. He loves you, and he wants the best for you."

He drew a deep breath. "The act of forgiving is for your sake, Leah. Not Manuel's."

A timer dinged in the kitchen. Leah stepped away, smiling sardonically. "Saved by the bell. I hope you're hungry. This recipe makes enough to feed a small army."

Jacobo watched her walk toward the kitchen, her shoulders squared in determination. She was fighting his words, and more than that, the word of the Lord. He wanted to talk to her more, to try to explain again what he knew to be true in his head even if he didn't yet know it in his heart.

But the window of opportunity had been lowered—though somehow, he sensed, not completely shut.

Leah lay in bed, listening to the night noises of her apartment. The refrigerator hummed in the kitchen, punctuated by the occasional sound of ice dropping in the icemaker. The wind whistled through a mulberry tree outside, and its branches brushed softly against her bathroom window. Two cats—no doubt Mrs. McLoughlin's tabby and Mr. Cormack's Persian—meowed and hissed at each other from a nearby ledge.

Safety. Familiarity.

Leah snuggled under the covers. The deep depression had gradually faded over the past months, leaving behind not quite hope, but numb optimism.

Jacobo had gotten her out of the apartment, out of hiding. First to the zoo, then the museum, then church, then myriad other places. Public places. Places where she had to interact with other people.

Especially church.

Leah doubted that anyone at Good Shepherd had ever met a stranger. From the first day she'd attended to the day she and Jacobo had talked to Nick about her working in the nursery, they had all been enthusiastic and cheerful. Friendly.

Joyful.

Infectiously joyful.

Truth be told, Leah hadn't thought her sorrow-filled life would fit in with the adults, so she'd contented herself with helping in the nursery. She'd quietly burped and diapered babies, wiped toddlers' tears when they'd taken the inevitable spill, and given juice to kindergartners.

And in between the diaper wipes and sipper cups, she'd found a tiny measure of peace growing in her soul. When she stopped to marvel at its presence, it would shy from her like a shadow trying to be caught by a child.

"You're so wonderful with Francesca," Marta Spinelli had confided in Leah. "Every Saturday she talks about coming to see Miss Leah the next day." She lowered her voice. "And it's such a blessing for me to have the time to worship with other adults for an hour."

Marta was a single mother whose boyfriend had run off long before Francesca's birth. She worked hard to support herself and her preschool daughter, but when she'd spoken to Leah, her face had looked unusually drawn.

"Is Marta all right?" Leah had whispered to Sylvia, another nursery worker. "She looks ill."

Sylvia fastened the top snap on wiggly Jonathan Simms's baby suit and held him lovingly against her body. "Marta has AIDS," she said quietly. "Some days are better than others for her."

"AIDS? But...but Francesca..."

"She's tested negative so far, but Marta's more concerned about what will happen to her if—"

Jonathan's mother had appeared at the doorway then to collect her baby, and Leah had been left standing alone in the middle of the colorful rag rug where they told Bible stories. Marta's situation made Leah want to sit down and weep, as some of the children did when their parents first dropped them off.

"Marta's talking to a childless couple in the church about adopting Francesca," Jacobo had told her later when she asked. "She thinks it might be best if a gradual transition is made before she becomes incapacitated."

"But she's always so happy! I never would have known anything was wrong if she hadn't looked ill."

"Marta knows the Lord is watching over her daughter. Nick's already promised her that he'll personally take care of Francesca, if necessary. Other people have volunteered too."

Lying in bed, Leah thought about Marta and others she'd met or heard about who were ailing. Besides Marta, others were stricken with incurable illnesses: cancer, multiple sclerosis, lupus. Others were going through painful marital problems: divorce, abandonment, spousal abuse.

If Good Shepherd seemed to be unusually joyful, it also seemed to have its own personal corner on suffering. Almost as if the two were connected.

"Impossible," Leah said to herself, rolling to her side.

The moon shone through a gap in the curtains, and she smiled. When she was a little girl, Daddy had told her the moon was God's night-light, symbolizing his watch over her while she slept.

If she believed Jacobo, God was still watching over her, caring for her. Loving her.

And not only that, but he had actually brought them together. To help each other.

Leah hugged her pillow close, savoring the remembrance of his kiss, yet feeling guilty for being in the arms of a man besides Perry.

But at the same time, she felt physically and supernaturally cared for—loved—as she hadn't felt in a long, long time.

Chapter Eighteen

When Jacobo pulled up in the driveway, he saw a light shining in the kitchen window. Dolores had waited up for him, even though it was well past the children's bedtime.

Any other day he would have been glad to spend time alone talking with her, but he wanted to think over his evening with Leah. During and after dinner, they'd spoken of minor subjects—a play the church youth were performing, repairs he needed to make to his bike, a project she was editing at work.

But always at the front of his mind—and hers, too, he suspected—was the kiss they'd shared. And the words he'd spoken about their being brought together.

Were they true? Or was he just so desperately lonely that he was taking advantage of a woman whose heart had already been cruelly broken?

Dolores held open the side door for him, shivering in her worn flannel bathrobe. "Come inside and warm up," she said in Spanish. "You must be miserably cold, riding around on that motorcycle."

Thinking of Leah 'the entire ride home, he'd actually been quite warm. "I'm used to it," he said, answering back in Spanish as he shut and locked the door behind him. "Why aren't you in bed?"

"I couldn't sleep."

Dolores seated herself at the table and stirred sugar into a cup of coffee. Jacobo grinned. "Drinking that won't help."

She shrugged, sipping on the brew. "I didn't figure it would matter. Morning comes soon enough, doesn't it? And I was hoping this would help warm me up. Maria and Rosita kept putting their cold feet on mine."

Maria and Rosita shared a bed with Dolores, while Marcos, Frankie, and Carlitos slept in twin beds and on a pallet in the other room. Jacobo slept on the couch.

He sat beside her at the table, weary, and accepted the cup she poured for him. Lacing it with sugar, he then sipped slowly. The warmth did feel good.

Dolores lowered her cup. "So how was Leah?"

"She was fine." He continued sipping, hoping that Dolores would take the hint and go back to bed.

"And she made you dinner?"

"Yes."

"So..." Dolores gestured, wanting more details. "Can she cook?"

King Ranch casserole had turned out to be some sort of cut-up chicken smothered in mushroom soup with a few green chilies. Filling, but rather bland. Nothing like the spicy tamales and *guisados* the women in the neighborhood prided themselves in creating. "Yeah, it was okay," he said.

"Just okay? Maybe it was the company that was worth staying so long for."

Jacobo set down his cup. "Yes, it was. Look, Dolores, I know you're curious about Leah. You've always been curious about women I dated."

"When you do date them."

She leaned back and lowered her voice. "You deserve a nice woman, Jacobo. Someone to settle down with and raise your own family." She paused. "After you get that precious law degree, of course."

Did she think he'd still be able to get one? How would he ever have the time? And as for settling down...

He cleared his throat. "Leah *is* a nice woman. And I'd like to bring her to meet you and the rest of the family. Maybe have dinner over here?"

"Sure." She studied her hands in her lap. "Even if she is Anglo, I should probably give her a chance."

"Yes." He took another sip, hoping the caffeine would give him extra strength. Now was the time, but he didn't want to tell Dolores the truth; he was already tired from going the rounds with Leah. "Dolores?"

"Hmmm?" She didn't look up from her mug.

"Leah..." Why was this so hard? "Before you meet her, you should know that Leah is the wife and mother of the man and child that Manuel killed."

Dolores stopped drinking but didn't lower the cup. She stared at him over the rim, her eyes dark and accusing. He had the absurd impression that she was putting a curse on him, and he nearly crossed himself, as Abuelita Felicidad used to do when she felt she'd been touched by the Evil Eye.

I'm yours, Lord. There's nothing that can hurt me under the shadow of your wings.

Except knowing that someone I love is hurt.

Dolores set down the cup and drew a deep breath. "Now I see what's happening. This Leah...she's the one who nearly hit Rosita. She deliberately tried to kill her!"

"No, Dolores. Leah risked her own life to avoid hitting her."

"Then what was she doing in our neighborhood?"

He wished he had a better answer; Dolores would never understand. "She was hurting. She thought if she could see where Manuel lived, where his family lived, that she might be able to understand why her family had been killed."

"And does she?" Dolores smiled bitterly.

"Of course not. There's no answer for that, not this side of heaven, anyway."

Dolores rose and stepped away from the table, away from him. She leaned back against the sink and crossed her arms. "The answer is that she's using you, Jacobo, and you're putting me and the children in danger. She wants to pay us back for what Manuel did, I know it. She's playing up to you by giving you what you want as a man just to get to us. And being a man, you're so taken with her, you probably won't even notice when she *does* hurt us!"

"That's not true." Jacobo tried to keep his voice low, mindful of the sleeping children. He gripped his cup. "She's not like that. What happened with Rosita was an accident. But the good that the Lord brought out of it was that Leah and I got to know each other. She has no desire to hurt you or the children. What good would it do?"

"What good?" Dolores laughed. "Revenge! The satisfaction of knowing that she hurt Manuel like he hurt her family. The joke would be on her, though, wouldn't it? Because Manuel wouldn't care in the least if anything happened to us."

"She doesn't want revenge. She just wants to get her life back...or what's left of it."

"Ha. She has a great life. I saw Daddy at the trial. He makes big money…some kind of investment counselor, right? What could she possibly need?"

Jacobo got to his feet, gripping the mug until his knuckles turned white. "She lost her husband and her son, Dolores. Do you think money matters? Do you think money can make a person happy?"

"I don't know," she shot back. "I've never had any. I've never had real love, either, so don't start lecturing me on how that's all we need to really live."

Jacobo drew a deep breath. *Lord, I can't deal with her anymore. She's self-centered and stubborn. She doesn't care what anyone's ever done for her. She doesn't even want to listen!*

Comfort her.

No. She won't care.

She's afraid.

Then you take care of her. You're the rock…the fortress…the deliverer. Not me.

Jacobo slammed his mug down on the counter beside Dolores, and she winced. "*No tienes vergüenza*, Dolores. You have no shame," he said. "I'm going to sleep. Good night."

"Jacobo…" Her face softened, and she touched his arm.

He shook it off and headed for the bathroom, where he got ready for bed. When he went to the front room, he could see the kitchen light was off. Dolores's bedroom door was shut.

He thought he heard her crying, but he settled into the lumpy couch—as he did every night—and turned his face away.

"I'm sorry she took it so hard," Leah said, suppressing a sigh so that Jacobo wouldn't hear on the other end of the phone. She swiveled toward the wall of her cubicle, lowering her voice. She knew the coworkers around her wouldn't deliberately eavesdrop, but sometimes voices carried.

"I wanted to introduce the two of you soon, but I don't think that'll be possible."

"That's all right." Leah wasn't certain she was ready to meet Dolores anyway.

She heard someone from the law firm ask Jacobo a question in the background, and he covered the mouthpiece and gave a muffled answer. "Look, I have to go," he said to her. "We're working on a big case here. Can I take you out for coffee tonight? I need to talk to you."

She leaned back in her chair, surprised. It had been four days since she'd last seen or heard from him—four days in which she assumed he'd changed his mind about her.

After hearing him detail the conversation with Dolores, she now wondered if he'd avoided phoning because his sister had changed his mind for him. "I'd like that," she said, swallowing back the suspicious question that came quickly to mind: *Are you going to let me down easy?*

"I'll be there at seven," he said. "Bundle up. It's supposed to be chilly."

"Okay."

As she hung up the receiver and listlessly opened a new file to proofread, she wondered what kind of chill he was referring to.

They shared the same side of a booth at the Purple Onion. Jacobo ordered two black coffees from a sour-faced dowager who had none of Louise's good humor. Leah's favorite waitress was nowhere to be seen, and Leah thought she remembered that Louise's shift was over well before the dinner rush.

When the coffee came, Jacobo didn't reach for his, but leaned back and studied her. "How've you been?" he said.

"All right." She blew lightly on the steaming brew, then took a sip. It scalded her tongue.

He leaned forward again. "I've been thinking about you, Leah. About us."

Just get it over with, Jacobo. "And?"

"And the deck is stacked against us."

Her heart tumbled, and she swallowed a lump rising in her throat. "I know," she whispered.

"Your mother doesn't like me; my sister doesn't like you... I know that in this day and age, families don't have the same influence that they used to. Maybe that's good." His mouth hitched up at the corner. "But in my culture—in my heart, especially—family means a great deal."

Leah set down her mug. "You don't have to say anything else. I understand."

"I don't think you do." Jacobo took her hands. "Leah, I've thought about you, prayed about you, for the past four days. And the answer I keep coming up with is that even though we have so many odds against us, even though we have a future that's no more certain than winning this Saturday's lottery, I don't want to let go of you. I want to see this relationship through until one of *us* says it should be ended. Not my sister, not your mother, not anybody else."

He studied her intently, and a worried look crossed his face. "That's how I feel, anyway. How about you?"

She nodded, finding her voice only now, as relief sank in. "The same. I value your friendship, Jacobo." She hesitated a moment. "I care for you."

He smiled slowly, a warm, tender expression that made her stomach dance. "I care for you too," he said softly.

Without realizing it, she leaned forward, and he kissed her— much more quickly than she would have liked, but then she remembered where they were.

Jacobo moved away a fraction, but didn't release her hands. She thought he would smile again, but his expression was sober. "Leah, we're going to have to go slowly. I don't want to substantiate what your mother and Dolores already believe about us. You deserve better, and maybe once they realize this relationship isn't based on physical desire alone, they'll get used to the idea."

"Maybe," she said, but felt doubtful. From the look on Jacobo's face, she could see he had doubts about their families too.

Fall moved into winter, and Leah found herself relaxing into a comfortable routine—work, life at her apartment, and time spent with Jacobo.

The work and habitat aspects of her life were pleasing. She got along well with her coworkers and even participated in department functions, and her home was no longer a cave of refuge from the world. She bought living greenery—spider plants, ferns, and ivy— Aztec-motif throw rugs, and brightly colored abstract prints for the walls. She played CDs while she cleaned and puttered around the apartment—Mozart and Beethoven, Oldies rock, Christian alternative, a Selena CD that Jacobo brought to jokingly educate her on Hispanic music.

Though she didn't think of life as great, or even good, it was better and somewhat less confusing.

Except where Jacobo was concerned.

Leah sensed a distinct shift in their relationship. It had deepened—and they saw each other as much as before—but there was something bittersweet. An undercurrent that they needed to enjoy their time together now because something might happen to change it.

No one knew better than she the fragility of life. Not a morning went by that she didn't awaken with Galen and Perry on her mind. The precious days they'd had together were gone, never to be retrieved.

When she looked at Jacobo, she saw a man she was growing to care for deeply, and she didn't want to make the same mistake twice. She wouldn't take him for granted as she had Perry. She wasn't going to worry about where their relationship was headed; she would simply treasure each day, each moment together, as a gift from God.

Another Christmas without Galen and Perry came, and this year she found herself, if not standing in the hopeful circle of the season, at least on its perimeter. Her mother was as cold as ever, refusing to sit with Leah and Danni as they giggled like schoolgirls during late-night popcorn gabfests in the kitchen.

"Don't you feel strange...knowing that he's related to that man?" Danni said as she and Leah converged at the table the night after Christmas.

"Yes, but Jacobo isn't like him. He doesn't even drink. He's a good man, Danni." Leah drizzled melted butter over a fresh batch of popcorn. "He'll make a good lawyer."

"What kind of law does he want to practice?"

"Criminal, I think."

"Prosecution or defense?"

Leah shook the last drops of butter from the pan. "I don't know. I never asked."

"Well, if he looks anything like that hunky Hispanic detective that used to be on *Law and Order,* he'll have a jury eating out of his hand... He's nice looking, isn't he?"

Leah stopped halfway to the sink, pan in hand. She thought about Jacobo and smiled.

"Aha! I thought so." Danni scooped up a handful of popcorn. "I predict you two will be headed for a different kind of justice one day...a justice of the peace."

"What, a wedding?"

"'What, a wedding?'" Danni teased, her mouth full of popcorn. She swallowed quickly and smiled. "Of course! And why not? You deserve some happiness, Leah. And if Jacobo's half as wonderful as you say..." She dropped her chin in her hands, sighing. "Does he *really* ride a motorcycle and wear a leather jacket?"

Leah laughed, returning to the table. "It's not as much for show as it sounds. Leather's the best material to wear in case you take a spill."

Danni winked. "Maybe he'll get you a matching jacket. You know...one that says something like *Biker Babe.*"

Laughing, Leah tossed a kernel of corn at her sister, and Danni quickly retaliated with her own popcorn barrage.

Hart Tyler shuffled into the kitchen. "Your mother thought a band of monkeys had gotten loose in the house."

"Oh, hi, Daddy," Danni said cheerfully, leaning over to pick a piece of popcorn out of Leah's hair. Leah returned the favor, and they broke into a fresh wave of giggles.

When they managed to control themselves, Leah held out the bowl to her father. "Want some popcorn?"

Hart smiled as he took a seat beside Danni. "No thanks. Butter's not on my diet anymore."

"It's not on my diet either, but that never stops me." Danni covered a yawn. "I'm heading for bed."

"You just want me to clean up the mess," Leah teased, pitching another kernel at her sister.

Danni picked it up off the floor and tossed it back at Leah. "Good night."

"Good night, honey." Hart watched her head out of the kitchen, then he turned back to Leah, his eyes still twinkling. "It's good to see you two laugh together. Like when you were girls."

"It feels good to laugh." Leah smiled slowly, sadly. "Sometimes I feel guilty…"

"Don't." Hart reached out and gripped her hand. "You should never feel guilty because you're alive." He smiled warmly at her and, still gripping her hand, rose. "Come here."

"What?" Leah said, following as he led her into the darkened living room. He motioned for her to sit on the sofa, and he plugged in the Christmas tree lights. "Oh, Daddy…"

She was tired of Christmas—she always had been the day afterward. This year, as last, she was not only weary of the holiday itself, but the entire Peace on Earth atmosphere.

The large multicolored lights glowed brightly, steadily. No light would dare blink on Emily Tyler's perfect Christmas tree. Leah could barely make out the evenly matched angel ornaments that decorated the pine branches, and she thought about the hodgepodge of ornaments she and Perry had accumulated during their short marriage. One of their final acquisitions had been a Mickey Mouse's Baby's First Christmas.

A tear slipped down her cheek, and she hastily wiped it away as her father sat beside her. He was silent a moment, staring at the tree, and she swallowed to keep more tears from rising.

"Isn't it beautiful?" he said softly.

"It's just a tree, Daddy." She didn't want to look at it anymore; she was glad the holiday was over. Christmas would never be the same.

"It's not the tree that's so beautiful, honey, it's the light."

She wiped away another tear. "It's just a strand from Kmart or Target or someplace. They don't even blink."

"They don't have to." Hart put his arm around her and drew her close. "I sat in here last night, long after everyone else went to bed, and I saw something I've never seen before."

"What?" She supposed she should humor her father.

"Do you remember when you were a kid, and you'd help me check the lights before we strung them on the tree?"

"Yes."

"Do you remember what would happen when one bulb wasn't working?"

"Yes, you'd curse a blue streak because we had to check every bulb," she said, smiling gently. She leaned against her father's shoulder, remembering the simplicity of life then.

He chuckled softly, remembering along with her. "I was furious because if one bulb wasn't working, the entire strand was useless. Each bulb depended on the others."

Leah swallowed hard. "They've improved lights since then, Daddy."

He tightened his arm around her. "Yes, they have. But they still do what they're intended to do, and that's what I saw for the first time last night. I can't believe it took me so many years to see it."

"What?"

"The top," he said softly. "Look at the top of the tree."

Leah raised her eyes to the crystal star Emily had carefully arranged on the uppermost branch. A white bulb glowed inside, and the crystal refracted its light in shining brilliance.

"All the other lights—the blues, reds, oranges, and greens— follow each other on one strand up to that light. They all shine together, each one its own color, but it's the star that lights the way. The star of hope, Leah. The star of life."

"Daddy…" Her throat tightened with emotion.

"Having the heart trouble made me think about life. And I realized that each one of us is like a light on that strand—each different in our own way, but leading upward."

"Not me," she said softly, choking back a sob. "I've been one of those burned-out bulbs for a long time now. Where do I fit?"

Hart took her in his arms. "You're the bulb closest to the star because you need its light the most," he said softly. "Don't you know how closely the Lord of hope has been watching over you all this time?"

"Daddy…" She buried her face in his shoulder. His words were so unlike her father, so spiritual. It sounded more like something Jacobo would say. Thinking of him made her feel guilty all over again, and she sobbed against her father's bathrobe. "Daddy, I miss them so much."

"I know you do, sweetheart," he said softly, smoothing her hair as he'd done when she was a child. "I miss them too. I spent all Christmas Day thinking about how much fun it would have been to watch Galen tear into his Christmas presents."

Leah couldn't help but laugh, even as she sobbed. "He really ripped into them that last Christmas, didn't he?"

"Yes, he did. He loved surprises."

"He was really surprised by that Fisher-Price farm set we gave him. He played with it all Christmas Day, remember?"

"And the Blue's Clues figures."

Leah laughed gently. "We had to pry Blue from Galen's hand after he'd gone to sleep. Then Perry set it down and we couldn't remember the next morning where it was, and…" She broke off, feeling a bittersweet sting. "Those are just memories. It'll never be like that again, Daddy."

"I know, but you'll make new memories, Leah. Different memories." He hesitated. "Danni told me you're seeing someone."

Leah stiffened. "What did she tell you?"

"She said that you seemed very smitten with this young man, and that if I wanted to know more, I should ask you."

Leah gently eased herself from her father's arms.

"Leah?"

She turned toward him and saw the light from the tree reflected in his eyes. He was watching her, a gentle expression on his face, and he reached out and took her hand.

Leah drew a deep breath and told him everything, starting from the time she'd run into Jacobo in the hallway of the courthouse during Manuel's trial, to three days ago, when he'd stood at her apartment doorway after they'd finished some last-minute holiday shopping and kissed her good-bye.

Maybe it was the soft glow of the holiday lights or the fresh scent of the pine tree that made her feel heady, but she found herself telling her father how much she cared for Jacobo and how he had made such a difference in her life.

When she finished, he was silent. Only then did she recall her mother's warning not to tell her father.

"Honey,…Leah," he finally said. "You haven't actually used the word, but it sounds to me like you love this man."

"I…I guess I do." She paused. "And I guess you're thinking, like Mom, that I've gone off the deep end."

He shook his head. "I was thinking more along the lines of your inviting him down here some weekend to meet us."

"Really?" She squeezed her father's hand. "You mean that?"

He nodded. "You're a grown woman, Leah. Do you think I don't trust your common sense?"

"You didn't right after Perry and Galen died."

"No, and I was wrong. Your mother and I both were."

"She thinks I'm still a little girl," Leah said bitterly. "She still won't admit I can take care of myself and actually make intelligent decisions about my life."

"She won't admit it to *you*, maybe, but she knows you're capable."

"Then why does she keep harping at me to move home?"

Hart smiled sadly. "One of the things you'll never know about Galen—though God willing, maybe you'll have other children— is the pain of watching him grow up."

"*Pain?*"

He nodded. "All you'll ever remember is a two-year-old you had to watch every minute to make sure he wasn't getting into the Drano or wandering outside the house. The older your child gets, the more you have to trust him to make his own decisions. Little by little he pulls away from you, out of the shadow of your parental wing, until he's ready to fly from your nest."

"And that's what I am. That's what I've been for a long time."

"Yes, but when a mother sees her child hurting—no matter

how old she is—her first instinct is to protect that child under her wing again." His voice softened. "And for someone like your mother, whose greatest joy and only goal in life was raising you kids, it's particularly difficult."

He kissed her on the forehead. "Don't worry about your mom. She'll come around. And now you'd better get some sleep if you don't want to fall asleep driving back to Fort Worth tomorrow."

"I'm not ready to go," she said softly. "I'd like to spend some more time with you, Daddy."

"You've got a job to get back to. And Jacobo." He smiled, cupping her cheek. "After the angioplasty, I realized how precious life is and how we should grab hold of the joy God's given us and not question it. Talk to Jacobo about coming here to meet us, okay?"

She nodded solemnly.

"Think he'd take an old guy for a spin on that motorcycle?"

She laughed, picturing her father in his best business suit on the back of Jacobo's bike. "Oh, Daddy."

He kissed her again, on the tip of the nose this time, and rose. "Good night, Leah. I love you."

"I love you, too," she said softly.

Sitting alone in the darkness, she hugged her knees to her chest and stared up at the colored lights and prismatic beauty of the crystal white star.

Jacobo had left a message on her answering machine, telling her he was going out with his nieces and nephews and wouldn't be back in until late.

He was sorry he hadn't gotten to talk to her—he wanted to hear about her Christmas. He'd be at work the next day and would probably be busy with a case, but he'd call as soon as he could.

He'd thought about her. He'd missed her.

Leah played the message twice, just to hear his words. She'd missed him too, missed his voice. She'd considered calling him from her parents', but she hadn't wanted to risk talking to Dolores.

He must have felt the same way about her mother because he hadn't called her either.

She tried hard to concentrate on work the next day, but every time the phone rang she jumped. Usually it was another coworker, inquiring about her holiday, but finally, thirty minutes before it was time to leave, she heard Jacobo's voice. "Merry belated Christmas."

She smiled, relaxing in her chair. "Merry Christmas to you, too. Did you have a good holiday?"

"The kids had fun. We bought a little tree and decorated it. Dolores made her special tamales."

Leah was quiet for a moment. "How is she? She must be close to delivering her baby."

"Less than a month. She's tired, but she's healthy. We're all healthy… That's a blessing."

"Is she still upset with you?"

"She's upset with life in general." Jacobo paused. "How were your parents?"

"My father and I had a very good talk. My mother didn't speak to me much."

"I'm sorry, Leah."

"My father wants you to come to Houston to meet them."

"That's a good sign. If he accepts us, surely your mother will too."

"I don't know…"

"Hey, I was thinking about heading out to the coast when the weather gets a little warmer. Maybe we could stop by Houston on our way…if you'd like to go with me, that is."

I'd love to. But she couldn't picture sharing a beach house together, being in such close quarters…

"I thought we'd ask my old roommate, Eric, and his girlfriend to go with us. You and Karen could share a room. You'd like her."

Leah let out her pent-up breath. "It sounds like fun."

"Why don't I come over tonight? I'm leaving here soon—I have to stop by the house, then I'll be at your place by six."

"Great. I'll make chili."

She hung up the phone, smiling, then started to head for Wanda's office to deliver a document. The phone rang, and she wheeled back to her cubicle, thinking of Jacobo as she picked up the receiver. "Don't tell me you can't make it after all," she teased.

"Leah?"

"Danni?" Leah could barely make out her sister's voice over the sobbing. She clutched the folder to her heart and dropped in her chair. "What's wrong?"

"It's Daddy! Mom…" She could barely speak. "Mom asked me to call you."

"Danni, get ahold of yourself." Leah said sharply, her stomach clenching with fear. "What's wrong with Daddy?"

"He's had a heart attack. He's in intensive care. Oh, Leah, I know you were just here, but you'd better come back. Quickly."

Chapter Nineteen

Numb with shock, Leah gripped the folder against herself and headed for Wanda's office. She ignored several coworkers' greetings, keeping her head down, hoping the tears didn't show.

Oh, Lord, not Daddy!

"Thanks for bringing this so quickly," Wanda said, holding out her hand. "I—" She took one look at Leah. "What's the matter?"

Leah bit her lip. She didn't want to say anything, didn't want to be a bother. Wanda was probably sick of her problems. "I…"

She glanced up at Wanda's sympathetic face and burst into tears. "My father's had a heart attack."

Wanda swiftly closed her office door and took Leah in her arms. "Oh, honey. I'm so sorry."

"I just…saw him!" she sobbed against the lapel of Wanda's immaculate business suit.

"He's not dead, is he?" Wanda said gently.

Leah shook her head.

Wanda set Leah down in a high-backed leather chair and handed her a box of Kleenex. She punched an office extension on the phone, tapping her foot. "Betsy. Leah's father has had a heart attack, and she needs to leave right away. Call American and get her a flight to…" she covered the mouthpiece and turned to Leah. "Intercontinental or Hobby?"

"Intercontinental is closer."

"Intercontinental, Betsy. And call me back when you know the flight time. Make it as soon as possible, but give her time to run home and throw some things in a suitcase. Yes, put it on the corporate account."

Leah dabbed at her eyes with a Kleenex. "That's very kind of you," she said, when Wanda hung up the phone.

Wanda glanced at the picture of her grandkids on her desk. "You just get there in one piece, okay? Do you know what hospital he's in?"

Leah nodded.

"Can somebody pick you up at the airport?"

"M-my sister's still in town for the holidays. I'll call her from the airport."

"Call her from DFW before your flight leaves. If I know Houston traffic, by the time she gets to Intercontinental, you'll already be there. Now, do you want me to take you to your apartment to pack a bag? You don't look like you should drive."

"I'm okay." Leah drew a deep breath and pressed a Kleenex against the rim of an eye. "I'll get Jacobo…my friend…to take me."

Wanda smiled and patted her on the arm. "Then get going. And call me tonight or whenever you get a chance and let me know how he's doing, all right? People here will want to know."

Leah nodded, knowing that they would. Not for curiosity's sake or for the opportunity to dissect her grief among themselves over the water cooler, but because they genuinely cared.

She gave her boss a kiss on the cheek. "Thank you, Wanda. You're the best."

Wanda put her hand to her face, her eyes wide with surprise. "Why...get on with you, girl." She waved at the door. "I'll call you at home with the flight information just as soon as Betsy calls me."

Leah headed for her apartment, then changed her mind and cut across two lanes to turn around. She didn't want to wait for Jacobo to reach her apartment, she needed him now.

Her hands were shaking as she pulled onto his street. She hadn't been here since she'd nearly hit Rosita. Mindful of that, she slowed down and drove carefully. Surely he'd had time to get home already.

When she didn't see his motorcycle in the driveway, her heart fell. She started to wait in the car, but then she realized he might park the bike around back.

She flew up the steps and rapped on the door. Someone opened it a crack, not even enough to pull the security chain taut. "Yes?"

Leah heard a TV blaring in a back room. She peered into the dim interior of the house. "Is...is Jacobo here?"

"You're Leah," the woman said flatly.

"Yes."

The door closed, and Leah started to rap again, but she heard the rustle of the chain disengaging. The door opened wider, and a pregnant woman stood beside it, with her hand on the knob. She jerked her head toward the room's interior. "Come on in."

"Th-thank you." Leah stepped inside, turning toward the woman, but she was no longer standing at the door. Confused,

Leah turned again, and this time she saw the woman bending over awkwardly to turn on a lamp.

"You're Dolores."

Her face unreadable, the woman nodded, moving forward. Leah instinctively backed up a step, but held out her hand. "I...I'm glad to meet you."

Dolores briefly slipped her hand into Leah's, then gestured at a ratty tweed sofa. "Please, sit." She smiled, but her eyes snapped with malice.

Leah perched on the edge of the sofa, curling her hand around its arm. "Wh-where's Jacobo? He told me he was coming straight home."

Dolores shrugged, flipping back a strand of long, dark hair. Leah could see the family resemblance in her facial features, but Jacobo's sister had nothing of his kind expression. "I don't know where he is. He doesn't tell me everything...even though eventually I manage to find out."

She leveled a look at Leah, who then dropped her gaze to Dolores's large abdomen. It twitched with the baby's vigorous kick, and Dolores ran her hand over the movement and placed her other hand at the small of her spine. She closed her eyes briefly and pressed her lips together.

Leah sympathized. She remembered how uncomfortable she'd been in the last two months of pregnancy. "Jacobo said your baby's due in less than a month," she said softly, trying to put aside the memory of Galen for now. Maybe she could at least engage Jacobo's sister in polite conversation until he got there.

Dolores's eyes flew open. "Probably more like any day now. Each one of my children has made an earlier appearance."

"Do you know if you're having a boy or a girl?"

"No, and I don't really care one way or another. I've had both, and they pretty much cry and go through diapers at the same rate."

"Leah!" Rosita ran into the room and raced to the sofa.

"Rosita! How are you?" Leah wanted to hold out her arms to the girl, but Dolores looked on with distinct disapproval.

"Frankie!" Rosita turned toward the hallway door. "Leah's here!"

"I'm busy!" he called from the back. The volume of the TV increased a notch.

Rosita's face fell. "I'm sorry."

Leah patted her arm. "That's okay, honey. Boys always seem to have something to do. I know my brother always did. But I'm glad to see you."

"You too! Mama, do you like Uncle Jacobo's friend? Isn't she pretty?"

Dolores folded her arms across the shelf of her stomach. "Yes, Rosita. Very pretty."

A motorcycle roared up the street and into the driveway. Leah was out the door and at his side before he cut the engine.

"Leah!" He removed his helmet and shook out his hair as he got off the bike.

Her eyes filled with tears. "My father's had a heart attack, and I need to get to the airport to fly to Houston. Will you take me?"

"Of course. Have you been home to pack?"

She shook her head. "I came straight here from work."

Jacobo glanced at the house. Dolores stood at the bottom of the steps. "How long have you been here?" he said to Leah.

She followed his gaze. "About ten minutes."

Jacobo sighed and, taking Leah's hand, started over to his sister. She shot them a disapproving look and headed back inside.

Jacobo turned to Leah with an apologetic expression. "Was she mean to you?"

"No." She hadn't been overly cordial, but she hadn't been outright rude either. "We got along all right."

Jacobo stared at the house for a moment, then turned. "Let's take your car, Leah. It'd be a cold, windy ride all the way to the airport on my bike."

As Leah threw some clothes into the suitcase, Jacobo listened to her telephone messages. They had to race to the airport to make the flight Betsy had arranged, but they made it just as the passengers were boarding.

Once he saw her safely on the plane and the plane safely off the ground, Jacobo headed home to make a few calls and to pack his bag.

Dolores stared at him darkly. "You're leaving," she said, her voice accusing.

Jacobo tossed his duffel bag on the couch and stuffed an extra pair of jeans at the bottom. "She may need me, Dolores."

"*I* may need you, Jacobo. What if the baby comes while you're gone?"

"Then you'll call a cab to take you to the hospital, and Mrs. Vasquez will watch the kids."

"What about your job?"

"I called and told them there was an emergency. I'm due a few days off anyway."

Dolores blocked his way as he headed toward the duffel bag, carrying a small stack of clothes. "I knew it would come to this," she said in a low voice. "I knew you'd choose her over us."

"I'm not choosing her over anybody! What's your real problem, Dolores?"

"The problem is that you're not like us anymore, Jacobo! You spend every night in this neighborhood, but you live in an Anglo world. You went to school there, you work there…now your love life is there too. You're one of them." Her eyes filled with tears. "How do I know you'll even come back this time?" she said in a ragged voice.

Exasperated, Jacobo set the clothes down. "Look, Dolores…" When he straightened, he saw that she had turned away, trying to hide the fact that she was crying.

Dolores was not a woman to use tears as manipulation.

Softening, he put his hands on her shoulders and turned her around. "Dolores…," he said gently, then lifted her chin with his hand.

She stared at him defiantly, and he smiled. It was easy to see where Frankie got his rebelliousness. Dolores had always been a fighter, had never settled for giving in. Jacobo wiped a tear from her cheek. "I'm coming back, Dolores. You can't get rid of me that easily."

"I don't want to get rid of you," she whispered. "You're all I have left. How would I manage without you?"

"You'd manage fine because you're a strong woman. But I'm not leaving you or the kids. Don't you know I'm committed to taking care of you?"

"What about *her?* Are you committed to her, too?"

"In a certain sense, yes. We haven't talked about any sort of future together, but it may be there. I hope that it is. But that doesn't mean I'm going to abandon you and the kids."

"Why shouldn't you?" Dolores angrily wiped away another tear. "Your life would be better without us."

For a brief moment, Jacobo considered the truth of the statement. Without Dolores and her kids, he could have whatever he wanted—law school, a place of his own, a *life* of his own. Leah.

But when he looked at his sister—hugely pregnant and exasperating though she was—or thought about his nieces and nephews, reality hit home.

He couldn't deny that which called him to be patient, to be kind, to bear all things, believe all things, hope all things, endure all things.

Lord, forgive me. None of those things mean anything compared to my sister and her kids. Even Manuel. My sin is against them for harboring unforgiveness toward their actions all these years, but more important, it's sin against you. Oh, Lord. Forgive me.

Jacobo smiled. "Why do I stay? Because you're *family.* Because I love you. That's never going to change no matter what happens, Dolores. Even if I choose to love Leah, too."

"Is that how you feel about her?"

"Yes," he said without hesitation. "And that won't change—I won't let it change—just because it makes you uncomfortable."

Dolores stepped away, her shoulders sagging with defeat, and gestured at the door. "Then go, Jacobo."

He stuffed the clothes in the bag, then kissed her on the cheek. "I'll call you when I get there. And I'll be praying for you while I'm gone, okay?"

She nodded. "I'll light a candle for her father," she said grudgingly. "You tell her that, all right?"

"I will." Jacobo gave her another kiss, then was out the door.

"They're controlling his arrhythmia with drugs," Danni said, the soles of her running shoes squeaking along the hospital linoleum. "But they had to use the defibrillators in the ambulance."

"His heart stopped?" Leah rushed to keep up with her sister. She dodged a candy striper pushing a metal cart filled with flowers and caught up with Danni at the elevators.

"No, but it was beating too erratically," Danni said as they stepped into the open elevator.

It quickly filled with people. Leah bit her lip, anxious to hear more but unwilling to discuss her father's condition around strangers. When they stopped on the cardiac-care floor, Danni pushed her way through the crowd, and Leah trailed in her wake.

"How's Mom?" Leah panted, trying once again to keep up as Danni race-walked down the corridor.

"She's not well. When I left to go get you, they were talking surgery."

Surgery! "Oh, Danni."

"Mom nearly collapsed when they took Daddy out of the ambulance. Owen's with her now, but I think she relies more on our support."

"But..." Leah's words were lost as Danni pushed through a frosted glass door into an empty waiting room.

A jolt of remembrance swept through Leah—the half-filled cold pot of coffee. The tweed furniture and table full of tattered magazines. The closed curtains.

She sat down on the nearest sofa and shut her eyes against the memories.

The door squeaked open. "Danni, Leah!"

At the sound of Emily Tyler's voice, Leah rose. "Mom!"

Her mother hugged her fiercely, her normally perfectly styled hair falling in unkempt waves around her face. "Oh, Leah, I'm so glad you came. I was afraid you wouldn't."

"I had to come, Mom. How could I stay away?" Leah drew back, puzzled that her mother would think her that callous.

Standing in the doorway, Owen cleared his throat. "I'll go check on the surgery time, Mom. Danni and Leah'll take care of you."

He disappeared before anyone could answer.

Emily laughed shakily. "Men are seldom useful in a real crisis. He's been hovering around me ever since you left for the airport, Danni. I'm glad you're back... I'm glad you're both here."

"Sit down, Mom." Danni directed her to the sofa, and Leah sat on her sister's far side. "What's the latest word?" Danni said.

"They're prepping him for surgery." Emily drew a steadying breath. "Apparently he's had damage to the mitral valve and they want to see if they can repair it. If not..."

She drew a Kleenex from her purse and held it against her nose. Her eyes watered, and she bowed her head. "They made me leave the room. I barely got to say good-bye."

Leah leaned across Danni to touch her mother's knee. "Mom..."

Her throat tightened. She wanted to say something, but knew nothing could ease her mother's hurt, nothing could relieve her anxiety. Leah couldn't tell her that he'd pull through; sometimes people didn't. She couldn't even say that things would be all right, because sometimes they weren't.

"Mom," she tried again, softly. "Mom, I love you. I'm here. We're all here."

Her mother raised her head. "Danni, would you please get me a cup of coffee?"

"Sure." She headed for the pot in the corner of the room.

"There's a vending machine in the lobby. I'm sure that coffee's much fresher. Do you mind?" Emily asked.

Danni looked at her mother, then Leah. She set down the pot. "I don't mind."

When they were alone, Emily hunched over, and a sob escaped her throat. Leah moved closer and drew her into her arms. "It's okay to cry. Let it out, Mom."

"Why did this happen to him? He's a good man!"

"I know, Mom." Leah held her mother tightly. "Don't give up. The doctors will do the best they can."

"It was so frightening. He was walking upstairs, and he just...fell. I heard the noise and came running. He was unconscious, and...I just stood there. I didn't know what to do. Thank God Danni was there to call 911 or he'd probably be dead."

She drew a ragged, tearful breath against Leah's shoulder. "He would have died because of me!"

"No, Mom. It's natural to go into shock. You would have reacted if Danni hadn't been there. I know you would."

"No! I'm not like you, Leah. I'm not strong enough to face bad things. You faced tragedy and came out stronger."

"Stronger?" Tears ran down Leah's cheeks. "Is that what you think?"

"You started a new life for yourself. I can't do that, Leah. If your father dies, I won't have anyone. You, Danni, Owen—you all have your own lives now."

"We'll always need you. I'll always need you." Leah's mouth quivered. "We all need each other, Mom. We're like a...a string of Christmas tree lights that won't shine unless all the bulbs are working."

"But you made it on your own. I thought you would need us, but you didn't."

"I did, but not in the way you and Daddy wanted. I only started living again when I let people reach out to me...and I reached out to them in return. Jacobo showed me that."

Leah paused. "I don't know what God has planned for Daddy, but I know the Lord loves you, Mom. And no matter what happens, he'll send people to help you."

Emily drew back and cupped her daughter's face with her hands. "Leah..."

Leah's eyes filled with tears. "I'm sorry I haven't spent more time with you, Mom. I thought you were trying to take charge of my life. I didn't realize you needed me."

Emily brushed back a strand of Leah's hair, smiling, her eyes wet. "All this time, we should have been grieving together. I've cried so much for Galen, for Perry...alone. Even without your father."

"Oh, Mom..." Leah wrapped her arms around her again in a fierce hug, and they held each other tightly, sobbing out their shared grief.

Jacobo pulled into the hospital lot and parked the bike close to the building. This time of night, there were plenty of spaces, especially for a motorcycle.

His legs foundered when he dismounted, and he realized that he was more tired than he'd thought. The holidays had been stressful enough, followed by a busy day back at work, then Leah's news. He'd stopped midway to Houston and phoned the hospital to check on her father's condition and learned he was headed into surgery.

The sounds of the busy street shattered any possible night quiet: the persistent buzz of a car alarm, the throbbing bass line of a rap song from a passing Mercedes, the blare of an ambulance's siren.

Jacobo rubbed his road-weary eyes and trudged toward the hospital entrance. Halfway there, he saw a Catholic church next door and stopped. He veered in that direction, climbed the solid stone steps, and opened the heavy wooden door.

Inside, all was quiet. And dim. He spent several minutes allowing his eyes to adjust.

Even at this late hour, several people knelt down front at the wooden railing, deep in silent prayer, their forms illuminated by a multitude of flickering candles. One elderly woman, her head covered by a lace scarf, raised gnarled prayer hands to an intricately carved crucifix above a marble altar. Two women gathered at the feet of a statue of Mary, while another lit a candle beside them.

Lining opposite walls from back to front, stone saints watched over the entire church.

Jacobo moved past the entryway, past the votive candles that had been lit near the Mary and Joseph statues at the back of the church. Without genuflecting, he took a seat on the back row, lowered the prayer bench, then knelt. Bracing his elbows against the pew, he rested his forehead against his clasped hands and closed his eyes.

For a moment, he didn't pray, just absorbed the quiet holiness of the sanctuary. The memories.

When his mother had taken him to church as a boy, he'd been moved by the sense-filling grandeur of mass: the feel of the holy water on his fingertips and forehead, the images of saints he believed he could never live up to, the pungent aroma of incense, the soothingly repetitive responses, the mystery of the Eucharist.

Church with his Protestant friends had seemed more like a pep rally than a privilege to enter God's presence.

Then, when he was a rebellious teenager, the reverence sifted away like sand between his fingers. He hung out with a fast crowd, staying out late, engaging in activities that he knew were wrong but felt helpless to avoid.

Though he knew it broke his mother's heart, he stopped attending mass and even threw away the rosary she'd given him for confirmation. The church had no place in his life.

But apparently God did. Just after his seventeenth birthday, Jacobo had wiped out on his bike and wound up in the hospital for a week with several fractures. Staring at the ceiling and the walls, bored, he'd had a lot of time to think.

His mother prayed over him daily, either at his bedside or at home, he knew. The hospital chaplain—a young Italian named Nick—gave him a card with the logo of a new church forming in the city.

"Why don't you check us out?" he'd said. "You can face God now, or you can face him later. It's your choice."

Reluctant to attend the church where he'd grown up, Jacobo nevertheless wanted to please his mother by going some-where, so he went to Nick's church that next Sunday. And then the next, and the next…until he met the Lord of the universe in his heart and realized that what he'd always called worship had been mere posturing before a God he'd never truly known intimately.

How many people offering prayers so late at night in this Houston sanctuary knew the Lord in their own hearts? For that matter, how many people in the Protestant churches sprinkled throughout the city knew him either?

Lord, I know that you dwell wherever hearts are open to you. Be present in a palpable way to each person here. Be present with Leah and her family.

His raised his head, and his gaze rested on the crucifix at the front. He shuddered inwardly at the sight of the suffering Christ, then remembered that the Lord he worshiped was no longer bound by the misery of a cross.

The women who'd stood before the statue of Mary shuffled down the aisle and out the door toward the hospital.

Jacobo clasped his hands tighter. *I don't fully understand suffering, Lord...why you had to suffer, why Leah has to. Please don't let her father die. Don't let him suffer. Don't let* her *suffer anymore. Hasn't she been through enough?*

He waited for a moment, hoping to see an answer written on the peaceful faces of the saints or blaze up in the assemblage of candles or even echo somewhere within the polished wooden pews.

But as was often the case, the harder Jacobo strained to listen, the more silence he encountered. He bowed his head again and this time listened for the still, small voice that spoke only, softly, in his heart.

A nurse stuck her head in the waiting room and told Leah and her family that they could see Hart as he was being wheeled to the operating room. They raced into the hall, and Leah hung back as one by one the others bent down to gurney level and whispered encouragement.

When it was Leah's turn, she groped amid the tubing and starchy white covers for her father's hand. He squeezed lightly, smiling crookedly from the narcotics.

"I love you, Daddy," she whispered, leaning over to kiss his forehead, just below the paper surgical cap.

He nodded once, slowly, then his face relaxed in unconsciousness.

They trudged back to the waiting room, and still they were alone. Danni brewed a pot of fresh coffee that no one drank.

Owen brought food up from the hospital cafeteria, but no one had an appetite. Now, near midnight, the egg rolls and steamed rice still sat in their Styrofoam cartons, untouched.

Emily stretched out on a sofa, exhausted. Owen headed to find a nurse for the latest word about the surgery, and Danni and Leah nodded off with their heads resting against their hands.

Leah was dreaming about ice skating under a cloud of brilliant white Christmas lights when she felt someone touch her shoulder. "Leah."

Her eyes opened. "Jacobo?" She smiled sleepily and rose, moving into his arms. His embrace was like a warm shield. "What are you doing here?"

"I thought you might need a friend." He glanced at her sleeping mother and sister. "I hope you don't mind."

"Of course I don't." She followed his gaze. Her mother had an arm thrown over her eyes, deep in sleep. Leah lowered her voice. "I'm so glad you're here."

Danni stirred. "Leah?" She blinked when she saw Jacobo, then straightened in her chair.

Leah smiled. "This is Jacobo, Danni. Jacobo, my sister, Danni."

He held out his hand, smiling. "We spoke on the phone when I called to give you Leah's flight number."

"Yeah. Thank you for calling." Danni smiled pleasantly, then when Jacobo turned his head, she mouthed the words *Law and Order* to Leah. Her smile widened. "Let me wake up Mom and…"

"No," Jacobo and Leah said at the same time. They stared sheepishly at each other.

"Let her sleep," he said. "Leah, do you want to stretch your legs and walk around the ward? We won't go far."

"Sure. Danni, you'll come get us if Owen comes back with news?"

She nodded, and Leah could tell she suppressed a smile.

Out in the corridor, several nurses bustled noiselessly at a nearby station, and an orderly pushed an empty gurney into a storeroom. Jacobo took Leah's hand and led her to a small, tucked-away lobby, and they sat close to each other on a cracked vinyl sofa.

She reached for him wordlessly, and he held her close. "How're you holding up?"

"I don't know. I think I'd really just like to get on the bike with you and head for the coast."

"Running away never makes problems vanish," he said softly.

How well she knew. She remembered the last time she'd driven, nonstop, to Galveston.

Leah swallowed hard. "I'm so scared. For my dad, of course. And for my mom. She's afraid of being alone if Daddy dies."

Jacobo kissed her temple. "Leah…"

"I know how hard it is. How alone you feel, how you feel like nobody really understands. Or cares."

Jacobo held her closer. "Before I left town, I called Nick," he said. "He promised to contact the prayer team about your father. Not five minutes later, Marta called, wanting to know what she could do."

Leah's eyes teared. "She has enough problems, Jacobo. Why would she want to help me and my family?"

"Why?" He curved his palm against her cheek, his eyes shining softly. "Because that's what the body of Christ does, Leah. That's what it means to be a member."

She shook her head. "I'm not a member of your church."

"The church isn't limited to a building or a particular form of worship or denomination. It's made up of everyone who follows Jesus' command to love the Lord, love one another. Everyone who believes in him. And when one member suffers, the body suffers with it."

He drew a deep breath, and his eyes misted. "I've suffered...so many have suffered...with you, alongside you ever since you lost Perry and Galen," he whispered. "I don't know why so much has happened to you and your family, but I do know that God loves you and holds you closely."

You're the bulb closest to the star because you need its light the most. Don't you know how closely the Lord of hope has been watching over you all this time?

I know the Lord loves you, Mom. And no matter what happens, he'll send people to help you.

Leah's pulse quickened. So many people, so many hurts, yet someone waited with outstretched arms for them all, walking across a sea of troubles and calling them to rise above and walk with him.

Take courage. It is I. Don't be afraid.

And like an echo, the simple command reverberated in her heart:

Come.

To him as to a living stone.

Come.

To the church of the living God.

Come.

Be fitted together to grow into a holy temple in the Lord, a dwelling of God in the spirit.

"Jacobo." Her mouth went dry. "When Perry and Galen died, I wanted to die too. I didn't think about others… I didn't know that I could help anyone else." She bowed her head.

Jacobo clasped her hands. "'I would have despaired unless I had believed that I would see the goodness of the Lord in the land of the living.'"

"I've seen it," she said softly, raising her head. She felt a tear slide down her cheek. "I've seen it many times, but I've never truly realized it until now."

Jacobo kissed her gently, then led her from the sofa and back down the hall. At the waiting room door, he paused. "I'll be close by, but I won't stay."

"Why?"

"You and your family need to be there for each other, without having to worry about an outsider." He eased the door open.

Emily Tyler stood by the coffee machine, and Owen was pouring her a cup. When she heard the door open, she turned, an expectant look on her face. At the sight of Leah and Jacobo, it fell. "Leah. I was hoping for a report. The nurse told Owen the surgery could be over anytime now."

Jacobo hung back, but Leah led him forward. "Mom, this is Jacobo Martinez. Jacobo, this is my mother, Emily Tyler. And my brother, Owen."

Jacobo shook hands with Leah's brother, then turned. "I'm sorry to meet you under such circumstances, Mrs. Tyler." He held out his hand again.

Emily glanced at Leah, then slipped her hand in Jacobo's. "It's very kind of you to be concerned. To ride all the way down here from Fort Worth."

Jacobo looked uncomfortable. "I should probably take off now, Leah...let you all be alone."

Leah touched his arm. She didn't want him to leave. She needed his strength, his presence. What if her mother started crying again? "Jacobo, please—"

Emily stepped forward. "You're welcome to wait with us." She cleared her throat.

Danni beamed at Leah over Jacobo's shoulder.

Jacobo glanced at Leah, then her mother. "Thank you, Mrs. Tyler."

Leah and Jacobo sat close together on the sofa. She wanted to ask whether Dolores had been angry that he'd taken off for Houston, but she didn't want to discuss it in front of her family. Instead, she twined her fingers with Jacobo's and rested her head against his shoulder, silent.

Danni flipped through a fitness magazine, the rhythmic page turns indicating she wasn't reading. Emily and Owen spoke in low tones about inconsequential matters—siding that needed to be repaired, a possible promotion at Owen's job, a neighbor's prized rosebushes. The drone was soothing, and Leah dozed off.

The door swung open. Leah jerked upright, then rose hastily at the sight of the surgeon, still clad in scrubs.

"Mrs. Tyler?" He walked straight away to Emily.

They rose, and Emily gripped Owen's hand. "How did it go, Doctor?"

"Just fine. There was some damage to a cusp of the mitral valve, but we were able to repair it. With a little bit of recuperation, your husband should be fine. He sailed through the surgery with no problems."

Emily sagged with relief, then turned into Owen's arms. Danni hugged them both.

Smiling, Jacobo hugged Leah.

Leah was too numb to speak. *Thank you, Lord.*

The surgeon fielded a few questions from Emily and Owen, then left. Leah and Jacobo held each other, murmuring their relief, then broke to speak with Danni.

When they turned to Emily, she embraced Leah. "The doctor said I could see your father once he's moved into the recovery room, so I'll stay here for a while. Leah, why don't you and Jacobo go back to the house and get some rest?"

"That's very nice of you, Mrs. Tyler, but I should probably get back to Fort Worth."

"Nonsense. You need some rest before you go all the way back up that highway." She laid a hand on his arm, and her face softened. "Hart wanted you to visit us. I argued with him about it, but I was wrong. I'd like to get to know you a little better."

Leah hugged her mother. "Thanks, Mom," she whispered. "Call us if there's any change with Daddy."

Emily held her close. "I will."

Leah kissed her on the cheek and tasted the salt of a tear, but when she released her mother, Emily was smiling.

Chapter Twenty

Jacobo waved hello to Frankie and a few of the neighbor kids playing football as he pulled into the driveway. He knew from the way Frankie ducked away, running farther down the street as if to throw a long pass, that he hadn't done his homework.

Jacobo sighed. *Welcome home. One day away, now it's back to reality.*

He pushed open the front door and didn't smell dinner cooking, even though it was six o'clock. Dolores was fastidiously punctual about mealtime.

In fact, the house was unusually quiet.

He stood in the middle of the living room, pushing down the fear that rose in his gut. "Dolores?"

To his great relief, Rosita ran into the room and threw herself at his legs. "Hi, Jacobo. We missed you."

He scooped her up in his arms. "I missed you guys too, *mija.* Even though it was only overnight. Where's your mama?"

Rosita scrambled down. "Oh, she's lying in bed. She said she didn't feel well."

"Is it the baby?" Jacobo tried to keep his voice calm.

"I don't know. Can I go outside and play?"

"Sure." He patted her on the back, distracted, and he vaguely heard her push through the front door as he headed toward Dolores's room at the back. "Dolores?"

The door was shut, but not completely closed. He rapped softly. "Dolores?"

He heard a groan and he pushed open the door. Dolores was seated on the edge of the bed, doubled over, clutching her stomach.

"Hang…on," she said to him over her shoulder. She got to her feet and braced her hands against the open closet door. She blew out four short, hard breaths, then let the air hiss through her teeth like the sound of a leaking tire. Four short breaths and a hiss. Four short breaths and a hiss. Over and over.

Bewildered, Jacobo moved to her side. Should he hold her hand? Get a washcloth for her forehead? Boil water?

Why hadn't he taken a Lamaze class so that he would at least know what women went through at a time like this?

She let out a long, even breath and straightened, clutching her hand to her back. "That was a hard one. We should have anywhere from five to ten minutes before the next one. My water already broke awhile back."

That didn't sound good, whatever it meant. "Five to ten minutes? Shouldn't you be at the hospital?"

She looked at him as though he were crazy. "Yes. I sent Frankie to get Mrs. Vasquez. Is she here yet?"

Jacobo suppressed a sigh of exasperation. *Frankie!* He started to call Rosita, then remembered that she, too, was headed outdoors. "Where's Carlitos? Maria? Marcos?" Why weren't they around when they were needed?

Dolores's mouth twitched. "They're down at Marisa's for the

afternoon. Relax, Jacobo. You act like I've never been through this before."

"*I've* never been through this before," he said. "Look… I'll go round up the kids and call a cab. Is there anything you need to take?"

She patted her abdomen. "Everything's right here. Why don't we just take the Plymouth?"

"It'd be our luck for it to break down now. It's a cab or my bike."

He hoped that would make her laugh, but she was already bracing herself against the door again, making those funny noises.

"Get…the kids settled," she said between two short puffs, then she groaned.

Jacobo ran for the living room and hastily phoned Marisa. She said that she already had Rosita in tow, and she could see Frankie out in her yard. When Jacobo explained the situation, she babbled a string of Spanish reassurances for him to pass on to Dolores, then agreed to keep the kids overnight, if necessary.

Jacobo's fingers trembled as he punched out the number for the cab company. He could hear Dolores panting as he explained the urgency of the situation to the dispatcher.

The cab arrived in record time, but by the time they reached the hospital, even Jacobo could tell Dolores was barely going to make it to the delivery room. He managed to convey that they couldn't wait to fill out forms and that since this was Dolores's sixth baby, unless the receptionist wanted the baby born right in front of her desk, she'd do well to get Dolores to a delivery room.

The receptionist found a wheelchair and rolled her in through the doors.

Jacobo sank to a sofa, exhausted. He'd spent all last night in the Houston hospital with Leah, then they'd headed for her house, and Leah and her sister had fixed him up in their brother's old room. But he'd been too keyed up to sleep, and he kept thinking about Leah sleeping in the room just across the hall.

He wondered how she was. He'd spent most of the day with her back at the hospital. She'd been allowed to see her father, and when she came out, her eyes were shining. She and her mother were deep in conversation about his recovery.

Jacobo had known then that he was no longer needed, so he'd headed back home in the late afternoon.

Your timing is wonderful, as usual, Lord. Thank you for bringing me home in time to help Dolores. Thank you for letting me help Leah, too, in whatever way I could.

He leaned his head back and closed his eyes. *Lord, it seems like a difficult task, but nothing's impossible for you. Please let Dolores and Leah see each other as you see them—wonderful, strong women with wounded hearts, but gentle hearts nonetheless.*

"Mr. Garcia?"

Jacobo jerked to his feet at the sound of the nurse's voice. "It's Martinez. Jacobo Martinez."

She looked puzzled. "Aren't you Dolores Garcia's husband?"

"I'm her brother."

"Oh. Is Mr. Garcia here?" She glanced around the semifilled waiting area.

"He's not here," Jacobo said, impatient. "Is Dolores all right?"

The nurse beamed. "She's doing splendidly. She's already delivered a beautiful, healthy boy. Would you like to see him?"

Jacobo sagged with relief. *Thank you, Lord.* "I'd like to see them both."

She smiled indulgently. "They're together. If you'll follow me…"

She led him through a maze of doors and corridors, to a small room, where she instructed him to put on a gown, mask, and gloves. "Don't want the little guy to catch any germs you might be carrying," she said cheerfully.

Then she led him to a small room. Dolores sat up in bed, smiling, holding out the baby for him to see as the nurse left them alone.

"Isn't he beautiful?" she said. "Would you like to hold him?"

Awestruck by the sight of new life, Jacobo accepted the swaddled baby. He'd held his other nieces and nephews when they were newborns, but never when they were only minutes old.

The baby was perfectly formed, from the shell of his soft little ear below a thatch of dark hair to the jagged fingernails on the fists he waved as he opened and closed his mouth in uneven mews.

"The Lord wove you, little one," Jacobo said softly. "You are indeed fearfully and wonderfully made."

When he looked up, Dolores was crying, holding out her arms. He handed her the baby, and she cradled him close. "To think that I wanted to get rid of him."

Jacobo sat on the edge of the bed and nudged the blanket back from the baby's face. "But you didn't, Dolores, and he's here. Have you thought of a name?"

"No. Manuel named the other kids. Do you have any suggestions?"

He thought for a moment. "How about Rafael?"

"Rafael. Rafael Garcia." She tried it out. "It sounds nice. What made you think of that?"

"Rafael means 'healed by God.'"

She smiled. "Are you sure you didn't think of it because of Rafael Palmeiro, the baseball player?"

"Well, that too." He grinned. "Maybe you'd like *DiMaggio* or *Mickey* better?"

She laughed softly, then stopped. She idly stroked the baby's cheek with a fingertip. "How was your trip to Houston? How is Leah's father?"

"He came through the surgery fine. She was glad to see me." He paused. "I met her mother and her sister and brother."

"Did they like you?"

"Yes."

Dolores unnecessarily retucked the wrap of the baby's blanket. "Why don't you invite Leah over to the house when she gets back home?—to see the baby, that is."

"And…maybe you?"

She glanced up, and her face softened. "Yes."

Jacobo smiled, then kissed her gently on the cheek. "I'll go call Marisa and let the kids know they have a little brother. Carlitos will be particularly happy—especially if Rafael has his own bear."

"Jacobo?"

"Yeah?" He turned at the doorway.

Dolores smiled shyly. "You've done so much…but can I ask a favor, for the future?"

"Sure."

"In a month or two…will you take me and the kids to Huntsville? To see Manuel?" She fussed with the blanket again. "He needs to see this baby, and I should probably talk to him."

Jacobo smiled. The Lord was doing quite a bit of healing lately. "Whenever you're ready, Dolores."

"He's beautiful, Leah. Just perfect." Jacobo's voice over the telephone was so animated, Leah was afraid he'd wake his nieces and nephews. He said he'd only recently put them to bed—they'd all had a late night oohing and aahing over the new arrival.

"I'm glad he arrived safe and healthy." She tried to sound enthusiastic herself, but she was having trouble speaking past the lump in her throat. She couldn't help but think about when Galen was born.

Jacobo laughed. "He almost was born in the cab. Honestly, Leah, I had no idea what you women go through to deliver a child."

Leah bit her lip, squeezing her eyes shut.

"Hey, I'm sorry. Leah?"

"It's okay, Jacobo. Women have babies every day."

"Yes, but not Manuel's wife." He was silent for a moment. "Dolores said when you get back to town, she'd like for you to come out to the house."

"That was nice of her," Leah said, without conviction.

"And I don't think I told you while I was in Houston, but before I left, she said she'd light a candle for your dad." He paused. "That means she cares, Leah."

Leah wrapped the cord around her finger. The empty space in her heart ached with the news of the baby's birth.

"How's your dad?"

Leah released the cord from her finger, relieved at the change of subject. "Much better. He's getting stronger every day. I'll probably head home on Sunday."

"Do you need me to come get you?"

She softened at his generosity. "I'll catch a flight. But thanks."

He was silent a moment. "I miss you, Leah," he said softly.

"Me too." She blinked back a tear. "Take care of yourself and those kids and…Dolores and the baby."

She hung up the phone and rested her elbows on the kitchen counter. *I'm glad the baby's here safely, Lord. But it's a painful reminder that my child is gone. Do you know how much that hurts? Why did it have to happen? Why did Galen die?*

She rested her head in her hands. *Jacobo says he doesn't understand either, but he says that you love me. And to be honest, I love him. But what about his family?*

What am I supposed to do?

When she got back to Fort Worth on Sunday, she was no closer to an answer. Physically exhausted from time spent at her father's bedside, she was emotionally exhausted from time spent with her mother, as well. They'd had several late-night talks over hot chocolate, and when Emily had tearfully kissed her good-bye at the airport, Leah knew that their relationship was moving to newer, more solid ground.

She wasn't so certain about her relationship with Jacobo.

It, too, seemed to be evolving, maturing, but with the birth of Dolores's baby, Jacobo had subtly taken on renewed concern for his family. She'd expected that, just as her father's surgery had drawn her closer to her own family, but a question stood between them now, lingering at the end of every telephone conversation they'd had while she was in Houston.

How much did she love Jacobo?

She saw the question in his eyes when he came to her apartment the first night back, bringing paper cartons of chow mein and egg rolls because he knew she was too tired to go out to eat. They talked of little else except their families, and she sensed the question again in the good-bye kiss he gave her before roaring off into the night on his motorcycle.

Did she love Jacobo enough to accept his family—*all* of them?

She was glad to go back to work, to keep herself occupied. Jacobo was busy every night that week helping Dolores with the kids, especially baby Rafael. Leah used the opportunity to entertain on her own, inviting Marta and her daughter, Francesca, over for dinner one evening and some of her coworkers the next.

The following night, Jacobo phoned to say that he and Dolores were throwing a neighborhood party Saturday in honor of Rafael's birth. Sunday afternoon would be his baptism.

"Dolores and I want you to come to both," he said, then paused. "Will you be there? I know I haven't had much of a chance even to talk to you lately…"

"I'll be there," she heard herself say. She knew she would probably regret it, but she had to prove how much she loved him.

Saturday night she drove to the north side of town. Amazed that there were so many cars, she had to park two blocks away. As she hiked toward Dolores's house, she heard the strains of Tejano music mixed with the playful shrieks of children, the patter of Spanish, and adult laughter.

Leah clutched the tissue-paper-wrapped bouquet of cut flowers she'd brought and slowed her steps.

Decorated with strings of Christmas lights, the yard teemed with lawn chairs, tables, a large, smoking grill, and people—old, young, younger still. A few Anglos and African-Americans, but most of them Hispanic. Some people sat, some stood, a few danced at the side of the yard, but all were happy.

Celebrating the birth of Dolores and Manuel Garcia's baby, who rested contentedly in his mother's arms as she sat on the porch steps and accepted adulation on his behalf.

Two houses away, Leah turned and headed back for her car.

"Leah!"

She heard Jacobo's voice, but she kept walking.

"Leah, hold on!" He gripped her arm, halting her movement. "Where are you going?"

She shoved the flowers at him, unable to look him in the eye. "I brought these for Dolores. I...I can't stay, Jacobo."

"Why?"

The simple one-word question echoed that which was already in her heart: *How much do you love me?*

She glanced back at Dolores, who laughed as someone took the baby from her arms.

"This is a party for Dolores as much as in honor of the baby," he said quietly. "She needs to know that people care about her. I invited everyone we know—neighbors, members of both our churches, coworkers, friends. And so many of them brought diapers and baby clothes—things that Dolores can't afford. She cries every time she opens another package."

"And I brought something impractical like flowers," Leah said bitterly, pointing at the bouquet in his hands.

Jacobo smiled. "She needs beauty, too, Leah." He gestured at the crowd. "Everyone brings something different, but each is needed."

Leah fought back tears. "Jacobo...I...I love you. But I don't know if it's enough—if I can handle being a part of your family."

She raised her head, for the first time looking him full in the face. His eyes were sad, but he smiled gently. "It's not a question of whether you have enough love for me, Leah. And it's not just my family you're uncertain you can handle."

"What do you mean?"

He touched the flowers. "If you're sure you won't stay, I'll give these to Dolores. She'll appreciate the gesture."

"Yes, I...I'd better be going." Leah frowned. What did he mean, it wasn't a question of whether she had enough love for him?

"I won't be at church tomorrow—I promised Dolores I'd go with her to talk to the priest about the baptism. Will you be at the baptism tomorrow afternoon? You don't have to stay for the reception afterward, if you're uncomfortable."

She considered his invitation. Jacobo's eyes pled with her and she melted inside. Church, even a Catholic church, she could probably handle, she reasoned. She'd slip in, see the baptism, and slip out. It would be a quiet affair that didn't require any social interaction, and her presence would make Jacobo feel better. "I'll be there."

"I'll be glad to see you." He drew her into his embrace, then kissed her warmly, gently, slowly. "I love you, Leah," he whispered.

"I love you too, Jacobo."

Her heart aching with uncertainty, she watched as he headed back toward the party and handed the flowers to Dolores.

It's not a question of whether you have enough love for me, Leah. And it's not just my family you're uncertain you can handle.

Leah tossed and turned in bed, unable to sleep. If it wasn't a matter of her love for Jacobo, or her ability to fit into his family, what did he think was troubling her?

Leah sat up in bed and swung her legs over the side. The pain inside was almost unbearable, gnawing her soul.

I can't stand feeling like this anymore. It's been there since Galen and Perry died, but it's more than just their deaths. Jacobo said it wasn't about my love for him or fitting into his family. So what is it?

She crossed her arms and pressed them hard against her stomach, as if she could press away the ache there. But the pain refused to subside, and no answer came.

In the nursery the next morning, she smiled and laughed with the children as usual, but her heart was tuned to the turmoil of her soul. She felt distant from everyone around her, so much so that several people asked her if she was feeling ill.

When she got back to her apartment, she thought she might actually be coming down with something. She lifted the phone to call Jacobo and tell him she wouldn't be able to make it to Rafael's baptism after all, then chided herself for being a coward.

She dressed for the event, her heart pounding.

What was she afraid to face?

What, indeed, had *really* troubled her about the party last night?

She sat on the bed, steeling herself. *I need to know. Show me what's underneath the surface.*

She put a hand over her heart. *It...it feels more like something between me and you, Lord.*

How much do you love me?

Leah drew a deep breath. *Is that it? Not how much I love Jacobo, but how much I love you?*

You shall love the Lord your God with all your heart, and with all your soul, and with all your mind.

I do! Is that all you want? A loyalty oath?

You shall love your neighbor as yourself.

The words stung, and the need to justify herself overwhelmed her. *Don't I? When have I not loved my neighbor? Who is my neighbor?*

Leah glanced at the clock. Late! She'd be late, and then Jacobo would think she wasn't coming. He'd already looked so sad yesterday—she didn't want to add a burden to the joyful occasion today.

She drove to the church, her hands sticky with perspiration on the wheel. *Love your neighbor as yourself.*

Didn't she? Why were those words like pinpricks to her soul?

The small Catholic church was tucked away on a side street near Dolores's house. Leah headed inside, wishing that she'd gotten Jacobo to agree to meet her outside. She didn't want to walk in alone.

But there he was, sitting down front with Dolores's kids, shushing them quietly, stilling an idly swinging foot, straightening Rosita's hair bow.

Leah smiled. He would make a good father, and it startled her that that thought was immediately followed by the realization that she wanted him as her husband, the father of her children.

Jacobo turned around and, seeing her, waved. He came up the aisle, smiling. His hair was pulled back in a ponytail, and he looked handsome as ever. She hadn't seen him in a suit since Manuel's trial.

He took her hand. "I was afraid you wouldn't come."

"I almost didn't." Her palms still felt damp, and she glanced around. Already people were filling the sanctuary.

"I saved you a seat with us."

"Are you sure? I don't really belong with your family."

"Of course you do," he said, leading her down front. He settled her next to Rosita and took the aisle seat himself.

"Hi, Miss Leah," Rosita said in a stage whisper. She folded her gloved hands across the lap of her starchy pink dress and tucked her legs, crossed at the ankles, under the pew. The other children were squirming, but Rosita seemed determined to act like a lady. Even when the little boy that must be Carlitos fidgeted, she showed him how to keep his hands in his lap and his feet still.

Love your neighbor as yourself.

Leah felt the need for solemnity as much as Rosita. She didn't know much about the Catholic Church, but she did know tradition was important there.

She leaned toward Jacobo. "Will you tell me if and when I'm supposed to say or do something?" she whispered.

"You don't have to say or do anything, but if you have any questions, I'd be glad to answer." He grinned. "First time in a Catholic church?"

"Maybe when I was a kid...but I don't remember."

"Do you know what *catholic* means?"

She shook her head.

"It means *the church universal.* Some would argue that it encompasses only those who follow the traditions and teachings of Rome, but others believe it means the entire body—no matter what denomination you worship with—because we're all children of God through faith in Christ Jesus."

He'd said as much in the hospital lobby during her father's surgery.

Jacobo took her hand. "Do you love the Lord, Leah?"

"Of course."

"Do you love the Lord's family?"

Was he still upset that she hadn't stayed for the party last night? "Yes, of course I love his family."

It's not a question of whether you have enough love for me, Leah. And it's not just my family you're uncertain you can handle.

Her mouth went dry, and her heart pounded. Jacobo smiled at her with gentle concern, then faced the altar, releasing her hand. "They're getting ready to start."

Dressed in vestments, the priest walked to the front of the sanctuary. He smiled at the congregation. "Would the family please step forward?"

For the first time, Leah saw Dolores, who rose from the front pew, the baby in her arms. An elderly couple rose alongside her, holding a small white garment and a white taper. Everyone was smiling.

"Those are the godparents, Jaime and Corina Reyes," Jacobo whispered. "They were good friends of my parents, and they own the bakery where Dolores works."

The priest smiled at Dolores. "What do you ask of God's church?"

"Baptism," she said clearly. Her face glowed with maternal love as she looked down at the baby. Rafael cried softly, batting his fists in the air.

Leah felt a small knot form in her stomach. She reached for Jacobo's hand, and he glanced at her before returning his attention to the front.

The priest spoke to Dolores and the godparents about the sacrament of baptism and their responsibility of raising the baby in the community of faith. He reminded them of their own baptismal vows, and they nodded solemnly. He traced the sign of the cross on Rafael's forehead, then had Dolores and the godparents do the same.

Leah glanced over the small congregation in attendance. Some of the faces she recognized from the party last night; a few she recognized as members of Jacobo's church.

Representatives of the church universal.

The church she had tried to hide from.

The priest moved the gathering toward the baptismal font. Dolores held the baby carefully, head tilted down, as the priest three times gently poured water over Rafael's forehead. Dolores bit her lower lip as if in concern.

The knot in Leah's stomach tightened.

Oh, God, God. How can she be worried? How can she know what real pain is? I'm so jealous of her, so jealous of Rafael's very existence.

The priest had the godparents slip a white garment over the baby to represent his newness in Christ, then anointed his tiny chin with oil. Rafael cooed and gurgled loudly, waving his arms with pleasure. Dolores pressed him to her body, smiling proudly.

Leah blinked back tears. *This should be a joyful occasion, not one where sadness is allowed. Why did I agree to come? I can't watch Dolores's baby symbolically die and be raised in new life!*

Just as she started to rise, Rosita slipped her hand in Leah's and squeezed tight. Leah shut her eyes and held back a sob.

Love your neighbor as yourself.

Slowly the layers were pulled back like fragile paper as she opened her soul and saw why she'd been afraid to join the party last night, why she'd been afraid to rightfully take her place in the body of Christ.

It hadn't been the crowd.

It hadn't been that she was only one of a handful of Anglos.

It hadn't even been the baby, Rafael.

The indescribable dam that had existed between Leah and the Lord cracked and shifted.

Oh, Lord, it's Dolores, isn't it? She *is my neighbor.*

Leah bowed her head, and a flood of emotions ran through her soul. *I've wished away Rafael, wished away Dolores, even, as Manuel's wife. I've harbored resentment, as though my sorrow were her fault, as though she were responsible for her husband's actions. Oh God, Jacobo's tried to tell me that she hasn't had it easy either, but I didn't want to listen. I've sinned against her not only because she's part of Manuel's family...but because she's part of yours.*

Oh, Jesus, forgive me!

Corina Reyes handed the white taper she'd been holding to the priest, who lit it from a tall candle near the altar. He handed the lit taper to Dolores. "Receive the light of Christ," he said, smiling down at Rafael.

Leah felt outward peace wash over her, followed by an inner sensation of warmth.

The priest said a prayer, then a blessing. Dolores held up the baby, smiling. The priest smiled also. "I present to you the newest member of our community of faith, Rafael José Garcia."

Someone clapped and cheered, then everyone was clapping and cheering. Jacobo put his arm around Leah, glancing down at her with concern on his face.

She smiled at him, tears in her eyes. "You meant Dolores, didn't you?" she said softly. "She's the one I needed to accept."

Nodding, he wiped away a tear from her cheek. "I wanted so much for you to be here, but I was beginning to think maybe you weren't ready after all. That seeing Rafael reminded you of Galen."

"He does. But I have no right to be upset at Dolores. Galen's death...Perry's death...they weren't her fault. She's been affected too."

Jacobo smiled, and in his eyes, Leah saw the answer to the question that had been between them. It was not how much she loved him or whether she could handle his family—it was much bigger, went much deeper, than the two of them. The living stone on which the spiritual building rested asked all its members how much they loved him and one another.

"Would you like to see the baby?" Jacobo said.

Leah nodded, and they pressed through the crowd toward the front of the sanctuary. Rosita, Frankie, and the other kids were already clustered around Rafael, proudly exclaiming over their newest sibling.

Someone pressed the white taper, still lit with the light of Christ, into Jacobo's hands. "Dolores," he said softly, trying to draw her attention from the multitude around them.

"Jacobo!" She turned from speaking with the godparents, Rafael in her arms. Her eyes narrowed when she saw Leah. She quickly passed the baby to Corina Reyes, as if she wanted to protect him.

Leah smiled gently. She and Dolores were strangers—enemies, some would say—but here at the altar, they shared common ground.

She took the candle from Jacobo and held it toward Dolores. "Peace of Christ," she said softly.

Dolores took the candle. Her hand trembled, and a tear slid down her face. "Peace of Christ to you," she whispered.

Jacobo took the candle and kissed Dolores's cheek. Dolores moved toward Leah, and they embraced. "I'm sorry, Leah," she whispered. "I'm so sorry."

Leah held her close. "I'm sorry too, Dolores. Thank you for including me on this special day."

Dolores turned and took the baby from Corina's arms. Her eyes shining, she handed him to Leah.

Leah took him in her arms and held him against her body.

Dressed in his white baptism gown, he stared up at her. His eyes were deep brown, matching the mocha color of his skin. He was no longer the son of her enemy, but a baby, innocent of his father's sin.

Jacobo wrapped an arm around her and looked down at Rafael. "What do you think?"

Leah's heart felt free. She looked up at Jacobo and saw that he was still holding the candle.

Leah smiled. "I think he's beautiful."

Two months later

Leah stood alone at the edge of the Gulf of Mexico and shaded her eyes against the rising sun. She and Jacobo had agreed to meet on the beach at four o'clock, and they'd huddled together with a blanket wrapped around their shoulders and studied the stars until they faded in the early morning light.

Somewhere beyond the horizon was a place of forgetfulness, a secret place where the words "Father, forgive them" forever sank and covered the flotsam and jetsam of broken lives.

And somewhere…somewhere this side of that horizon, Jesus was walking toward her across the sea with outstretched arms, smiling, speaking the one word that spoke true hope to wounded souls: Come.

And somewhere…somewhere high above the troubles and pain of the earth were Galen and Perry, happy and whole. She would be with them one day, but for now—in this life—other fragile hearts needed attention.

Leah drew a deep breath of the salty air. The tide washed against her bare feet, and she pulled up the ankles of her sweatpants to keep them from getting wet. Shivering against the cold, she burrowed into her jacket.

"Cold?" Jacobo wrapped his arms around her from behind.

She leaned back against him, into his strength. "Not anymore. How was your walk down the beach?"

"Very good. I used it as my prayer time."

"Praying for anything in particular?"

"Lots of things." He kissed the top of her head. "Mostly you."

"For me or about me?" she teased.

"Both." He released her so that he could face her. "It's a good thing Eric and Karen are staying with us and that you have Karen as a roommate. Temptation's great enough as it is."

Leah smiled. She knew exactly what he meant. Since Rafael's baptism, their relationship had deepened emotionally and spiritually. The physical yearning had increased as well.

"I told Dolores that my plans are to move out as soon as possible—to get my own place."

"Oh?" She raised her eyebrows and smiled.

He grinned. "Relax. I don't have any designs in mind. I just need my own space. I love her and the kids, but I need some quiet time for myself."

"I understand. You've taken care of them a long time. You've sacrificed a lot."

Jacobo was silent a moment. "Eric's trying to talk me into going back to law school."

"In Austin?"

"No, in the Metroplex. Maybe Texas Wesleyan—they have a night school. Or even SMU. It all depends on scholarships and grants."

"I'm glad, Jacobo. It's your life dream."

He smiled slowly. "My life dream is to be obedient to the Lord—*día a día,* as my mother used to say. If law school is in his plans, fine. If not...I'm satisfied." He took her hand in his. "I'm more than satisfied. I'm happy."

"Me too," she whispered. "I didn't think I ever would be."

Jacobo cleared his throat and gazed out at the gulf. "Leah, I know it's too early to ask anything definite, but I've been thinking lately about our future. Manuel won't get out of prison for twenty years, but even then—you need to consider that if we have a permanent relationship, you might have to stare at him over the Christmas turkey..."

She squeezed his hand. "I've been thinking about a permanent relationship with you too. And that if you're willing—and if Dolores is too—I'd like to meet Manuel. I've heard something about victim-offender reconciliation programs." She drew a deep breath. "Well, it would be a start, wouldn't it?"

Jacobo smiled broadly. "It would be a very good start."

"I know what the Lord calls me to do, even if I don't completely understand it," she said. "What Jesus did, I have to do."

"It may not be easy. It'll take time."

She turned and smiled up at him. "Sí, Jacobo. But forgiveness begins with one step. All he asks is that I let him lead, then he'll take care of the rest. *Día a día.*"

If you enjoyed *The Living Stone*,
ask for Jane Orcutt's *The Fugitive Heart*,
available at your local bookstore.

Chapter One

Kansas
Spring 1864

The sun stung Samantha Martin's wet eyes as she fled the house for
the barn's dark refuge. Everybody probably thought she was childish for bolting from the Sunday dinner table, but she didn't want
her family or the Hamiltons to see her tears. She was fourteen now,
too big to cry.

The stock had been turned out to graze, and she stumbled into
an empty stall. Choking back sobs, she braced her arms against a
weathered post and buried her face against her clean calico dress
sleeves. The pungent smell of lye soap mingled with the barn's
familiar odors of animal, harness leather, and hay. How could Pa
talk about leaving? Didn't he know how much they needed him?
How much *she* needed him?

It had only been a year since the grippe took Ma. Since then Samantha had had no mother to confide in about the embarrassing changes in her body, no mother to warn her she was growing up. Pa certainly hadn't bothered to talk to her about that. Or a great many other things, it seemed.

The barn door creaked open. Samantha muffled her sobs and wiped a sleeve across her eyes. It was probably just Caleb coming to accuse her of being a baby. All her life her older brother had teased her about one thing or another.

"Samantha?"

Her breathing slowed, and she cautiously peered around the stall. Sixteen-year-old Nathan Hamilton, her best friend and neighbor, stood in the shadows, watching her, waiting. As far back as she could remember, he and Caleb had been a big part of her life. When she was little, Samantha toddled after them, joining in their boyish games on the adjoining farms. Years went by, and the games evolved into far-flung expeditions down to the river and beyond. Caleb was disgusted at the intrusion, but Nathan urged her on: climbing the big cottonwood to the best lookout branch, tightrope-walking the fallen log across the water, racing through the wheat fields. Higher, farther, faster.

And when she'd failed or, worse yet, cried after too much of Caleb's teasing, Nathan had tended her skinned knees and comforted her bruised feelings. He'd read countless books to her and shared his dreams of becoming a doctor and seeing the world— even opening her own window on it by teaching her to read long ago. He was her champion, and she'd known since she was seven that she wanted to marry him.

Nathan opened his arms in silent invitation, and she went to him without question. Sobs welled anew and spilled out. He stroked her hair, his hand curiously strong yet gentle. "Shh. It'll be all right."

"Why didn't they tell us? Pa...and your pa...are joining the army! They're going to the war and leaving us!"

"Shh."

"They might...get killed!"

His arms tightened around her. "Cry it out," he whispered against her hair. When her sobbing stilled, he said quietly, "I have something to show you."

She drew back, sniffling. "Wh-what?" He'd always known how to stop her tears.

He smiled down at her, then ran the pads of his thumbs across the wet trails on her cheeks. "Come see, Sam."

She swallowed the last of her sobs, and her stomach warmed with pleasure. *Sam.* Nathan was the only one who called her that. Trusting as always, she followed him out of the barn and around the newly growing wheat field.

She looked at him as he walked ahead of her. His gait was quick with the vigor of youth, his body strong from years of hard farm work. When had his shoulders grown so broad? All of a sudden he looked...different. Like a stranger, a grown man, yet somehow still the Nathan she'd always looked up to.

He led her all the way to the edge of the woods, then knelt. Bewildered, she got down on her knees beside him.

"Look." He carefully eased up a thatch of loose grass. Four tiny bunnies snuggled together in a shallow bed. Their ears were pressed flat against their bodies, and Samantha could see the quiver of their little hearts.

Awestruck, she reached to scoop one up, but Nathan stopped her. "Don't touch them. The mother will abandon them if she smells your scent."

Samantha drew back. "Why isn't she here?" she whispered.

"She's probably watching from the woods." Nathan gently replaced the grass, then smiled. "This is our secret. I'll check on them every day and make sure they're safe. Will you help me?"

She nodded, solemn. Nathan had taken care of every stray, lame, or sick animal that crossed his path, but this was the first time he'd ever asked for her assistance.

Nathan took her hand, and she glanced up, startled. His green eyes were luminous. "When my father told me he was enlisting, I told him that I wanted to go too. But he won't let me. He says I need to stay here."

She shivered. "I'm glad. You might get hurt." She blinked back tears at the thought of Pa in the army.

"Sam, I'm tired of waiting for something interesting to happen around this dull place. I want to go out and see the world. If I have to go to war to do it...well, at least it's for a good cause."

Samantha swallowed hard. "I...I'd be sorry if you went, Nathan."

His eyes deepened. "Would you?"

"Y-yes." His gaze was doing strange things to her—her heart rang hot like a blacksmith's anvil, but her feet and hands felt as cold as the winter ice she chipped from the horse trough.

Nathan gently took both her hands. "Would you be sorry because I wasn't here to chase you and Caleb to the river anymore or because you would miss being alone with me?"

"Both," she whispered, confused. Had she revealed too much of her heart?

Nathan smiled, and her hands felt heavy and clumsy in his. Unnerved, she turned her face away, trying to sort through her tangled emotions.

For years they'd played together, laughed together, and her world had been orderly and happy. Now Ma was dead, and Pa was leaving. Even Nathan, her rock, was changing. And in the process, somehow she was changing too.

He turned her chin back with a gentle finger. "I've always cared about you, Samantha," he said softly. "I wouldn't hurt you."

She blinked back unshed tears and swallowed hard. "Then tell me why you want to leave. Why our pas want to leave."

His eyes searched hers, and she could see he was struggling for words to explain. Their fathers' imminent departure had something to do with Nathan wanting to go too, and a greater sense of loss swelled over her. Everyone was sweeping right by her when all she wanted was for things to stay the way they were.

"Samantha…," he said, then moved closer and wrapped his arms around her. Her heart hammered like the bunnies', and she rested her cheek against Nathan's shoulder. She felt his cheek, then his lips, brush against her hair. His arms tightened, and she relaxed, feeling protected. He would keep her safe.

"Nathan!"

Samantha wrenched free, inexplicably mortified at the sound of Mr. Hamilton's voice. He stood at the edge of the field yet made no move to come closer. His expression softened when he caught her eye. "Your father's looking for you, Samantha," he said. "He's concerned."

Nathan touched her hand and smiled. Her stomach twisted on itself like a clumsily knotted rope. Her face flushed warm with embarrassment, and she ran past Mr. Hamilton so quickly that her long hair streamed around her shoulders. She glanced back, and she could see Nathan still standing by the bunnies' nest, watching her.

Nathan shifted on his knees in the straw covering the barn floor. He wiped the newborn lamb's nose so it could breathe, and when it exhaled with a soft bleat, he smiled sadly and wiped the rest of its small body. When the lamb was dry, he held it, still bleating pitifully, against the ache in his chest.

"The ewe died?" his father said behind him.

Nathan nodded, his throat tight. The old ewe had been his mother's favorite. Hannah Hamilton refused to slaughter any of the few sheep they raised, valuing them instead for their gentle companionship and warm wool. Nathan had tried valiantly to save Buttercup during her lambing, but the birth had been breech. The ewe had bled to death before the spindly lamb could even nurse.

Nathan felt his father's hand on his shoulder. "I know you did everything you could, Son."

Nathan didn't answer. With great effort, the lamb lifted its small head, but it flopped back against Nathan's chest. He laid the newborn down in the warm box he'd prepared and waited.

Bawling, the lamb hunched up, and Jonathan critically examined its body. He eased his forefinger into the lamb's mouth, shaking his head when it refused to suck. "I don't think this one'll live. Even if his ma had made it, he's too weak. His mouth is even cold."

"I'll tube-feed it cow's milk until it's strong enough to take to one of the other ewes or a bottle."

Jonathan raised his eyebrows. "That's a lot of work, and cow's milk isn't always enough. God doesn't make mistakes; sometimes we have to let him have his way in these things."

"I've saved lives before, and I can save this one with or without God's help," Nathan said stubbornly. He knew what his father would say to that, so he rose quickly to fetch the equipment he'd need.

As he gathered the milk bucket and tube, he glanced out the open barn door and saw that night had fallen. His father lit another lamp and hung it near the sheep pen, then dragged the ewe's carcass outside. Nathan stared wistfully at the darkened sky and the stars that began to twinkle seductively. He arranged the milking stool beside the cow and pressed his cheek against her warm flank while he milked. His mother had taken over the milking years ago when his father deemed him old enough to handle more vigorous work, but Nathan secretly missed the daily chore. When he finished, the cows always stared at him with their great appreciative eyes, and he felt he had truly done them a favor.

But as much as he loved caring for the animals, he felt trapped on the farm. Sometimes he'd run past the orderly rows of corn and wheat to where the grass and sky gathered, smooth and unbroken. He'd stare longingly at the edge of the world, miles beyond, where freedom surely lay. Past the imprisoning prairie to forests and mountains, big cities and small, books and love and dreams and plans fulfilled in the life he was meant to lead.

His father had taught him everything he knew, not only about the farm, but about academics. For years he'd encouraged Nathan to consider going back East when it was time for college, and last year Nathan had decided to become a doctor.

Then Jonathan Hamilton and Robert Martin announced they were leaving to join the army.

When he finished milking, he knelt beside the lamb. It squalled piteously, and Nathan eased the tube down its throat. The lamb protested weakly, and Nathan cradled it against his body. "Come on, little one," he murmured. "You need this to live." The lamb looked up at him as if in understanding and stilled at once. "That's it, lie back. You'll make it."

Jonathan smiled faintly. "You have such a gentle touch, Nathan. Why do you want to fight a war?"

"Why do you?"

"Robert Martin and I want to see an end to slavery. We feel called to help preserve the Union."

"And I feel called to see what war's like."

"You need to keep at your studies if you want to go to college, Nathan. The war has taken enough boys."

Nathan bristled. "I feel the same about this country as you do, Father. I'd like to see justice served."

"There are other battles for justice than war. I know you want to act on the beliefs God's given you, but—"

"God didn't give me anything. *You're* the one who made me read the classics and study the philosophers. You taught me to think for myself."

"And tried to teach you love for God's Word. I thought you would see that intelligence and faith are compatible."

"I don't need a supreme being, Father. I can handle myself. *And* this lamb. You'll see."

Jonathan's eyes flickered. "Your compassion for healing comes from a gentle heart, Nathan, but you allow pride to rule you."

"I know what I can do on this farm. And now I want to know what I can do out in the world beyond it!"

"War isn't the answer to your wanderlust *or* your search for freedom. At your age, you think you're immortal, but war is death."

Nathan jerked his head at the bloody spot where the ewe had lain. "*Life* is death, Father. Isn't that what you read in Ecclesiastes? No matter how you live your life, it all comes to the same end. Death. 'All things come alike to all…'?"

"You're right, Son, but it also says that God will bring everyone into judgment for every secret thing we've done, whether it's good or evil. It's not a matter of what's right in our eyes but what's right in his."

"So how is it that *you* know what's right for me?" Nathan said bitterly, staring down at the lamb. Nourished for the time being, it had fallen asleep. Nathan removed the tube and gently placed the lamb in its box. Sighing, he rocked back on his heels and ran a hand through his hair. Despite his bravado, he was afraid the lamb might not make it after all.

At least arguing with his father took his mind off his fear. As far back as he could remember, they'd argued philosophy, the Bible, politics—even farming techniques. He always thought of them as merely disagreements; he never suspected that his father egged him on to force him to think. But now he realized that the spirited discussions were intended to hone his beliefs, to steer him to faith in God.

Nathan felt a hand on his arm, and he turned. His father's gray eyes were soft. "How do you feel about Samantha?"

"I'm going to marry her one day," Nathan said automatically. During the past year, she had figured into his plans by day and his dreams by night. "I love her."

"She certainly is turning into a beautiful young woman."

Embarrassed, Nathan glanced away. He'd noticed lately that

Samantha wasn't the rugged tomboy she'd appeared to be over the years. At times she was as elusive as a butterfly and twice as fragile. He'd hugged her thousands of times before, but today there had been something different in her touch.

He'd never before noticed how soft her hair felt, like kitten fur against his work-roughened hands. He'd wanted to loosen the ribbon at the back of her head and feel the weight of her hair in his hands, then touch her smooth cheek and reassure her everything would be all right. She evoked a strange protectiveness from his heart, a fierce desire to abandon everything for her. A gentle desire to hold her closely, shielding her from all harm. A warm desire to be all things to her.

He would go away and find his freedom. Then he would come back and make her a part of it.

Jonathan smiled gently. "The feelings you have for Samantha are perfectly natural for your age. And your mother and I have always hoped you two would eventually marry. You've grown up together, and you're good friends. That's important for a marriage."

He sighed. "But for now, I need you to stay on this farm. There's been talk of bushwhackers coming across from Missouri. Robert and I are known abolitionists, so I'm counting on you to protect your mother." He paused. "Once the mortgage is paid off, no matter what happens to me, the farm will be yours."

Nathan started to say he'd never have any use for it, but he glanced at the lamb. It shivered in its sleep, and he laid his hand over its small body. He'd forfeit his own rest tonight and settle for dozing every few hours in between lamb feedings. "Go on to bed, Father. I'll watch out for things here."

Jonathan smiled and put his arm around his son. "This lamb

of yours might make it after all. I'll stay here awhile in case you need some help."

Nathan felt a smile work its way to his mouth, but a cold ache formed in his stomach. His father wouldn't be around the farm much longer to help.